"Audrey, I can't—"

He broke off, shaking his head.

He was about to pull his hand away from her face, but she grasped it before he could move. Her pulse raced, and she could hear the alarms in her brain again, cautioning her that she wasn't being careful enough. That her heart might rupture with emotion for Kieran at any minute.

That's not going to happen, she thought, turning over his hand. She stared at the intersecting lines on his smooth palm, wishing she was a gypsy and could tell the future from the criss-crossed marks. Instead, she brought his palm to her lips, kissing the skin gently. She inhaled, taking in his leather-and-spice smell. She clung to his hand, kissing it repeatedly, working her way from his palm to his fingertips, taking note of how his body had gone rigid, how his breath had turned ragged.

"Audrey." It sounded like a plea. But whether for her to keep going or to stop, she wasn't sure . . .

And Then He Kissed Me

A White Pine Romance

By

KIM AMOS

FOREVER

NEW YORK   BOSTON

Copyright © 2015 by Lara Zielin
Excerpt from *Every Little Kiss* 2015 by Lara Zielin

Forever
Hachette Book Group
1290 Avenue of the Americas
New York, NY 10104

www.HachetteBookGroup.com

Printed in the United States of America

First Edition: July 2015
10 9 8 7 6 5 4 3 2 1

OPM

Forever is an imprint of Grand Central Publishing.
The Forever name and logo are trademarks of Hachette Book Group, Inc.

The Hachette Speakers Bureau provides a wide range of authors for speaking events. To find out more, go to www.hachettespeakersbureau.com or call (866) 376-6591.

The publisher is not responsible for websites (or their content) that are not owned by the publisher.

ATTENTION CORPORATIONS AND ORGANIZATIONS:

Most Hachette Book Group books are available at quantity discounts with bulk purchase for educational, business, or sales promotional use. For information, please call or write:

Special Markets Department, Hachette Book Group
1290 Avenue of the Americas, New York, NY 10104
Telephone: 1-800-222-6747 Fax: 1-800-477-5925

For Rhonda, my cheerleader. No one can top that.

Acknowledgments

Many thanks, once again, to the numerous people who continue to help breathe life into White Pine, Minnesota. I'm especially grateful to my editor, Michele Bidelspach, and my agent, Susanna Einstein—both tireless supporters. Huge thanks as well to Alex Kourvo, who read the early drafts and provided so much insight and help. And a gigantic Harley-sized thanks to Stephanie Smith, who patiently answered all my questions about motorcycles and Harley culture. I'm so glad the book gave us a chance to reconnect!

I'd also like to give a shout-out to the delightful, magical town of Empire, Michigan, which hosts an annual asparagus festival and provided the inspiration for White Pine's quirky tradition. There really is such a thing as asparagus beer, and it really is delicious. Right Brain Brewery out of Traverse City, Michigan, makes it and you can taste it the third week in May every year.

Enjoy!

And Then He Kissed Me

$\mathscr{P}$ROLOGUE

$\mathscr{A}$udrey Tanner suddenly understood why people hated Mondays. Sure, she'd dreaded them sometimes, maybe even been frustrated by them. But now she fully grasped the sheer loathing of them.

She stretched, savoring the warmth of the covers, and thought to heck with the day job. Eyes closed, ignoring the daylight streaming against her lids, she debated calling in. Faking sick. Telling the high school that she was under the weather and they should call a substitute. They could feed the kids in her gym classes chips and soda and chocolate for all she cared.

She never used her sick days, but then again she never used her body like she had last night, twisting it around Kieran Callaghan in such a way that their cries of pleasure rattled the windowpanes. She smiled to herself, hoping the neighbors hadn't heard. Then thinking she didn't care if they had.

Reaching out, she felt across the bed for Kieran. For the body she'd only just discovered but felt like she'd known for years. Her fingers spread, anticipating the hard planes of his muscled flesh, every valley and contour both new and achingly familiar at the same time. How was it that they'd only just met two weeks ago? Kieran was a jumble of contrasts that should have left her reeling and confused, but instead everything about him only made perfect sense. Being with him created an incomprehensible rightness that her affordable house and her steady job and her sensible grocery list had never come close to.

She smiled sleepily, anticipating his touch all over again, even though they'd been up long enough the night before to see the stars fade. Even though she had to go to work. Even though she was supposed to be helping with the Good Shepherd Walk later that afternoon.

Oh, but she'd throw it all into the Birch River for him. She'd shed every part of her practical life to feel this much excitement—this much love, if she was honest—every day.

But when her hand reached his side of the bed, all she came up with were cold sheets.

The fog of sleep dissipated instantly. Audrey opened her eyes and squinted against the bright May sunshine streaming through her curtains. There was a dent in the pillow where Kieran's head had been resting next to hers. The thought of his dark red hair flaming in color against her plain sheets made her smile. She strained, listening for the sound of him making coffee. Brushing his teeth. Cooking them eggs.

But the house was quiet.

Throwing back the sheets, she padded quietly to the bathroom and peeked out the window, figuring she'd find him outside tinkering with his Harley. Maybe they'd even go for a ride. She smiled, thinking about the wind in her hair, the sun on her skin, and how wild and alive she felt pressed up against Kieran on the open road.

Then again, maybe she'd just beckon him back to bed instead. She'd pull his workman's hand away from the engine and lace her fingers with his. "Ride me instead," she might whisper.

An unthinkable phrase from her lips two weeks ago. Now, double entendres seemed a natural part of her vocabulary.

Her naked skin prickled in the morning air; her muscles ached in the most delicious way possible. You didn't get this feeling after a typical workout, she thought.

Of course, last night had been anything but typical.

She belted the cotton robe she'd left hanging behind the bathroom door and wondered about getting something silky. Something naughty. She pictured lace and leather and the way Kieran would undress her with his eyes when she wore it. She shivered, savoring the thrill of emotions he churned up inside of her. He ignited an electric current, as if a part of her that had been shut off was suddenly thrown on, casting white-hot light on everything.

Like the narrow table in her hallway, for example. She could picture him lifting her on top of it, slamming it into the cream-colored walls with the force of their bodies coming together.

Or the white stools around the small island in her kitchen. She studied them as she entered the room. He could sit her on top of one and spread her wide, doing unspeakable things that pulled her apart and put her together again so she felt like a Picasso painting. Altered and magical and beautiful.

Or the kitchen counter, where—

She stopped. A small yellow Post-it was stuck next to the coffeemaker. She smiled, wondering at his thoughtfulness. How was it possible that a man clad in so much leather, who rode the biggest motorcycle she'd ever seen, could know the words that would open up her heart? He'd been leaving scraps of poetry around the house all week.

Bright star! Would I were as steadfast as thou art!

She'd had to google the line. John Keats, as it turned out.

The fullness of your bliss, I feel—I feel it all.

She'd googled that one, too. William Wordsworth.

She pulled the Post-it off the counter, musing whether he'd left her Shakespeare or John Donne. Instead, her vision rippled as she took in the two words he'd penned.

I'm sorry.

She blinked, then blinked again.

Sorry for what?

She looked around. Kieran was of course here and would explain all this momentarily. She called his name in the quiet house, but there was no answer.

Her heart pounded. Adrenaline surged.

Sorry for what?

Walking quickly to the front door, she threw it open just as Kieran's motorcycle rumbled to life. The noise was deafening on the quiet street. A distant, practical part of her wondered if the neighbors would be angry.

The most present part of her wondered what in the world Kieran was doing. He was astride his bike and had it pointed down the street, away from the house. His saddlebags were zipped and buckled, his chin thrust forward.

"Kieran!" she called. His head turned sharply toward her. He revved the throttle like he was going to speed away, and her stomach lurched. *No,* she thought. *What are you doing?*

She wanted to kick herself for the crazy way she was acting, running down the sidewalk in her robe like some madwoman. Except that her fear wouldn't relent. Not when Kieran's pale green eyes stayed so far away as he looked at her, and not when his body went stiff under all that leather.

Dirty jeans. Scuffed boots. Rugged and wild. She thought she'd harnessed his attentions, the same way he'd brought out some of the wild girl in her, itching to break free. They'd balanced each other perfectly.

Hadn't they?

"Where—where are you going?" she managed, raising her voice slightly above the engine's purr.

"I have to go."

"Now?"

"Yes."

Their staccato words were too short, too sharp. Underneath them was a mountain of dialogue that terrified her. What was he saying? Where was he *going*?

"What is this?" she asked, raising the Post-it into his line of vision. He winced as if she'd flicked scalding water at him.

"I don't expect you to understand."

"Try me," she said, thinking of how they'd bared their souls to each other these past two weeks. How underneath his Harley leather and her P.E. teacher track pants they'd both been so much alike. She'd let him into her home, into her heart, into her bed. What was there left to hide? Surely nothing they couldn't tackle together. They were a team. A unit. She knew this as surely as she knew he was sitting in front of her at this very moment, about to make a terrible mistake.

"I have to go. I'm not coming back."

Her body seemed suddenly too heavy. As if it couldn't support her.

"*No.* Whatever you think you need to do right now, you don't. Just slow down. Let's talk."

"It's—I can't—" Kieran swallowed several times. And then, to her horror and dismay, he kicked the Harley into gear and sped down the road.

His name was a cry on her lips as she raced after him. Her legs pounded the blacktop. She would catch him at the next stop sign. Or at the light in town. She was fast. Athletic. Fit. She could do this. Because there was no alternative. If he left, he took a part of her with him that she'd never get back. He would leave a fathomless black hole where for two weeks there had been nothing but stars.

She sprinted, muscles burning, lungs heaving. If neighbors stared at her, eyes wide, she didn't notice. If commuters rolled past her, eyebrows raised, she paid them no mind. Kieran was her goal. Her destination. Both the starting and the ending point.

It was a sliver of glass that had finally stopped her. A piece so jagged and dirty that she couldn't quite tell where the glass ended and the blood and dirt started. She glanced from her heel to the point on the horizon where the road disappeared into sky.

The pain came then. It wasn't just one wave, it was two—first physical, then emotional, both of them so black and thick that she almost lost her breath. She was half naked, barefoot, at least a mile from home. People were staring at her.

She wanted to duck in shame. Instead, she forced herself to feel everything. She let the pain focus her rattled mind and sharpen her senses.

She'd chased him like a dog running after the family station wagon, and he'd never let up on the throttle. Not once.

Oh, God. Had she really been so stupid? So foolish?

So wrong about everything?

Surely not. What they had was *real*. Which meant he'd be back. He just needed time. Give it a day or so. He would come rumbling back and she'd be furious, but she'd forgive him.

That was what people in love did. They made mistakes, and then gave each other the grace to make things right again.

She turned back toward home, limping until a neighbor asked if she was okay. His glasses were square. She thought his name might be Andy. Maybe-Andy offered to give her a lift. She started to wave him off, then thought better of it. She should get home. Clean up. Get ready for Kieran.

Because he'd be back. He *would*.

Minutes later, she wobbled unsteadily up the front walk, pushed open the door that she'd left ajar.

She called in to work after all. Told them she was sick. It wasn't a lie, the way it had been fifteen minutes ago.

And then she stayed home and waited, ears straining for the sound of Kieran's motorcycle as each passing hour melted into the next.

$\mathcal{C}$HAPTER ONE

Five years later

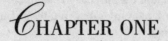ieran Callaghan wasn't used to being questioned. Considering that the source of the interrogation was his boss, he knew he needed to allow it. But he didn't need to like it.

"You're pissing your panties about this opportunity… why, again?" Lorne asked, running a hand through his salt-and-pepper hair. Across the wide conference room table, it was clear he was agitated, and rightfully so. Kieran wouldn't understand the situation himself unless he was smack in the middle of it.

"White Pine is tiny. Full of farmers. Why should I waste my time there at a Harley dealership that's doomed to fail?"

The lie burned inside him. He'd loved White Pine. More particularly, he'd loved one very specific thing about White Pine. He shoved aside the memory.

"The local economy can sustain this dealership," Lorne

fired back. "We've done the due diligence. They just need some help getting it rolling. Same as every other Harley you've ever helped jump-start *because it's your job.* You telling me you don't want your job anymore?"

"Of course I want my job. I'm telling you I don't want this *assignment.*"

Lorne sat back in his leather chair. He studied Kieran with a practiced eye. He'd known Kieran for too long to allow this bullshit. Kieran could see it in the arch of his brow, the curl of his lip.

"You got some skeletons hiding in Minnesota you want to tell me about?"

A graveyard full of them, Kieran thought. But he wasn't about to say that. As much as Lorne knew about him, he didn't know everything. Certainly not the darkest parts.

Which was how Kieran liked it. He'd rebuilt himself. *Transformed.* And he wasn't about to go looking back over his shoulder if he didn't have to. He caught a glimpse of himself in the shiny surface of the conference room table. Clean shaven. Collared shirt. A businessman with a staff of employees and a title to match: Advancement Director.

Fine. So what if he had to go back to White Pine? He could handle it. The town was small but not that small. It wasn't like he'd be face-to-face with his past every day. He could avoid . . . certain people if he needed to.

"There's an ownership opportunity there, too," Lorne said, folding his hands. "If you're interested."

"No, not there," Kieran said, angry that he sounded so defensive. Good Christ, how had he ever stayed cool around a betting table long enough to win? He lost his composure too easily these days.

Worse than all that was the fact that he was nervous. He

could feel the sweat collecting at the base of his neck. It was a thread of emotion he wasn't accustomed to winding through him—not for a long time, anyway.

"Suit yourself." Lorne shrugged. "But I need you there in a week. This dealership just opened and if they don't get their shit together now, the odds against them are stacked."

Odds. Betting. There was language he understood. And if he were still a gambling man, he'd go all in on the fact that this was a terrible idea. He should stay as far away from White Pine, Minnesota, as possible. Instead, he found himself nodding yes.

"Whatever you need, Lorne."

"There's the Kieran Callaghan I know. He'll get there eventually, but he's gotta be a pain in your ass in the process."

"Hey. This pain in your ass has made sure Harley dealerships all over the country are running as smooth as a baby's bottom."

"Yeah. And White Pine better not be any different."

Kieran's temper flared. He suddenly wanted to tell his boss to fuck off. To say that he'd had enough successes to earn a pass. To say that either he bowed out of this assignment, or he bowed out of the job as a whole and Lorne could go find someone else to fill the position.

But Kieran held his tongue. He hadn't come this far just to throw it all away now.

He tamped down the sharp jab of emotion that pierced his gut. If he was going to White Pine again, he'd better keep his damn head down. He was going to be a cool, calm professional like always, and he was going to launch a successful Harley-Davidson dealership, same as ever. And then he was going to return to Milwaukee and forget about it all. Just like he'd forgotten about White Pine five years ago.

It was simple, really.

"I'll be there by next Thursday," he told Lorne. He had his secretary on speed dial, and had mentally packed half his things already.

But deep inside, his emotions churned. A whole sea of them, and it felt like the only thing holding them back was a wall of brittle glass that might shatter at any moment.

* * *

Fletch Knudson's eyes were roaming up and down Audrey in a way few men's pupils ever did. For a moment, she felt like the sales manager was appraising her, a little like a farmer looking over a cow before taking it home to his barn. She shifted uncomfortably.

"I'm just here to drop off my résumé," she said, shoving the thick paper at him. "For the showroom spokesperson?"

Both Fletch's daughters had come through Audrey's P.E. classes years ago. So it was strange to think of this dad of two as being an ogler. But he was definitely staring.

"You'll have to do," he said finally. "Follow me."

"Excuse me?" she asked, but he was off, striding into the offices behind the showroom where the new-paint smell of the freshly built building still lingered.

Had she really just gotten the job? If so, she had laundry in the dryer at home that she needed to get back to. They'd have to make the paperwork quick. In spite of this, she felt a flutter of excitement. Her career wasn't dead after all. *She could do this.*

As long as Fletch wasn't some kind of staring pervert, that is.

She expected him to lead her to the conference room, maybe even to their HR person, but instead he stopped at a closet behind one of the new steel desks.

"Look, we filled this job days ago," he explained, rifling through the hangers, "but the girl we had lined up quit. Literally just walked out the door."

"Literally?" Audrey asked. "Because a lot of people misuse that wor—"

"She's gone," Fletch interrupted, his dark brows pinched together with frustration, "and you're about her size. With some help, you might do. The makeup artist is here now—she'll teach you what you need to know. After today, you're on your own, so listen to her. The gig is Monday through Friday, ten to four. Stand there, look pretty, make the hogs look even better."

It took her a moment to grasp what he was asking. "This isn't a...sales position?"

"Sure. In a manner of speaking." He shook the clothing in his hand. It was a leather bustier and some chaps. It wasn't just immodest. It was downright scandalous.

Her face heated. She looked down at her long-sleeved T-shirt and track pants. Her typical uniform. If she was going to wear anything for this job, she'd thought it would be a pin-striped suit. "You want me to wear *that*?"

"It's not hard and it pays thirty bucks an hour. You want it or not?"

Audrey blanched. That was close to what she'd made as a teacher. With a master's degree.

She thought about her dwindling bank account. Her piles of unpaid bills. Beggars couldn't be choosers, it was true, but at that rate she wouldn't be a beggar for long. No matter how humiliating it would be to march out there dressed like Mad Max crossed with Victoria's Secret.

She studied the skimpy clothing. "Okay?" she said, hating the doubt in her own voice, hating the alarms that were firing, saying *Leave now*.

This didn't have to be so bad, she reasoned. After all, there had been a wilder version of herself that had loved being on the back of a Harley. That Audrey would have grabbed these clothes and worn them with pride.

But that Audrey had existed a long time ago. And she'd been very short-lived.

Even so, Audrey took the garments Fletch handed her. "Get changed in the employee bathroom down the hall. The makeup artist is two doors down from there."

The leather squeaked in her grip, as if protesting as much as she wanted to.

* * *

"Isn't this a little much?" she asked ten minutes later as Deborah, the makeup artist, volumized her eyelashes to about seventy times their normal length.

"Nope," Deborah said. "It looks good." Audrey wondered if she should trust the source, considering that Deborah's bloodred lips were hammered through with thick posts.

"You can just leave my hair," Audrey said as Deborah undid her ponytail. "It's hard to do much with."

"I have secret weapons," Deborah replied, grabbing a nearby can of hairspray. "Close your eyes."

"But I—" She tasted hairspray and shut her mouth.

When Audrey tried to take notes about when to use the eye-shadow primer and where to apply the bronzer, Deborah pulled the pen and paper out of her hands. "Watch, don't write," she said.

Audrey didn't know how to tell Deborah she didn't *want* to watch any of this. She didn't want to witness the humiliating aftermath of losing her job and having to dress for a part that felt downright embarrassing. But here she was. She locked eyes with the reflection in the mirror and tried not to blink.

"Look," Deborah said, softening after a minute, "this might not be your jam, but you need to look as dramatic and styled as those motorcycles out there. Your drugstore lip gloss isn't going to cut it."

Audrey didn't have the heart to tell Deborah it wasn't even gloss—it was ChapStick.

But as Deborah continued to work, Audrey found her words of protest drying up.

The dusting of blush made her soap-clean face look sunkissed. Her brown eyes, suddenly outlined in black, were both enormous and mysterious. Her hair cascaded around her shoulders in a way that reminded her of a waterfall— fierce and a little reckless. Audrey studied the changes silently. If she were honest with herself, she had to admit she looked good.

No, scratch that. She looked *hot*.

"How do you like it?" Deborah asked.

It was a wild, breathtaking look she'd only ever considered once before. And then locked away permanently.

"I take it your silence is good?" Deborah asked.

"Very good," Audrey replied finally, almost smiling.

"All right, tiger. Go get 'em."

She tottered out to the showroom floor in her new heels, part of her wondering if she was going to make it—and if everything was going to be okay after all.

* * *

Three hours later, Audrey could feel her underwear riding up her backside. Sweat was trickling down her thighs in rivulets. Skin-tight jeans were nearly cutting off her circulation, and leather chaps on top of the denim were raising her core body temperature enough to make her light-headed. A girl could be uncomfortable or embarrassed, she thought, but to be both at the same time was a special kind of torture.

She cringed at how alien she felt. What part of her had thought this was a good idea? Sure, she needed a job, but this wasn't employment, it was torture.

Bright light sliced through the showroom's enormous floor-to-ceiling windows and Audrey squinted, allowing that maybe this had been a mistake. She was a fish out of water in these clothes and with this hair—or maybe it was more like a monkey in a costume.

But it was either perform or walk. And Audrey had no other options.

She placed her hands on her hips, determined to look alluring just like Fletch had asked. Leather fringe on her cuff links fluttered like strips of ribbon in the wind. Standing next to one of the Harley-Davidson motorcycles in the showroom, she wondered what, exactly, alluring was. Track coaches didn't get much practice with things like that.

Former track coaches, that is.

A sharp pain pierced the tender place just behind her breastbone. She gritted her teeth. *Smile more, think less.*

The murmurs of the customers filled her ears. People swarmed amid the shiny chrome and sleek black lines of the motorcycles lining the floor all around her. For the past few hours, drivers had been thundering up and down the road just beyond the towering showroom windows, like cowboys riding handlebarred horses.

The noise from the engines was nearly loud enough to drown out her thoughts. Which was a good thing, considering that the only thing her brain wanted to focus on was the question of what in the heck she was doing here. And whether or not she should ever come back.

"Audrey?"

She turned. It must have been the sixth or seventh time she'd heard the question since she started her shift, the vowels and consonants of her name laced with disbelief.

This time, it was Red Updike. He'd sold her grass-fed beef from his farm for years. He stared at her, flannel shirt tucked into his well-worn Levi's, his mouth pulled slightly downward.

Her spine stiffened with embarrassment and something more. Frustration, maybe. It was one thing if Audrey wanted to feel out of place in these clothes and with all this makeup, but why did the people of White Pine have to stare at her like she was a circus freak with three heads? She imagined tongues were already wagging down at the Paul Bunyan Diner about her changes.

The thought made her want to stick the heel of her stiletto through one of the motorcycle tires and listen to it deflate with a satisfying hiss. She was irked enough with her situation without her community piling insult on injury. Instead of using her heel like a steak knife, Audrey plastered on the smile she'd perfected through a lifetime of agreeable rule-following.

"Hello, Mr. Updike," she said as professionally as she could. "Are you looking for a Harley today?"

He shifted. Right then, the only thing he was looking at was *her*. Probably wondering where the town's track coach and physical education teacher was hiding under all the hair and makeup.

Blame district downsizing, she wanted to tell him. But she held her tongue.

"This, uh..." Red seemed to be searching for a question that didn't involve a query about what she was wearing. His head, more square than round, tilted to the side.

Audrey fought off an eye roll. She almost liked it better when strangers from Marston or New Prave or Faldet or any of the surrounding towns would give her a once-over and a low wolf whistle. It might be chauvinistic and objectifying, but at least their jaws didn't go slack and their eyes round with bewilderment. For crying out loud, she thought, was it really so impossible that she could work her...assets a bit?

She didn't need the folks in her hometown to stand up and slow clap for her, but she wished they could be a bit more supportive.

Because, truthfully, there *was* a tiny part that didn't hate this. Deep down she felt a crackle of energy where a thrumming sliver of her was somehow more awake in these new clothes. More present, perhaps, as if their contour and shape were bringing her to the forefront of her own life just a bit more.

She kept it buried, though. Audrey knew all too well

where such wild-hearted blazes could lead. And she wasn't about to go down that road again anytime soon.

Red cleared his throat. "What's the, ah, front-tire speed rating on this hog?"

Audrey brought herself back to the job at hand. She flashed Red the smile she'd taught herself at the beginning of the day when it dawned on her that she'd be spending her time in a Harley-Davidson dealership and she knew nothing about most things on two wheels.

"I can find out about that tire rating for you, Red. In the meantime, can I show you some of the features of this one right here?"

She had no idea what any of the mechanics were on the Harley Street Glide she was pointing to, other than it was a beautiful, inky black that reminded her of a moonless night, and the seat was a scoop of leather deep enough to throw on a horse and call a saddle.

"These are the...handlebars," Audrey said, tottering over to the front of the motorcycle in her heels and wishing momentarily for her sensible running shoes. "This is where you steer."

The lines on Red's forehead deepened in a confused crinkle. Audrey was never going to be any kind of help to the dealership if she kept this up. She straightened, and looked at Red square on.

"Honestly, I never would have guessed that a Harley was your kind of ride. Tell me what you like about them."

Red's expression relaxed a little. He stared at the bike. "Oh, well, you know. Machine like this is quality, a real piece of craftsmanship. And—a fellow can dream, I suppose."

Just goes to show how little I know, Audrey thought.

She never would have figured a Harley store in a small town like White Pine could make it. After all, her community comprised everyday folks who were farmers and teachers and small-business owners. But White Pine Harley had been open for a few weeks now, and it seemed to be doing fine. Today, there had been a constant, steady trickle of people in the showroom. And more sales than she'd expected. Ben Howell, her dentist, had bought a three-wheeled Electra Glide. And Lester Lawsick, the local large-animal vet, had bought a used machine off the back lot.

I may have been wrong about everything, Audrey realized suddenly, wondering how well she really knew her hometown. If the community could fire her from her dream job, stare at her like a freak when she found a new one, and support a Harley dealership, what was next?

"They've got used ones, too, if you're interested," she said, trying to help Red think about his options, if price was an issue.

"I suppose I'm just browsing," Red replied. "Though I do like the idea of change. Riding this around instead of my old truck. Can you imagine?"

Audrey felt herself smile—this time for real. Part of her *could* imagine Red whipping along White Pine's back roads, the rumble of the Harley echoing over the hills, the smell of hay and grass on the wind as he sped past fence posts and freshly painted barns.

"Sometimes we all need a little change," Audrey agreed, speaking the words for her sake as much as Red's. A few short weeks ago, she'd been coaching long-legged girls over hurdles to get the whole team to the state finals. As a P.E. teacher, she'd been teaching volleyball and softball and lacrosse. Then, the principal had told her that the district had eliminated P.E. from the curriculum due to emergency budget cuts that would avoid a district shut-down. Paul Frace, the bearded English teacher, would be taking over coaching duties. She didn't even get to finish out the remainder of the school year.

"No child left without a huge behind," she'd quipped to some colleagues about the disbanded P.E. program as she packed up her things. It was either joke—or bawl.

And now, here she was, standing next to a motorcycle thanks to the fact that she'd been a runner, an *athlete*, and she could look good in some chaps.

She caught a glimpse of her body in the showroom's large display mirrors. Every curve of her was pressed against leather and denim, every piece of her glossy auburn hair had been sprayed to tousled perfection. She looked like a different person.

Maybe that wasn't such a bad thing.

She smoothed the front of her leather bustier, wondering if she should have been strutting around Harleys all along. She figured she would at least have had more fun.

"You have a good day now," Red said, jolting Audrey back to the here and now. She blinked, worried she'd missed conversation with him while staring at herself. But Red had been looking at the motorcycle and was probably lost in his own fantasy, too.

He walked away, his workman's boots clomping on the white-tiled floor. That left Audrey alone for the moment. She lifted her face to the afternoon light that slanted into the showroom. It sparkled on chrome fenders and warmed the buttery black leather of the motorcycle seat enough to make her want to lie down and nap. Not that she was going to do any sleeping anywhere in her current attire. But she could sit for a while.

Grasping the motorcycle's handlebars and pitching herself forward, she scooted and shimmied until one leg was over the seat. It wasn't graceful, and she was pretty sure there were titters coming from customers in the showroom, but at least she was off her feet in those heels.

She readjusted herself on her machine, trying to ignore the pinch of jeans on her flesh. She'd just gotten comfortable when she heard her name again, spoken from behind.

"Audrey."

This time it wasn't a question.

A shiver ran through her, as if the air conditioners had suddenly kicked in and icy gusts were coursing through the room. Beneath the bustier, her heart began to pound so hard she worried for a moment the stays might not hold and she'd come toppling out of the whole contraption.

Her nerves tightened with adrenaline, both hopeful and fearful at the same time. It couldn't be…

"*Audrey.*"

She struggled to breathe. Steadying herself as best she could, she turned and stared into the pale green eyes of Kieran Callaghan.

Her whole body swayed. If she hadn't been sitting down, she would have certainly fallen like a tree in the middle of a clear-cut.

Kieran Callaghan.

Dear God.

He was wearing a dark leather jacket and jeans, standing with both hands in his back pockets as if he were reclining on life itself. His eyes were the color of new blades of grass reaching toward the spring sun. They searched her face as he likely tried to figure out what in the world she was doing in front of him, butt cheeks on a Harley.

With every ounce of composure she could muster, Audrey straightened her spine. She tried not to focus too much on the cleft in his chin, or how the afternoon light ignited hints of gold in his dark red hair.

She spoke the first three words that came to mind: "You're an *asshole*."

The insult was out before she could take it back. Not that she wanted to, but the vehemence behind it jolted her. *Maybe it's the new clothes,* she thought.

Or maybe it was five years of anger finally getting a chance to vent.

Kieran raised a brow at her. He opened his mouth, but she found herself leaning forward, the words coming hard and fast. "I've been waiting five years to tell you that. And I have no idea what you're doing back in town, but you should leave this store. Right. *Now*."

Kieran's wide mouth twitched. Audrey tried not to stare at the movement, tried not to think about how much she'd once loved that mouth.

She narrowed her eyes. "Well? What do you have to say for yourself?"

Kieran grinned—a goofy, toothy motion that had her insides fluttering.

"Well, since you're asking," he said, his eyes traveling slowly along her body from head to toe, assessing her curves and attire like *she* was what he wanted to ride, "I suppose I should tell you that I'm your boss."

Audrey stared. "Excuse me?"

"And calling me an asshole is grounds for firing."

Audrey's brain buzzed, trying to process how in the

world her ex-boyfriend was standing in front of her claiming to work here.

Kieran Callaghan didn't hold down steady jobs. He didn't stick around anywhere for very long, in fact. That was a lesson Audrey herself had learned the hard way.

She stared at the expensive leather jacket covering his broad shoulders, the fine cut of the jeans he was wearing, the thick silver watch on his wrist. Audrey had pictured Kieran in her mind's eye a thousand times over the past five years. He had been both handsome and intelligent when they'd met, and she figured he'd simply become less so as time went on. In her imaginary picture of him, he'd grown thin and ragged. In her version, leaving her had been the thing that had broken him.

In her wildest dreams he'd never improved. He was even more chiseled somehow, and his eyes held a depth—a wisdom—that unnerved her. Audrey's breathing turned uneven, and it wasn't just because of the corset.

"I don't believe you," Audrey said, trying to keep the turbulent emotions off her face. "There is no way you work here."

"Now you're accusing your boss of lying. You're not really getting off on the right foot."

The rule-obeying part of Audrey's brain raised an alarm. If there was a chance Kieran was telling the truth, she needed to shut up now. In fact, she'd needed to shut up five minutes ago when she called him an asshole.

"It's good to see you," Kieran said slowly, his voice low enough so that Audrey swore she could feel the reverberations of it on her skin. "But we certainly can't work together. I'm going to have to ask you to leave this position."

A roar started in Audrey's ears. She reached out to the motorcycle to steady herself.

Kieran Callaghan was *not* going to storm back into her life just so she could lose two jobs in two weeks. She was not going to just accept her pink slip and march out of here like the good girl everyone expected her to be. She was wearing eyeliner and stilettos, for crying out loud.

Kieran might be inside this dealership looking altogether different, but, by God, so was she.

"I'm not going anywhere," Audrey said. She straightened on the back of the motorcycle. "I don't care what your job is here. Do whatever you want. But this? Right here? Is *my job*."

She marveled at the words coming out of her mouth. As if she spoke this way to people in authority all the time.

"Audrey, listen—"

"No, you listen. I don't know who you think you are, but you'd better back off. Or there is going to be some serious trouble."

Kieran's eyes flashed. "Are you threatening me?"

He leaned in farther, and Audrey's blood pounded. His strong jaw, his high cheekbones, his warm skin—it was all mere inches away. Some deep, reckless part inside wanted to throw herself against him, inhaling his scent and putting her lips on his like she had five years ago. Instead, she channeled her energy and looked him square in the eye.

"Why don't you find out? *Asshole*."

CHAPTER TWO

$\mathcal{K}$ieran Callaghan tried to focus on the fact that he'd just been called an asshole in his own showroom—twice—rather than admit to the overwhelming emotions that came with seeing Audrey Tanner again after all these years. He steeled himself against the searing heat flaming every one of his nerve endings. He forced himself to relax, to play it cool. He hadn't anticipated running into her here, of all places, but that didn't mean they had to be near each other for very much longer.

The back of his throat tightened, the way it always did when he was gambling and on the verge of either a crushing loss or an enormous win. He gave her the same easy smile he used to give the other card sharks around the green felt table, and ignored his churning insides.

I have to get her out of here, he thought, fighting the pull toward her. Good Christian mother of Mary, the woman looked like she'd just popped off the pages of a magazine—

and not the kind they kept in doctors' waiting rooms. Back in the day, he'd been unbearably turned on when she wore running shorts and a tank top. Now that she was clad in leather and tight jeans, he worried his hands might reach for her before his brain could tell them not to.

"I'm not sure you understand," he said, summoning every ounce of professionalism he had, "but this isn't a negotiation."

"Then it's a war," Audrey shot back. "Because you cannot fire me." Her brown eyes, normally warm and welcoming, were flinty with irritation and anger. She placed a hand on the lean space where her hip met her waist. He tried not to stare, tried not to imagine his own fingers on that curve, moving slowly upward to—

"I am *talking* to you." Her voice was tight with emotion. The sound of it echoed in the high-ceilinged showroom— a gunshot in what was supposed to be an oasis—and a few customers turned to stare.

Kieran arched a brow, letting that be his only reaction. He didn't want customers suspecting that anything was amiss. But underneath his leather jacket, his whole body was a jumble of nerves. He was going to have to get her off that motorcycle and into a space where they could talk.

That is, if he could get control over himself long enough to get more than a handful of words out. Because seeing Audrey again was like being hurdled from a warm, dry room into a freezing hailstorm. It was shocking, jarring, and more painful than he'd like to admit. Emotions from the past pummeled him—guilt, affection, remorse.

Five years ago, he'd ridden a Harley into White Pine during its annual Asparagus Festival, fallen head-over-heels for Audrey, and then left after two weeks.

Since then, he'd worked hard to forget her, building a
life for himself and letting five years of new experiences
fill the space in his mind that she'd once occupied. He assumed he'd succeeded.

The tightening in his chest at the sight of her was telling
him otherwise. Audrey might look completely different, but
her effect on him was exactly the same as he remembered.

The only difference was that now he wasn't a wild and
reckless rider tearing up the open road and doubling down
every chance he could. That was a lifetime ago, which
meant that no matter what feelings were bubbling to the
surface, he couldn't let Audrey's nearness affect him. He
was a professional, dammit. And this was his showroom.
No one called the shots in here but him.

He was in the process of telling her to leave again when
his eyes landed on the top of her bustier, and his words
got lost somewhere between his brain and his mouth. Her
breasts were practically sculpted over the top of the leather,
forming twin mounds that had lust rolling through him in
hot waves.

"Up here, Callaghan," Audrey said, pointing to her face.

His eyes snapped to hers. What the hell was wrong with
him? He was a professional manager, for crying out loud,
not some horny teenager. "Get off the hog, and let's go
talk," he said, trying to regain control of the situation.

"No. You have no right."

"As this dealership's advancement director, I sure as hell
do." His tone was icy, clinical. Underneath the bustier, she
stiffened.

"What's an advancement director?"

"I make sure new Harley-Davidson dealerships get up
and running right."

"This one seems fine."

Her beautiful mouth, small and bow-shaped, was knotted tightly.

He'd never seen her mouth in such a state. When they were together, she'd used her mouth to smile, or to kiss him so eagerly he thought he'd snap from the desire between them. He was long gone by the time she'd frowned that deeply, he supposed.

Dammit, he should have expected to see her again instead of assuming he could avoid her. He should have planned better, strategized more. He could practically hear Lorne laughing at him for his stupidity. "You fuckin' blockhead," his boss would say, smacking him on the back of his head. And then he'd guffaw until Kieran was laughing, too, unable to help himself.

"You think this is funny?" Audrey demanded. "You think it's hilarious to come in here and threaten someone's job?"

"You already have a job," Kieran answered, instantly refocusing. "You're a gym teacher. You shouldn't be here."

Audrey's face paled. "That—that's not the case anymore. I work here now."

The news surprised him; the broken note in her voice disarmed him. But he pushed past it. "Not for much longer you don't. Get off the hog and follow me, or I'll call security."

"No."

"Suit yourself."

He was reaching into his back pocket for his cell phone when she thrust her hand forward to stay his. The feel of her fingers on his skin had him seeing dark spots in his peripheral vision.

"Wait."

He didn't dare meet her gaze again. Instead, he stared at her fingers, at the short, trimmed nails that were so plain and practical in contrast to the rest of her. They were still a gym teacher's nails, he thought, wondering what in the world had happened to Audrey to make her shimmy into tight clothes and sit on a motorcycle for pay.

"I can't," Audrey whispered, leaning closer to him. Her scent reached him—fresh detergent and a hint of vanilla— and it was all he could do to keep his face a mask of indifference.

"You can't what?"

"I can't get off this bike. Literally. And I'm not misusing the word."

"You're stuck?"

"Something like that."

"How'd you get on the bike, then?"

Audrey pulled her hand back, and he noted its absence acutely. "I did a little shimmy thing, sort of pitching myself forward."

"So do that again, but in reverse."

"Well, I would except…" She tucked a piece of glossy brown hair behind an ear, stalling.

"Except?"

"I felt a button pop. On my jeans. And I'm afraid, if I do it again, that…" She lowered her eyes and studied the seat's black leather. Kieran worked to keep a straight face.

"You're afraid that if you get up, your pants will fall down?"

"Not fall down, no. They're too tight for that. But split open at the front? Yes."

He could see her cheeks color, even under the makeup. It made the light dusting of freckles across her nose even sexier, if that was possible. He shook his head, trying to stay focused.

"Well, that's no problem," Kieran replied casually, even though the idea of Audrey's pants bursting open had his cock hardening against the fabric of his jeans. "We'll just do this."

In one smooth motion, he scooped her off the Harley and into his arms. He shook his head when he saw her getting ready to protest. "You yell or whine, and I'll carry you outside and lock the doors on you. You stay quiet, we can talk in the back room. Agreed?" He saw an angry muscle working in her jaw, but she nodded nevertheless.

And then, just like that, Audrey Tanner was back in his arms.

He'd been so sure that he'd be able to return to White Pine and avoid his past altogether. So how he came to be *carrying* part of it in the form of Audrey Tanner, how her arms came to be looped around his neck, how her smell was everywhere, intoxicating him as he stormed toward the back room, was a turn of events he could never have predicted. It was also a dangerous set of circumstances, and he never should have let it get this far.

He had a job to do, dammit. He was here to build on his future—not relive the past.

When he reached one of the back offices he kneed the door open, then placed her roughly on the floor. She stumbled a little in the heels, but righted herself, glaring at him. He was about to tell her to change clothes and get out of the dealership when he heard a pop. Something on the bustier came loose—he wasn't sure what—and before Audrey could stop it, the front panel covering her chest slid downward. Her mouth made a horrified little O as her breasts sprang from their constrictive covering. Her nipples pebbled at the sudden exposure to cool air. Kieran got a hungry eyeful before Audrey scrambled to cover herself with a mortified "Oh!"

Instinctively, he reached forward to help her. "I'm so sorr—" he started before she swatted his hand away.

"Stop it!" she cried. "Get back!"

Just then, Fletch Knudson walked through the office door, and pulled up short. His neat moustache twitched. His ice-blue eyes flicked back and forth between them. "What in holy hell is going on here?"

"It's nothing," Kieran said, stepping away from Audrey.

Fletch's face was bunched with concentration, trying to make sense of what he was seeing. His gaze settled on Audrey.

"Did he hurt you?"

Audrey clutched the broken bustier to her chest. "No, of course not," Kieran interjected. "It was just an accident."

"I'm waiting for *her* to answer," Fletch said.

Audrey's knuckles whitened around her handful of clothing. Kieran realized right then that she held all the cards. Her hand trumped his.

She could take him down with a smattering of words, could pretend this had been more than it was, and put his job at risk. Kieran forced his breathing to be steady—in and out, calm like it wasn't the last play of the game—and tried to remember that the woman he'd lost his heart to five years ago had a blazing white soul, the stark opposite of his black one. She wasn't like him; she wasn't always calculating how to turn the odds in her favor.

Audrey had been so kind, so willing to trust him and believe the best. But even her shining golden goodness—her love for her friends and family and her hometown, her faith in the people around her—couldn't lighten the darkness inside him, though five years ago he'd wanted it to.

Underneath the makeup, Audrey's face was pale. "No," she said, "he didn't hurt me. It's just a misunderstanding."

Kieran let out a breath he didn't know he was holding.

"But I'd appreciate it if you'd tell him that he can't fire me. I need this job."

Fletch's face was slack with relief. "I'm glad this isn't what it looked like. It's Kieran's call, though, about your job."

Kieran's throat was dry. "I think—" he began, but couldn't put the rest of the sentence together. Thinking around Audrey Tanner had suddenly become downright difficult.

"Let her stay, Callaghan," Fletch said. "The model we had lined up quit, and Audrey jumped in like a champ. She's doing fine out there."

There was a time when a situation like this—one that knotted his thoughts and tied up his insides—would have had him running to the betting table. There, he'd place his money with the dealer, again and again, until nothing remained in his brain except the game. Except winning.

Only, more often than not, he came out losing.

Those days were behind him, thank God. Yet, even if he let Audrey keep her job, he couldn't allow her to think that being here was a good idea. Being around her was a reminder of a past he needed to forget. He had a new life to keep on building, and in order to do that, he had to get her gone. Even if it wasn't today, it would have to be soon.

He pulled himself up to his full height—six foot three—and stared down at Audrey. Her hands shook as they held the broken leather tight against her chest. But, to his surprise, she didn't back away from him. Instead, she lifted her chin and stared at him square on. Audrey might have the same goodness illuminating the inside of her, but she *was* different than the woman he knew five years ago.

"If you stay, then you stay out of my way," he growled at her, working hard to sound intimidating. "Understand?"

"Or *you* can stay out of *my* way," she replied, her brown eyes narrowing. "Last I recall, I was here first."

Kieran was getting ready to dress her down with a lecture about still being her boss, but Fletch stepped in. "All right, you two. Enough. Let's call it a truce. Audrey, you're done for the day. Go on and head home. We'll see you tomorrow."

With a final glare at Kieran, Audrey walked away—one hand holding up her broken pants, and one hand gripping the broken bustier. She tilted her chin high enough to make him wonder what in the world had happened to the Audrey he knew—the fresh-faced gym teacher who had stolen his heart with her feet placed squarely in practical running shoes. Why she was now clad in makeup and leather at a Harley dealership was beyond him.

Apparently he had a lot to learn about the new Audrey Tanner.

Not that he would afford himself that luxury.

He clenched his fists and steeled his resolve. As much as he might want it to be different, the most important thing to know about Audrey Tanner was the simplest thing: He was going to have to stay as far away from her as possible.

CHAPTER THREE

$\mathscr{A}$udrey hung up her new clothes in the dealership's back closet and felt a small pang as she walked away from them at the end of her shift.

She tried to push the emotions aside. It was silly to think that just changing your outside could change your insides.

But she couldn't deny she felt different after a day of looking like someone else.

She slid into her car in the parking lot and stared at the beige interior. It seemed so dull after the glossy colors and shining chrome of the dealership. She wondered briefly about getting one of those mirror balls that hung from the rearview, but she could already hear her sister, Casey, telling her it was ridiculous. Inefficient. Excessive.

She couldn't even imagine her sister's reaction when she told her about the new job. She swallowed, figuring she'd just avoid that topic altogether for a while.

The image of clean-cut, handsome-as-ever Kieran filled her mind as she pulled away from the dealership. Her skin flamed at the memory of being carried off the dealership floor in his arms, and of her bustier flying open minutes later. Her stomach flipped at the raw power of being in his arms, of being close to him again.

Careful, her brain cautioned. She took a calming breath. She wasn't about to let five years of pain disintegrate like paper on a wet sidewalk. Kieran was an unhappy part of her past that didn't vanish easily.

Good for me for calling him an asshole, she thought. She giggled involuntarily. What had come over her? It was as if stepping into the clothes was stepping into someone else's body. It was a person Audrey didn't know very well, but someone with whom she was excited to become more acquainted.

A spring wind whipped through town as she headed into Lumberjack Grocery to get food for tonight's Knots and Bolts recipe exchange. The crisp air snapped the American flag outside the library as she turned down Main Street. When she stepped out of the car, the wind pulled at Audrey's already tousled hair.

She headed for the bakery, hoping to grab something prepared. She'd had plans to bake raspberry bars for tonight, but the unexpected turn of events today had meant all the baking ingredients were still intact at home.

Her thick-soled running shoes hardly made a sound on the grocery store's tile. Her track pants didn't pinch at all. She wondered suddenly what it would feel like to stride down the smooth floor on her stilettos, the fringe on her leather sleeve fluttering. She was so lost in thought that she nearly crashed into Evelyn Beauford head-on.

"Oh, excuse me," Audrey said as their shoulders bumped. "I'm not watching where I'm going."

Evelyn's eyes seemed to widen along with her smile. "Goodness, Audrey! I'm not sure I would have recognized you if we hadn't collided. Have you done something new with... your hair?"

Audrey had changed her clothes, but apparently her hair and makeup on their own were enough to startle people. "Just trying out a different look."

The creases in Evelyn's lined face deepened. "Well, what perfect timing to see you here. I was hoping to bend your ear soon about the upcoming Good Shepherd Walk."

Audrey groaned inwardly. The annual Good Shepherd Walk was a fund-raiser for the local Catholic church, and she somehow always found herself on the planning committee for it. Never mind that she wasn't Catholic, and charity walks weren't exactly her thing. Everyone just assumed they were because she taught P.E.

Or used to, anyway.

"This year, I thought we'd start down by the river and end at the church, instead of the other way around," Evelyn said, her soft, powder-smelling hand reaching out to grasp Audrey's.

Audrey stared down at Evelyn's wrinkled skin, her insides knotting as she wondered for the seventh year in a row how to tell the older woman that she did not, in fact, want to help with the Good Shepherd charity walk.

"I—that is—this isn't a good time for me," Audrey stumbled. "As you probably know, I lost my job. Things are a little difficult."

Evelyn nodded solemnly. "Of course. Which is why it's more important than ever to give. When you're in need, that's when you serve the most. 'Give and it shall be given to you.'" She smiled warmly, and Audrey's heart sank.

How could she argue with this sweet, Bible-quoting old lady?

But that was the problem. Audrey wanted to argue. She wanted to tell Evelyn that she loved running, but not walking. That the crowds made her a little dizzy. That every year, she tried to make the registration process electronic, but the group insisted on paper forms and it was always a mess.

Only Audrey never said those things. Not to anyone. Not to her school's principal when he'd insisted Audrey serve on the superintendent search committee, even though Audrey was already on the community outreach committee. Not to her hairdresser when Audrey had asked for bangs and her hairdresser had said they were out of fashion, no matter that it was Audrey's choice. Not even to the waiter the other day when he brought her a roast beef sandwich instead of a turkey club, but Audrey ate it politely so she wouldn't raise a fuss.

Maybe it was time for her to start speaking up. She pictured herself in the clothes from the dealership and tried to recall the boldness she'd felt in them.

"I just don't think I can, Evelyn," Audrey said. Her voice shook but she pressed forward. "Not this year. I'm very sorry."

"Oh." The old woman's face fell. "We just need your help so badly."

"I know, but—"

"I'm not sure we can have the walk without you, frankly."

Guilt washed over her. She stared at her running shoes. She couldn't leave them in the lurch like this. Could she?

"Perhaps I could find my replacement? Would that help?"

"Well, I suppose. How long do you need, dear?"

"A couple days. I'm sure I can find someone."

"We hate to lose you. You've been such a blessing."

"I'm sure I can find someone who is equally as... blessed," Audrey bluffed. After chatting for a few more minutes about Evelyn's tulips this spring, she waved goodbye to the older woman and headed for the bakery. She hadn't gotten out of the Good Shepherd Walk entirely, but she felt a twinge of pride that she'd made some baby steps in that direction. It was a start, anyway.

The rich scent of bread and yeast had her stomach growling as she stared at multiple cakes and pies. She figured she ought to grab the apple pie because it was the dessert most people would enjoy. What Audrey wanted, however, was the twelve-pack of powdered-sugar donuts on the nearby shelf. They were like dusty soldiers all lined up in their plastic tray, ready to march into her mouth.

The pie would be more suitable. More people would like it.

But wasn't it her dessert to bring?

"Come to Mama," she whispered, and grabbed the donuts. She headed for the checkout before she could change her mind.

* * *

In the cozy back room of Knots and Bolts, Audrey sipped a velvety red wine, grateful to finally be gathered with her friends after the day she'd had. She sighed with contentment just as her friend Betty eyed her across the table.

"You look like a Minneapolis hooker," Betty said. Her friend's clear skin and rounded cheeks were nearly angelic in the warm light. Which was only appropriate, Audrey supposed, since Betty was now the wife of the local pastor.

Audrey put a self-conscious hand up to her face.

"Oh, leave her be," Willa Masterson—now Olmstead—replied. Willa poured more red wine into Audrey's glass. The splash of the liquid was a comfort, and Audrey smiled gratefully. Willa, the most recent addition to the weekly recipe exchange in the room at the back of Betty's fabric store, had returned to White Pine recently after years in New York, and had opened up the White Pine Bed and Breakfast in her family's old home on Oak Street. The charming B and B was thriving, and so was Willa's marriage since she'd rekindled her romance with her high-school sweetheart—and one-time house contractor—Burk Olmstead.

Audrey felt a small twinge of jealousy as she studied her friend's laughing green eyes, her radiant smile, and the sparkling ring on her left hand. She tried ignoring it, but the splinter of emotion just buried itself deeper: this feeling that Audrey had lived in White Pine her whole life, played by all the rules, and hadn't found love, but Willa had managed to swoop in, find a guy, *and* start a business in a matter of months.

It's because Willa takes risks, Audrey thought, recalling how hard Willa had worked to change her attitude and open her heart to Burk. Not to mention learn how to fix up old furniture.

"Earth to Audrey," Betty was saying, tapping the table with her finger.

"Sorry, what?"

"You went away," Betty said, her corn-yellow hair so soft in comparison with her no-nonsense tone. Betty pushed a plate of hot dish toward Audrey—a Minnesota version of casserole and a favorite of the recipe exchange—and arched a brow. "What aren't you telling us? And does it have something to do with why your face looks like you survived an explosion at the cosmetics factory?"

"Betty!" Willa scolded.

Audrey laughed. She and Betty had known each other since high school, and she understood that her friend meant well. It was just that Betty could be shockingly direct sometimes, which was precisely why Randall Sondheim, pastor of the town's Lutheran church, had asked her to marry him. They'd tied the knot at Willa's B and B last fall.

"I'll fill you in on my face," Audrey said, "but let's wait until the other girls get here." Burk's sister, Anna Palowski, and Stephanie Munson, another high-school friend, were usually running late—but they got a wide berth because they were also the moms in the group.

As if Audrey had summoned them with the mention, the Knots and Bolts back door opened and the fresh, early-summer air rushed in with the two remaining women.

"Sorry we're late!" Stephanie sing-songed, dropping herself into a chair. In addition to the stains her clothes usually sported from her five-year-old twins, there were now paint flecks in her bright red hair, thanks to her new job helping Willa rehab furniture and sell it. Audrey stared at her friend, wondering how she did it all. *I don't even want to make time for a church walk,* she thought. And here Stephanie was, raising twins and working for Willa.

"I just dropped Juniper off at drum lessons," Anna said, referencing her daughter. She reached for the wine, the movement dislodging some of her ebony hair from its messy up-do. "Can you believe it? Sam met her there and is going to bring her home after they're done. He thinks our daughter has innate talent, and I swear he's already thinking about how to be her manager. And all I can think is, our daughter is *three*."

"Your husband's just having some fun," Betty reassured her. "And Juniper will probably be awed that adults are telling her it's okay to bang on some stuff for a while." Betty stood, walked to the back room's small kitchenette, and returned with two more steaming plates of hot dish. The scent of warm cheese and ham had all the women *mmm*-ing appreciatively. Betty had been experimenting with "southern style" hot dishes, so this particular casserole was laced with grits and collard greens.

"Betty, I swear you make the best hot dishes," Audrey said, lifting her fork just as Anna dropped hers.

The clatter of the metal on wood jerked everyone to attention. "Sorry," Anna apologized, reaching for the errant utensil. "It's just—Audrey, your *face*. I didn't realize—I'm just not used to seeing you like, like—"

"Like she should be dancing on one of those poles at the Outlaw Bar?" Betty finished for her.

"Oh!" Stephanie said, finally taking a good look at her friend. "Audrey, that's more makeup than I've seen you wear, ever. Do you have a date?"

Audrey sat up straighter. "No, but I do have a job."

There was a beat of silence. Betty opened her mouth to speak, but a swift kick from Willa under the table silenced her.

"Congratulations!" Willa said, grasping Audrey's hand. Audrey squeezed, grateful for the support. After she had been fired, Willa had taken the brunt of Audrey's tear-choked phone calls.

"Is your job—" Betty started.

"Why don't we let *Audrey* tell us what her new job is?" Willa interrupted.

Audrey speared her hot dish and thought about how to explain what had happened. And the fact that Kieran Callaghan was back in town.

"It turned out that the Harley dealership in town was hiring. I went in to submit my application for a sales position, and they gave me one. It's just, I'm not selling the bikes as much as I'm...modeling them."

"Modeling them how?" Anna asked.

"Well, like, sitting on them."

"Wearing pants and a T-shirt like right now, huh?" Betty asked.

"Not exactly," Audrey replied, thinking about the leather bustier and jeans she was going to have to pour herself back into tomorrow. "It's more like motorcycle attire. Jeans and a leather corset. Some chaps. And stilettos."

Betty whistled. "Damn."

Audrey flattened her palms on the red table. The bumps and knots of the old wood were like Braille, hiding messages in the grain. Maybe even one confirming it was time to be done being so mousy. She thought about the incredulous looks she got from the White Pine customers on the showroom floor, and how they were so similar to the looks her friends were giving her now. Was it really so impossible that she could be...*sexy*?

She drew a breath. "Listen, I know it's not what anyone pictured me doing—hell, it's not what *I* pictured me doing—but it pays really well. And I don't have a lot of options here. So if everyone could just be supportive for five seconds, I'd really appreciate it."

The room went silent. The only sound was the wind whispering through new leaves on the trees outside. Betty set down her fork. "Sweetheart, I'm sorry. I get ahead of myself sometimes. I don't mean to run my mouth like I don't support you."

"We *all* support you," Stephanie said, "and we want you to be happy. If this does the trick, then go for it."

"There's something about it I like," Audrey said, remembering how empowered she'd felt staring at her reflection in the showroom's mirrors, "but the truth is, I almost got fired from this job, too."

"What?" Willa asked, her green eyes wide. "Why?"

Audrey steadied herself, because the memory of Kieran Callaghan saying her name, of him pulling her into his arms and carrying her to the back room, and of him looking hungry enough to devour her when her bustier flew open, was about to topple her off her chair.

"It turns out Kieran Callaghan is back, and he's the manager of the place or something. He didn't want me there, and he tried to fire me, but Fletch Knudson backed me up, and I was able to stay."

"Kieran Callaghan?" Betty asked, her tone laced with anger. "The same Irish jerk who broke your heart?"

"The very same."

Betty set her jaw. "I will pickle his balls for him if he messes with you."

Audrey burst out laughing. "Betty! It's fine. I can handle him."

Willa studied her. "Are you upset he's back?"

Kieran Callaghan had torn her apart, and she'd rather

chair ten Good Shepherd Walks than have to be near him again. But he didn't upset her in the way Willa was asking, because out of all the people in the showroom today, he was the one who'd studied her in a way that made her feel like a painting: as if her skin was some kind of gilded frame and he was peering through to her insides, trying to find meaning there. It was the same way she'd remembered him looking at her five years ago, so intent on taking her all in. So intent on taking everything in, frankly. On the back of his motorcycle, he'd point out things he was always catching with his sharp eye: the tail of a fox disappearing into the brush, for example, or the white head of an eagle soaring in the sky overhead.

Of course, she could be as nostalgic as she wanted about who he'd once been or how he looked at her now, but their chance at being together was gone, stripped like a field of wheat after a brittle, unrelenting rain. Five years ago, she'd fallen so hard so fast that her heart had plummeted before she could catch it. She'd thought she'd found true love, while he'd fled after penning a hastily scribbled note— without even a *good-bye*—and she was still struggling to make sense of it.

Audrey realized Willa was staring at her, waiting for her to say something.

"Kieran being back is nothing," she told her friends. "He's still a jerk. And I'm not going near him if I can help it."

"But won't it be weird, working with him?" Stephanie asked, her ginger hair flaming in the light.

"We're working together, not sleeping together," she replied, even as part of her imagined their bodies twisting in the sheets.

"More power to you," Anna said. "Stick it out, and show Kieran what he's missing."

"Absolutely," Willa agreed. "Make him pine for what he lost. I mean, you look like a different person rocking that makeup. Your eyeliner alone is amazing. You look practically Egyptian."

"She'll make Kieran wish he could raid her tomb," Betty said.

"Or make him wish he could unwrap her mummy." Stephanie grinned.

"After a week, Kieran Callaghan will be *dying* see her Nefer-titties," Anna said, slapping the table.

"He'll want to water her fertile crescent!" Willa cried.

Audrey snorted. "I already know he has a big...sarcophagus."

Everyone around the table collapsed into fits of laughter. After long minutes, they finally collected themselves, sipping wine to recover. Audrey reached into her bag and placed the donuts on the table. "Didn't want anyone to think I forgot dessert."

The women stared at the prepackaged food.

"I thought you were bringing raspberry bars," Betty said.

"I was going to. But instead of baking I sat on a Harley all day."

"I didn't even know you liked donuts," Willa said.

Audrey picked up a white ring and stared at it. Powdered sugar drifted onto her fingers. "That's the thing. I love donuts. Like, really love them. I never eat them, though."

"Until now," Stephanie said, taking one for herself.

"Until now," Audrey agreed, biting into the dessert. The

powder and cake exploded in a sugary mix in her mouth. She groaned with pleasure.

Empty calories, her sister, Casey, would say. Instead of feeling empty, however, Audrey felt energized, full of something she couldn't place. Like standing on the edge of a windswept cliff and staring into the churning sea. The thundering roar of all that tumultuous water would fill anyone up with strange yearning.

Not that Audrey had ever seen anything like that in real life. She'd never left Minnesota, actually.

But that night when she got home, when the spring wind howled all around her and shook the tree branches above, she stood on her porch for a few extra moments with her eyes closed. If she concentrated, she could just about picture her feet on a craggy outcrop and the water frothing below.

The image stirred something inside of her. But what it was, exactly, or what it was leading to, she wasn't quite sure. Later, she lay in bed and let the wind's rattle sweep all thoughts of Kieran Callaghan far, far from her mind.

CHAPTER FOUR

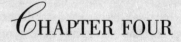

The wind had died down the next morning when Audrey got to work. There was no rattle against the windows or howl in the trees to distract her from Kieran across the showroom floor. She tried to tear her eyes away from him, but was somehow unable to make her pupils move.

A dark wool sports coat hugged his broad shoulders in a perfect fit. Instead of a collared shirt, he wore a T-shirt underneath it, and Audrey swore she could almost see the outline of his rock-solid abs through the cotton material. She licked her lips distractedly, thinking about lifting the shirt from the waist of his jeans and sliding her hands underneath, running her palms over his ridges, the heat from his skin warming her through and through.

The idea made her shaky, not to mention irritated. There was nothing about Kieran that should make her hotter than she already was under these blasted showroom lights. Especially after the way he'd treated her.

She stuck out her hip in an effort to make the nearby motorcycle—a small, compact Night Rod that looked like it could race the wind itself—appear even more appealing. Inside, she was dying for a hamstring stretch.

Kieran was showing a husband and wife the features of a pumpkin-orange Ultra Limited—a massive machine built to carry two very comfortably. She tried to ignore the conversation, but bits of it reached her anyway.

"This windshield is going to make your ride much quieter," he was saying, pointing to the piece of glass between the handlebars. "Plus these hard bags on the side"—he pointed to the storage compartments in the back—"are going to let you carry a lot of what you need with you."

Audrey marveled at his expertise, at his clean look, at his authority in this place. This morning, she'd spotted him through the conference room windows *leading a meeting*, and she even heard one person call him "sir."

It was certainly a far cry from the man she once knew. Five years ago, Kieran's dark red hair had been shaggy, curling just below his ears—not at all like the trim cut that framed his head now. His jeans had been clean but the cuffs were frayed, and his jaw had been shadowed with stubble. He'd still had his broad shoulders and big chest, but he'd been thinner somehow, leaner and harder.

Audrey had watched him walk into the dance tent at the Asparagus Festival, her eyes never leaving his form. The music had retreated to the edges of her hearing, drowned out by a wave of quiet, as if the world had slowed, pausing momentarily while she took him in. The whirling figures on the dance floor spun into distant blurs, and the lights receded. Before spotting him, she'd been standing to the side, stiff and awkward, wishing she could just go home already, but forcing herself to stay since she wanted to enjoy the festival, whether or not she had a date.

Kieran had turned to her then, maybe feeling the intensity of·her gaze or just sensing that she was staring, unabashedly, and came directly toward her. His wide mouth stretched into a slow smile. The angular lines of his face were partially shadowed in the dim light, giving him an air of mystery. She marveled at his perfect lips, and the small cleft on his chin where she suddenly wanted to place her finger, just see how the tiny dent felt.

"Porta-Potties at this festival probably smell worse than most, don't you think?" he'd asked. "All that asparagus pee?"

Later, she'd recall how odd it was that his first comment to her was about *urine*, and how improbably funny she'd found it. A bubble of laughter sounded from her throat.

"I suppose it's better that the pee smells like asparagus, versus the other way around," Audrey had replied. "Otherwise we'd never eat it."

It was Kieran's turn to laugh then. She'd watched, fascinated, as he threw his head back, flashing bright white teeth. She felt her pulse quicken, felt the presence of the sky above and the hardness of the earth below and believed, in that moment, she was exactly where she needed to be.

Kieran glanced at the asparagus beer she was holding. "I imagine that must be like drinking boozy V8, what with all the vegetables. But the way you're sucking it down, maybe there's a chance I'm wrong."

"Very wrong," Audrey said, lifting the nearly empty glass. Asparagus beer was her favorite, which was a tough break since she could only get it for a few weeks each year. "You should try one—the beer tent is just next door."

Together, they'd walked to the beer tent, where Kieran

bought two fresh pints, and they drank them under the stars. And when he loved it—when his light green eyes brightened even more—Audrey thought she felt the whole world tilt slightly, realigning itself just for her.

Just for *them*.

"What's your name?" she asked as they finished their beers and headed back into the dance tent.

"Kieran Callaghan, of the Callaghans of Cashel, descended from the Irish king of Munster."

"How very noble."

"And you?"

"Audrey Tanner," she'd replied. "Of the…Minnesota Tanners."

He held out a hand. "May I have this dance, Audrey Tanner?"

She stared at his outstretched fingers, at the lean, calloused shape of them and hesitated for only the briefest of seconds. *She hardly knew this man. This was unwise. He could be dangerous.*

Nevertheless, she'd reached for him. The moment their fingers connected, lightning struck her spine. She wondered if she'd be able to remain upright, the electric surge of it all was so much, but then his arms were around her, holding her tight, and she found she'd been made strong, not weak. It turned out she could dance for hours and hours and hours.

"Miss?"

Audrey started. She blinked to awareness, realizing there was a woman staring at her.

"Yes, I'm so sorry. How can I help you?" Audrey attempted a smile at the short woman in front of her with paper-white skin.

"None of the sales staff here seems to want to wait on me," the woman said, frowning with pale lips that nearly matched her pallor. In contrast to all this was the crop of dark chestnut hair that jutted from her head at an impossibly stylish angle.

"Oh, I'm so sorry," Audrey said. "Let me get—"

"No," the woman said, cutting her off. "Can I just talk to you?"

Audrey collected herself. "Yes. Of course."

"The thing is," the woman said, "I don't think anyone here *wants* to help me. I've been standing over there by that Softail Slim"—she jerked her small head at a stout, flat gray bike—"and I think people assume I'm like you."

"Like me?" Audrey asked, wondering if the woman meant broke.

"A model. I think they think I'm here to look pretty. And even if I couldn't afford a bike, which I *can*, the gear in here sucks. It's a joke."

Audrey's eyes flicked over to the women's section, taking in the tiny rack of baby T-shirts, bikinis, thong underwear, and a bustier just like the one she was wearing. It was a fraction of the total retail space. In contrast, there was a whole section with boots, leather jackets, chaps, and hats for men.

"I guess I could wear a leather jacket cut for a small dude," the woman said, her pale cheeks pinking with irritation, "but the thing is, they make bike gear for women now. Lots of it. So why don't you carry any of it? And why am I standing around not being waited on? It's like this place is straight out of *Mad Men* or something. The only woman who works here is a model, and I half expect the boss to ask me for coffee."

"Well, I'm just here temporarily," Audrey said. "I was a gym tea—"

"Nobody's judging," the woman interrupted. "We all have to do what we have to do. But this place? You guys are missing the mark. Big time."

And before Audrey could stop her, the woman turned and left. Audrey followed after her in spiky heels, but couldn't even get close. The dealership doors swooshed shut before Audrey could even ask the woman her name.

"Shit," she muttered. She teetered into a nearby corner, feeling terrible. But as she watched from the shadows, she realized the woman was right. Men were talking to men. Women were on the periphery, picking at fingernails, looking around, seemingly lost. Good heavens, how many of them were potential customers? And they were being ignored!

The shining chrome of the machines was a blinding reminder of the fact that she didn't ride, but maybe if she could, she'd be more help to the woman who'd just come in. And all the other women like her. She gritted her teeth, not wanting to let herself remember how exhilarating it felt on the back of a bike with the scenery whipping past, the sky wide overhead, and how, with Kieran, she thought she was always riding toward something.

"Is there a problem here?"

Audrey turned to find Kieran in the small space with her, hands on his hips, staring.

"Did you offend that customer?" he asked before she could say anything. "She walked out of here looking angry after talking to you. What happened?"

There were lines of tension around Kieran's mouth she

couldn't remember seeing yesterday. Dark circles ringed his eyes, as if he hadn't slept much the previous night.

"I was trying to help," she answered.

He inched closer. Her heart thundered. "Then what happened? Why did she bail?"

"She couldn't get one of your sales associates to talk to her." It came out more testily than she wanted. Kieran's nearness unnerved her.

"What did you do about it?"

Audrey bristled. "As the *advancement director*, I'd think you'd be in more of a position to help than someone in chaps and a leather corset."

Kieran folded his muscled arms. "All right," he said after a long moment. "Tell me specifically what occurred so I can address it."

Audrey blinked in surprise at Kieran's tone. He'd switched into professional mode. He was being a manager. And not a terrible one.

"I couldn't catch up to the customer to stop her," Audrey said. "But the problem's bigger than that. She was pointing out how all the gear in the store is the kind of thing I have on. And I can hardly get so I can sit on one of these things, much less drive one. She was frustrated by our approach to women, and I don't blame her."

Kieran studied Audrey then, a look that pierced her with its thoughtfulness. "Fair enough. I'll talk to my sales managers. Maybe they need to be reminded that women are our clientele, too."

Kieran had turned, ready to leave, when Audrey grabbed his hand. The graze of fingers was electric enough to send a jolt through her. "But maybe the situation's bigger than that?"

Kieran raised an eyebrow. "How do you mean?"

Audrey pulled her fingers away from his, surprised at how reluctantly they moved. "What if it's not only about the sales guys? I mean, maybe you need to rethink what kind of stock you're putting out for sale. Retrain some people. Do some surveys and find out what women want. Make the solution more...comprehensive."

Like teaching me how to ride, she thought but didn't say.

"And you'd know because ex–gym teachers have so much experience with this kind of thing?"

He may have meant it as a joke, but the dig stung. Before Audrey could fire off a reply, an administrative partner with a long, blonde ponytail hustled up to where they were standing. "The contracts for your two o'clock conference call came in, Mr. Callaghan. Do you want them now?"

Kieran glanced at the pile of papers in her hand. "Thanks, Dawn, but I'll get them in a few minutes. Just put them on my desk, if you will."

Dawn nodded and trotted away. Audrey watched her go, unable to shake how successful *Mr. Callaghan* was now, how he exuded a kind of leadership and authority that were only glimmers when they'd met. A small, brittle part of her wanted Kieran's life to have fallen apart when he rolled away from White Pine five years ago. How had it happened that his life hadn't shattered but rather blossomed?

"I'm sorry. Did you have anything to add about our disappearing customer?" Kieran asked, checking his watch.

A shard of old hurt sliced at something deep inside. "Funny, how all of a sudden people *leaving* bothers you," she said.

She couldn't tell if he'd paled slightly. Part of her didn't care.

He leaned into her, so close that his breath was on her skin. The small whispers of air felt like gale-force winds, threatening to knock her to her knees.

"Careful," he said in a low voice. "This is a business, and I'm your employer. I'm not interested in rehashing the past."

They were unbearably close. "And what makes you think I am? The day you rolled out of my life was the day everything got a hundred percent better." It was a lie—and a terrible one at that—but she didn't retract it.

She expected him to fire back at her, but instead he smiled, ever so slightly, as if he knew she was bluffing. The movement, tiny as it was, undid her. The muscles in her body were set to unravel, leaving her in a slack heap on the gleaming white floor. Her very center quaked, reminding her what an incredible physical specimen Kieran was. How every contour of his body had seemed downright sculpted when they'd been in bed together.

She found her hunger for him building, even as they stood there. But she forced herself to be still, to keep her breathing even and controlled. She wasn't about to lose herself a second time to him.

She summoned all her strength and pulled away, putting cold air between them. "Your female customers deserve better than what you're giving them. I'd say that's probably true for all the females in your life, but I'm trying to focus on things that aren't a lost cause."

A muscle flexed in his jaw. His green eyes pierced hers. "If you don't like the way I run things, by all means, there's the door. It's your choice."

She actually laughed at that. She supposed there was always a choice; it just didn't feel that way. He hadn't given her any options when he'd left before, and now that he was back, her only options felt like either this job or food stamps.

She flicked her head toward the rack of women's gear. "For the record, your choices are terrible."

Kieran pulled on the cuffs of his smart wool jacket. "I'll let you know when I need your opinion. In the meantime, this is the last time you mention anything related to our past here. Understood?"

He didn't even wait for her to answer. He simply turned on his polished heel and left.

Audrey stood there trembling in his absence. Her heart—sinking and pounding at the same time—didn't make the past seem like it was safely tucked away whatsoever.

* * *

Kieran splashed cold water on his face in the dealership's white-bricked bathroom and tried to get hold of himself. Above, the hum of fluorescent lights matched the vibration of his nerves after the close encounter with Audrey in the showroom.

Fighting Saints of New Orleans, the woman was infuriating. Standing in the showroom with her brown eyes flashing and her chest heaving, she had talked to him like no other employee did—ever.

She had also made some of the most intelligent, insightful points he'd heard any of his staff make. Her ideas about expanding the female demographic were so smart he'd fired off the insult about her being an ex–gym teacher just to put her in her place.

It made him the worst kind of jerk. He groaned, wishing instead he'd complimented her on her insight. On her strategy. On all the brightness and cleverness she'd always shown—ever since they'd met.

Instead of cowing her, he should have just done what he wanted, which was to pull her to him and kiss her until the past was so far behind them that all they had was the pleasure of the present.

He hadn't, of course. Because Audrey didn't want him.

He stared at his reflection in the bathroom mirror—hard jaw, even harder eyes—and told himself he deserved it. He'd left like a coward five years ago, and insulted her five minutes ago. She had every right to be angry and to want nothing to do with him.

His leaving had been the best thing that had ever happened to her—she'd said it herself.

He leaned against the porcelain sink and fought the shame bubbling up from deep within. People around here called him "sir" and they saved the seat at the head of the conference room table for him, but Audrey was a reminder of who he really was—someone who'd barely clawed his way out of hard times.

He tried to picture the diploma on his office wall, the glowing reviews he'd received from his own managers in the past, and the ever-growing numbers on the calendar marking his time in recovery.

But all he could see was the dark shame that followed him around like a cloud. His face was shadowed enough to remind him of his childhood days when he and his older brother, Auggie, used to go hungry, bones jutting at all angles. There were grim weeks when his dad would lurch away, leaving only his mom to try to scrape together enough for all of them. She'd pull Auggie and Kieran close and kiss the tops of their heads, whispering her wish to be able to fill them up with love, because then they'd never be without. She'd sew, clean, or do anything she could for money or food, all of them waiting for their dad to come stumbling back, hopefully with a pocketful of winnings but, if not, he'd eventually go back to delivering furniture with his cousin's company.

Kieran closed his eyes, tired of his reflection. Auggie had pulled out of the tailspin of their childhood early on, first by joining the navy, then by going immediately into the police academy. Today, he was an officer in the Boston Police Department. Kieran grimaced, knowing his own transformation had taken much longer, and it had come at a terrible price. It had involved not only losing his mom, but carrying a secret he could never tell Audrey, which meant he could never be honest with her.

And if his addiction meetings had taught him anything, it was that honesty was a pillar of any strong relationship. As much as his fingers yearned to touch her cheek, as much as he longed to pull her close to his chest and feel her warmth against him, and as much as he wished he could atone for the past, it could never be.

He sighed, wishing Audrey could just evaporate, like mist when the sun warms the air. It seemed unfair that his heart could swell so much in her presence. It was a wonder that it didn't come exploding out of his chest.

He turned off the tap, listening to the water drip, trying to focus on the sound.

The longer he was around Audrey, the more he wanted to atone for his actions. But coming clean with her would mean she'd find out that he was once an addict who, five years ago, had accepted a terrible deal at a desperate cross-roads. It would also ruin her closest relationship—and he wasn't about to go causing any more damage to Audrey than he already had.

He glanced at his reflection in the mirror—all angles and edges. Not soft with emotion. Not soft with *anything*.

There had once been a day when he'd been good at bluffing. Good at pretending.

His gambling days were behind him—he'd made damn sure of that—but he needed one more lie. He told himself he didn't care for Audrey Tanner one whit.

And as he stared at his shadowed face in the bathroom mirror, he almost believed it.

CHAPTER FIVE

The next morning, streetlight reflections glimmered on the wet blacktop as Audrey jogged through her neighborhood. The rain shower from the night before had cleared the early May air, leaving the smell of fresh dirt and pine and grass on the wind. Audrey inhaled deeply as she wove her way through streets lined with still-sleeping households. In the east, the sky was transitioning from black to a dim rose, and stars were fading above.

It was her favorite time to get a workout in—to be alone and let her legs move while her brain unfurled its coiled ideas—but today she wasn't so sure she liked how much her focus kept shifting back to Kieran Callaghan.

She desperately wanted to think that after five years, her searing desire for him would have cooled a little bit. She'd always told herself that she couldn't resist a bad boy—but Kieran wasn't acting like a bad boy now. And a prickling unease reminded her that she wasn't sure he ever had been. Sure, he had ridden a motorcycle and didn't seem to have any kind of full-time job when she first met him. But he'd never seemed downright...nefarious. She'd stereotyped him that way later, after he'd left her. Her hurt had rewritten the story of their brief time together, and after a while she'd figured she must have imagined his blend of tenderness and muscle, and how a jumble of contrasts could exist in one man: strength and softness, intelligence and bravado.

Audrey wiped her forehead and hoped her thoughts of Kieran would be wiped away, too. All these mental gymnastics and flutters in her stomach didn't mean anything, except maybe she needed to get laid. Never mind that she'd never had a one-night stand in her life. Even after such a short time with Kieran, when they came together, she'd believed she was in love. But if there was any time to shake things up, it was now.

Not that it had to be sex that changed things. She pushed a strand of sweaty hair away from her forehead. When it came down to it, there were thousand ways to change her life that didn't have to involve a man. She could change out her wardrobe, or take lessons of some sort. She could get another degree, or train for a triathlon.

She could learn to ride a Harley.

The options pumped through her in time with her heartbeat.

Audrey crossed the Birch River, its water dark and rustling, and then headed toward the high school. If she kept going straight, she'd hit downtown. After that, up a gentle hill, was Willa's neighborhood, where White Pine's biggest homes were built. Audrey lived on the other side of the river—in a simple one-story house she loved and had bought herself—though she favored runs through Willa's quiet streets where ancient oaks arced over her like protective giants. Many of those grand homes had been built by White Pine's early bankers, lumber barons, and railroad executives. The structures were still stately and lovely, with old ivy crawling up the sides and long, curved driveways that seemed to smile as she raced by.

Not today, though. Audrey was going to hit the track at the high school and do sprints, then run the metal bleachers. She needed to squeeze into her work attire every day, and the regular recipe exchanges—especially the ones to which she brought donuts—weren't going to help anything stay buttoned or fastened.

As she ran across the damp football field toward the track, she thought she saw a dark figure silhouetted in the shadows of the bleachers. She blinked and tried to focus, but it was still too early—there wasn't enough light to really tell. Nevertheless, she pushed her shoulders back and kept her head high. *Look strong so your attacker will think twice,* she'd read once. She'd never felt unsafe running alone in her beloved small town, but it was good to be aware nevertheless.

Thinking ahead. Covering her bases.

She exhaled, suddenly frustrated with being so logical and practical and predictable. She had forced herself to play by every rule in life, and it had left her single and fired from her dream job. Irritated, she pushed herself to sprint the last bit of distance to the track, then went right for the bleachers. Up, up, up to the top—her legs burning and her lungs heaving.

When she turned to trot down and do it again, she

screamed at the hooded figure standing at the bottom of the stands, waiting for her.

"I am armed!" she cried, glancing around for an exit strategy, "and I will hurt you."

The figure waved its hands. She couldn't make out exactly what it was saying, but when it finally pushed its hood back, she relaxed. A dark ponytail cascaded from the top of the figure's head, curling at the ends around the shoulders. From Audrey's vantage point, it looked like Alexis Belten.

"Ms. Tanner!" the figure called. "It's just me! Sorry if I scared you!"

Audrey trotted back down the stairs, her heartbeat slowing and her muscles relaxing.

"Alexis?"

Sure enough, the track team member and one-time volleyball player was standing there in the dark, nervously shifting her tall, lean frame from one foot to the other.

"I'm so sorry," Alexis said, "but I had to make sure that it really was you out here, and then you screamed and I was like, *oh crap* she thinks I'm a *murderer*, but then I remembered my hood was up so I pushed it back so hopefully you'd know it was me and not, like, Jack the Ripper."

Audrey nodded. "That's all fine. But what are you doing here? The sun's not even up."

"No, I know," Alexis said, twisting her hands together. "That's the point. Not that it's dark, I mean, but that you're here and this is when you work out sometimes and I want to work out with you. I came yesterday and the day before, because I know you do bleachers at least one day a week, I just didn't know which day. I wanted to join you is all."

Even in the dark, Audrey could see Alexis's forehead

crinkling with nervousness and something else. Worry? Why hadn't the girl just called or e-mailed her?

"Of course you can run with me," she replied. "We could tackle these bleachers together if you wanted."

The pretty, rounded apples of Alexis's cheeks plumped with happiness. "That would be awesome. Hard, but awesome."

"Why don't we walk around the track once, just to get you warmed up," Audrey suggested, her heart pinching at how easily her coaching instincts kicked in. And at how happy it made her.

The pair set off, taking the quarter-mile in quick, brisk steps. "So is everything all right?" Audrey asked after a moment, glancing sideways at Alexis. As she did, the screen lit up on the slim phone tucked into the running band on the girl's arm. It glowed eerily in the fading darkness. Audrey figured it for a text message. Her students texted like they breathed. "Things okay with you?"

Alexis's ponytail bounced as she worked her arms and legs. "Um, I guess they're okay. The new coach, Mr. Frace? He's *such* a joke. He barely makes us do anything, like he's so worried that we'll break a sweat or something. It's like he thinks we're swooning ladies in those books he teaches—*Pride and Prejudice* or whatever."

Audrey smiled, though her chest tightened to think about the girls' track team barely practicing. They'd never make it to district finals at this rate—never mind State.

"You're signing yourself up for two practices today, you know," Audrey said. "Just because you're running with me this morning doesn't mean you get out of Mr. Frace's practice later, no matter how lame it is."

"I get it," Alexis said, her mouth pulling downward.

"If it's too much, you can always run with me on the weekends. I always get a good workout in on Sunday mornings."

Alexis flashed a smile, which disappeared as quickly as it came. "That would be great. Because the whole team misses you, you know. It's stupid what they did to you. And I…"

Audrey arched a brow as the girl's words faded. Alexis bit her lower lip and appeared to have more to say.

"And?" Audrey prompted gently.

"Nothing," Alexis replied, shaking her head. They were back at the bleachers, and the slender girl put her hands on her hips. The screen on her phone lit up again.

"Is someone trying to get in touch with you?" Audrey asked. "Seems awfully early for texting."

"No, it's fine."

The screen lit up again. Audrey paused, inviting her to say more, but Alexis pushed past it.

"God, running these bleachers is going to suck," she said instead.

"Sure you want to?" Audrey asked, allowing Alexis to change the subject. She figured out early on in her career that pushing teenage girls to talk would get you nowhere. Best to let Alexis reveal what she had to say in her own time.

"Oh, heck yes. And I bet I can beat you."

"Oh, you think?" Audrey asked. "On your mark, get set—"

"Go!" Alexis cried, taking off ahead of her. On her arm, her phone's screen glowed again, dimming as the girl raced away.

Audrey followed, letting Alexis get a big head start.

She watched Alexis hurtle herself up the bleachers, and couldn't help but be impressed. Alexis would win their race today for real.

And Audrey figured she'd find her own way to win today, too—or, at least try something totally new—at the dealership. She was going to shake up her life somehow. It was time.

Whether or not it involved Kieran Callaghan was an entirely different issue altogether.

* * *

An hour later, Audrey watched the steam rising from her mug of coffee as she waited for her sister, Casey, to pick up the phone. Outside her kitchen windows, birds darted from tree branch to tree branch, trilling and singing in the pale sun. They'd finally returned from their long winter somewhere far away from White Pine.

Welcome back to the best place to be, she thought. Her gaze traveled from the birds to the battered notebook resting next to her coffee. She used it for coaching, and it was scrawled with drills and practice ideas. It included everything from weight-lifting regimens to how to divvy up the workouts to ideas for getting enough protein into athletes. She'd pulled it out after her run with Alexis, wondering if she'd have the chance to really use it again.

The thought had her smiling slightly when Casey finally answered.

"Hello." The word out of her sister's mouth was a statement, a period in a conversation that hadn't even started yet.

"Hi, Casey," Audrey said. She heard the rustle of papers

in the background. "Are you at work already?" It was barely eight o'clock.

"I'm doing a round of tax prep for some of the companies with extensions past April fifteenth," Casey said, sounding distracted. "The date for filing never moves, but you'd be amazed at how many people can't get it together."

Audrey pictured the rows of manila folders in her home office, each one neatly labeled thanks to her sister, and knew she'd probably be one of those late-filers if it weren't for Casey.

"Long day, then," Audrey said, trying to sound sympathetic, even though she knew her sister loved her job. Casey worked as a corporate accountant about an hour up the road in Eagan, a suburb of Minneapolis. She spent most of her time in a small office on the sixth floor of a glass-walled office building that had a shallow man-made pond out front. Audrey never could get past the smell of the place—a mixture of paste and paint—or the way the plastic leaves on the fake plants in the atrium collected dust. But Casey was there day in and day out, promoted again and again, and never seemed to tire of the columns, spreadsheets, and forms that comprised her successful career.

"Any movement on the employment front?" Casey asked. The question's phrasing had Audrey picturing soldiers lined up to do battle, pressing into enemy territory.

"It's, um..." Her eyes tracked the birds fluttering past her window. "It's not what I expected." Her stomach sank at the evasion. It wasn't a lie, not technically, but guilt still weighted her insides.

"There's nothing in that town," Casey said. "You need to move up here."

Audrey forced a smile, reminding herself that if her sister was opinionated, it was only because she was used to playing the role. The two girls had lost their parents when Audrey was ten and Casey was thirteen. They'd gone to live with their aunt Lodi, who was struggling to get by on her own—never mind having two girls around. Casey was the one who'd had to grow up too quickly and become the adult, making sure Audrey ate, making sure she had clean clothes, making sure Audrey did her homework and stayed out of trouble. It was because of Casey that Audrey had tried out for the track team in high school and had gone to college on a track scholarship.

It's because of me she's in that office right now, Audrey thought, her heart constricting. If Casey hadn't had to care for Audrey for so many years, maybe she wouldn't have grown to expect that responsibility was always hers to shoulder—a trait she never lost. These days, she applied it to her job, working almost constantly. Audrey pictured her sister's bare left hand and swallowed back still more guilt. Would her sister be married if it wasn't for Audrey? Would she be happier?

"I'd love for us to live closer," Audrey hedged, "but I'm still looking into a few job opportunities in White Pine. There's more than you think."

Casey sighed. "Well, in the meantime, I've got some potential leads for you up here. I'll keep you posted."

Audrey clutched the phone. She tried to summon the boldness she'd felt in her Harley clothes, the same emotions she was able to channel at Lumberjack Grocery, in order to tell her sister she didn't want to move to Eagan. She'd loved so many things about her P.E. job—the kids, the parents, the other teachers—but the thing she'd loved most about all of it was being in White Pine. Doing all this work in her hometown had her feeling like she was making a difference in a place that mattered to her. Doing that somewhere else—it felt like forcing two puzzle pieces together that just didn't want to fit.

But the argument died on Audrey's lips. Her sister was trying to help her—that was what she always did—and Audrey should be grateful instead of combative.

"Sounds good," she lied. The picture of Kieran Callaghan was filling her mind, and she knew she should tell her sister about him, about the temporary position at the Harley dealership that was helping buy her more time in White Pine. Casey hadn't liked Kieran five years ago—and she wasn't about to get excited about him now—but her sister should know the truth. Or, at least part of it.

"Just so you know, Kieran Callaghan is back," she said, trying to sound as nonchalant as possible. She dragged a finger along the linoleum counter. "I hear he works at a Harley dealership." She left out the part about how she worked there, too.

There was a long pause. "You don't say."

"I saw him with my own eyes."

Casey exhaled, long and slow. "I hope this goes without saying, but you should stay away from him."

Audrey laughed, though it was forced. "Of course. Don't worry about me."

"I mean it."

"So do I." She knew she sounded defensive, but no one needed to worry about her and Kieran.

"Good. Then are we still on for lunch next week?" Casey asked. "I'll come down there if it's easier. You're probably trying to conserve gas money."

Audrey bit her lip. The numbers in her bank account were

disastrously low—worse than even Casey knew. But instead of conserving gas money, she suddenly felt like pulling out her credit cards and going shopping. It was what a bold woman in high heels and leather corset would do—someone who eschewed the practical for the pleasurable. She pictured new shoes and an oversized handbag. She could almost taste the crusty baguettes at the expensive French café that Willa had taken her to once, which she suddenly wanted to visit again. She'd order a bottle of wine for lunch, and maybe even dessert, too.

She shook her head. She was losing it. She strained to focus.

"I would love to see you down here," Audrey said. "I'll meet you at the Paul Bunyan Diner next Saturday."

"See you then," Casey said. "Love you." With a soft click, she was gone.

Audrey stood there holding the phone, watching the leaves twist on the trees outside. A distant sparrow caught her eye, a dark speck against the bright horizon. She watched it plunge, a breathtaking fall from the sky, and then at the last minute beat its wings once—a powerful thrust—and fling itself back upward.

She gritted her teeth. The birds were having a more exhilarating time than she was. It didn't seem fair.

Audrey glanced at the clock. It was time to get ready for work. *It's time for Kieran,* she thought. A chill raced up her spine. She shivered. Already the idea of being near him again was overpowering.

She tried to push past it, to ignore it entirely. To listen to her sister's cautionary words. But it was as if the sparrow she'd watched had become trapped in her chest and its fluttering wings were setting the electric tempo of her heartbeat.

CHAPTER SIX

*A*udrey was just coming out of the women's bathroom—makeup on, and bustier laced, and ready for work—when Kieran came striding around the corner from the other direction. Audrey pulled up short, thinking that the sight of Kieran could stop any woman in her tracks.

He was wearing a white collared shirt that had *Harley-Davidson* embroidered above the breast pocket. The crisp material set off the dark-flamed color of his hair and the impossibly pale green of his eyes. He'd tucked the shirt neatly into jeans with a black leather belt, and he wore black, thick-soled Harley boots on his feet.

It was the perfect blend of professional and edgy—that same mix of contrasts that she'd once found so appealing about Kieran—and she stared longer than she should have. *Just walk past,* she commanded her legs, but they stayed rooted on the spot.

"Little late, aren't you?" he said gruffly, glancing at his watch.

It was 9:55, and work didn't start until ten o'clock. But instead of firing back, she gave him a slow smile. The kind of smile a woman who regularly dressed in a leather bustier might give a man she wanted. *I can pretend I have an alter ego,* she thought suddenly. She could be a different Audrey altogether—a badass, sexy Audrey—who could ride a motorcycle because Kieran would teach her. She'd tilt-shift Kieran Callaghan's world, instead of the other way around, and get him to do what *she* wanted for a change.

The idea was ludicrous—and thrilling.

In spite of the alarm bells sounding in her head, she inched closer to him. Her pulse ricocheted just beneath her skin, and she prayed she wasn't sweating visibly. "Maybe I'm right on time," she whispered.

His eyes widened in surprise. She could already feel moisture collecting at the small of her back. Internally, she repeated *Shut up* to the part of the brain screaming to stop what she was doing already and get to work.

She was ready to turn away when Kieran made an animalistic sound in the back of his throat. It froze her in place like prey in the wild. His eyes flashed dangerously. *She'd had an effect on him.*

"This isn't how you get ahead in businesses that I run," he said, low and gravelly.

"That's because," she demurred, "maybe you're talking about the wrong kind of head entirely."

If he started to smile, he pinned it back quickly. "I don't remember you being so forward."

"A lot can change in five years."

He looked her up and down. His gaze was ravenous. "Clearly," he said.

The raw emotion coursing through her was suddenly carnal enough to spark fear. It jolted the logical part of her brain into action. What was she even doing? This was downright reckless. It was *tawdry*. She could lose her job.

"I should..." she started, but the words faded away into less than a whisper.

She should what, exactly? A few weeks ago, she thought she knew how to answer that question: She should work hard at a job that would reward her efforts. She should try not to make waves. She should put others first. She should guard her heart so no one like Kieran Callaghan would come roaring into her life ever again.

Which had all led her here. Broke. Underemployed. Restless. And with Kieran Callaghan staring at her like he wanted to devour her.

Turn away, her internal editor commanded. *Go to work.* But instead she simply watched as Kieran's hand grasped her upper arm, and he pushed her straight back into the women's restroom from which she'd just emerged. It was just a single stall and a sink, a cramped space, which felt smaller still from the heat of Kieran's body and the overwhelming mass of him. Had he always been this tall?

He turned the lock with a satisfying click.

Then his lips were on hers in a searing kiss that left every part of her scorched with pleasure.

* * *

Kieran backed her against the bathroom door roughly. The handle dug into the small of her back, the metal frigid against her exposed skin. But none of it mattered when his enormous hands grasped the side of her face and held her while his mouth claimed hers.

Her internal cries of *don't*s and *can't*s were muted against a rush of surprise and then desire. Oh, how easily it came back to her—the feel of him, the touch of him. In five years, she'd never once been kissed like this. It was as if Kieran wanted to taste not just her mouth, but to taste the very things that comprised Audrey's essence.

Her hands traveled up the crisp cotton of his shirt, feeling the corded hardness of his forearms, his biceps. She inhaled his spicy scent and the bleach of the clean bathroom just underneath.

The bathroom.

Good God, she should be horrified at losing herself like this in a bathroom, of all places. With colleagues from the dealership just outside, no less! If people found out, everyone in town would be gossiping about it.

She squeezed her eyes shut against the whispers in her head and pressed herself fully against Kieran's body. She could feel his hardness through the fabric of her jeans. The thick stiffness of it made her heart pound. He groaned and ran his hands down her corseted sides. Sparks ignited behind her eyelids. It didn't matter one bit what anyone said, she realized, sucking on his lower lip. For the first time in years, Audrey felt alive.

Memories that she'd shut away for too long came surging forward with the power of ocean waves: In vivid high definition, she could still remember how Kieran had peeled off her clothes as they tumbled into bed together and then stared at her as if she'd been a Renaissance sculpture. The seconds had ticked in her head—was he horrified by what he was seeing?—but the awe on his face was unmistakable. He'd run his hands over every part of her: calves, thighs, stomach, arms, even hands and feet. She'd wondered what he was doing, but then he'd murmured into her ear how he'd begun to doubt if she was real, and touching every part of her was the only way he'd know he wasn't dreaming.

Kieran was a mass of angles and muscles that thrilled her, but it was when he'd quoted Emily Dickinson to her in bed—"I had been hungry, all the years, my noon had come, to dine"—that she'd found herself swept up in an explosion of affection, a glittering supernova of emotion for this man. He could have just been another hot body in a leather jacket. But Kieran was something else entirely, something that had pierced right through her in a way she hadn't expected.

And now, as if reading her thoughts, he murmured into her ear, "Boldness be my friend," and lowered his head to place his lips against the rounded top of her breast.

Was that *Shakespeare* he was quoting? But suddenly it didn't matter, because he'd freed her breasts from the corset and placed the tip of one in his mouth, sucking gently. Hot sparks lit up her body. She moaned, biting her lip against the sound, against the improbable rightness of his touch.

She plunged her fingers into his dark red hair and arched against him. His lips were hot on her skin, his tongue was alive and wild. Audrey was the verge of losing herself completely when his cell phone rang. The shrill noise echoed off the cold tile of the bathroom, shattering the moment.

"Dammit," Kieran mumbled, fumbling for the device in his back pocket. It rang again, high and loud, and Audrey heard laughter outside the bathroom door. "Folks taking calls in the bathroom, what's next?" someone said. It sounded like Fletch.

Kieran ignored the call and shoved the phone back into his pocket. He studied her for a long moment, his broad chest rising and falling like he'd just run a race. Audrey was keenly aware that her breasts were still exposed, her nipples taut and high in the cold air. A hungry part of her wanted Kieran's mouth on them again, even though another part of her cried out that this had been a terrible mistake. They'd both lost their heads.

Slowly, cold dread replaced Audrey's hot lust. Had she really played the fool and let Kieran take what he wanted from her all over again? And in a company bathroom, no less?

Her cheeks burned. She fumbled for her corset and pulled it over her aching breasts. Kieran watched her but didn't offer to help.

Damn him, she thought bitterly. *But damn me more for being so stupid.*

Her brain raced, searching for a way to salvage her dignity. She straightened, determined to seem as though this had been no big deal. Like she did this thing all the time.

"I wanted to ask you something before we got... distracted," she said. "It's important."

Kieran arched a brow. "Oh?" Before she could answer, he grabbed her wrist. His thumb rubbed a gentle circle. The movement made her knees weak.

"I want—that is, I should learn to ride a motorcycle. That should be part of the job."

"You really want to ride a Harley?" Kieran asked. Audrey glanced just past his left temple, unsure of how to address the question. Was it really so improbable?

He pulled her even closer, and her breath caught. "If you want to learn," he murmured into her ear, "then I'm happy to show you."

She stared into the green depths of his eyes. *This is what she'd wanted.* Kieran was going to teach her to ride. But the reality of it had alarm bells sounding in her brain. Being around Kieran clearly made her lose whatever composure she had. What would happen when they added the romance of the open road and a powerful motorcycle to everything?

He traced a line from her wrist to her palm and back again. She found herself staring at Kieran's wide mouth, at the perfect color of his lips against his golden skin.

Would it really be so bad if she let him be her teacher?

Just be alter-ego Audrey, she reminded herself. It wouldn't be that hard to play the part.

"I'm looking forward to seeing if I'm as good a student as I was a teacher," she replied.

Hunger flashed in his eyes, but before he could do anything, his cell phone rang once more, sharp and loud. He pulled it out and grimaced as he looked at the number.

"I have to go," he said abruptly, not meeting her eyes.

His energy shifted suddenly—going from hot and predatory to cold and something else. Regretful, perhaps?

Audrey's heart constricted. He wasn't eager to be away from her already, was he? Whatever his reasons were, he'd flipped off his desire for her like a switch. The effect left a confused ache in her chest.

You can't trust this man, she thought. Never mind that her heart lurched toward him as if ready to trust him implicitly.

"I'll talk to you later," he said, pulling the door open an inch to ensure the hallway was empty.

And then, when the coast was clear, he was gone. He'd left as quickly as he'd pulled her into the small room. His absence should have been a relief, but instead it left her as cold as the white tile all around her.

* * *

Kieran strode down the hallway toward the dealership's used lot, bursting out the back door with enough frustration to make the heavy steel groan.

Archangel Michael and his heavenly host, Audrey Tanner was going to *undo* him.

He ran his fingers through his hair, swearing under his breath. The truth was that he didn't mind Audrey unraveling him. The feel of her curves against him in the bathroom had been so unbearably pleasurable he'd worried for a moment he might spill himself right there in front of her.

He wanted this woman, there was no doubt about it. No matter their past, no matter his mistakes. He felt more for Audrey Tanner than he had for any woman in five years— or, hell, his whole life. Oh, the things he would do to her if he had his way.

What he didn't want, though, was any connection with her sister.

He glanced at his phone, where Casey's number flashed as a missed call. Freezing dread filled him. The picture of his mom, riddled with cancer and struggling for breath, flashed in his mind. All the scheming, all the lies, only to lose Mom after all. He shook his head, trying to clear the image.

The smart thing would be to walk away from Audrey right now. She and her sister were at the center of things he wanted buried forever. He should fire her, get her out of his sight, and never have any contact with her again.

But could he do it?

He paced the blacktop, pulling on the cuffs of his shirt as if the answer was in the cotton. He'd been a first-rate jerk to her, leaving just as they were falling in love, and he figured she'd have nothing but ire and anger for him. But, wouldn't you know it, she was as open-hearted as ever. She should have shoved him away in that bathroom, told him to get lost and never touch her again, but instead she'd made demands on him, same as he had on her. She was playful and bold instead of bitter. And he'd been able to kiss her until they were both breathless.

The memory of it had his jeans tenting all over again.

Audrey still felt something for him. He knew it as surely as he knew his own feelings for her had come roaring back unexpectedly, a tidal wave he hadn't prepared for, but that had taken him under anyway.

He stopped his manic strides and took a deep breath. All around him, used Harleys sparkled in the light, lined up like soldiers ready for battle.

If he'd had more time, he would have pushed Audrey against the wall and licked the long, graceful line from her collarbone to her ear until she shuddered with tenderness. He would have kneed apart her legs and placed his raging erection between them—pressing the long ache of him into her until she gasped—and then taken her to his apartment to finish what he'd started.

He shuddered, thinking about the past, when their bodies had come together. They'd been passionate but exploratory, just getting to know one another. The realization hit him that he didn't know whether Audrey preferred back rubs or foot rubs, if she liked to be held in the morning after lovemaking or turned loose to start her day, or how many times she could come apart in his hands—*with* his hands, and with other things—in a single night.

He clenched his fists. He could not go on like this, being tormented.

But he couldn't face Casey again. She not only knew about his black past, but they'd made a terrible deal together. One that he'd thought would save his mom.

In the end, he'd lost both Mom and Audrey.

And now—if he told Audrey the truth, it might come at the unbearable price of shattering her.

He raked his hands through his hair, wishing desperately for some way around this impasse. He wanted to pull Audrey close, to be near her.

Except…*no.*

Kieran gritted his teeth. The thought was *impossible.* The idea of being with Audrey Tanner was like wishing for the moon. You could stretch and stretch, you could imagine your fingertips brushing its chalky surface, but in the end you'd just come away with empty space.

And yet, he had to admit he'd had fantasies about what life could be like in White Pine—permanently. He'd allowed himself to imagine the things in his life that would be possible if he had someone like Audrey believing in him. Now, with her so close, with five years of trying to forget her undone in a matter of days, maybe it was time to make the fantasy a reality. At one point he'd been the man she wanted. Now, perhaps he could work to be the man she deserved.

He shook his head. It was insanity, he told himself.

Then again, how many times had he taken ridiculous

odds and come out ahead? He could still picture the bet he
took in a back-hole gambling den in Reno. The dry desert
wind had rattled the thin walls of a shabby room that was
cobbled onto the side of a dark bar. He swore he tasted
sand every time he swallowed. Around him were four other
players, but only one of them was still in the game with
him. It was the last card of a hand of Texas Hold 'Em. The
river card.

He was all in. He'd bet everything on a terrible hand,
starting with a smattering of low cards. But they were
black, everything in his hand was black (some days he felt
like everything in his goddamn life was black), and as the
cards turned over on the table, he began to think he could
pull together a straight flush. All spades.

Spades to dig him into a hole, or dig him out of one.
Naturally.

The meat-fisted man across the table had stopped rolling
the toothpick from side to side in his mouth. It was his
"tell," the physical tic he exhibited when things were going
his way. He had a good hand.

The dealer reached out, ready to flip the river card.
Kieran tensed. He was drawing to the inside. He needed
a four of spades. The odds were beyond bad. And even
if he got it, who was to say that the other player didn't
have a straight flush of his own, but with higher cards?
Kieran's straight was as low as it could go, starting with
a two.

The card had flipped and Kieran had swallowed back a
whoop of ecstasy. He'd stayed stone still, a quiet so practiced that no one would ever be able to read him. They
showed their hands. Toothpick man had a full house. Incredible cards.

Only Kieran's were better.

That day, he'd used both arms to scrape his winnings off the table. He'd tested the universe, challenged the odds that the impossible was possible, and he'd won. It was what he loved about gambling, what had drawn him to the tables even when it had passed from being a hobby to a sickness. Even when his luck had turned and he'd lost everything.

No, he thought. That wasn't true.

He hadn't lost everything until he'd lost Audrey.

The thought rattled him. If he wanted to try to win her back, he would have to confront Audrey's sister, and that was a dangerous prospect indeed.

The idea sent a cold chill through him despite the warm sun all around.

He grimaced at his odds. He'd have to bring the past to light to have any chance of being with Audrey. And once he did, would she even want him?

He stared at the wide blue sky, the color of dawn breaking over Moccasin Lake, and wondered if he could ride away from this place and never come back. He'd done it once, but nothing in him was convinced he could do it a second time.

Audrey Tanner was pulling on him with a force stronger than gravity. Was it time to finally stop resisting? He closed his eyes, imagining himself letting go and crashing into her. The impact would shatter them both. But perhaps there was a single entity they could put together from the pieces of their separate selves.

Maybe it was time to place one final bet.

* * *

Later that afternoon, whatever distracting thoughts Audrey had about Kieran vanished as she walked into the show-room after her two o'clock break and saw three teenage boys elbowing one another and laughing.

The click of her heels on the tile slowed, then stalled.

These were White Pine High School kids.

Oh, Lord. She'd told herself that she wasn't in any danger of seeing former students since she worked during school hours. But of course that wouldn't account for spring break, or teachers' conferences, or any of the other days that had students running around White Pine when they were normally in classes.

She didn't want it to, but her whole body heated with mortification. *They were going to see her.* Maybe they'd even come to see her. The lure of a former teacher strutting around motorcycles might be too good for a bunch of hormonal teenagers to pass up. After all, she was sure the rumor about her fate at the dealership was all over school by now.

Nevertheless, she batted back the creeping embarrassment. She should be proud of the fact that she was seeing students. She'd taught many of them and had cared about all of them. She had nothing to be ashamed of just because her career prospects had changed.

She looked down at the tops of her breasts mounding over the bustier. She tried to ignore two good reasons for being self-conscious staring her in the face.

She squared her shoulders. No sense in avoiding them. No sense in being scared of them, either. They were kids. If they judged her, it was because they were young and silly. When they were her age, they'd understand how life could take turns you didn't expect, and how one day you were wearing gym shorts and the next day you were wearing chaps.

The boys were gathered around a bright red SuperLow, a motorcycle that reminded Audrey of the movie *Easy Rider*. They were smiling, pointing at different features, and of course pretending to hump the back tire.

Typical.

She strode forward. "Boys," she said, just as one of them—Braden Acola, if she remembered correctly—pretended to jerk off one of the long handlebars. Their howls of laughter faded as she approached. "These machines aren't toys. Either you act respectfully around them, or I'll need to ask you to leave."

She looked from Braden to Cody Sims to Hunter Haglund. All faces she knew. They stared back at her—or at least at parts of her. Their open-faced, teenage ogling was almost humorous. Almost.

"Ms. Tanner, you work here now?" This question was from Cody, whose white-blond hair flopped so far forward it was nearly hanging in his eyes.

"I do," she replied, thinking that they *knew* this already. She gritted her teeth. Was it wrong that she just wanted them out of here? She could be as altruistic about it as she wanted, but deep down she hated this mixing of her past and present.

She lowered her voice in her best I-am-the-teacher tone. "Unless one of you is going to buy a motorcycle today, then you need to stop goofing off and leave."

The boys didn't move. "Aren't you supposed to be helping us?" Braden asked. His round face and thick body reminded Audrey how much she'd had to push him to do anything in gym class. "Aren't we your customers now?" He smirked at Cody and the two of them burst into laughter.

The third one, Hunter Haglund, stayed stone still. He was a sharp-jawed kid who hadn't spoken much in gym class. Audrey had remembered thinking he was a good, quiet kid who was sometimes too serious. It was a fact that was evidenced now by his furrowed brow and dark look.

"You're only customers if you buy something," Audrey said. "And I'm not sure you can afford anything in here."

"Hunter can." Braden smirked. "He's a customer."

"Yeah," Cody added. "Hunter wants a bike."

Audrey studied Hunter again, this time taking in his crisp shirt, his jeans that probably cost more than she made in a month. It reminded her that the Haglunds lived up by Willa. Hunter's dad was a ... surgeon, maybe? He worked in medicine, anyway, practicing nearer to Minneapolis.

"Then perhaps Hunter should talk to a sales manager while you two wait outside," she said.

"We could wait with you," Cody said, his eyes shining with laughter. "Seems like you have a super cool job now. You could tell us about it." He and Braden cracked up all over again. Audrey inhaled, ready to give them her best I'm-still-the-teacher lecture when Hunter intervened.

"Knock it off," he said. His eyes were obsidian with seriousness. His friends wiped the smirks off their faces immediately. "We're leaving."

Hunter turned his dark gaze to Audrey. She wanted to thank him for his maturity, but instead found that a cold prickle of unease rendered her wordless. This quiet, introverted boy had just helped her, and here she was, muted with something she couldn't explain. She gave him a small smile instead, the best she could do, and watched as the three boys exited the showroom.

When the door closed shut behind them, she gripped the nearby motorcycle and steeled her resolve. Those boys were the first students to come ogle her, but they wouldn't be the last. She straightened her posture while mentally recalling her list of all the tricks she knew to get kids to pay attention, to listen, and even to fear her if needed. She'd be darned if, next time, she was anything except ready.

CHAPTER SEVEN

That Saturday, Audrey turned her face to the sun as she walked to meet her sister for lunch. Her new wedges—a burnished silver color that glinted in the light—were from Willa, as were the hip-hugging jeans and her designer T-shirt.

Her friend had given them to her, along with a pile of other fashions, claiming she was getting rid of many of the clothes she'd bought when she'd lived in New York. "Early on in New York." Willa had laughed, her emerald eyes sparkling. "I've gained weight since then."

Audrey had tried to refuse. After all, these were designer clothes—they must have been worth a fortune. But Willa had insisted, and Audrey had finally accepted, admitting she was ready for a wardrobe change.

The clothes were more form-fitting than what she was used to (everything was, compared with yoga pants and track jackets), but the expensive material landed on her curves just right, helping Audrey feel the same boldness she did in her dealership attire without showing all the skin. Audrey had taken time today to apply some makeup as well. Again, not as much as what she wore at the dealership, but even a little gave her a sense of boldness from the inside out. It wasn't the makeup per se, but the idea that she could change if she wanted to. She wondered if this was what it was like to feel beautiful—an in-your-skin kind of power that had her wondering what this new version of herself was capable of.

She hummed a little as she approached the Paul Bunyan Diner. The awnings on Main Street flapped in the breeze, and the scent of warm soil and new grass was everywhere. Bonnie Lufson slid a wooden asparagus into the window of Loon Call Antiques, its smiling face reminding Audrey that in another two weeks, the White Pine Asparagus Festival would be in full swing. The trees lining the sidewalk would be wrapped in green crepe paper, kids would careen around with their faces painted green and asparagus crowns on their heads, and the local restaurants would begin serving their custom dishes: asparagus pasta, asparagus focaccia, asparagus pizza, asparagus ice cream, and, of course, her favorite, asparagus beer.

Not even the experience of Kieran could dim her love for the Asparagus Festival. She smiled to herself until she spotted Evelyn Beauford a few yards ahead, walking right toward her. The sight of the older woman, her pale blue coat flapping behind her like wings, sent Audrey's stomach sinking. She still didn't have a replacement for her role on the Good Shepherd Walk committee, and she was sure her lack of backup meant she was going to have to just suck it up and do it again this year.

As the older woman got closer, Audrey steeled herself for the inevitable. She stood waiting for a wave, a smile—any sign of recognition—to begin the dreaded conversation, but it never came. When Evelyn was just a few feet away, it hit her: She didn't recognize Audrey.

Whether it was the clothes, the hair, the makeup—or a combination of all three—it didn't matter. Audrey suppressed a giggle as she turned her back and pretended to be window-shopping at Loon Call Antiques. Evelyn Beauford walked right past her without so much as a glance.

Audrey stood there for a moment until she was sure the older woman wasn't going to turn back. Then she let out a chuckle and headed for the Paul Bunyan Diner, wondering if anyone else would fail to recognize her, and feeling excited about the prospect.

* * *

The cowbell over the door of the Paul Bunyan Diner clunked as Audrey entered. She took note of the giant stuffed asparagus propped up next to the hostess station as she slid into a knotty pine booth and smiled at her sister. "I'm so glad we could meet up!" she said, reaching across the white ceramic coffee cups to take her sibling's hands.

Casey started to reply, then stopped. Audrey watched the hard lines around her sister's mouth deepen with shock. Casey pulled her hands back as if she needed them to steady herself.

"What happened to you?" Casey asked. She glanced around the diner as if she thought one of the other customers might have an answer for her—or perhaps the rusty saws or old frying pans on the walls might talk, or the gingham curtains over the windows could offer some enlightenment. Audrey followed her sister's gaze, thinking how they both might share the same dark brown eyes and hair, but that her sister's face had been shaped by more cares and worries. It was all too visible in the wrinkles around her sister's eyes, the stubborn thrust of her jaw, and the strain in her neck. A thousand spa treatments for a thousand years might never ease this look off Casey's face; it was part of her now.

"You don't even look like yourself," Casey whispered, as if trying to keep Audrey's new look a secret. "Are you all right? I have some workout clothes in the car. You could change into those if you need to."

Audrey blinked. She'd expected her sister to have some comments about her new look, but she was surprised at how vehemently Casey seemed to think it was a mistake.

"I got these clothes on purpose," Audrey said, trying to make her voice light. "And I did my makeup like this intentionally, too. I kind of like it. It's better than the old lip stain, right?"

She smiled at Casey, willing her to remember the cheap gloss they'd bought when they were teenagers, just ahead of the homecoming dance. They hoped the makeup would make them more noticeable, so that at least one of them would get asked to go. The gloss had dyed both their lips a red bright red that they'd loved at the time, thinking it was glamorous. A few weekends ago, however, they'd pulled out pictures from that time, catching sight of their clown-looking lips and laughing so hard that they could hardly breathe.

Audrey wanted Casey to laugh, to make a reference to Bozo, to pretend to squirt water from an imaginary flower in her lapel. Instead, Casey's eyes roamed from Audrey's styled hair to the form-fitting T-shirt to the sparkling silver bangles on her wrist. The perpetual V-shaped wrinkle between her eyebrows grew more prominent.

"Why would you do all this?" she asked.

"I'm shaking things up," Audrey replied, grabbing the menu and pretending to study the breakfast options. "A little change will do me good."

"If you're trying to find long-term employment, then I don't think this is a good—"

"Do yah know what you want today?" the waitress asked, interrupting the conversation.

"Coffee," Casey answered briskly, "one egg over hard, and rye toast with margarine on the side."

The waitress jotted it all down, then looked at Audrey. "What can I get for…"

She stopped in mid-sentence, her pen poised. "Audrey Tanner, for gosh sakes, is that you?"

Audrey smiled up at Pauline, who had worked at the diner for years. "Sure is," she replied, "in the flesh."

"Well, my goodness. Don't you look glamorous!"

"Thank you," she replied with a pointed look at Casey, as if to say *See, other people think I look just fine.*

Pauline's bright blue eyes squinted with happiness. "Really. You look great. I mean, you always did, but you're just fantastic now."

Audrey felt her cheeks pink with the compliment. "You're being too kind."

"Am not," Pauline insisted. "Cripes, looking like that, you should throw your hat into the ring for Asparagus Queen this year. It's always a pretty young thing that wins it."

Audrey smiled. She'd watched the contest for years now. Women between the ages of twenty-four and forty would line up onstage, talk about how much they loved White Pine and what they'd do for the community as queen, and a panel of locals would pick the winner. The queen got a satin sash, an asparagus bouquet, and a thousand dollars in prize money.

"Thanks for the vote of confidence," Audrey said, "but I think I'll forgo any pageant gowns just now. I will take a Paul Bunyan omelet with a glass of orange juice, though."

Pauline winked at her. "You got it."

When they were alone again, Casey took a deep breath. "There's a job opening in Eagan, not too far from where I live. I already talked to the assistant principal about it. It's head track coach, boys and girls, but there's no teaching—only coaching. They're top of their division and you get an assistant coach, plus athletics has its own secretary. You'd have administrative support as well as coaching staff."

Casey finished just as Pauline came back to pour coffee and drop off Audrey's orange juice. Audrey was grateful for the interruption because she wasn't sure what to say.

Of all the scenarios she'd imagined when she got fired from her job, her least favorites were the ones that had her leaving White Pine. Her stomach twisted at the thought. But what else could she do? She couldn't stay at the dealership forever, dressed in leather and working with Kieran Callaghan. But could she really put on her old track pants and go back to coaching again?

I have no idea what I want to be when I grow up, Audrey thought.

"Well?" Casey asked after a minute. "What do you think?"

Audrey took a steadying breath. "Thank you for looking

out for me," she said. "I am so grateful for the help, but I'm
not sure I'm ready to pack up and leave White Pine. Losing
my job was hard, but it's also given me time to—I don't
know, explore my options. I think I'll always want to teach
and be around people, but maybe there are other ways to
do that besides coaching."

"Nonsense," Casey said, waving a hand. "You have a
master's degree and you need to put it to use. You can always stay with me until you get settled." When Audrey
didn't answer right away, Casey reached for her hand, giving it a quick squeeze. "But if you simply *had* to stay in
White Pine, you could always commute."

Audrey considered this, wondering if she'd be happy
spending so much time in her beige car every day. She
thought about the crowded school hallways and the anemic
paychecks. Was that what she wanted? She stared at her orange juice, unsure.

"You're not glad we live far apart, are you?" Casey
asked after a moment. Her tone was teasing, but Audrey
could hear the concern just underneath.

When Casey had first moved to Eagan for her accounting job, Audrey would have happily considered abandon-
ing White Pine altogether. She'd missed her sister terribly,
an ache that for a long time didn't want to subside. But
Casey's absence had forced her to branch out in her friendships, and eventually she'd reconnected with her high-
school pals Betty, Stephanie, and Anna—and then Willa.
The separation from her sister had forced her to expand her
family, and she had a new sisterhood as a result. She wasn't
at all sure she wanted to walk away from that, especially
when she was still in the process of figuring out what she
wanted to do next.

"I don't want us to be separated by miles and miles," Audrey hedged. "I just wonder if I can make a go of it here."

"Doing what, exactly?"

Audrey shifted in the wooden booth. "That's the thing. I may have found employment for right now. The pay is good, by the way."

"Is it teaching?"

"It's more like sales." She stared at the scalloped edges of her paper placemat. "At the new Harley dealership in town."

Casey went very still. "Where Kieran works?"

"He's there, yes."

Casey eyed her sharply as Pauline delivered their food. Audrey picked up her fork, but her sister's hawk-like gaze was quickly eroding her appetite.

"Audrey. Whatever game you think you're playing, just stop now. You need to leave that job immediately. Kieran Callaghan was bad news the first time around, and nothing has changed."

Maybe I've changed, Audrey thought, staring at her puffy, golden omelet.

"Kieran's not an issue," she said. She wanted to believe it.

Casey scraped a tiny amount of margarine over her toast. "No, he's trouble. He is going nowhere fast, and you shouldn't let him take you down, too."

Audrey's insides sank. Casey had given her the same lecture before—after Casey had met Kieran for the first time. Casey had grilled him about his past, about how much he had in his savings account, even chiding him at one point about not having a Roth IRA. Kieran had played it cool, but Audrey had been mortified.

Later, she'd confronted Casey, saying she didn't care what Kieran looked like on paper, that her feelings for him wouldn't be swayed. Casey had fought right back, saying Audrey was making a terrible decision that she'd regret soon enough.

To her credit, when Kieran left, Casey had never once said "I told you so."

Audrey set down her fork. "Kieran aside, the hours are good and it pays well. And I think I can make a difference there."

"Doing what, exactly?"

"Well, a few days ago, for example, there was this woman who came in and no one spoke to her. Not *one* salesman. So I went over and helped her as much as I could, which wasn't a ton, but at least I talked to her. And I was thinking this dealership isn't targeting women very well as a point of sale. So what if I got some training—"

"No."

"Excuse me?"

"Audrey, just stop right there. You are not going to spend your time thinking about how a motorcycle dealership can sell bikes to women. It's ridiculous."

Audrey bit the inside of her cheek. It hadn't felt ridiculous when she'd thought of it. In fact, the only reason she hadn't moved forward with pursuing her idea was because Kieran, who had promised her riding lessons, had been racing from meeting to meeting, taking lunches with executives, and even getting his hands dirty in the service bays while he chatted with mechanics. She figured she'd use their lesson time to pitch the idea of women's sales to him, only there hadn't been any lesson time. Yet.

"I know it might sound a little odd," Audrey admitted,

"or at least very different from what I've been doing, but I think this position could work."

"Right. Because everything you do around Kieran works out so well for you, doesn't it?"

Audrey stared at her food, silent, until Casey set down her fork and folded her hands. "Come on," Casey said, "look at me."

Audrey raised her eyes and found her sister's matching pair, shining with concern and love, staring back. "I know I sound like a jerk," Casey continued, "but I'm worried about you. Losing your job was tough, but you're talented and hardworking. I don't want to see you throw away good opportunities so you can stay in White Pine and get hurt all over again. At least, if you stay, find something else besides that awful dealership with him inside of it."

Audrey shook her head. "I appreciate your concern, but I like it there."

Casey lifted a brow. "And I suppose you like all that makeup and this new wardrobe of yours, too?"

Audrey shrugged. "Who knows? I'm trying some things out. I need to be able to do that without feeling like you're disapproving every step of the way."

"I *am* disapproving every step of the way."

Audrey almost smiled. "Then disapprove all you want, but let me live my life. If I don't do it exactly the way you think I should, then that's just something you have to come to terms with."

Casey sat back. Audrey knew she didn't usually disagree like this with her sister. But enough was enough. She was ready to shake things up, and if it meant she had to fight with her sister some, so be it.

"Fine," Casey said. "But when someone else gets this great opportunity in Eagan, I can't help that. And I may not be able to help find a different opportunity by the time you're finally ready to face the facts. There's a good chance you'll be on your own. Is that what you want?"

Cold unease crept along Audrey's skin. Her sister may have support and love behind her intentions, but right then she sounded downright threatening. "I'll happily live with my own decisions," Audrey replied, sitting up straighter in the creaky booth. "And if I make some mistakes, that's part of figuring it all out."

Casey took a sip of coffee instead of replying, but her disapproval was there, as plainly as if she'd spoken it.

Audrey adjusted the sparkling bangles on her wrist and prayed she wasn't falling headlong into disaster all over again.

CHAPTER EIGHT

*K*ieran watched Audrey exit the Paul Bunyan Diner, observing from the edge of a nearby alleyway. She glided away from the diner in tight jeans and a hot little T-shirt that had him sucking in his breath. She was impossibly beautiful. Several other heads turned her way on the street, leering across overstuffed planters and asparagus signs. She looked like the kind of woman who could do better than him. She deserved an investment banker, he thought. Or a lawyer or a doctor. Someone who didn't have to keep his past hidden.

But today, he was willing to confront his mistakes and his past and try for her. He had to do at least that much, or risk wondering *what if* for the rest of his life.

And it started with her sister, Casey.

Audrey moved away, up the street toward Knots and Bolts, while Casey came toward him, her pace brisk, her sensible heels clunking along the sidewalk. Given the way she walked, Kieran wondered if she went anywhere without a purpose. But whatever her mission was today, he was about to interrupt it.

"Hi, Casey," he said, stepping out in front of her.

She pulled up short to avoid plowing into him. But if she was surprised or caught off guard, she never showed it. The woman could play poker with the best of them if she wanted to, Kieran thought.

She regarded him with her brown eyes—the same color as Audrey's, technically, but so much flintier. He wondered briefly if his hurting Audrey had added to her hardness. He couldn't blame her if it had.

"Kieran," she said. One word, flat and solitary.

"We should talk," he said. "It's been five years. There's so much to catch up on." His words were easy, even though his brain was buzzing with a lost sense of time. It felt like this interaction was years old, and he'd been here before.

"There's nothing we need to say to one another," Casey replied, trying to push past him. But he blocked her way on the sidewalk.

"I've paid back my debt," he said, lowering his voice. "And I care about your sister. So let's bury our secret once and for all, because I'm going to try and win Audrey back."

Casey's head shot up. Her features knotted in disapproval. "No." From her lips, the word had a finality to it that chilled Kieran. Suddenly, the day's sunlight was too thin around them, shifting from warm honey to weak white. Her chilly manner froze him through.

"Let's go and talk about it," he offered, shoving his hands in his pockets like this was any other conversation, and she was any other person. Like the stakes weren't unbearably high.

"Where?"

"Just up the sidewalk here. Black Bear Bar—we'll have a drink."

"No." The word came too easily from her lips, over and over. "I don't want to be seen with you. Come to my car. It's just down the block here. We'll talk there." She brushed past him with an assurance that belied her small size—five foot five, just like Audrey, and rock hard to boot, only not from muscles. From life, he thought.

Kieran inhaled to steady himself, and followed her down the sidewalk. He stayed a few respectable paces behind. When she slid into her car—a compact silver machine that looked as sensible as it was boring—she already had the key in the ignition. She wasn't going to give him much time, it was clear. He opened his mouth to speak, but she beat him to the punch.

"You will stay away from my sister," she said. "There's no discussion to have. You need to agree, then get out of my car."

Kieran had to admire Casey's bravado. The woman was half his size but acted like a mob boss.

"Or you'll do what, exactly?" Kieran said. He settled into his seat, indicating he wasn't going anywhere.

"You know what I could tell Audrey. You understand the deal we made."

Kieran chuckled, even though his palms were clammy with nerves. Even though the memory of trying—and failing—to save his mom's life had his heart grinding with pain in his chest.

He had to call Casey's bluff, and pray it worked. "If you tell your sister about the deal we made, it makes us *both* look bad. Are you willing to risk that?"

"I'll deny it."

"Except I still have copies of the checks I wrote to pay you back. There's a paper trail that links us."

"So?"

"Your funds were conditional. You offered them up so I'd leave. Which I did. You think Audrey's going to look past that?"

It was Casey's turn to laugh. "That may be, but I'm her sister, Kieran. You're just—I don't know—some guy she banged a few years ago. I'm her flesh and blood. Do you really think she won't forgive me? We're family. But you? I wouldn't be so sure. There's no guarantee she'll want anything to do with you when she knows the truth."

Kieran wanted to rebuff her words, even though part of him knew she was right. Casey had looked at him with the same disapproving stare five years ago, after tracking him down in his shabby hotel room at the Great Lakes Inn.

"Guys like you always have an angle," she'd said at the time. "So I'm asking: What's yours?"

Back then, not knowing what a calculating monster Casey was, Kieran had tried playing her with his winning grin. "Lady, I know you don't like me, but your sis—"

"I have money," she'd interrupted, her blank expression never changing. "Plenty of it. And if you need some, then we should make a deal. You should take it, and in return, I never have to see you again. My sister, either."

Kieran had tried grinning again, but he could feel the wrongness of it. He figured he looked like a leering jack-o'-lantern.

The truth was that he did need money. Lots of it. And he did have an angle, because he was trying to cobble together enough money to get his mom chemotherapy treatments for her cancer. The only problem was, he couldn't walk away from the gambling table. He was addicted, and his sickness meant he was losing more than he was winning. And with every loss, his mom's cure became more distant.

Casey was right about him being desperate. The only thing she didn't know—*couldn't* know—was that Audrey wasn't part of any game.

"I googled you and you came up in a few low-level poker tournaments," Casey had continued, her eyes traveling over his open suitcase, shirts and pants spilling everywhere. "The thing I can't put together is why you're in White Pine, when all the real poker games are north of here, closer to Minneapolis and the big casinos."

Because I lost so badly there, he thought. He'd made a scene and they'd kicked him out. Not that he was going to tell Casey that. "Just traveling through," he'd told her, shrugging, trying not to let this frigid woman unnerve him.

"My sister likes you," Casey had continued, picking at a hangnail as if she was bored, "and I don't. So tell me: What will it take to never see you again? I know you need money. So let's negotiate."

If Kieran he could go back and do it all over again, he would shove her out the door and tell her to get lost. He would find some way to come clean with Audrey and fix his problems with her help. But Casey was Lucifer herself, meeting him at the crossroads of his bad choices, offering him what he needed most—money to try to cure his mom, who was without health care and without medical help. He and Auggie had pooled together what they could. But every time Kieran won at the tables, every time his luck had piles of money stacked up and his mom's treatment in sight, he kept betting. His luck had shifted, and soon his pockets were empty.

God help him, he'd gambled away his mom's cure. And five years ago, when Casey had offered him money in exchange for his soul—or at least his heart—he'd agreed. He wouldn't have to return to Auggie and his mom ashamed and desperate. And he could get his mom the medical help she deserved.

In return, he'd tried to push his feelings for Audrey Tanner away forever.

The memories had Kieran's stomach watery with anger and irritation. And shame, if he was honest with himself. Casey was right—Audrey might never forgive him when she discovered the truth of what he'd done. Even someone as generous and kind as Audrey had limits.

His jaw clenched as he stared out of the window of Casey's car. But, dammit, he had to try. Even though part of him couldn't blame Casey for wanting better than him for Audrey, it wasn't her place to stand in the way.

"I'm going after her, Casey. I'm going to try and love her the way I should have five years ago. If she'll have me, I'm never going to let her go again."

Casey's face paled. Her lips pursed. "You'll lose her when I tell her the truth."

"I could always tell her first."

Casey glared at him. "You wouldn't."

Kieran met her ferocious gaze. He knew that if he wanted a real chance with Audrey, he would have to tell her. Eventually. Honesty would have to be a pillar of their new relationship. If he could even get that far.

"I still have feelings for Audrey. And I believe she feels

things for me, too. Do whatever you have to, but my path is set."

"You're making the biggest mistake of your life," Casey said.

Kieran heard the threat in her voice, but he still wondered: Would Casey really come clean with Audrey when the truth made *her* look so bad as well?

This would be the bet, then. This would be the hand he'd play: he would call Casey's bluff.

Who knew when it would all play out, but he'd once played a round of poker that lasted three hours. He was used to long games.

He was even more accustomed to long odds.

"Bring it on," he told Casey, and stepped out of the car.

* * *

Before work the following Monday, Audrey found herself striding down a south-facing hallway at White Pine High. Her gaze was locked on the room ahead, her steps easy as if it were no bother for her to be in her former place of employment. She could smell the disinfectant tang of the hallways mingling with the doughy aroma of lunch food. She took in the corrugated fronts of lockers and the banner over one hallway reminding seniors to buy their class rings before the school year ended. She walked on, her throat tightening with the knowledge that this was a place she'd loved but one she could never come back to.

Today, however, the school secretary, Janet Rifflemore, had let her in easily enough. "I'd like to talk to Paul Frace," Audrey had said, standing at the front desk of the administrative offices. She figured the truth was better than any falsehood she could come up with for seeing him. "I wondered if he might want some pointers about coaching the girls through the last of the track season."

Janet's long face had brightened. "Oh, I bet he would. He was just saying in the teachers' lounge how tough it is, how much time it takes in addition to grading the spring tests. Here, let me pull up his schedule."

Audrey had already found it herself in a stack of papers at home. She'd saved the contents of her old desk, which had included administrative filing. If his schedule hadn't changed much in the past few weeks, then Paul would be on break before the next class. Which gave her something close to thirty minutes during which to speak with him.

"What do you know," Janet said, "he's got some time between classes right now. If you want, you can check his room, down in the English wing, to see if he's there. Otherwise, try the teachers' lounge."

Now, as Audrey headed toward his classroom, she prayed silently that he'd be in the first locale. Because no way could she face the teachers' lounge, answering questions of *how was she doing* and *what was she up to* and *were things going all right?*

She would happily tell them she worked at a Harley dealership, modeling motorcycles. They probably already knew, frankly, considering how word got around in White Pine. She would even try telling them about how different she felt on the showroom floor, how it was helping her think about changes in the rest of her life. She could explain all about how she was excited to see if she couldn't improve sales for women there. But once she started chatting about it, she knew she'd see pity in their eyes or hear it in their voices while they all sipped sodas and graded papers and shook their heads at how unjustly she'd lost her job.

It might have been a low blow, it was true. But she was determined not just to move on—but to thrive. Never mind her sister. Never mind Kieran, even. She was going to live life as she saw fit, right here in White Pine. She wanted to buy fresh donuts at the Rolling Pin and listen to the church bells sounding across the Birch River on Sunday morning, and meet with her friends at Knots and Bolts, and go to the Asparagus Festival every year. She wanted to live in the town she loved more than anything else. More than any man, more than any job, this town had been with her since she was little, and she knew the streets and sidewalks as well as she knew herself. She would stay here. Because she felt like she could make a difference here. She just had to figure out how.

The night before, she'd been researching statistics about women and their purchasing power, and she was awed at how many females were taking up Harleys of their own. In Minneapolis they had an all-women riding club she'd found online: the Magnificent Hogs. She knew she needed to get White Pine Harley to see the potential customer base here—and she was determined to be more than a hot ass in some leather chaps.

It might be time for a new Audrey, and for a new start. But in order to get there, she had to visit Paul Frace.

She tapped on his classroom door, then pushed it open gently. "Paul?"

She heard the shuffling of papers, the scrape of a chair. "Yes, how can I help?"

The next thing she knew, she was face-to-face with the bearded English teacher. They had once been tied together for a three-legged race, she recalled suddenly, during a fall carnival. She didn't know what year. A long time ago, that was certain.

"Uh, hi, Paul," she said, twisting the handle of her purse in her hands. "I don't mean to bother you, but I wondered if we could talk?"

"Audrey!" he said, his bushy eyebrows raised in surprise. "What a pleasure! My, don't you look different." He cleared his throat. "Please, come in."

He ushered her into the room with the manners of someone hosting a dinner party, or inviting her to have a drink. She remembered the way Paul would put his napkin on his lap before eating his brown-bag lunch, or how he'd hold the door for her with spine-stiff formality. Even if he wore pressed khakis and a plaid shirt and tie, Paul Frace seemed like a man who would be comfortable in breeches and a top coat, more suited for the manners of the late 1800s than the current day.

"To what do I owe the pleasure?" Paul asked.

"I hope I'm not intruding," Audrey said, noting the papers and textbooks scattered across his desk. He sat behind the metal behemoth while she slid into one of the kids' chairs, feeling suddenly small and ridiculous. "I wanted to talk with you about the track team."

Paul shook his head, a beleaguered smile on his face. "I couldn't be more glad to have your company on this topic. It's been such a nightmare since they let you go. I don't feel like I'm doing these girls any kind of service. More of a disservice, actually. Is it wrong that I just want the last few weeks of the school year to be over so someone else can do the job next year?" He leaned his head on an ink-stained hand. "I fear I've been an abysmal replacement in your absence. The budget cuts that forced you—" He shook his head, stopping himself.

"I'm sure you're doing a fine job," Audrey said, skirting the issue of her dismissal. "It's just that I started running with one of the girls, Alexis Belten, and she seems to think the team isn't being challenged enough. I wondered if my old coaching notes would help?"

She reached into her purse and pulled out her small notebook filled with practice drills and ideas. The weight of it was so familiar in her hands, the pages battered from years of love and scribbling. She tried not to clutch it too tightly. Paul needed it more than she did, after all. "It's nothing formal, but I'm not using it and I figured it might be of service."

Paul took the notebook gingerly, handling it as if it were the Holy Grail itself. "This is such a gift," he marveled, "such a generous move in light of what...occurred."

Paul was too polite. He wouldn't utter the words about her being let go. He didn't know how to say it, and she wouldn't know how to reply if he did, at a loss to explain how she was ready for what was next, ready to face new things, and holding on to this notebook was only anchoring her to the past. The small book looked so strange in Paul's hands, but maybe strange was okay. Maybe strange was a door that led to new and exciting things. She blinked against the image of Kieran that flashed in her mind.

"I care about the girls," she said, trying to stay focused, "and I want them to finish the season strong. We were on a good path. These girls want to be challenged. Just remember that."

Paul nodded thoughtfully. He stared at the notebook, then set it down on his already cluttered desk.

"Can I get you a drink?" he asked, his denim blue eyes finding hers in the dusty room.

"No, I'm fine. I don't mean to keep you. I just wanted to drop off the notebook and—"

"I meant a drink outside of here. Outside of the school, that is. Ah, perhaps after work sometime?"

Audrey's mind raced. "But you have a girlfriend. I forget her name, but..."

"Camilla. She—that is, we broke up."

Audrey got the distinct feeling Paul had been dumped. And now he was asking her out.

She stilled in her chair, coming to terms with the idea. The crazy thing was, a month ago she would have said yes. Paul was nice. He had a job and he was smart and kind. She could certainly do a lot worse in White Pine.

But she was ready for something more. The memory of Kieran against her in the bathroom had heat searing her spine.

Not that Kieran would be the reason she would say no to Paul. The truth is, she didn't want to date a teacher. A remnant of her past. She especially didn't want to date a romantic Englishman trapped in a twenty-first-century teacher's body, who might cut off locks of her hair and press them into envelopes with wax seals. If that was, in fact, what romantic Englishmen did.

"Thank you, Paul. I'm so flattered. But I think I'd better pass."

"Are you seeing someone, then?" he asked amicably enough.

Audrey bit her lip. She saw Kieran every day. But they weren't anything to each other. "No, I wouldn't exactly say seeing."

"But there's someone, then?"

"I can't say—"

"Does he know how you feel?"

Audrey's cheeks heated at the line of questioning. She was no prude, but it felt unbearably awkward to be in this classroom with Paul, answering his questions. What was more, the bell for the next class was going to ring, and she needed to duck out of the school before any other students or teachers saw her.

"I—I'm not sure we're really anything," she said finally.

Paul nodded. "I see. I don't mean to pry, it's just that you're so lovely, Audrey. Coming back here like this, giving me your coaching notebook. It's astounding, really. I've admired you for a great while. I'm sorry that whomever you seem interested in isn't throwing themselves prostrate at your feet, begging for the honor of being loved by you."

Audrey couldn't help but smile. It was a sweet compliment, and the idea of Kieran at her feet was nearly snort-worthy. "I'm afraid I have a complicated past with the person of interest," she admitted.

"Complicated? Well, rest assured, then. All the great romantic writers gave their heroes and heroines complicated situations. Austen. Hardy. Brontë. And they still got their happy endings."

Audrey knew she wasn't going to get a fairy-tale ending with Kieran. "I'm not sure I'm in the market for happily ever after. But thanks anyway."

Paul shrugged. "You give me your notebook, I give you best wishes that your life ends up like an eighteen-hundreds novel. That seems about right." He smiled with genuine warmth, and Audrey found herself returning it. She stood up.

"Thanks, Paul."

"Thank *you*, Audrey," he said, walking her to the door. "And if you change your mind about that drink, please give me a ring."

Audrey nodded. "Will do," she agreed. But inside she was thinking that she was leaving connections at her school behind, and forging ahead with something new entirely. That left her feeling just as breathless as she'd been with Kieran in the bathroom.

Which was saying something.

CHAPTER NINE

Casey would die if she could see me now, Audrey thought as she and Willa elbowed through the crowd at the Wheelhouse Bar. Audrey trailed behind her friend, keeping her eyes fixed on Willa's dark blonde hair, and worrying she might lose her in the packs of people gathered at the bar, on the dance floor, and at tables all around.

The Wheelhouse on a Saturday night was the place to be in White Pine. Never mind the wilted cardboard coasters or the discarded peanut shells crunching underfoot or the filmy windows that looked out onto a flat, halogen-lit parking lot.

"There are so many folks around!" Audrey said above the din of the jukebox. The music made the crowded space feel even more packed. "Half of White Pine must be here." Audrey had eaten lunch and dinner there hundreds of times—but rarely had she bothered to patronize the place after nine o'clock at night.

Willa eyed her. "If you think this is a crowd, you should have seen the night Redfish Sushi opened in Midtown Manhattan, and who I pushed out of the way to get a table. Trust me, this is nothing."

Willa squeezed into a place at the bar, pulling Audrey along with her. With a few charming smiles at the men all around them, Willa soon had both of them seated on cracked-leather barstools, drink menus in hand.

"You're so good at this," Audrey said, unable to help noticing the way men's eyes roamed along Willa's every curve. Her friend had always been glamorous to a degree, even in high school, but these days she was downright sophisticated. Not to mention beautiful. Tonight, Willa was making jeans, boots, and a herringbone sweater look like they were runway-ready.

Audrey swallowed, feeling suddenly like a cubic zirconia next to a diamond. Willa's hair was sleek and shiny, whereas Audrey's was tousled. Willa's makeup was minimal, whereas Audrey had donned her "Egyptian" eyes again. And Willa was in jeans, whereas Audrey had on a knee-length leather skirt, another one of Willa's castoffs.

Willa made it all look so effortless, Audrey thought, her face beginning to warm. The idea of moving to Eagan was suddenly in her mind, if only for the fact that the city was big enough so everyone she knew wouldn't see her mortifying machinations as she tried to shake up her life a little bit.

She tried to remember that she'd felt good when she left the house. That shouldn't change just because she was sitting next to her friend, who'd always known how to dress well.

"Heya, Audrey."

Dave the bartender was smiling at her from the other side of the polished wood. Audrey blinked at the brightness of Dave's teeth in the dim space. She'd never noticed what a nice smile he had, which seemed odd. The pair had known each other for years. He leaned his muscled forearms on the bar and closed the space between them.

"Hi, Dave. How's the asparagus beer coming?" Every year, Dave crafted his special brew for the Asparagus Festival, and each year, people came from all over the state to drink it.

"Coming along just fine. I've got some here if you want to taste it."

Audrey felt her eyes widen. "But it's not supposed to be out until the festival. And the festival's not for another two weeks."

Dave winked at her, and there was something about the motion that sent hot sparks along her skin. Was he... *flirting*? "If you promise not to tell, I'll get you some. But this has to be between us. Can you keep a secret?"

Audrey stared at Dave—at his short, raven-black hair, and at the lines of his handsome face that were a flattering mix of boyish and masculine—and managed to nod. She'd known Dave since middle school. She'd been to the Wheelhouse countless times. And not once—ever—had he winked at her.

Maybe she wasn't such a cubic zirconia after all.

Willa tapped the bar before Dave could walk away. "Hi, Dave. Can I get a cranberry juice?"

Dave nodded distractedly. "Yah, sure. Coming right up."

"He barely even remembered I was here," Willa said as Dave headed off. "Did you see that? The whole bar faded away and it was just you and Dave Englund."

Audrey couldn't help but smile. "I'm flattered. He's a nice guy."

"Just not the guy you really hoped to flirt with tonight."

"Excuse me?"

"Oh, come on. Like you aren't craning your neck every five minutes to see if Kieran Callaghan is here."

Audrey straightened. "I am not."

Willa's green eyes sparked with amusement. "Okay, Tanner. Whatever you say."

Audrey was indignant. "Listen, if I have any interest in seeing Kieran, it's only to pitch him on a business idea I had."

"Does this plan involve taking off his clothes?"

"What? *No.* It's about targeting women more as a demographic for sales."

Willa faced her friend fully. "Are you trying to tell me that if he walks in here tonight, that the two of your are going to talk about gender demographics?"

"It makes sense for the dealership. It's just a business plan."

"Well that business plan has you staring at the door an awful lot. Do you know something I don't?"

Audrey blushed, wondering how to confess that she'd overheard Kieran telling Fletch about his plans to hit the Wheelhouse that weekend. And when Willa said she wanted to go out this weekend as well, Audrey might have suggested the same bar. But it wasn't to flirt with Kieran on the off chance she saw him. It was only to have a conversation with him so he'd see the potential of women at the dealership. And to get those lessons scheduled already.

"I might have heard something about him being here," she offered, "but I'm interested in seeing him for *business reasons* only."

Willa's gaze searched Audrey's face. "You sure about that?"

Under her friend's direct stare, she shifted. She wanted to answer that Kieran was in the past, a mistake she wasn't going to relive anytime soon. But the words wouldn't come.

Instead, she grabbed Willa's hands. "Look, whether I see Kieran or not, I'm over the moon to be out with you on a Saturday night. Your B and B has been so busy, and job stuff with me has been nuts, and it's nice to get a chance to see you, one on one."

Willa squeezed her friend's hands. "You know that's the truth."

Just then, Dave came back with the drinks. Willa's asparagus beer was nearly overflowing in a tall pint glass. He set it down in front of her and took care to wipe any overage with a bar towel. Willa's cranberry juice arrived unceremoniously in a plastic cup.

"You need anything else," Dave said, looking straight at Audrey, "you let me know. And remember, that beer is our secret."

"I won't tell a soul," she said, and lifted the glass in a toast to Dave.

Willa cleared her throat. "What do you want to bet that pint doesn't show up on our tab tonight?"

"Really? You think he'd do that?"

Willa laughed, just as the jukebox kicked up a fiddle-heavy country song that had people lining up on the dance floor. "Oh, honey. I think he'd give you a whole keg if he thought it might get you interested." Audrey shook her head, disbelieving. First Paul Frace, and now Dave? It didn't seem possible.

She took a sip of her favorite beer and closed her eyes as the tangy, bright ale hit her palate. For fifty-one weeks every year, beer was just beer—but for one week, during the Asparagus Festival, beer was downright heavenly.

"God, this is good," she said appreciatively.

"We can go home now, I think, and call your night a success."

"How's your..." Audrey looked down at her friend's drink. "Cranberry juice?"

"Tart. But fine."

"No vodka? Don't you drink cranberry and vo—" She stopped in midsentence as the realization hit her. "Oh my God, are you *pregnant*?"

Willa laughed. "I think you just told the entire bar my news."

Audrey flew off her barstool to hug her friend. Tears of happiness pooled in the corners of her eyes as she gripped Willa ferociously. "Oh, you are going to be the best mom ever! You and Burk must be so happy. Do you know what you're having?"

Willa clutched her friend back. "It's a little early for that. But I think I'm hoping for a boy, based on what a hellion of a daughter I was."

Audrey climbed back up onto her own barstool. "You were not," she protested. "You just rebelled for a little while. And if your parents were around now, they would be so proud of you. Just like everyone is so proud of you. And happy for you. And I can't stop talking because I'm so overjoyed at this moment!"

Audrey touched her pint glass to Willa's plastic cup. "To new arrivals," she said, her eyes pricking with fresh tears.

Willa arched a brow. "Don't get all sappy and emotional

on me right now. You are going to be an aunt, it's true, but tonight is not about your responsibility. It's about getting you some. Maybe hooking you up with someone for hot, steamy sex."

"Willa!"

"I'm serious. When is the last time you got laid?"

Audrey nearly spit out her beer. She swallowed, then gasped, "You sound like Betty!"

"Sometimes, Betty says things that need saying. When was the last time you were, as they say biblically, *with* a man?"

Audrey stared at her golden ale, mortified. But if she couldn't tell Willa, she couldn't tell anyone. "Kieran. Five years ago."

Willa set down her plastic cup. "For real?"

"Yes, for real. I wouldn't make up something that embarrassing." She didn't add the part where she'd kept taking her birth control steadfastly, just to cover her bases, even when the possibility of anything happening was so remote.

"Oh, sweetie," Willa said, shaking her head, "that *is* a dry spell. Well, here's hoping it ends tonight. Or at least that it starts sprinkling in the desert, if you know what I mean."

Audrey laughed, just as Dave placed another beer in front of her. "I noticed your asparagus ale was getting a little low," he said. "Thought I'd refresh it."

"Thank you," Audrey replied, feeling the warmth of the beer spreading through her. "It's delicious. I love it."

"I grilled sixty pounds of asparagus this year," Dave said, pride turning up the corners of his mouth. "Took me days, but it got a roasted note into the beer that I love.

And can you taste the honey? There's just a tiny bit in there to add sweetness so the whole batch doesn't get too bitter."

Audrey shook her head. "I'm afraid my palate isn't that sophisticated. I just know that one time each year, I drink something that I wish I could get *all* the time."

Dave reached out and, to Audrey's surprise, touched the tips of his fingers to hers. "If you're still around later, when things slow down for me at the bar, maybe we could hit the dance floor?"

Audrey blinked. In his form-fitting black T-shirt, Dave would hardly be a bad way to end the evening. Lean and tall, Audrey could almost picture how his long, sinewy muscles looked underneath his clothes. She felt a thrill deep in her stomach and smiled.

"I think that would be nice."

Dave turned to wait on another customer, just as someone elbowed into Audrey's space. "Excuse m—" she started to say, but was cut off by the massive form of Kieran Callaghan standing over her. Golden strands of his dark red hair ignited in the bar's overhead lights. Behind them, his reflection fragmented in a hundred bottles lined up on the wall. He was everywhere, it seemed. In the warm bar, Audrey suddenly shivered.

"I'm surprised to see you here," Kieran said, his eyes raking over her, taking all of her in. No *hi, so nice to see you*. No *fancy meeting you here*. It was brusque, even for Kieran. It almost didn't matter, though. *He was right in front of her*. They were sharing the same space again.

Not that Audrey was about to let herself get carried away. "Hello to you, too, Kieran," she said. "This is my friend Willa Olmstead. She lives in town here and runs the

White Pine B and B. Willa, Kieran is my, uh, boss at the dealership."

She made the introduction like Willa had no idea who Kieran was, like they hadn't just been talking about him. A current of nervous energy had her wondering what to do with her hands. She grabbed her beer glass, then set it down again.

Poised and elegant, Willa didn't miss a beat. "It's nice to meet you," she said. "Any friend of Audrey's is a friend of mine."

Kieran glanced at Audrey's beer, and his eyes widened slightly. "Is that what I think it is?"

Audrey nodded, realizing that she'd had pints of asparagus beer in the past five years, but that Kieran's first—and last—swig of it would have been when they were together. "Asparagus beer," she said, liking that Kieran seemed jolted by the liquid. As if he'd forgotten it existed but seeing it now was dredging up memories long forgotten.

"Let me get you a pint," Audrey said, and flagged Dave, who came over quickly.

"Another pint?" Audrey asked. "For my boss here?"

Dave barely glanced at Kieran. He let his fingers touch Audrey's for the briefest of moments. "Coming right up."

Kieran's jawline hardened. "You know him?"

"That's Dave Englund. He makes the asparagus beer every year. He's a friend."

"Friend?" Kieran replied, his voice rough. The sound brought the hairs on the back of her neck to attention. "Is that what the kids are calling it these days?"

His reaction was unexpected. Was Kieran...jealous? Audrey glanced at Willa, who was sipping her cranberry juice in an effort to keep from smirking.

"He asked me to dance later," Audrey said with an offhanded shrug.

She wasn't sure what she expected Kieran to do. Maybe shrug in return, tell her to have fun. Or maybe just stalk away. But the next thing she knew, he'd placed both hands on Audrey's waist, lifting her off the barstool in one motion. "Excuse us," he said to Willa. "I'd like to get a few numbers in before *Dave Englund*."

Audrey started to protest, but the words died on her lips when Kieran laced his fingers through hers. It was more thrilling than holding hands should be.

Dancing with him could be even better.

She smiled to herself and let him lead the way onto the dance floor.

CHAPTER TEN

The song blaring from the jukebox was a quick, twangy country song, but Kieran ignored it and crushed Audrey to him as if it were a slow dance. Bodies whirred past, but he paid them no mind. He needed Audrey close to him. Damn that bartender, and damn her sister, Casey, most of all.

He gripped Audrey more tightly, wondering what in the world he was going to do. He'd play his bluff, but, in the end, this might be his last chance to hold her, and he was determined to savor it. Her nearness made his muscles sore. His heart filled his rib cage and ached against his sternum.

"Kieran, I can't breathe."

She struggled and he reluctantly relaxed his grip. Pulling away, Audrey rubbed the part of her face that had been pressed into his shirt seam. "What is going on with you?"

Kieran ran a hand through his hair. Shit. She was staring at him with a bewildered expression.

"I didn't mean to make you uncomfortable," he said, "I just…" He trailed off. What could he possibly say?

For a moment, she just stared at him, befuddled, until someone bumped her from behind on the dance floor and she landed awkwardly against his chest. He steadied her in his arms, longer than necessary. She didn't fight him.

"What gives?" she asked finally, her warm brown eyes melting him. "Are you all right?"

Hell no, he wasn't all right. He was berating himself for being such a simpleton, approaching Casey like he had. Had he really thought she would just let him pick up where he and Audrey had left off? What foolish part of him had believed that if Casey saw him, if she just *talked* to him, she'd realize he and Audrey had a shot at something real? Secretly, he'd thought that she'd shake hands with him, let the past be the past, and give him her blessing to start anew.

But Casey wasn't having any of it. She didn't want Kieran within twenty feet of Audrey. Kieran's muscles tightened, knowing that, now, if he wanted to try to be with Audrey, he was going to have to risk losing her in the process.

"Just—just dance with me a minute, okay? I promise I'll let you breathe."

She nodded and this time he pulled her to him with more decorum. With one hand around her small waist and the other holding her hand out to the side, he forced himself to inhale and exhale normally, to close his eyes against the tide of emotion ripping through him. He lowered his heartbeat the way he had practiced around the poker table, and put on his gambler's face. This time, he had to bluff against himself—against his very own emotions.

"Did something happen?" Audrey asked.

He studied her face—her tiny, pert nose and her sweet, bow-shaped mouth—and knew he could lie and tell her everything was fine. He could play the gambler around her, again and again, or he could show her his cards. And his hand was terrible.

"I'm fine right now," he said, bending down so he could speak directly into her ear, above the noise of the dance floor. He inhaled her clean vanilla smell and resisted nibbling on her delicate lobe. But he let his words come out with enough breath to make her shudder.

Her muscled legs were unbearably sexy in her leather skirt, and her thick hair was tumbling around her face like she'd just been walking in the wind. She looked wild, frankly, and he wanted to tame her in his arms. In his bed, if he could.

He was very aware of the fact that his weren't the only set of eyes at the Wheelhouse trained in her direction. And he'd be damned if he'd let another man put his hands on her in his presence. Certainly not that bartender, Dave Englund.

Audrey studied his face, her warm eyes tracking back and forth across his features. He could feel sweat breaking out across his brow, in spite of his plans to remain calm and cool.

"Kieran, what aren't you telling me?"

God, the woman could read him. Technically, he'd spent less time with her than he had with that waitress in Wichita, or that tour guide at Yellowstone, who had joked about his "Old Faithful." And yet, when Audrey looked at him, she seemed to peer all the way into his soul—into the black depths of him that somehow didn't frighten her, when they certainly should have.

Those black depths had frightened her sister, Casey, that was for sure.

Kieran tightened his grip on Audrey's waist and pulled her an inch closer, wracking his brain for the best way to answer her.

He lifted his hand from Audrey's waist to touch her cheek. He ran a single finger down her smooth, sun-kissed skin and formed the words of the truth in his throat, ready to confess everything:

Five years ago my brother and I had pooled some money to get medical treatment for my mom, because she had cancer. We agreed that I should try to increase the little bit we had, since I was a shrewd poker player. I agreed, and, at first, I was doing great. I was winning and I was going to bring enough home to help Mom. Except I kept playing, even when I was up. I couldn't walk away. And as a result, I lost nearly everything. That's when your sister found me, and she offered me money to help Mom, as long as I'd stay away from you. That was the deal. And, God help me, I took it. I got clean after that. But we still lost Mom, and in the end I lost you. And I'm sorry, because if I could go back and change how this all went down, and if I could change the way I left you, I would.

Only the words wouldn't come. They were stuck in a shame-filled part of him that wanted to keep the past hidden forever from the woman in his arms. She deserved better than him, and he should just leave her alone. Even if she hinted at wanting him, seemed interested in rekindling what they had, it could never be.

Suddenly, Audrey froze in his arms. He blinked, bringing himself back to the here and now, only to find Audrey gazing up at him furiously.

"What?" he asked.

She never answered him. Instead, she reached up, grabbed the back of his neck, and brought his lips down on hers.

CHAPTER ELEVEN

Oh, God, what was she doing kissing Kieran Callaghan? Heaven help her, she had been undone by his expression, the way he'd stared at her with a mix of sorrow and desire on his face like nothing she'd ever seen before. The raw vulnerability there had been a shocking thing to witness on this biker of a man, and it hinted at the truth kindling in her heart: that there were depths to Kieran Callaghan. And right now, she couldn't resist inching closer to those possibly unknowable fathoms, daring to wonder at what was going on underneath his enormous exterior.

Kieran deepened the kiss, cutting off her thoughts. All that was left was the feel of his warm lips, of his tongue joining hers, and of his arms gripping her as if they'd never let go.

Kieran released one of her hands to plunge his fingers into her hair. He twisted the tendrils and tilted her head back slightly. Audrey submitted to the motion, allowing him more access to her lips, to her tongue, to her warm breath coming in ecstatic gasps.

She was dimly aware they were making out on the Wheelhouse dance floor like a couple of drunk teenagers and she didn't even care. The electric feel of Kieran touching her again was all she cared about.

Audrey heard herself saying "yes" out loud. The word surprised her. And yet, this felt so unbelievably right. She wondered briefly how she'd ever managed to walk by him on the showroom floor without doing *this* each and every time.

Kieran broke the kiss to breathe into her ear. "I can't make out with you like this. Not here. I can't guarantee I'll be able to control myself, and I won't embarrass you in public." The inches he suddenly placed between them felt like cold miles. Desire rolled through her, a turbulent wave that had her closing the gap. But he held her stiffly in his arms.

His light green eyes were serious as he stared at her. The magic of the moment was slipping away, and Audrey was desperate to hold on to it. She wanted the wood dance floor to be sticky with fairy dust, not spilled drinks. She wanted the overhead lights to flicker because they were stars, not because they were shorted out. And she wanted to be this close to Kieran Callaghan again simply because she could be, not because she needed to be.

"Kieran, come on, let's just dance—"

Dancing would lead to more kissing. And more kissing would lead to more of everything that could unravel this coil of desire inside of her.

"No." He grasped her ass and pressed against her, so she could feel the full force of his erection. Instantly, the space between her legs warmed with longing. "Make no mistake," he growled, "I want you. Saints help me, though, I won't do anything more tonight. You deserve better."

His features softened as they stared at one another. He swallowed visibly. "Let me take you to dinner. Let me walk with you in a park. You deserve a date."

Audrey blinked. What was Kieran saying? Right then, she wanted the opposite of dinner and a park. There was a hot, ready part of her that wanted to tumble into bed and fuck, for crying out loud. She placed her hands on his broad shoulders, in part to steady herself as the memory of Kieran inside her, their naked bodies joined together, came roaring back.

For so long, she never thought she'd be this close to him again. Now that she was, she wasn't about to force him to *court her* when they both knew that wasn't Kieran's MO. He didn't owe her anything, and she didn't want his penance.

"No," she said, lowering her hands from his shoulders to his thick biceps, sliding her fingers teasingly to his hands. His skin was hot. She could practically feel the warm blood just underneath the surface. She laced her fingers with his. "You and I are not about dinner. We are not about parks. We are about something else entirely."

She licked her lips, where the taste of him still lingered. His eyes followed the motion of her tongue. He was wound so tight she wondered that his muscles weren't cramping. "I don't want to date you, Kieran."

She let the words hang there, her heart thumping. His expression didn't change, but his grip on her hands tightened. Something like pain flashed across his face, but then it was gone so quickly she wondered if she'd imagined it.

The seconds stretched out, and she wondered suddenly if she'd said something wrong. "All right," he said finally, his eyes still on her mouth, "no dating. But I am going to teach you how to ride."

Audrey arched a brow. "A motorcycle or something else?"

Kieran threw back his head and laughed, a rumble that was as true as it was deep. Her heart constricted. She loved how happy he sounded. He unlocked their hands and flat-palmed his way from her waist, up her rib cage, grazing the sides of her breasts before cupping her shoulders.

"I'll teach you how to ride a *motorcycle*. Just like you wanted. Tomorrow. Sunday. Pick you up at noon."

Audrey frowned. "What about tonight?"

"You don't get to make all the rules, Tanner. Just some of them."

Audrey exhaled with frustration. Her nerves were frayed from being this close to Kieran. She wanted a re-lease, and dammit, he wasn't going to give it to her.

He bent down and placed his lips gently on hers. She tried to ease her tongue into his mouth, to heat up whatever Kieran was trying to cool off between them, but Kieran re-sisted. Their breath mingled, and even this chaste kiss had Audrey seeing spots of color behind her closed eyes. After a moment, Kieran pulled away.

"I'll leave you and Willa to your ladies' night. Until tomorrow." He tipped an imaginary hat toward her, and disappeared into the crowd. For a moment, Audrey stood there, dazed, until the sound of laughter brought her back to the here and now. It was Willa, giggling her head off as she watched Audrey stand there in shock.

Her face deepening to crimson, Audrey walked off the

dance floor with as much dignity as she could muster. Dear God, everyone must have seen her with her tongue down Kieran's throat. She lifted her chin like she didn't care.

She just hoped the bar was dark enough so her flaming cheeks wouldn't betray her real feelings. She was mortified.

Once seated, Audrey smoothed out her hair and skirt. Her outsides felt like they were in as much disarray as her insides.

"It looks like you pitched your idea and it was a productive business discussion," Willa said, grinning.

Audrey groaned. "God, I didn't even talk to him about the dealership. I totally spaced it."

"Really? I'm *so surprised*, because you two looked so professional out there."

Willa cracked up all over again, and Audrey looked for Dave, hoping for another asparagus beer. Unfortunately, he suddenly wasn't as keen to wait on her.

Shocker.

She placed her forehead on the bar's sleek wood. "Ugh, what have I done? I just made out with Kieran in front of the whole town."

"Oh, screw it," Willa said, rubbing her friend's back. "Who cares what anyone thinks. Did you have a good time?"

Audrey straightened and faced Willa head-on. "That is the most fun I've had in five years."

Willa hooted. "Well, there you go."

"I wanted to keep having fun, if you know what I mean, but he left."

Willa's smile faltered. "Like, *left* left?"

"No. Nothing that dramatic. He said he's going to pick me up tomorrow and teach me to ride a motorcycle."

Willa's grin widened. "You don't say. That sounds down-right respectable."

"I just—for a second there, I wanted it to *not* be re-spectable tonight. You know?"

Before Willa could answer, Dave approached them and cleared away their empty glassware. "Need anything else?" he asked.

"Dave, I'm sorry about that," Audrey said, her face red-dening all over again. "I kind of have a past with that guy and—"

"It's fine," he interrupted, even though he didn't sound like it was fine. "No big deal. Would you like another drink?"

"Probably just the check when you have a moment," Willa said.

Without missing a beat, he slid the paper ticket across the bar, then walked away.

Turned out, he'd charged Audrey for both beers.

Willa eyed her friend sympathetically. "Okay, so you ir-ritated Dave Englund a little bit. He'll get over it. In the meantime, we have a big reason to celebrate."

Audrey tilted her head. "We do?"

Willa raised her plastic cup. "Absolutely. I don't know if you felt it, but it started sprinkling in the desert tonight."

CHAPTER TWELVE

Audrey jogged to the track the next morning with the throaty sounds of birdcalls in the trees all around, and the first daffodils pushing their way up through the moist ground. The damp air refreshed her lungs, which were hot and dry, working overtime to keep up with her legs.

Every step she took, she could hear Kieran's name on the pavement.

Kie-ran, Kie-ran—left foot, right foot, mile after mile. She was increasing her pace, trying to outrun herself, trying not to hear his name. But the sound of it was in her ears, in her mind, and on her lips.

No matter how fast she jogged, she could still feel his hands pulling her close on the dance floor. No matter how much she pumped her arms, she could feel his breath on her skin, and the rippled tension of his thick muscles underneath his shirt. She moved her legs faster still. Somewhere inside, Audrey was aware that she was trying to outrun not the way Kieran made her feel, but her own ridiculous response to him. It was as if he were a magnet clad in leather and clean cotton, and she was made of shreds of metal that clung to him anytime he came around. For heaven's sake, he'd nearly had her taking off her clothes on the dance floor last night, and that was only from kissing.

She gritted her teeth, remembering how, five years ago, his lopsided smile had had her throwing back her duvet and inviting him into her bed. She'd been so trusting, so naïve. She'd thought it was love, when really it was just a steamy couple of weeks.

Well, she'd be darn sure she didn't make the same mistake this time. She was smarter and wiser now—and didn't need a full-blown relationship to have some fun.

She wove though White Pine's streets, which were quiet as families readied for Sunday service at the Lutheran church, and relived the moment Kieran had asked her for a date. His green eyes had stared into hers so earnestly she almost believed him.

A date. Like normal couples have.

She clenched her fists. If she was honest with herself, she wanted a date with Kieran. She longed for dinners, movies, even the stupid walks in the park Kieran had mentioned. A giant, Harley-Davidson-sized part of her yearned to do the things that regular folks did when they had feelings for each other.

But she knew that wasn't Kieran Callaghan. *That* man did not date. Five years ago, she'd made the mistake of thinking he did, and it had nearly torn her heart apart. This time, she'd be more careful. No matter how vulnerable and raw he seemed, no matter how intrigued by him she became, she'd set her expectations accordingly, and not get disappointed when it was time for him to leave again.

Wouldn't she?

Audrey wiped away sweat from her brow, wondering if she was truly capable of keeping her heart protected if her body was flinging itself headlong into pleasure. Her breath came in raspy gulps as she turned onto the last street before the track, her feet pounding the blacktop.

She pictured Willa's cranberry juice from the night before, the happiness in her eyes as she announced she was pregnant, and felt a pang of longing. At some point, Audrey knew she wanted that, too. A husband. Kids. A family.

Kieran Callaghan was never going to give her those things. So why was she wasting her time with him? She should be out there looking for a man who would give her everything she wanted.

The only problem was, she wanted Kieran. She wanted his spicy scent all around her, wanted his warm breath in her ear whispering poetry while his strong body claimed hers.

It was Kieran or no one.

The thought jolted her. She pushed herself harder, trying to outrun her emotions. But they kept pace with her, refusing to be left behind.

She pumped her arms. If she had feelings for Kieran, she just had to get them out of her system. She had to get *him* out of her system. Then she could move on.

Right?

A gust of spring wind swept across the track. She turned into it.

Five years ago, she'd been a gym teacher, convinced that things were going to work out because anything except a happy ending was too hard for her to fathom. Now, she knew better. She could still believe that Mr. Right was out there.

In the meantime, though, she'd take Mr. Right Here Right Now.

As she raced toward the track, she craned her neck, searching for Alexis's tall frame, and was surprised to see multiple shadows instead of just one. She pulled up closer to the metal bleachers and realized Alexis had brought company: Sonja Jorgenson and Caitlin Granlund, two more girls from the track team.

"Ladies, what are you doing here?" Audrey asked, hands on her hips as she worked to catch her breath.

"We heard Alexis was running with you," Caitlin said, her blonde hair in braided pigtails, "and we wanted to come, too."

Audrey glanced at Alexis, hoping for some illumination, but the girl just shrugged.

"I'm happy for the company," Audrey said after a moment, "and you're welcome to join me on Sundays. But on school days, you need save your energy for practice with Mr. Frace."

"We are," Caitlin said. "We promise. We saw he was carrying around your old coaching notebook, and he's gotten a little better. But even with the notebook, he's still way different."

"Yeah, we totally miss you," Sonja added.

Audrey's stomach knotted. She missed these girls, too. But she also believed Paul Frace would find his way—eventually.

"Let's stick to Sundays, then," she said. "We'll run together and push one another, and you'll still be Paul's during the week. Sound like a plan?"

"Totally," Sonja agreed, her wide eyes bright. "But if my mom ever comes, can we slow it down for her? Just for the first few runs?"

Audrey tilted her head. "Your mom wants to run with us?"

"Kind of. She wants to get in shape and I told her to come today, but in the end she got scared and stayed home."

Audrey knew Sonja's mom, Faye Jorgenson, and liked that the woman always cheered for Sonja at track meets, and made sure to bring her daughter lots of extra Gatorade.

"Tell your mom I'd be happy to run with her anytime if she's interested," Audrey said. "I could help her out. It would be fun."

"What, like a personal trainer?"

Audrey blinked. She'd never thought about that label before.

The idea left her a little breathless. "Sure," she answered. "If your mom wants to get in shape, why not?"

"When you're done there, talk to *my* mom, too," Caitlin added, playing with the end of one blonde pigtail. "She's always like, 'Oh, Caitlin, if only I could use all this exercise equipment we have at home,' but she never gets her butt in shape enough to do anything."

Audrey trembled, but not from the cool morning. Could it be that there was a personal training niche in White Pine she'd never thought about?

She took a breath, the idea filling her mind.

"When you get home, tell your mom I'll give her a call," Audrey said to Sonja. "I'll see if we can't set up a schedule. You tell your mom the same thing, Caitlin."

She was amazed at the words coming out of her mouth. Was she really going to cold-call two parents and see if they wanted some training help?

Then again, she'd already walked into a Harley-Davidson showroom and held her ground, in spite of being totally unprepared for the job. She'd also proved she could bring more than just her body to the gig, now that she had a whole host of ideas about how to reach more female customers.

So why couldn't she find a few personal training clients as well?

"That would be so awesome," Caitlin said. "My mom has been so annoying about getting in shape. If you finally get her to stop talking about it and do something, I would owe you big-time."

Audrey was about to tell the other girl she didn't owe her anything when an idea flashed in her mind.

"How about doing me a favor right now? Since I'm leading this running club and all?" Audrey asked.

Caitlin arched a brow. "Like what?"

"Like help out with the Good Shepherd Walk this year. I don't want to do it, but I want to find a replacement."

"Isn't that the walk where they have all the cakes and baked goods at the end?" Sonja asked.

"They do," Audrey agreed.

"Doesn't Elliot Singer go to that church?" Caitlin asked.

"Totally," Sonja said to her friend. "And I bet he'd be there."

Caitlin flipped her pigtails. "What would we have to do?" she asked.

"Help put up flyers. Do the registration forms. They're all paper and kind of a pain, but it's manageable. Help get everything set up the day of. Make sure all the people doing the walk have water. That kind of thing."

"Sounds intense," Caitlin said.

Audrey nodded. It wasn't the easiest of volunteer activities.

"You know what else is intense, though?" Sonja asked. "Elliot Singer's eyes."

Caitlin giggled. "And his abs. I got a glimpse of them in gym class once."

"I'll help if you do it," Sonja said.

Caitlin's white teeth flashed as she grinned. "All right, count me in."

Audrey almost burst into laughter. She never would have imagined that finding not one but *two* replacements would have been so easy.

"All right, let's get going," she said, as much for the group's benefit as her own. Part of her was worried the girls would change their minds if they dawdled too long. "Three miles, and we'll do intermittent thirty-second sprints along the way."

She was already running before she'd finished the sentence. She was grinning to herself, and bouncing that much more with each step.

* * *

The girls were pushing themselves on the three-mile run, and Audrey felt a swell of pride toward her small group. The clump of runners crested a small hill to the south of the school, about a half mile from the finish. "You got this!" Audrey called to the girls to encourage them. "Not far now!"

They were returning to town along the back roads, with farmland rolling all around them and dark tree branches cresting over the top of them. Audrey had clicked on her portable flashlight, even though the sky was pinking to the east. Better safe than sorry out here.

As if in response, headlights popped up behind them, and the rumble of an engine sent a cluster of birds flapping into the weak morning light. "Everyone to the far side of the road," Audrey said, flicking her flashlight beam so the car would be sure to see them. They were in the opposite lane, facing oncoming traffic, giving the car a wide berth. Still, she dropped behind the girls, so the flashlight beam would illuminate the entire group.

The engine rumbled closer, and Audrey waited for it to pass. But the deep, vibrating sound remained right behind them. She turned her head and stared straight into two white headlights. She blinked, trying to clear the painful glare.

"Girls," she said, "stay together. Nobody race ahead right now."

"Who is that?" Sonja asked.

"I don't know," Audrey said, slowing to a walk. The other girls did the same.

Suddenly, Alexis was next to her. "Ms. Tanner," she breathed, "I think that's my boyfriend, Hunter."

"Hunter Haglund?" Audrey asked, remembering her brief encounter with him at the dealership. "What's he doing out here?"

"He—sometimes he follows me," Alexis said, her eyes wide. As if on cue, the phone tucked into her armband flashed with a message. "He texts me, too."

A thousand questions and concerns flashed through Audrey's mind, but she pushed them all aside. Hunter was a good kid, she told herself. This was no big deal. "Listen to me carefully," she said to the group. "I want you all to stay together on the side of the road here. I'll go have a talk with Hunter. You stay put. Got it?"

"Yes," they replied in unison.

The engine rumbled louder, as if Hunter were revving it. Audrey pivoted around to face Hunter's car. The rest of the girls pressed themselves along the edge of the road, nearly losing themselves in the trees.

All of them, that is, except Alexis.

Audrey didn't have time to tell the girl to step back. The car rolled up and inched to a standstill. Alexis stood next to her, trembling.

She kept a protective arm on Alexis as the driver's-side window on the shiny new Dodge lowered.

The intricate dash and smell of new leather hinted at what an expensive vehicle it was. Inside the car's elaborate interior, shadows snaked from Hunter's chin to his eyes, emphasizing the hard lines of his face. He stared at Alexis then slowly, agonizingly, turned his gaze to Audrey.

"Something we can help you with, Mr. Haglund?" she asked.

Hunter didn't reply, just returned his focus to Alexis. His sand-colored hair looked black, his eyes appeared bottomless. "I worry about you. You know I worry about you."

Alexis's trembling deepened. "I was out for a run. *Am* out for a run. You need to stop following me like this, Hunter."

"I'll do what I have to do to make sure you're safe."

Audrey stepped in front of Alexis, pushing the girl behind her. "Safety is not what you're doing right now, Hunter. You're being reckless. You just endangered four women, and you need to knock it off."

Hunter's mouth stretched slowly into a smile that was colder than winter. "Or you'll do what, exactly?" he asked.

"Turn you in to the cops for one," Audrey replied. "Get a restraining order against you for two. How does that sound?"

"You're not a teacher anymore. You can't do anything."

The budding branches of the trees overhead scraped together as if in agreement. Audrey's blood heated.

"Do *not* tell me what I can and can't do, Hunter. If I see you around Alexis again, you are going to be in deep trouble. Do you understand me?"

Hunter scoffed. "Trouble. Very funny coming from a motorcycle model." He turned his eyes back on Alexis.

"I love you, baby. I'll see you soon."

Alexis shook her head, her dark ponytail swaying. "If you keep doing this, I don't know if I can stay with you."

Audrey saw Hunter's knuckles turn white around the steering wheel. "Please don't say those kinds of things."

"She has every right to stand up for herself," Audrey said, "and a breakup will be the least of your problems if you keep this crap up."

He glared at Audrey. "Whatever," he said, starting to roll up his window. "I'll text you soon, Alexis."

Audrey had just enough time to push Alexis a few feet back before the car tires squealed, fishtailing dangerously close as he sped away.

The silence on the road was deafening after the car's rumble was gone. Twigs snapped and grass rustled as Caitlin and Sonja came bursting out of the trees next to the blacktop. "Oh my God, why is Hunter being such a creeper?" Caitlin asked, her twin braids sporting thistles and bits of leaves. She stared at Alexis, then Audrey.

"Is he following you?" Sonja asked.

"He wanted to make sure Alexis was okay," Audrey said, trying to diffuse the girls' rising panic, "and went about it in an unorthodox way. It's okay, everyone. We're all right. We've got just a short distance left until the school, and then everything will feel a lot better. So let's finish this thing, okay?"

Her limbs were weighted with concern as she jogged, and questions started stockpiling in her mind. Was Hunter stalking Alexis? Did the poor girl feel in danger? Audrey remembered suspecting during their first run together that Alexis had something she wanted to talk about—and wondered suddenly if this was it. Was she looking for a way to get out from under Hunter's thumb?

The sky was ribboned in pinks and golds when they got back to the high school. Birds trilled and swooped all around them, and the morning would have been downright breathtaking if their stomachs and minds weren't churning with anxiety.

"Did anyone drive down here, or did you all jog down?" Audrey asked as they stretched their quads.

"I drove with Caitlin," Sonja replied.

"Then can you take Alexis home, too?"

"Sure, but what about you?"

Audrey smiled in what she hoped was a reassuring way. "I'm fine. Don't worry about me. You guys just get home safely." They all nodded and started toward the parking lot, but at the last minute Audrey grabbed Alexis's arm.

"I'm going to drop by to see you at home later. We need to talk." Audrey spoke the words knowing that visiting Alexis was going to cut into her date with Kieran. But the girl looked terrified. She was pale enough to pass out.

Alexis nodded. "I'm sorry about this. I wanted to tell you before, I just didn't know how."

"It's all right," Audrey replied. "No need to apologize.

Whatever is happening is not going on because you did something wrong."

"It's just that he texts me all the time. He says he's trying to help me. But I'm getting scared."

Audrey gave the girl a quick hug. "We'll get it sorted out. Just lay low and don't talk to Hunter if you can help it. Does your mom know any of this?"

Alexis's panicked eyes flew to meet Audrey's. "No, and you can't tell her. She'll be at work this afternoon so it's fine if we talk, but I'm not supposed to even be dating boys, much less seeing someone seriously. Hunter and I have been together for three months now. At first, I thought he was so mysterious and I loved that—I loved *him*. But now, he's just, he's changed, and I can't—"

Alexis's words were lost in a dry sob. Audrey's heart erupted with pity. She put a comforting arm around the girl. "We'll get it worked out. If you have to go anywhere today, try and go with other people, not by yourself. Promise me you'll do that, okay?"

Alexis nodded, and Audrey gave the girl's shoulder a final squeeze. "I'll see you this afternoon," she said, making sure Alexis got in the car safely with Caitlin and Sonja.

When they'd driven off, Audrey began her jog home, her mind and body both exhausted. All she wanted was a warm shower and to crawl back in bed for a few minutes before meeting Kieran.

If Alexis was in danger, she had to help the girl. But her brain was so foggy she could hardly think about how. She blinked and pushed on—then told herself it was exhaustion that was causing her to think she saw Hunter's Dodge disappearing around the corner ahead of her.

CHAPTER THIRTEEN

The thunder of Kieran's Harley-Davidson echoed up and down Audrey's street, shattering the Sunday silence. He almost felt badly for the roar of his engine, the way it rattled windows and door frames, except it was the only thing keeping the sharp barbs of truth from piercing his thoughts.

He was going to have to explain the past to Audrey.

He was going to have to come clean and pray she'd have him anyway.

He was going to have to gamble—one final time—and hope his horrible hand could still net him a win.

He cut the engine. The silence was deafening until the squawk of blue jays in a nearby tree pierced the air. Their blue-and-white wings darted against the bright midday sky. The sun was warm on his black leather jacket. He lifted the helmet from his head and breathed in White Pine's clean air. In front of him, Audrey's squat brick house was trim and neat. Bright tulips dotted a small landscaped bed off the front steps.

It looked the same as it did the last time he was here.

He braced himself against the realization that last time he was in that house, he had been in Audrey's bed. Pictures flashed in his brain in high resolution, as if it had been minutes ago, not five years. Her glossy chestnut hair cascading across the pillows. Her limbs twining with his, leaving her scent everywhere on his body. The delicate spray of freckles across her skin had reminded him of brown sugar, and he'd run his tongue across them, tasting sweetness.

He'd thought they'd been starting something. Until he'd taken Casey's money and ended whatever it was that had just been beginning.

His hands tightened around his helmet. There was no getting around the fact that he was going to have to tell her the truth. About his past. About Casey. About the reason for the way he'd left her.

And he would tell her. *He would.*

Just not right now.

This afternoon, he was going to let them have some time together—the one luxury they hadn't been able to afford, because he'd robbed them of it. But he would give it back to them now. He couldn't scale much when it came to the mountain of mistakes he'd made, but today he could climb a few steps. He could hold out his palm and offer a handful of coins against the enormous debt he owed them both.

He could give them the scraps of one unencumbered afternoon. A date, even though Audrey said she didn't want one.

She might not want one, but she certainly *deserved* one.

He glanced down and noticed his hands were shaking slightly. An obvious tell. He closed his eyes, drawing in a slow, steadying breath. When all of him was still—save for his hammering heart—he walked the short distance to the front door, and rang the bell.

●

* * *

Audrey had watched Kieran from the kitchen. Past the living room she could see out the plate-glass window to the edge of the front walk where he was just—standing. Even at a distance she could tell he was studying her house like it was a series of pieces he was trying to fit together, and not a solid structure already in existence.

She leaned against a wall to watch him, wondering what he was thinking. Without his helmet on, his rugged face was exposed to the sun. Her breath paused as the light hit his strong jaw, illuminating the stubble there. The cleft in his chin was a divot of perfection; his green eyes were glinting like pale ocean waves. No, not the ocean, she realized—the *sea*. They were the color of the water when light hit the backs of waves that rolled onto white sands. She could see it in her mind, even though she'd never experienced anything so exotic in real life.

When it dawned on her that Kieran was no longer standing at the edge of the sidewalk, she straightened, knowing he must be headed to the front door. She tugged on the hem of her black fitted T-shirt, so her midriff didn't show. She was too old for that nonsense, though she did have on a pair of dangerously short cutoffs. She was glad to show her legs—she was proud of those—and for a moment imagined them wrapped around Kieran's muscled torso. If he were standing, she'd have them looped around his waist, and perhaps he'd lean her against a wall and—

The doorbell rang and Audrey swallowed, realizing she was already flushed. "Good God," she muttered. At this rate, all Kieran would have to do is lift a finger and she'd be shimmying out of her threads in no time.

She concentrated on relaxing her features and adopting an air of nonchalance. She'd be darned if Kieran would know how much he rattled her.

Apparently, she didn't need to wonder if Kieran was having any of the same pre-outing jitters. He took one look at her and burst into laughter.

"What in the world are you wearing?" he asked, his eyes dancing with amusement as he took in her T-shirt and shorts.

Audrey found herself tugging on the hem of her shirt again. A thousand smart answers crowded the tip of her tongue, but she held them back. Instead, she brought her hands to her sternum, then began moving them downward. Slowly, slowly, her hands descended over the front of her shirt. The heat of her own skin was a source of energy. She was powerful and beautiful and she dared him to say otherwise. Her brain screamed at her to stop, her practical side was mortified, but the hungry look on Kieran's face fed the movement. Under his gaze, she came alive.

When her hands reached her breasts, she arched her back a little, but kept up the languid march—down to her abdomen and then to the front of her shorts. She stopped there, but never broke eye contact with Kieran. *Look at me and see more than my clothes,* she demanded silently. The muscles in his jaw tensed.

"Is there a problem?" Audrey asked after a moment. She felt bold and daring, and she'd be damned if she let him, or any man, make her feel otherwise.

Kieran stepped forward. He reached out and hooked one finger through the belt loop of her shorts. He pulled, and Audrey allowed herself to be tugged forward. Her front door was still open, and she wondered if the neighbors were getting an eyeful of Kieran Callaghan standing there while she felt herself. Good grief, what was she *doing*?

Her thoughts were cut off as Kieran pulled her closer still. Their torsos were almost touching. The scant inches between them were filled with electric tension.

He will never give you what you want, she reminded herself. Not devotion. Not commitment. Not love or a family.

His touch nearly said otherwise. He put a gentle hand on her cheek, cupping her face as if she were the most precious, tender thing in the world.

Kieran tilted his head toward her. She parted her lips slightly, wondering if his mouth was going to demand everything from hers again, the way it had the night before at the Wheelhouse. But instead of kissing her, he brought his lips to her temple. The delicate touch had her shivering.

"You will die if you wear that," he murmured against her skin. His finger, still hooked through the belt loop of her shorts, tugged again. His torso pressed against hers.

She inhaled the smell of him—leather and pine and clean cotton—and the scent cut right to her heart. She could be with a hundred men, she thought, and none of them would smell this perfect.

"You cannot ride a motorcycle like that. I need you to change."

Audrey pulled back, suddenly grasping what he was saying. "My outfit is dangerous?"

"That outfit is very, very dangerous," he said, his eyes on her chest. "You need to change."

"Into what?"

Panties only. A negligée. Nothing.

If he'd said any of these things, Audrey wondered if she would do it. Instead, Kieran removed his hands from her and straightened, putting space between them. Audrey hated the additional inches of nothingness.

"What you wore before when you rode with me."

The mention of the past had Audrey's muscles trembling. "That was a long time ago. You'd better be specific."

"Jeans. Boots if you have them, no laces. Wear a long-sleeved T-shirt. And a jacket over that if you have one."

Audrey didn't like the directive. It might have been fine for her five years ago, but now it sounded like the only thing missing was a chastity belt and a habit. She wondered suddenly about all the pictures she saw at the Harley dealership, of women in bikinis on the backs of bikes. The dealership was giving women mixed signals. They were supposed to be sexy when they rode, but sexy wasn't necessarily safe.

"Are you sure about this?"

"You can't go on a bike with bare skin showing. If we take a tumble, your skin will get scraped off like—well, just trust me. This is safer." Kieran reached out and twined a lock of her hair in his fingers. He was unbearably gentle. "I'm sorry I laughed," he said quietly, his eyes locking on hers. "It came out wrong. I want you to be safe. That's all."

Audrey nodded. "Sure. I unders—"

His gaze intensified. "Let me be clear. If we have another date, I want you to wear what you have on right now. *Exactly* that. Okay?"

Audrey nodded, though she already knew there wouldn't be any more dates. Kieran didn't date women.

Something inside her plummeted at the thought, but she ignored it. If all she had with him was today—*one day*—that was enough. She wasn't going to let herself get attached again. She'd take what she wanted, what she needed, and let that be enough.

"Be right back," she said, forcing a smile.

She could feel Kieran's eyes on her—the pressure of those green waves against her heart—as she walked to her bedroom and closed the door softly.

CHAPTER FOURTEEN

When Audrey was clad in what felt like enough layers to ride a motorcycle in Antarctica, she and Kieran exited her front door and made their way down the short walk to his gleaming bike.

From afar, his looked like any number of other motorcycles in the dealership showroom. But up close, Audrey found herself faltering as she stared at the bike's exquisite details—minutiae she'd buried from five years ago, but which were now laid out before her, a reminder of the first time she'd seen this bike. The first time she'd seen Kieran, for that matter.

There was the way, for example, Kieran still hung his sunglasses crookedly from the brake stem. Or the way the deep blood red of the cycle's fenders and body glittered in the sunlight. She'd believed at one point that the color must have matched that of her heart, when it beat inside her chest for Kieran. The leather was soft and well maintained, but it still sported a series of small creases. Like a thumbprint, she'd once thought: a specific mark that Kieran's body had left on the rich material. And her body had left its mark on the material, too. She'd ridden this bike as well, her arms clutched around Kieran's waist, her head inches from his broad shoulders. The wind had taken her breath away, the speed had thrilled her senses. Being with Kieran had given her a rush she hadn't come close to since.

The bike was like a living memory—a scrapbook on two wheels—and she was having a hard time turning the pages without feeling overwhelmed. By the past, by the present— by all of it. She reached out and grasped the leather grip on the end of one handlebar to steady herself.

"You all right?" Kieran asked, studying her closely.

"Yes, fine," Audrey answered, stretching her lips in what she hoped was a convincing smile and not an awkward leer.

Reaching into a saddlebag, Kieran pulled out a second helmet and handed it to her. "Safety first."

Audrey took it without complaint. She'd only recently discovered that plenty of Harley riders who came into the dealership refused to wear helmets, but Kieran had always made it a priority.

"How come you wear a helmet when so many other riders don't?" she asked, fastening the nylon strap under her chin.

Kieran turned over his black helmet thoughtfully. "I suppose it's because a good gambler knows when the pot is too rich. I could play the odds, but even if I lose once, that's potentially losing everything. A limb. Some skin. Part of my brain. It just seems like an awfully steep payment."

Audrey smiled at the metaphor. "That's good logic. Too bad I never figured you for a gambler."

She said it lightly, teasingly, but something in those words had Kieran's face darkening. "There's a lot about me you don't know."

Audrey blinked at the sharp note in his voice. The words sliced through her. He was right, of course. She didn't know nearly as much about him as she wanted to, because he hadn't given her the chance. He'd left. And now she was playing at the dangerous game of believing she didn't need to know him. That she could simply want him for his body. For some fun.

Kieran shoved the helmet onto his head and mounted the motorcycle, revving it to life. She climbed on behind him, thinking it was fine by her if Kieran wanted to have secrets. There was plenty he didn't know about her, thank you very much.

She was going to learn to ride this hunk of rubber and steel and chrome and that was going to be the end of it. No melancholic memories. No significant sentiments. It was going to be a blast—pure and simple.

Out of the corner of her eye, Audrey caught the slow movement of a dark vehicle at the end of the street, and it reminded her of her promise from earlier.

"Hey," she said, ignoring the way her thighs grazed Kieran's hips, and how her hands slid neatly around his waist, "I need to take a detour with you. Can you drive me over to a student's house?"

Kieran nodded, and she pointed the way there. The Harley rumbled to life beneath her as they took off, and for a moment it was impossible to tell where her own tremors ended and the machine's powerful vibrations began.

* * *

Kieran silenced the engine and tried not to think about the way Audrey's body slid against his as she climbed off the bike. Her curves were still evident, even through all the layers of clothing. And her smell—clean vanilla and detergent—reached him in unexpected moments, unsettling him. She would move her arm, or turn her head, and there it would be. He wanted to bury his face in that smell, to pull her toward him and inhale the sweetest parts of her, but he wouldn't. He'd vowed that nothing could happen until she knew the truth. She deserved that. And, dammit, she deserved a date, too—a real outing where she was doted on and cherished, and he'd give her that as well, come hell or high water.

She pulled her helmet off and shook out her glossy hair. The bright afternoon light lit it like a halo, and his chest tightened. The sight reminded him keenly that she was an angel, and he was among the fallen. A sinner with a past who didn't deserve her.

Kieran set the kickstand and helped Audrey off the bike. "Whose house is this?" he asked.

"A student from the track team, Alexis Belten," Audrey answered. Concern created a little wrinkle between her brows, and Kieran wanted to place his thumb on the crease. He would smudge it away if he could, then kiss the tender skin there, easing her worry.

"Everything okay?" he asked instead.

Audrey shook her head no. "This morning her boyfriend, Hunter Haglund, followed her on our run. She says he's been stalking her. I think she needs help."

Kieran's body heated with protective concern. "You were there? Did he hurt anyone?"

"No," Audrey said, her eyes darting nervously to the

small white house with black shutters. "Everyone was fine, but this kid is a dark horse. I can't tell if he's just mixed up or if he's actually bad news. Either way, I want to help Alexis to think about her options."

Before she could walk to the front door, Kieran caught her arm. She looked down at his hand, at the way his fingers wrapped around the many layers of clothing she was wearing, but she didn't pull away. She had never pulled away, he realized, even when others did. Five years ago, if he hadn't forced her to release her grasp on him, she might never have pulled away at all. The thought made his muscles ache.

"You're still running with your students?" he asked, searching her face.

"On Sunday mornings. Just to supplement their track workouts until the end of the season."

"And you're stopping by to see this girl, to help her?"

Audrey smiled slightly. "Why all the questions, Sherlock?"

"Just thinking it's pretty amazing that you're still involved, helping your students when you're not even officially on the school's payroll anymore."

"I was good at my job. I guess it's hard for me to just walk away from these kids, especially when they might need me. You know?"

His fists clenched, thinking of how giving Audrey was, even when she'd been hurt, been dismissed.

It was true of her school.

It was true of him.

"It's incredible, how much you care," he answered honestly. "If I can help, I will."

"Thanks," Audrey said, looking toward the house. An

asparagus wreath hung on the front door. "I'll just be a minute."

He released her arm and kept a careful eye on her as she headed up the short sidewalk. He pushed down the thought clamoring inside his brain: the idea that he wanted to keep an eye on Audrey Tanner forever. If only he could.

* * *

Alexis answered the door wearing fuzzy pajama bottoms and an oversized White Pine High sweatshirt. Her long, dark hair was damp, presumably from a recent shower. In spite of her relaxed appearance, Alexis's face was pinched with worry. Her hazel eyes were ringed with shadow. Her lips were tight, even as she tried to stretch them into a smile.

"Hey, Ms. Tanner. Who's the hunk on the bike?"

"A friend," Audrey said. "Can you talk for a few minutes? Is this a good time?" She knew she was being brusque, but they could address questions about Kieran on next Sunday's run.

"Sure, we can chat now," Alexis said, lacing her long fingers together nervously. Everything about the girl was long, Audrey realized—from her legs to her arms, even her neck. She made an exceptional athlete, and also a stunning one. Audrey could understand why Hunter Haglund was obsessed with her.

"What happened this morning," Audrey began carefully, "was super scary, and I can only imagine how stressful this is for you. I want you to know that I'm here to help, but that if you feel threatened or if Hunter's behavior is escalating, we need to let other people know. Especially if this isn't the first time Hunter has followed you, or made you feel unsafe. Does that make sense?"

Alexis leaned against the white door frame as if she were exhausted. Behind her, a television murmured with voices and applause. "I guess. I mean, it's not the first time he's followed me, but the thing is, he's never hurt me. You have to know that. He just says he wants me to be safe. At first he called a lot, and I thought it was sweet, how protective he was. But then he started calling and texting so much, and he'd get mad when I didn't pick up. One time, he saw me talking in the hallway with Jeff Uster and I thought he was going to just lose it. Like, *bananas* crazy."

"Are you afraid of him?" Audrey asked gently, even though she could see the answer clearly on the young girl's face.

Alexis nodded. "Yeah. Now I am."

"Then he's hurting you. It might not be physical, but emotional hurt is still hurt. You shouldn't have to live in fear, and what's more, we need to stop him before it escalates. I'm not saying it will, but we should be sure."

"All right," she said after a moment. "So what should I do?"

Audrey took a breath. She'd counseled kids on a thousand things—first dates, bad grades, athletic scholarships—but this was the first time she'd had to talk to someone about a stalker. "First, you have to tell your mom. I know she doesn't want you dating, and that it's not going to be an easy conversation, but you have to tell her you've been seeing Hunter."

The girl groaned, but Audrey pressed on. "How about your dad? Is he around and do you need to tell him, too?"

She shook her head. "They're divorced. He lives up in Coon Rapids with his new wife. I don't see him much."

Audrey took the girl's trembling hand in her own. "Okay, that's fine. But you also need to tell your guidance counselor and probably Mr. Frace, just because you have him for English and track. He's probably the teacher who sees you the most, right?"

"Yeah, probably."

"First thing tomorrow at school, talk to them both. In the meantime, keep your cell charged at all times. And don't hesitate, I mean even for a second, to call the police about Hunter. If he starts lurking around you or your house tonight, get them on the phone."

Alexis blinked back tears. "Will he go to jail?"

Audrey squeezed the girl's hand. "Whether he does or not isn't your concern. Your only concern is being safe. And the police can help with that if need be. Now, when does your mom get home?"

"She finishes up her shift at the hospital in a few hours."

"When she gets back, you guys need to talk. Tell her to call me if she has questions. I can vouch for what happened this morning. And if I need to, I can tell her what a good kid you are."

"She's just going to yell and get mad. She has stupid rules that don't make any sense, and all she's going to hear is that I broke them."

Audrey smiled sympathetically. She didn't have an overprotective parent, just Casey, and that was hard enough. "Just remember, your mom set those rules for you because she loves you and she wants the best for you."

Alexis's hazel eyes narrowed. "No, she sets those rules because at my age, she was knocked up. Her parents made her marry my stupid biological father, and she was miserable. And she keeps acting like I'm going to do the same thing, even though I'm not her."

From the corner of her eye, Audrey saw Kieran shift, leaning more of his weight on the bike. She could feel his gaze on her, watching. For some reason, it made her feel safer, and somehow stronger. She returned her focus to Alexis, and gave the girl's hand another squeeze.

"You, me, and your mom all want the same thing here— for you to have a bright future where scary boys aren't making you feel frightened. We can all do that if we work together. You agree?"

Alexis nodded, but fear still shadowed her face. Audrey hoped that the girl's school counselor would do a threat assessment and then take appropriate next steps based on the outcome—ideally calling Hunter's parents, and getting their help disciplining Hunter. Audrey figured it would be hard for him to cruise around in his shiny new car scaring Alexis if they just took it away. If that didn't work, she hoped the school would work with the police.

Audrey pulled out her cell. "Here," she said, handing it to Alexis. "Put your number in there. I'm around if you need me, okay?"

Alexis keyed in the digits. "Thanks, Ms. Tanner. You're awesome. I wish I could still see you at school. It sucks they fired, like, the *one* teacher who cares."

"Lots of teachers care," she replied. "Keep me posted after you talk to the school and your mom. Maybe text me?"

"Yeah. Totally."

"Okay. Be safe." She gave the girl a hug, hoping to reassure her.

When Alexis closed the door, Audrey exhaled deeply.

She took a moment to ground herself—to remind herself she'd done right by her former student. She gazed from the tiny blades of new grass between the pieces of pavement at her feet to the wispy clouds fading into a jewel-blue sky above.

Hunter had scared them all, it was true, but at least Alexis had told her what was going on. And now, thanks to her prompting, Alexis would tell others, too. With any luck, and with the school's help, Alexis would be free of Hunter shortly.

Audrey was encouraged by the thought. Things were on a better path than they had been that morning. And that was something to be thankful for. The shard of fear inside Alexis (and inside herself, if she was honest) would dull soon enough.

Audrey looked down the sidewalk and found Kieran watching her, his gaze steady, his frame tall and strong.

Her insides quaked at how his gaze never left her. His stare was unshakable and protective in a way that gave her a deep thrill—at least until she reminded herself that she was probably reading too much into him. Nothing about Kieran was unshakable or steadfast. He was probably just staring at her because she looked like a lumpy mess in all her riding clothes.

Even so, her heart pounded with every step she took down the sidewalk, until it was a drubbing mess by the time she was once again at his side. Never mind that for all the past hurt that was between them, today he was being downright gentlemanly—or at least his version of it. And never mind that a click was sounding in her brain, a noise like the tip of a branch against glass when the wind blew. Like the sound of something snapping into place.

No, never mind any of it, Audrey thought. She put her hand on the bike, but looked straight at Kieran. "I think it's time for that ride," she said.

Kieran's wide mouth broke into a grin. "I'm looking forward to teaching you how to handle this bike."

She thought he was going to make a joke—maybe a crack about what she would have between her legs the rest of the day—but instead he brushed a wisp of stray hair away from her face. "I'll keep you safe, though. I promise."

And it was the gentleness of his words, the sweet protection in them, that had her emotions flaming all over again. Her heart hammered a beat she swore she could hear over the rumble of the engine.

CHAPTER FIFTEEN

Holy Saint Francis of Assisi, Kieran thought as he steered the motorcycle toward the parking lot behind the Elks Club. *If Audrey shifts again, I am going to lose it*. The press of her body against his was unbearably hot. With every bump or turn, a different part of her connected with a different part of him. The little motions had exposed raw thoughts he knew he had to set aside.

He was here to give them a date. An afternoon of just being together, getting to know one another. Nothing physical.

Taking a deep breath, he concentrated on getting them to the little paved stretch that overlooked the Birch River. It would be the perfect location to teach Audrey the basics of riding a motorcycle. But as the pavement rolled underneath them, his mind was like a boomerang, returning again and again to wondering what being with her again would feel like.

He'd peel off all her layers of clothing, one by one, in an exquisitely painful march to bare flesh. He would kiss the rounded end of a shoulder, the tip of a finger, the back of one knee—random places because he could. Because he would take his time savoring her. He'd allow his hunger to build until she was stripped naked before him, her hair cascading past her neck and her freckled skin nearly glowing in the soft light. And then he'd place her on her back, lifting one of her long, strong legs and placing it on his shoulder. She would be open to him, her softness his for the taking, and he'd ease himself into her—

"Hey. The light's green."

Kieran jerked. Audrey was tapping his arm. Ahead of him, the traffic signal had turned, and cars were moving. Behind him, a horn blared. Shaking his head, he kicked the motorcycle into gear and let the spring wind scrub his mind.

Nothing could happen between them until Kieran came clean. He had to confess the past and tell Audrey the truth. He wanted their hearts and their minds and, hell, even their souls—his dark one and her lovely, light one—to be honest with each other, laid bare and free from the past.

He picked up speed, and the Harley's rumble was suddenly like laughter. A deep, resonate chuckle at Kieran's unrealistic goals.

He wanted too much. He knew it, and he understood it wasn't fair to ask Audrey for anything. Why should she forgive him when he'd made such a calculating decision five years ago to choose money over her? And colluding with her sister on top of everything else was going to be a hard tale to tell.

No, as much as he wanted to, it wouldn't be fair to

give in to his current desire. He couldn't—he wouldn't—complicate things with sex before they'd had a chance to discuss why he'd left the first time.

They were riding over the Birch River now, the dark water sliding past the vibrant green of new leaves and grass along the shores. A cluster of geese rooted for bugs by the banks. Puffy yellow goslings waddled behind their parents, beaks opening and closing to demand food.

On the other side of the bridge they hit Main Street. Green banners flapped happily on light posts, heralding the arrival of the Asparagus Festival the following week. The fountain in front of the library splashed playfully in the afternoon light. A sign in front of the Rolling Pin bakery announced asparagus donuts for sale.

Kieran marveled at how picturesque the whole place was. It had been this way five years ago, too, when he'd arrived to find a backroom poker table where he could try to win back money for his mom. And then he'd met Audrey, who had cracked him open, enough so that the darkness inside of him had slipped out. Well, *some* of it, anyway.

But not enough so he stayed put and told her the truth.

After he took the money from Casey, he'd returned to Boston and his mom had started chemotherapy. But the cancer was too advanced, and she was in hospice a few short weeks later.

After she died and he and Auggie had buried her on a sodden, overcast day in July, he'd left again. He'd intended to ride to the other side of the country—to the sunshine of California, maybe—but in the end he'd only gotten as far as Wisconsin. He had parked himself in Madison and started attending addiction meetings. Then he sought help with his finances. He started working toward his undergraduate degree at a community college, and got help from a volunteer career counselor creating a sensible résumé out of the fractured pieces of his life.

When the Harley-Davidson headquarters in Milwaukee asked him in for a job interview, he'd ridden north expecting them to laugh him out of the room. They offered him employment instead, the best gig he could have hoped for. The only thing he could think as he shook hands with his new bosses was that Audrey was still with him—at least the part of her that let good things come into his life. It was silly, he knew, but still. Two weeks with Audrey had changed him. Had changed *everything*.

All this time he'd tried to ignore it. He'd tried to pretend that their meeting was just a fluke, and that he would have been able to land on his feet in spite of her. Being back in White Pine, however, made it all too clear. Audrey Tanner was one of the few truly good things that had ever happened to him. This place had happened to him, and so had these people. He liked it here. He liked what it did to him.

The only question was, did anyone else feel the same about him?

Most importantly, did Audrey?

* * *

Audrey leaned in closer to Kieran, her face inches from his. She could turn and kiss him, she realized, placing her lips on his wide, wonderful mouth, but she held back. Right now, she was actually interested in what he was *saying*.

"The bike has to be in neutral before you can start it. And this light here says whether or not that's the case." He pointed at a small indicator on the motorcycle's dash, to the right of the speedometer.

Audrey followed the motion of Kieran's hand, noting the thick, dark-red hairs that covered his forearms and faded to a light blond on his knuckles. Past the motorcycle and down a gentle slope, the Birch River splashed by. The Elks Club parking lot was empty, save for the two of them, and Audrey found herself delighted by the quiet, private lessons.

"How do I get the bike in neutral, then?" she asked, peering at all the instrumentation.

Kieran grabbed the left handlebar. "You press this lever in. It's the clutch, and that will let you shift gears. But the gearshift is down by your left foot. So you have to press the clutch with your hand, then use your foot to shift. Does that make sense?"

Audrey glanced at Kieran's thick-soled black boot, which was hovering over a small lever near the kickstand. "I sort of wish it were an automatic," she replied.

"It takes some getting used to, that's for sure. But you're smart—you'll learn in no time." He winked at her, and her skin heated at the unexpected compliment.

"The brake is on the other side of the handlebar," Kieran continued. "When I was first learning how to ride, I grabbed the brake instead of the clutch." He grinned, showing his even, white teeth. "It didn't end so well."

"When did you learn?" Audrey asked. "Who taught you?"

"Tim O'Donnell," Kieran replied, his green eyes sparkling with the memory. "His brother would ride his bike down to Finnegan's bar, and Tim and I would steal the hog once his brother was inside. Tim had an extra key, and we'd be gone for hours while his brother was getting sauced. It was months before we ever got caught. We had a ball."

"Where was that?" Audrey asked, realizing with a sinking feeling that she didn't even know where Kieran had grown up.

"Southie. Er, South Boston officially, I guess."

"Do you miss it?"

"I miss my mom, mostly. She died a few years back."

"I'm sorry to hear that. Do you have any other family?"

"My brother, Auggie. He's a police officer. My dad, I don't talk to. He lost a lot of money gambling when we were growing up. It's part of the reason—"

Kieran stopped suddenly. The only sound was the wind rustling the leaves on nearby trees.

"Part of the reason what?"

Kieran shook his head. "I'll tell you, I will, but not now. Today, we're going to get you on this bike, and we're going to have fun, and that's all there is to it."

Audrey opened her mouth to protest, but Kieran shook his head. "Nope. No arguments. Now, look over here on the right side of the bike. That's your rear brake. So you've got two brakes total, okay? One on the front, that you engage with your hand, and one on the back, where you use your foot."

Audrey let Kieran redirect the conversation, in part because she wanted to believe that he really would tell her about himself later.

A warning flared in the back of her mind. *Careful,* it signaled. If she got to know him, really know him, she might develop feelings for him all over again. Feelings that went well past raw physical desire.

So instead she focused on the bike. For the next

twenty minutes Kieran instructed her about how to engage the clutch, when to use the front brake and when to use the back brake, reminded her to check her mirrors and always wear a helmet, and to "ride like you're invisible and they're drunk." When he finally let her hop on the bike and start it up, her head was swimming in details. How would she know what gear she was in? What if she let out the clutch too fast? What if she hit the gas too hard and did a wheelie? Or, worse, what if Kieran's bike tipped over with her on it?

"You're in neutral now," Kieran said, putting a strong, steadying hand on her shoulder. His touch was firm, reassuring. She relaxed slightly. "And you need to shift to first. So pull the clutch in, and then shift down to first gear."

She let out the clutch slowly, just an inch, and the bike started to roll. Her heart rolled along with it. "Is this normal?" she asked nervously.

Kieran walked alongside the slowly moving bike, laughing. "Don't panic. It's fine. Now, pull the clutch back in, and shift to first."

He let go of Audrey, who instantly missed the pressure of his hand. She tried to remember the steps. *Think*, she commanded her rattled brain.

She pulled the clutch back in. Nothing happened. What was next?

"Shift with your foot. First gear. Press down." Kieran walked alongside the bike, watching her.

She did as she was told, and Kieran clapped. "Good job. Now, give the bike a tiny bit of gas and let out the clutch slowly. Nice and smooth, like I showed you."

Biting her lip, Audrey concentrated on letting out the

clutch with her left hand and giving the bike gas with her right. Easy, easy...

The next thing she knew, the bike was rumbling to life and she was moving—actually *riding a Harley*—across the parking lot. She surprised herself with an ecstatic whoop. It felt amazing! Incredible! So freeing! She glanced down at the speedometer and laughed out loud. She was barely going five miles per hour.

At the end of the parking lot, she turned the bike gently, back toward Kieran. He was smiling broadly. She braked like he'd showed her, using her foot. When a hiccupping sound started in the engine, Kieran called out "Press the clutch again!" With her left hand, she engaged the clutch and the shuddering stopped. The bike purred underneath her.

"Well done," Kieran said as he approached her. His eyes squinted as he grinned.

Audrey laughed again—an ecstatic sound. She couldn't wait to do all this again, to go faster next time, and race down open roads.

"*Yet knowing how way leads on to way, I doubted if I should ever come back.*" Kieran winked, and a sharp pang of affection nestled just underneath Audrey's ribs.

"Was that more poetry?" she asked.

He nodded. "Frost. *Two roads diverged in a wood and I—I took the one less traveled by.* Seemed about right, since you looked like you might ride off and leave me. Leave everything, maybe, since you were having so much fun."

Audrey blinked at him. That was exactly how she'd felt. And here he was, putting her emotions into verse. Her stomach twisted in a way she couldn't explain.

"How do you know those poems?"

Kieran shrugged, staring at the rumbling bike. "A cousin came to visit us when I was about ten. She was in college—the first of anyone in the extended family to go—and she was studying literature. She left behind this book of poems, and I nicked it."

"You stole your poetry?"

He grinned. "I said at least thirty Hail Marys in repentance."

She could imagine his fingers sliding along the glass rosary beads, quick and smooth. "To be fair, I read that stolen book cover to cover, and memorized nearly every single poem. Just because I liked the sound of the words."

He was so casual, so offhand about being a rough-and-tumble kid who discovered he loved poetry. The idea of this tender-hearted boy growing up memorizing a stolen book of verse was enough to have Audrey's whole body trembling.

"Did you have a favorite?" she asked.

Clouds drifted overhead as he gave the question some thought. "Probably Coleridge. The things he imagined were so incredible. Fantastical and so beyond anything I'd ever dreamed at that point. I mean, a poor Boston kid reading about Kubla Khan? I found out later that Coleridge had an opium addiction. So maybe that explains where his mind was."

He grinned and the joy in his expression made her muscles weak.

"Now, enough Frost," Kieran said, oblivious to the emotional tides threatening to sweep Audrey away. "One more time around the parking lot. Go on, then."

Audrey did as he asked, and the poems were forgotten

in the rush of riding the bike again. She felt as if she was cutting through the spring day, slicing it open and experiencing it in a new way. Good heavens, no wonder men chose Harleys as their go-to in a midlife crisis. The machines were downright liberating.

The thought reminded her suddenly of her business plan for the dealership. Since she hadn't exactly been able to present her idea to Kieran at the Wheelhouse, she figured there was no time like the present.

"I loved that," she said after she'd come to a full stop again. "And I bet I'm not the only lady who would be at home on one of these bikes."

"Definitely. They're built for men and women."

"So let's make that a reality at our dealership."

"How do you mean?" he asked, reaching down and turning off the engine.

Audrey lifted her helmet off so she could see Kieran fully. "We're ignoring fifty percent of the population. We've got to target females as a demographic. I mean, think about the clothes we carry. The items for women are ridiculous—that stupid bustier you make me wear, for example. Those clothes aren't functional. You said so yourself. Think about if we actually sold clothes that made women feel sexy and tough *and* safe. And statistics say that a lot of women earn more than men these days. There's big potential for them as buyers."

She paused to take a breath. Kieran was watching her, the lines around his eyes crinkling. "You've spent some time thinking about this."

Audrey shrugged. "I have lots of time to think when I'm just sitting there, modeling the bikes. And I can only watch women walk out on us so many times."

"I didn't realize it was such a pressing problem."

"Maybe you just don't have the right lens," Audrey replied.

She expected him to tell her they'd talk about it tomorrow, back at the dealership, but instead he was just staring at her. His jaw flexed. His gaze grew intense.

"You think of others all the time," he said after a moment. "Who you can help, what you can do." He reached out and took the helmet from her hands, then hung it from the handlebars. "You're always trying to make things better." His throat worked, and Audrey watched the movement, mesmerized. Was Kieran getting *emotional* about all this?

She straightened. Surely not. Or, if he was, it was over the dealership, not her.

He reached out and touched her face, and she drew in a breath. Every nerve ending in her body ignited not from his touch, but from the impassioned look on his face.

"Audrey," he said gently, "I can't—" He broke off, shaking his head.

He was about to pull his hand away from her face, but she grasped it before he could move. Her pulse raced, and she could hear the alarms in her brain again, cautioning her that she wasn't being careful enough. That her heart might rupture with emotion for Kieran at any minute.

I will not let that happen, she thought, turning over his hand. She stared at the intersecting lines on his smooth, white palm, wishing she were a gypsy and could tell the future from the crisscrossed marks. Instead, she brought his palm to her lips, kissing the skin gently. She inhaled, taking in his leather-and-spice smell. She clung to his hand, kissing it repeatedly, working her way from his palm to his fingertips, taking note of how his body had gone rigid, how his breath had turned ragged.

"Audrey." It sounded like a plea. But whether for her to keep going or to stop, she wasn't sure. "*Sweetheart.*"

At the sound of the endearment, her mouth stopped. Her eyes flew to his. He had never called her anything before except her name.

The pained look etched onto his face had her insides plummeting. What in the world could be causing him such distress? How could he look so passionate and so heartbroken at the same time?

She clutched his hand. Oh, there were depths to this man. It was such a shame he hadn't trusted her with those depths five years ago. Maybe things would be different now if he had. Instead, Audrey was facing him on the blacktop, not pulling him into her arms even as she longed to. Her body stilled, resisting the urge to grab him and never let go.

As it turned out, Kieran had the opposite idea.

Lifting her off the bike, he crushed her to his broad chest, her name a coarse whisper on his lips. He kissed her hair, her forehead, then found her mouth with an intensity that made her weak-kneed.

His wide mouth captured hers as he plunged a hand into her hair, tilting her head back until their lips were perfectly aligned. Hunger flared inside of her at his touch, and she opened to him, letting his tongue explore, letting his free hand unzip her coat and remove the layers of clothing between them.

She was seeing spots behind her eyelids—great bursts of desire that exploded when he nibbled on her lower lip, or when she wrapped her arms around his neck and he groaned in the most exquisite way.

Fire heated the space between her legs. But, more alarmingly, an ache began to spread through her chest. It pressed against her sternum and wouldn't relent. It was the pang of wanting more. *Wanting more from Kieran than just his body.* Heaven help her, she wanted to hear about his life and his likes and his experiences in Southie and what other poems he'd memorized. She wanted to know him, and not just physically. She wanted all the things she never got five years ago, because he fled.

But I can't have those things, she reminded herself, trying to diffuse the pain in her chest. He was never going to be the guy who let her in for long, who stuck around so that something lasting could grow out of their time together.

And he's going to leave this time, too, she reminded herself sternly.

She looked down. Her coat was in a heap at her feet. Kieran had his hands under the cotton of her long-sleeved T-shirt, working his way up her sides, stopping just underneath her bra. His thumbs arced over the delicate lace there, and she sucked in a breath as his strong, calloused fingers brushed her nipples. He grasped the tips of her breasts, worrying her flesh gently, sweetly. She saw stars and grabbed his body so she wouldn't topple over. She threw her head back and said his name. "Kieran."

His mouth found her exposed neck. His tongue licked her from clavicle to ear in a delicious, hungry motion.

"I love it when you say my name," he growled. Pushing up her shirt, he bent down to suck on her through the lace of her bra. He nipped the end of her breast, pulling it between his teeth. It was a mix of gentleness and pain that scrambled her brain. She couldn't think straight.

She reached down and placed her hands in the thickness

of his hair. She grasped the sides of his head and tilted his face to hers. His expression was one of both pain and desire. She licked her lips.

Kieran stood slowly. He towered above her, his body coiled with an energy she couldn't quite read. "I don't think I can stop myself if we go much further."

Her body hummed. She nodded. He was right: They should stop everything right now and end this. Walk away.

But instead of saying or doing any of that, she watched her fingers assume a power of their own and land delicately on his groin. His rock-hard penis was right there on the other side of his jeans. She gasped at the way it jumped at her touch.

An animalistic sound escaped him. Audrey pulled off her long-sleeved shirt so that she was standing on the blacktop in her jeans and bra. The breeze was cool on her skin. She watched Kieran take her in, his green eyes dark with hunger.

"What are you doing?"

She barely knew herself. Going this far was a mistake. And yet she was powerless against her desire for him.

She grasped his leather jacket and peeled it off his body. Next came his shirt, so that his strong, muscled chest was exposed to the afternoon sun.

"Audrey, wait. I can't—"

She ignored him and palmed her way over his pectoral muscles, feeling his downy dark-red chest hair against her hands. She kissed his smooth skin, circled his broad shoulders with her arms and pulled him close.

She licked him, so hungry for his body she wanted to bite and taste him for hours. She stroked her tongue over his bare chest again. He shuddered.

She licked again, flickering her tongue, imagining herself a serpent. The snake of temptation. He groaned deep in his throat.

She licked again, once more, and he broke.

She could feel the river of it washing over her, the current of it sweeping them both away. It was his resolve, she realized. Whatever had been holding him back was gone. Whatever walls of resistance he'd built, she'd successfully pulled them down.

His mouth came down on hers so violently she lost her breath. He captured the sound, not letting it escape. His hunger was a heat, flaming through them both.

"Not here," Kieran said, breaking the kiss to lift her into his arms. She twined her arms around his neck, savoring the feel of his flesh against hers, of how easily he carried her to the grassy bank leading down to the river. His body was taut and corded. His pace was brisk enough to make her wonder if he wanted to take her before he could change his mind.

A few steps down, off the pavement, the tall prairie grasses would shield them from any prying eyes. The only clues to their existence would be their piles of clothes next to the motorcycle, but Audrey hardly cared.

He placed her roughly on the riverbank's green carpet, following immediately with his own powerful body. There was a rock digging into her backside, and a twig near her head. She paid them no mind as Kieran kneed apart her legs and shoved his massive form between them. Through his jeans, his erection pressed against her flesh. She clutched his shoulders and drew him closer. If he thought he was being rough—being *hasty*, even—then she would show him she didn't mind. She kissed him eagerly, lifting her hips against his.

"I need you." The way Kieran hissed the words, she wasn't sure if it was an oath or a curse. He matched her hunger with his own, tearing his lips from hers so he could bite her neck, her clavicle. The little nips of pain were delicious, leaving her crying out for more. He lowered himself to her breasts, unlatching her bra with one deft motion. He tossed the fabric aside and palmed one nipple while taking the other rosy tip in his mouth.

He was not gentle.

Thank goodness, because she did not want him to be.

Audrey cried out as the electric pleasure of his rough mouth coursed through her. He responded by suckling harder, biting her when her fingernails raked across his back.

She gasped with pleasure as he took off his own pants and then tore off—*literally*—her panties. She was wet and already craving him in her deepest parts. He was on his knees between her bare legs, and she had a clear view of his raging member, thicker and harder than she ever remembered. It stood erect, straight and true, from a bed of dark red curls. A thrill raced through her. She felt her lips part in a delicious smile.

There would be no slow, gentle reconnection. There would be no sweet lovemaking. If ever she'd wanted him to take her, she was going to get her wish.

Kieran was watching her watch him. His eyes were dark, his lips slightly parted. His skin rippled over muscles drawn tight with desire. He placed one hand on either side of her head, then lowered himself, grinding his body into hers. Audrey gasped as the tip of his cock found her wet, aching center. She was feverish, shaking like an addict who needed a hit. Kieran was her drug, and she wanted the high he would bring her.

He claimed her mouth, his tongue fierce and hot. She wrapped her legs around him, drawing him closer. "Now," she whispered into his ear, wanting him to fill her up until all she felt was him. The tip of his shaft spasmed against her center, and she felt it so deeply she arched against him.

He answered her call, grasping her buttocks and entering her with a force that had her seeing stars of pain and pleasure. The sound that emitted from her throat was so primitive, so visceral, that she wondered if she had transformed into some kind of animal, taking a mate on the forest floor. In that moment, she was carnal and she was spiritual; she was broken and she was whole; she was past and she was present.

She thought she could feel him in every cell. He was everywhere inside her, and unyielding on top of her. His body pressed down on her, while his thickness stretched her to the point of breaking. She let her legs fall to the side, surrendering to the length of him, willing her body not to fight his thrusts.

The hot pain receded quickly, replaced by a sensation that built at the base of her spine. She writhed against him, demanded everything from his flesh. If part of her had wondered if she'd find tenderness when their bodies met, she buried it now. She was getting what she wanted.

It would be plenty.

Kieran's mouth was on hers again, his lips demanding as much from her as she was taking from him. She twisted her hands in his hair, pulled him closer still, daring him to give her more. Her tongue met his, stroke for stroke, her hips met his thrusts every time.

Kieran's fingers dug into her bottom, pulling her against him until he was fully buried. He held her tight as he thrust still more, penetrating her even while he was engulfed to the hilt. She had never been so thoroughly consumed before in her life. Audrey's fingers raked wildly along his back, driving him deeper, crying out for every last ounce of him.

He gave it to her. His movements were so strong, so ferocious, that they unleashed the ocean of pleasure that had been pooling at her spine. It roared through her with tsunami-like force, drenching her in glittered ecstasy. She was drowning in it. She howled, carnal and wild, and didn't even care. As her orgasm broke, Kieran redoubled his efforts, riding her hard, unforgivingly. His own pleasure erupted moments later, the volcanic heat of it spilling through them both.

As Kieran's body stilled, Audrey found herself relaxing. Her desire was slaked, her hunger fulfilled. Her thoughts were clearer now, less like typewriter keys clanking out incessant ideas and more like bits of paper floating on water. She inhaled deeply.

She'd forgotten how life-altering great sex could be. Even rough sex. Maybe even especially rough sex. She smiled to herself, thinking it would be fun to plan this again. Maybe with more candles and fewer rocks, like the one digging into her scapula right this minute. She shifted underneath Kieran, wondering if she should ask him if she could sit up. But he rolled off her before she could get the words out.

She was relaxed, buzzed with pleasure, and expected Kieran to be the same. But the way he hastily pulled on his pants and wouldn't look at her spoke of regret, not satisfaction. When his eyes finally found hers, she saw sorrow, not contentment.

Her happiness unfurled into confusion. Did even just

fucking her make him sad? Did everything about bringing her pleasure make him remorseful?

"What?" she asked, grabbing at her bra and torn panties. "What is that look?"

"I'm sorry," he said, running a hand through his dark-flamed hair. "I didn't mean for that to happen. I should have—I wasn't—I'm sorry."

Her mind reeled. Was he seriously sorry already? Before, he'd at least waited a few hours before walking out on her. Now, it would be instantaneous.

She stood. She'd told herself this could happen. She'd told herself that Kieran Callaghan was exactly this man. This was hardly a surprise. She steeled herself against any part of her mind that wanted to think otherwise.

"Be sorry all you want," she said coolly. "I got what I came for." Snapping on her bra, she walked boldly back into the parking lot. She could hear Kieran rustling through the grasses behind her.

"Audrey, you misunderstand me," he said as she strode toward her pile of clothes.

"Oh, no, I think I *absolutely* understand you, Kieran," she said, pulling on her jeans and tucking her ruined underwear into a pocket. "I think we're pretty much crystal clear at this point. So why you're sitting there with a hang-dog look is beyond me. You don't owe me anything. I don't need anything more than what you just gave me. So, really, thank you."

Kieran shook his head. He gazed past her, to the rustling tree line and the cold river, and took a deep breath. "Audrey, I told myself I wouldn't do this. I don't regret being with you, but I do regret that it happened without you knowing the truth."

She blinked. "What truth?"

"The truth about what really happened five years ago."

What happened was he left, plain and simple. What more could there be?

"I want to tell you what really went down when we first met," he continued. "I want us to have a chance, if it's not too late. And in order for that to happen, I have to tell you about the past."

"A chance?" Audrey faltered. Her insides twisted. Was Kieran actually talking about them being together in the present tense? She must have heard him wrong. "I don't follow."

"I mean I care for you, Audrey. But for us to have a shot, I need to talk about what happened. I want you to have the full picture—the *true* picture—of what occurred after we got together."

A buzzing started in Audrey's brain. A tide of emotions wanted to burst forth inside her. Surprise. Hope. And skepticism, too. They were all rolling together into one mass that was pressing against her heart. Vaguely, she was aware of Kieran saying her name, staring at her with concern.

"You want to be with me?" she finally managed to ask.

"Very much."

Affection swelled, but she pinned it back. "But you have to tell me something in order for that to happen?"

Kieran nodded. "And I have to warn you, it won't be pleasant to hear."

Audrey's throat felt suddenly scratchy. She wanted water. She swallowed.

Kieran watched her, his pale green eyes never leaving her face. Her mind raced under his gaze. He wanted her to hear his confession.

So that they could be together.

Confusion darkened her vision. The only question was: Did she want to be with *him*?

She still felt dizzy from their sizzling sex, the exquisite release he'd given her. But her jumbled emotions signaled a warning that anything more than a spicy romp in the grass was a bad idea. Maybe it wouldn't be so bad if he just kept his secret and they stayed friends of a sort. Or colleagues. Dread chilled her as she wondered what he could possibly have to say.

Should she really give Kieran Callaghan her ear? Five years ago, she'd given him everything. And he'd ridden away without a glance backward.

Now, he was asking her to risk her heart again.

"I—I'm not sure this is a good idea," she whispered.

"It may not be, but I can't think of another way." Kieran's muscles were taut with tension just under his skin.

"I think you should take me home." She held out her hand for her coat. He handed it over slowly.

She shrugged into it, ignoring the hurt creasing his face.

"Audrey, please. If you'll just give me a chance..."

She shook her head. The truth was, she had given him a chance. And he'd squandered it when he left.

"Whatever happened, I think it's best if it just stays in the past. We had our time five years ago. I'm not sure there's anything left for us." Her brain reeled as she spoke the words. Was that true? Did she even believe what she was saying?

Oh, but she couldn't let this man try to win her back. Five years ago, maybe they could have worked out. But that was a long time ago.

Things were different now.

There was a prickling behind her eyes. She turned from him to blink away any tears. The pain surprised her. She wanted to feel more relief, more assurance that she was doing the right thing.

You are, she told herself. *You are.*

When she turned back, his face was shadowed.

"We should go," she said, her voice hollow in her own ears.

Wordlessly, he nodded.

She slung a leg over the motorcycle and grabbed her helmet, fastening it while he climbed on. The engine rattled her mind, her body, shaking loose a torrent of thoughts. Was she making the right choice? Was this all a terrible mistake?

Afternoon light dappled the new leaves on the trees, but Audrey couldn't find any beauty in it. The wind was raw in her face, her seat on the motorcycle lumpy and unforgiving. In front of her, Kieran's back was as straight and hard as a two-by-four.

A lump rose in her throat. She studied his rigid muscles, his unbending frame, and told herself it wasn't so bad.

She wasn't the same Audrey Tanner she was five years ago, and this had proved it. Kieran's steeliness wasn't her enemy. It was her reward.

She should embrace it.

The motorcycle turned away from the sun, into the long afternoon shadows.

Audrey fought a deep, unforgiving chill that went straight into her marrow.

CHAPTER SIXTEEN

The next day, a mist hung in the air, turning the sky and trees the same flat color as the cement under Audrey's feet. Not even the bright green asparagus cutout she'd spotted in front of Lumberjack Grocery—featuring a smiling mom, dad, and baby asparagus—could offset the flat, dull gray all around.

The thick, muddled air matched her mood more than she wanted to admit. Since her conversation with Kieran yesterday, Audrey's thoughts had been clouded, her whole being more than a little off kilter. Her mind had replayed the fiery sex and his unexpected profession in the parking lot over and over, wondering what "truth" Kieran could possibly need to tell her.

There was a splinter of doubt embedded deep inside about the way she was reacting to all this. It rubbed her emotions raw with every breath. Had she made the right choice by not hearing him out? She still didn't know, and the uncertainty was making her weary.

As she headed to the Dane County offices, she trembled at the memory of the intensity with which they'd come together next to the river. As hot as it had been, she wondered if there could be more between them. There *had* been more, five years ago, the first time they'd made love.

But that had ended in disaster and heartbreak.

She shook her head. She'd tried to ignore the soreness in her chest that had been there since they'd parted. But every time she thought about the emotions storming in the pale green seas of Kieran's eyes or remembered his words of affection, the ache would start all over again.

Desperate to take her mind off of everything and needing time away from Kieran, Audrey had called in sick to the dealership and instead turned her focus to her recent conversation with Sonja and Caitlin. The idea of helping more people in White Pine become fit—not just high-school kids—was her one bright spot right now.

Earlier that very morning, on a whim, she'd decided to head down to the YMCA.

The soggy day had only looked worse in the dull morning light. But inside the clean, carpeted lobby, it had been a colorful mix of oranges and greens. She'd smelled chlorine from the pool, and it reminded her of hotels and vacations.

"Can I speak with a personal trainer?" she'd asked. Briefly she wondered if she was being too brash—did you need to make an appointment before you saw a trainer?—but the woman behind the front desk simply nodded.

"Sure thing," she replied. "Let me get Greg."

A few minutes later, a short, compact man entered the

lobby, bouncing on the balls of his feet as if he were warming up for a race.

He held out a hand to Audrey. "Greg Freeman. How can I help?" She shook his hand. He continued to bounce.

"I have a few questions," Audrey said. "I was hoping I might be able to speak with someone about training?"

His gaze flitted up and down her body. Assessing, she realized.

"Are you training for something specific? Trying to build up to a new fitness level?"

"I—actually, I was thinking about *becoming* a personal trainer. But I wanted to talk with someone who was actually doing it. I know you're busy, so I'm happy to make an appointment if that's helpful. Or maybe buy you coffee for your time?"

To her delight, he had twenty minutes before his next client, so in exchange for an energy drink out of a vending machine, he let her pick his brain about which certifications would be necessary, whether she should specialize in a specific kind of training, and how she should go about getting clients.

Greg's chatter was as nonstop as his bouncing. Audrey listened and took notes, pausing only when Greg mentioned how much the certifications cost.

"It'll probably run you about a grand," he said, pounding back the last of his energy drink. "There's certification and there's testing, too. And sometimes you need specific equipment. Heart rate monitors, for example."

Audrey's heart sank. She decidedly didn't have a thousand dollars lying around for any of this.

"Don't let the cost get you down," Greg said, reading her expression. "Some places offer scholarships or financing. I funded mine by entering a bodybuilding contest. I took second, which was almost eight hundred bucks in prize money."

His comment instantly ignited an idea in her mind. She could feel herself grinning as she thanked him profusely for his time.

Now, a manila folder under her arm, she was headed into the Dane County offices to see about making her dream a reality.

Her phone rang just as she reached the building's front doors. She fished the cell out of her pocket, then held back a groan. It was Casey, who had been trying to reach her for days. She'd ignored the calls, largely because she knew Casey would ask about Kieran, and Audrey didn't want to talk about him. What had happened on Sunday was surprising and confusing—but it was also private.

She could still feel Kieran's mouth on her breasts, could still feel his warm hands on her flesh, could still feel him stretching her until she thought she'd crack wide open. She shivered. She could never tell Casey about any of that. And the parts of Sunday's fight she *could* tell Casey about would just have her sister saying what Audrey had already come to terms with—that there was no hope for her and Kieran in the present.

Still. She had to speak to her sister at some point. She hit talk, silently praying that Arvid Faltskog would be working the county desk when she was done with the call. Arvid was always efficient with paperwork—even if he was grumpy about it.

"Hey, Casey," she said, forcing brightness into her voice. She stepped into the building's foyer, out of the dreary day.

"I've been trying to reach you. Where have you been?"

I'm fine, thanks for asking, Audrey thought. "Oh, just busy," she said instead. "I'm on my way right now to enter the Asparagus Queen pageant. Wish me luck."

There was a pause. "Why would you do that?"

Audrey looked down, staring at the swirls in the marble floor. Whites and browns intertwined in the rosy stone like ribbons of marshmallow and chocolate. *There are sweet things everywhere if you just look,* she thought to herself.

"Technically, I qualify," Audrey replied carefully, "since I'm between the ages of twenty-four and forty, and I have lived in White Pine for more than five years. Those are the rules."

"Those may be the rules, but it's still a pageant. Honestly, are you going to wear a gown and give a speech?"

"I will wear a dress," Audrey said. "And if the judges ask for a speech, I'll tell them how much I love White Pine."

Casey surprised her by giggling suddenly. "No ventriloquism, though, right? Because that would be *nuts*."

Audrey stopped walking. "Are you seriously bringing up Mr. Chippy right now?"

Casey laughed harder. "I'm sorry, I know I shouldn't. But…I haven't heard from Mr. Chippy since that Hawaiian vacation he took to find some *coconuts*."

Audrey tried to summon irritation at being teased, but instead she laughed at the shared memory of how she'd uncovered a chipmunk puppet at a garage sale when she was eleven, and convinced herself she was a ventriloquist. Casey had helped her write a whole skit with "Mr. Chippy," which she'd performed at her middle school talent show. Needless to say, the kids loved the endless jokes about nuts—but the teachers, not so much.

"My nuts are so cold, I'd better hide them in this *wood*." Casey hiccupped, losing it now.

"Casey!" Audrey cried, laughing even more. "Come on. I'm serious. I want to do the asparagus pageant."

"You *know* Chippy's momma always had her cheeks full of nuts."

Audrey clapped her hand over her mouth to hold the laughter back. "Oh my God, stop it right now."

But the sisters wound up giggling to each other for several more moments. When she could finally breathe again, Audrey was instantly lighter and more clear-headed. Her sister could be prickly at times, but she was also the only person who could make Audrey laugh until tears leaked from her eyes.

On the other end, Casey exhaled. "Listen, do what you want, but I just worry about you, Audrey. The pageant is fine, but I just want to make sure it's not a distraction from finding a real job. And by real job I don't mean this silly dealership thing."

Audrey clutched the phone, wondering how she could explain that part of her actually agreed, and that the pageant was all part of a much bigger plan. She was going to enter the Asparagus Queen pageant—and take back her career by using the prize money to pay for training certifications. After all, it wasn't as if she were desperate to get back to the dealership anytime soon and face Kieran on the showroom floor.

"All I'm trying to do," Casey was saying, "is help you out a bit. Can you understand that?"

Audrey blinked. Casey had been talking for a while now, but she hadn't really been listening. "Uh, of course," she answered blindly.

"Good. Then let's meet on Saturday for lunch."

"Saturday is the pageant. I have to be onstage by one."

"It will still work. Especially if we meet at the Paul Bunyan Diner by noon. Sound okay?"

"All right," Audrey agreed, her mind as swirled as the marbled patterns at her feet. She hung up the phone, and pushed Casey out of her brain as she strode to the county desk to file her pageant paperwork.

When Arvid Faltskog looked up from his post at the county desk and harrumphed a hello, she took it as a good sign.

* * *

He'd lost her.

Kieran let the cold mist batter his face as he raced his bike over rolling farmland, knowing he'd shown his hand and gambled with his terrible cards—and it was no surprise the pot wasn't his. Audrey Tanner wanted nothing to do with his sad sob story, and he couldn't blame her one bit.

Wind threaded through his hair and he savored the feeling. His helmet was locked in the saddlebags on the back, and for once he didn't mind. He let the clean Minnesota air rush over him fully, thinking that soon he'd be in a different state, helping another dealership.

He wouldn't try to stay in White Pine. He wouldn't try to make his position here permanent. No, he'd move on and let Audrey be free of him, and that would be that.

Except that he felt like a coward—like a loser, honestly—for giving up so easily. Had he really conquered so many demons in his life only to lose Audrey before he could even tell her the truth?

His stomach knotted for the hundredth time at the unfortunate reality that he'd thrown her on her back on the riverbed and released the tension between them for a few glorious moments. But she still didn't know what had really happened five years ago.

And, very likely, he'd made things worse by not being able to keep his dick in his pants. He grimaced, thinking of how carnal their sex had been. He'd lost himself totally in her, unable to resist, taking her with a force that had surprised him. And she'd responded passionately and eagerly. So much so that the moment they'd finished, he'd wanted to take her again. But he knew he couldn't until he confessed, and he'd never gotten the chance.

The truth of it all left him feeling hollowed out and a little bit rotted, too. Like a pumpkin that's sat on the porch for too many weeks after Halloween.

He slowed the bike, pulling over to the side of the road. Distant green fields were covered in cottony mist. He could hear cows mooing, but couldn't see them. They were lost in the haze.

Kieran set his jaw. *The truth will set you free.* Wasn't that the expression? It had been his intent on Sunday to tell Audrey what had really happened five years ago, to tell her what a mistake he'd made and how he'd turned his life around, but he'd only gotten as far as banging her, then wanting something from her. Wanting a future with her, specifically.

That much, he'd said. It was bad timing. It was idiotic, and if this were a test, he would have failed.

He pondered the worst card a gambler could hold. A deuce? A mismatched face card? No. The worst card he could hold would be a joker. Not even a card at all.

Still, he had to put the joker down on the table. Somehow, he had to get her to hear the truth.

He clutched the handlebars. He had such a ruinous tale to tell, but in ruin there was always redemption. His and Casey's both, perhaps.

And if Audrey didn't see it, well, she could walk away from him. *Then* she could hate him.

But he had to try again.

He revved his engine and pulled back out onto the damp road. It was madness, pursuing Audrey like this. He was risking her heart as well as his own, since this story involved her sister. It involved family. But she needed to know.

He would ask her once more to hear his story.

He wasn't sure what she'd say, but, come hell or high water, he would attempt it.

If there was anyone out there who could know the worst about him, and dare to love him anyway, it was her.

Whatever happened, he would show her that joker.

* * *

On Thursday, Audrey was rushing down the sidewalk to Knots and Bolts, clutching a Mexican hot dish to her chest, when a dark figure slid to her side and began to keep pace with her.

"Hi, Ms. Tanner."

Audrey stopped cold. In the dim afternoon light, with the mist swirling, she faced Hunter Haglund, trying not to show her surprise.

"Hunter," she said, taking in his clean, pressed clothes and polished shoes. She caught a whiff of cologne in the air.

Hunter stepped in closer, and Audrey looked down the

sidewalk toward Knots and Bolts, just a hundred feet away. Golden light poured out of the large window at the front, glittering onto the wet street. It looked warm and inviting—and impossibly out of reach at that very second.

"Do you have to go somewhere?" Hunter asked. His dark eyes searched hers; strands of his sandy hair swayed in the wind.

Audrey straightened her spine. "What do you want?" she asked, ignoring his question.

She thought Hunter would smile creepily, maybe say something menacing, but he surprised her by dropping his gaze to the sidewalk. "I wanted to say, the school talked to me, and my parents talked to me, too. I didn't mean to freak you out the other day. You or Alexis. I guess I just wanted to say sorry, and it won't happen again."

Audrey studied the boy. Alexis had been texting her about Hunter earlier in the week, so she knew the school had gotten involved. She knew Hunter's parents had been told about the boy's behavior. What she hadn't known was that Hunter would be so easily altered. She narrowed her eyes. She wasn't sure she believed it.

He backed away slightly. "I'm sorry if I startled you. I just wanted to apologize. For the incident on the road." His mouth was pulled into a contrite line.

Audrey wasn't sure what to say. She certainly hoped the school and his parents had knocked some sense into him.

"I'm glad you understand the situation," she said after a moment. "That's a good first step. From now on, respecting Alexis's boundaries is not a request, it's a rule." She didn't want him thinking that he was off the hook because he was sorry. What he needed to do was totally and completely stop pursuing the poor girl.

Hunter nodded. "That won't be a problem."

"Good." Audrey shifted the Mexican hot dish in her arms. At this rate, it was going to be frigid by the time she got to Knots and Bolts. Hunter just watched her, which made her skin prickle with unease. The kid really, really needed to pick up on more social cues. "All right, then. I need to go. Good night, Hunter."

She began walking away. Hunter didn't move. "Good night, Ms. Tanner," she heard him say to her retreating back.

She would have given him a wave, but both her hands were wrapped around her hot dish. She supposed it was just as well.

CHAPTER SEVENTEEN

$\mathcal{T}$he dreary afternoon was forgotten the minute Audrey stepped inside Knots and Bolts. The back room's bright red table was adorned with a large crystal vase filled with cheerful spring flowers—grape hyacinths, soft-petaled irises, bold tulips, butter-yellow daffodils, and bluebells. Their colors were a perfect match for the tones in the room's homey, braided rug. Best of all, Audrey's friends were already gathered in the cozy space, sipping coffee or tea or wine, and murmuring at the warm, spicy smell wafting in from the kitchenette. It was Betty's tortilla soup, the perfect complement to Audrey's Mexican hot dish.

"Good thing you're here," Betty said, wiping her hands on her apron as Audrey shrugged out of her coat. "I was worried you'd gotten stuck on a motorcycle again and couldn't get off."

Audrey blushed. She seriously had to stop telling them

everything that happened at the Harley dealership or she'd
never hear the end of it.

"Aw, now, I'm just teasing," Betty said, eyeing Audrey's
pink cheeks. "Come on in and let me heat up that hot dish
for you. We'd better serve it soon, or Pregzilla is going to
chew through the walls."

"I am *not* Pregzilla," Willa protested as Betty took the
hot dish from Audrey. "I'm just tired. And hungry. Good
Lord, being with child takes it out of you." She was sitting
at the table with her feet up, sipping some kind of sparkling
juice. Audrey laughed, happy that Willa had told everyone
her wonderful news.

"For crying out loud, you're still in the first trimester,"
Stephanie said. "Just wait until the third." She shook her
head, no doubt reliving the memory of carrying her twins.

"Don't I know it. Barely a few months in, and I'm already such a mess. Burk is going to ship me out of state. I
swear it."

"Out of state?" Audrey asked, shaking her head. "No
way. Pregzilla is Japanese. You're going to have to go *over-
seas*."

"Oh, she's not going anywhere," Anna said. "I see how
my brother looks at her. If Burk thought Willa was beautiful before, Willa pregnant is doing him in. He can hardly
speak around her. It's disgusting. And adorable."

"Come on, Sam must have looked at you that way,"
Stephanie said, pulling her bright red hair into a quick,
messy bun. "He must have been over the moon when you
were pregnant with Juniper."

Anna's dark blue eyes crinkled with a happiness that
swelled Audrey's heart. Was it really possible to be adored
so thoroughly? That even when pregnancy made you fat

and gassy and swollen, a man could love you more than anything? She suddenly had a hard time swallowing, wondering if anyone would ever love her that much.

"Sam liked it, I guess," Anna said evasively, taking a sip of wine.

"Oh, I'm sure he more than liked it," Stephanie said. "I bet he had your pregnant self every which way he could get it."

"Steph!" Anna cried, laughing. "You sound like Betty!"

"Sometimes Betty says things that need saying," Audrey chimed, quoting Willa from the other night at the Wheelhouse. Her friend winked at her, and Audrey grinned.

"I do what now?" Betty asked, stepping out from the kitchenette, where she'd been reheating Audrey's hot dish.

"You just tell it like it is," Willa said, "and that's why we love you."

Betty huffed. "Damn straight I do."

Minutes later, forks were clinking on mismatched plates and spoons were scraping bowls as they ate and talked together. Anna told them that Juniper's drum lessons had her banging her and Sam awake each day, whacking them both out of bed with wooden spoons. Betty said her pastor husband had become addicted to a reality show about drag queens and thought there were good life lessons in the program that he should preach from the pulpit, though he wasn't sure how the congregation would feel about the show as a metaphor. And Stephanie regaled them with a story about how one of her twins had dumped all of her expensive packets of chocolate protein powder into the tub and then mixed in enough water so he could take "a mud bath."

Audrey laughed and ate and listened, but inside was

wondering at what point she should jump in and talk about Kieran—or if she should at all.

Kieran and I had sex.

He told me he has feelings for me, but I don't trust him.

Sometimes, in spite of everything, I fantasize about the two of us being together.

I don't know everything that happened five years ago.

But I'm not sure I want to know now.

It all sounded so ridiculous. Betty would probably tell her to stop giving it any thought at all—that Kieran Callaghan could fuck her eight ways until Sunday, tell her he was a prince with a flying carpet, and it wouldn't matter one whit.

Except it didn't feel that way. She was working so hard to tell herself not to pay attention to Kieran, not to let him affect her, that it was exhausting. Her head hurt and large swaths of her ached.

"You okay over there?" Willa asked, elbowing her gently.

Audrey lifted her eyes from her hot dish and forced a smile. "Fine. Just thinking about the Asparagus Festival. I submitted my paperwork for Asparagus Queen today. I guess I'm just nervous."

"You don't say!" Betty cried, her blonde hair bouncing. "Good for you!"

"Audrey, that's perfect!" Stephanie said. "You're coming out of your shell in spades. How wonderful!"

"I'm thinking of using the prize money to pay for some personal training certifications. To maybe start my own business here in town. That is, if I win."

"How fabulous! I'll be your first client," Willa said. "You can help me lose my baby weight."

"Even if you don't win, I suppose you could work and save for a while to get the certifications that way," Betty said.

Audrey wasn't sure how to tell them that she'd eventually have to find a job that wasn't at the dealership because of how complicated things had become with Kieran. She'd called in sick every day since Sunday. It was irresponsible and gutless, and if she kept it up, Kieran would surely have to fire her. She would have to go in tomorrow, no matter what, just to ensure she wouldn't get canned until she had something else lined up. The thought steeled her resolve for her new line of business.

"I'm really more interested in using the pageant to help my business. Or, that is, my would-be business. This is just a way to build on the personal training interest that's already out there. The whole town will be watching the pageant, after all."

"Are you thinking of asking them to add a swimsuit competition or something?" Stephanie asked. "Show your figure a bit?"

"No, nothing that dramatic. I was just thinking I could talk about wanting to be a small business owner up on that stage. Really come across as a professional. Help people see I'm serious."

Betty sat back thoughtfully. "It's a good start. Afterward, you could put up some flyers in the grocery store and advertise in the *Loon Trader*."

Audrey nodded. Betty was a savvy businesswoman, and she ran an online Halloween shop in addition to Knots and Bolts. She'd taught Willa the basics of the business plan that had helped the White Pine Bed and Breakfast get off the ground.

"The pageant plus the additional advertising could be really powerful," Audrey agreed. "It could prove to the whole town that there's new life in this gym teacher."

"There's new life in you either way," Anna said, smiling. "Whether you win at the pageant or whether you start your own business, we're so proud of you."

"Thanks for your confidence," Audrey said to her friends. "I wish you were all on the voting committee. This crown means a lot, actually, especially if I leave the dealership."

"Hold on," Willa said. "Who said anything about you leaving the dealership? I thought you liked it there. I thought you had some business ideas for the place."

Audrey bit the inside of her cheek. Darn it, she'd gone and spilled too much. "It's fine," she hedged, still not wanting to talk about Kieran, "but I don't want to be there forever. It's a gig, not a career."

She could feel the women all staring at her, doubtful. "Why do I think this all has something to do with that Irish boy?" Betty asked.

"Did something happen during your date on Sunday?" Willa inquired.

"Wait, you had a date on Sunday?" This was from Stephanie.

Audrey rubbed her temples. This was going in exactly the direction she wanted to avoid. "Yes, I had a date with Kieran on Sunday. It was..." she tried on different words to describe the day.

White hot. Thrilling. Maddening.

All of the above.

"I don't know what to say," she finally admitted. "Kieran and I—that is, he told me he has feelings for me, and it's thrown me into a tailspin. Five years ago, I would have given anything to hear him say that. Now, I just want to avoid getting hurt again."

"So that's why you want to leave the dealership," Betty said matter-of-factly.

Audrey traced a pattern on the red table's smooth surface. Was it self-preservation that had her leaving the dealership? Or was it something else entirely?

Cowardice.

The word lodged in her throat and she couldn't swallow it down.

She was running away from Kieran because she was scared: fearful of the way he made her feel, frightened of the emotions she was afraid would burst through her heart and overtake her, and, worst of all, petrified of what he would say about the past. Because what if it changed her mind about him? What *then*?

To her horror, she felt a tear begin to slide down one cheek. She wiped it away, hoping no one would see, but everyone around the table picked up on it.

"Oh, honey," Willa said, putting a warm hand over Audrey's. "It's going to be all right. You're going to get through this."

"I'm just so confused," Audrey said, taking in a shuddery breath. In a matter of weeks, Kieran had gone from storming into the dealership and threatening to fire her to professing his affection for her. He was a mass of mind-boggling contradictions. "I keep deciding how to feel about Kieran, what box to put him in, and then he goes and moves everything around."

"Love is kind of like that," Betty said gently.

Audrey lifted her eyes. "This isn't love," she said. "I don't know what this is, but it's not love."

"Okay, okay," Betty said, holding up her hands in an *I surrender* gesture. "Sorry about that."

Audrey massaged her forehead. Her skull felt like it was going to split into eight thousand pieces, and fragments of her would forever be lost in the braids of the carpet underneath her chair. "Can we talk about something else?" she asked. "Please?"

"I have dessert," Anna said, standing. She began to collect the dinner plates, and Audrey quickly followed, glad for the distraction.

"What did you make?" Stephanie asked, helping switch the conversation.

"It's a tart." Anna moved into the kitchenette. When she returned, she was carrying a lovely pastry with a flaky crust and a golden orange middle.

"Oh, that looks heavenly!" Willa said, staring at the dessert. "What kind is it?"

Anna locked eyes with Audrey. "Passion fruit."

Audrey had to grin. "Well, that figures."

"You get an extra big slice," Betty said, serving Audrey. "You need it."

Audrey picked up a fork, and didn't argue.

CHAPTER EIGHTEEN

Friday morning, Audrey stepped out her front door with a hastily scribbled to-do list in hand. Its length had her wondering if she was going to be able to accomplish even half.

She had to pick up a dress from Willa for the pageant, then beg the local cobbler, Landon Valcheck, to fix the broken strap on the one pair of high-heeled shoes she owned. After that, she had to swing by Lumberjack Grocery to buy detergent so she could do the loads of laundry that were spilling out of her hamper. Oh, and she still had to make it to work by ten o'clock. Which meant she needed to get to the Rolling Pin, pronto, for a much-needed cup of coffee.

Audrey's mind was so preoccupied that she almost didn't notice the rose petals on her front steps—at least until her heel slipped on one of them. She caught her balance and looked down to find the crimson bits of flower scattered everywhere outside her front door, down the stairs and small sidewalk, all the way to her car.

She stilled. In her mind's eye, she pictured dark hair licked with flames and sea-green eyes.

"Kieran," she breathed, smelling crushed rose on the day's warm breeze. The clusters of red had bits of poetry racing through her brain, the lyrical words Kieran had recited to her from his stolen book. Especially one of her favorites: "But he that dares not grasp the thorn should never crave the rose."

She'd always loved the Anne Brontë poem about being courageous in spite of failure. And of course she'd made no secret about loving roses.

Her muscles trembled. Had he really done this?

She stared at the sea of tiny red waves and inhaled sharply. Who else could it be?

No one was the answer.

She closed her eyes briefly. Good grief, why did he have to be so damn romantic? Why did he have to confess his feelings and then leave her rose petals in a grand emotional gesture?

Audrey clutched her to-do list in her hand, wondering how she was ever going to get anything done with the vision of rose petals in her brain all day. She would have to find Kieran at work and thank him. She hadn't been sure what to say to him all week. Now she knew she had an opener.

"I'll just tell him this was nice," she murmured, making her way along the petal-littered sidewalk to her car. She stopped to pick up a single crimson arc, inhaling its sweetness and fingering its softness. "This was lovely."

Even as she spoke the words, she could feel the dam beginning to crack in her heart, letting rivulets of emotion seep through.

If the dam burst, she might feel too much—and never be able to construct the edifice again. She'd had five long years to build this one, stone by stubborn stone. In spite of her best efforts, Kieran was chipping away at her protective wall. Oh, there was part of her that wanted to help him tear away the barriers. To let everything she felt for him just come roaring through—the passion, the affection, the rainbow of emotions for him that colored her insides.

But did she dare? Could she trust him?

What if he had secrets from five years ago that would undo her all over again?

She climbed into her car and started the engine. *That may be,* she thought, *but I can still talk to him.*

The question was whether it would really just be a conversation—a polite chat where she'd thank him for the flowers—or if she'd find herself wanting to hurtle her body at him all over again.

* * *

Two Rolling Pin coffees in hand, Audrey trekked past clusters of golden daffodils, up the sidewalk to the White Pine B and B's wide front porch. The wooden planks had recently been painted a rich brown—no doubt Burk's doing the minute winter's grasp on Minnesota had loosened—and the new floor color was complemented by sky-blue wicker furniture, plus an assortment of cushions in flowers, stripes, and paisleys. It should have been an odd arrangement, but the whole thing had a unique, charming quality that was threaded through the entire B and B. "I call it Minnesota chic," Willa had joked once about her style. "Manhattan meets the Midwest."

Before she could ring the bell Willa pulled open the door, smiling. "I saw you drive up. Come on in."

Audrey handed her a coffee as she stepped into the warm space. "Decaf, for the mom-to-be."

Willa took it and inhaled the aroma. "Giving up wine for nine months will be hard, but giving up caffeine might just kill me."

"You'll be able to drink it again when you really need it. I hear those midnight feedings can be brutal."

Willa's emerald eyes flashed playfully. "You know you're going to be the one I call when I'm up with the baby. Two o'clock a.m., your phone rings, it's me wanting to talk to pass the time while my boobs get sucked on."

"By someone who is not Burk."

Willa snorted. "Touché. By someone who is not Burk." She turned toward the magnificent staircase that led up to some of the guest rooms, as well as Willa and Burk's room. "Speaking of boobs, let's find you a dress that shows yours off." She and Audrey began the climb up the gleaming wooden steps. "I pulled out a box from the attic with some more of my New York wardrobe in it. The pickings are slim—I threw out so much—but there's one in there that just might work."

Ten minutes later, Audrey was standing in the middle of Willa's bedroom wearing a sparkling charcoal dress that hugged every inch of her body. The hem was hand-beaded with exquisite crystals, daring anyone to look away. The scalloped top plunged into a V at the front, but it was taste-ful, not tawdry. The bulk of the material was in the fitted sleeves, which came all the way to Audrey's wrists. It was a perfect blend of sexy and elegant.

"You wear it better than I ever did," Willa said, studying her.

Audrey turned in front of Willa's large, gilded mirror. The dress must have cost a fortune when Willa bought it new, and Audrey could understand why she'd kept it. It was also everything Audrey wanted it to be: a mix of gorgeous and eye-catching in a way that would have everyone looking at her—for all the right reasons. Her stomach fluttered at the idea that she'd be modeling this in front of the entire town.

As if reading her thoughts, Willa came and stood next to her. "You can win if you wear jeans and a T-shirt," she said gently. "You are so beautiful, and this town loves you. No matter what you have on."

Audrey fingered the dress's glittery material. "I appreciate that," she said. "I'm just ready for something different. I want people to see me in a new way."

"People plural or person singular?"

"Come again?"

"Do you need *everyone* to see you in that, or just one person in particular? The person whose name rhymes with Kieran Callaghan?"

Audrey fought to keep the color out of her cheeks. This was most decidedly not about Kieran. "It's actually the opposite," she replied, turning back to the mirror. "I'm doing this because I need to move forward with a new career. A job where I'm not around him all day long."

Willa took a sip of coffee. She stared at Audrey's trim figure in the mirror, but her eyes were farther away, focused on something Audrey couldn't see.

"I hurt Burk pretty badly when I left for New York," she said after a moment. "I was horrible to him. And I wasn't exactly wonderful to you when we were teenagers and ran track together."

Audrey blinked at the abrupt change in conversation. "Willa, that's so many years ago. It's water under the br—"

"I can't think where I'd be if Burk hadn't forgiven me," she pressed on. "If he hadn't opened his heart to me and risked believing that I'd changed. Or at least that I was trying to change. I'm just saying that five years is a long time. And people don't always stay the way they were."

Audrey stared at her figure in the silver dress. She certainly couldn't have imagined herself wearing this dress six months ago. Hell, six weeks ago it would have been a stretch.

Willa put a warm hand on her friend's shoulder. "I don't know what I would have done without your forgiveness, too. You always see the best in people, and it's such a blessing. To me, to the people in your life. I'm just saying, don't lose sight of that."

Audrey's throat thickened. Willa and Burk were so happy together that it was tough to recall that their relationship had been a struggle. But Willa was right. She had been mean, selfish, and cruel to the people around her. Audrey and Burk included. Audrey had forgiven it all because she was willing to trust that, down deep, Willa's heart was tender enough to change. She'd been right, of course. And now thinking about Willa being anything except her dearest friend in the world was jolting. Discombobulating, even.

Her insides pinched. She wanted so much to believe that

Kieran could be the same way. That, like Willa, he deserved a second chance. She pictured the rose petals, heard his poetry, saw the kindness in his face. But the stakes were so high.

She knew she could love Kieran again, but if it didn't work out, she wasn't sure she could survive the heartbreak again.

"What if I'm wrong about Kieran?" Audrey asked, searching her friend's face. "What if I just end up getting hurt again? And he rides off, like last time, leaving me in the dirt?"

"That's a legitimate concern. He absolutely could do that. There are no guarantees he won't."

"Then why do I even want to risk it?"

"Because that's what faith is. That's what *love* is. You believe, even when you're not sure what you're going to get in return. And you trust it will work out for the best. He told you he wants a future with you, right? Then you believe him. You take the leap with him."

Audrey groaned. That seemed like an awfully tenuous answer.

Willa smiled. "I'm just saying, think about it. In the meantime, you need to get to work, and I need to get lunch started for our guests. Would you believe, we have six more people checking in this afternoon for the Asparagus Festival."

Audrey shimmied out of the silver dress, hugged her friend, and set off for the dealership. As she drove into town, her throat was crammed with all the words she wanted to say to Kieran.

Thank you for the roses.

I am afraid of how much I could care for you.

In five years, there's never been anyone else.

If it wasn't for the fact that she was behind the wheel, she would have closed her eyes in order to sift through the tangle of phrases. As it was, she pressed down the accelerator and hurried to her job.

CHAPTER NINETEEN

*K*ieran was standing over Fletch Knudson in the dealership's windowed conference room, pointing to a product catalog. "This is what I'm talking about, Fletch. Practical stuff, not high heels and bustiers."

He placed his finger on the page, next to a black leather jacket—fitted and feminine, but safe as well. Next to it were thick riding gloves, tapered and sleek but completely functional. This was the way forward. The dealership was going to carry better attire for women. And it wasn't going to ignore them as customers anymore—it was going to target them. In short, the dealership was going to execute Audrey's ideas in full.

On the conference room table was a file folder with Kieran's recent research on how many working female professionals there were in the area. He'd gathered statistical and demographic data, and the results were astounding. Vets, doctors, office managers, entrepreneurs—all women.

Now, it was his aim to train the sales staff to target these women, plus carry stock that actually appealed to them. If they could do it, the dealership could be doubling, maybe even tripling, its profits.

Fletch smoothed his bristly moustache. He didn't look convinced. "You say Audrey came up with this?"

Kieran nodded. "Audrey was the one who realized tha—"

He stopped as Audrey walked by the conference room on her way to the dealership floor to work. The points of her stilettos clicked on the hallway tiles, and the fringe on her cuffs fluttered like prairie grass. He stilled, surprised to see her today. He'd begun to wonder if she'd ever return at all, and if he'd have to fill the role with someone else. Frankly, a more shrewd manager would have fired her by now. Four days of calling in sick without an explanation was more than enough grounds for dismissal. Because, of course, he knew why she hadn't been in, and it wasn't the flu.

She'd been avoiding work so she could avoid *him*.

He watched her with a protective vise gripping his heart. Her athlete's body was poured into the same jeans and fitted leather top she always wore, but he suddenly hated her attire.

He wanted her clad in safe riding clothes, not sexy ones. He wanted her to sport a helmet that would protect her incredible mind. He wanted her fingers covered by gloves so that her hands wouldn't be soiled by the messy, dirty world around them.

He wanted her in something that reflected as much care for her insides as her outsides.

He leapt to his feet and dashed to the conference room door. Audrey saw him through the floor-to-ceiling glass and stopped. He pulled open the door. "You got a minute?" he asked. "Fletch and I were just meeting about your idea."

Her brown eyes widened. "You mean my business idea?"

He nodded. "The very same. I was just showing him a product catalog especially for women. Wondered if you wanted to weigh in."

Audrey's bewilderment turned to delight in the space of a half second. And that was exactly how long it took Kieran's heart to crumble into dust and settle at the bottom of his rib cage. If he could, he would spend his life working so that Audrey always looked this happy. He would toil for years to make her eyes glitter like this, if that was what it took.

Trying to stay focused, he ushered her into the room and seated her next to Fletch.

"Kieran was just saying you think the ladies need some different things from us," Fletch said, the tone of his voice indicating he still wasn't convinced. He slid the catalog over to her. "More like this?"

Audrey's eyes flicked briefly to the pictures on the pages. "That's just a small part of the big picture," she replied. "Women are earning more than they ever have, and we should be going after their business. I was looking online, and did you know that one in four motorcycle riders is a woman? But when they come into our showroom, we largely ignore them. We have racks of clothes for guys, but only a few items for women, and those pieces are a joke. Bikinis, baby-doll T-shirts, ridiculous shoes. They need *attire*. Actual riding gear. And if we carried it—if we actually respected and acknowledged that women were more than an accessory—I think it would be good for business."

Fletch shook his head. "I mean no disrespect, but it's a little ironic, hearing this from a woman who we're paying to be an accessory."

The edges of Kieran's vision darkened with anger. He was ready to storm Fletch, to take him by the throat and rattle him, but Audrey just laughed. "I get that," she said, "and add to that the irony that I never would have even *noticed* any of this if I wasn't out there sitting on a bike dressed like a female member of the Village People."

Fletch chuckled. "I can't say I've ever taken advice from anyone wearing a corset. But I know you know this town. You really think this can work?"

Audrey nodded. "I do."

Kieran wanted to pull Audrey into his arms, wanted to kiss her brilliant head and put his hands over her stunning heart, but instead he cleared his throat, businesslike. "I can recommend the initial changes, but Fletch is the one who will need to really implement them. He might need help. You up for that, Audrey?"

Audrey started. "Like really work with him on this whole thing?"

Kieran shrugged. He didn't want to push Fletch too far, but he also knew that this project could use Audrey's oversight. "Don't see why not. We could get you out of those chaps and into a business suit. Full time. Salaried."

He glanced at Fletch, whose eyebrows were arched with surprise, but at least he wasn't angry or irritated. His gut clenched with hope. *This could work.*

Audrey's thick lashes fluttered. "I don't know. I was thinking of starting my own business. This is—I don't know."

She was visibly flustered, and Kieran desperately

wanted to hold her, tell her to take her time deciding. "It's all right," he said instead. "Nothing has to be decided today. I just wanted to pull you into the conversation and make sure you knew your idea was being taken seriously."

From across the table, Audrey trained her eyes on his. The warmth there heated him from the inside out, sent hot flames dancing along his skin.

"Thank you," she said. "This means a lot."

Fletch's phone beeped, and he excused himself to answer it. Within seconds, it was just the two of them, facing each other across the wide conference room table.

Kieran glanced at the surface. It was smooth and plain and flat—the perfect surface on which to turn over his last, terrible card.

"Audrey," he said evenly, "there's something else I need to ask you."

* * *

Whatever else Kieran Callaghan might say to her, Audrey wasn't sure she was going to hear it. The stays on her corset were strained to breaking, and she couldn't get enough air into her lungs. Her heart felt like it was expanding by the second inside her chest.

He'd offered her a job. A real job because she had an exceptional idea and he'd *listened* to it. If her clothes would let her, she'd dance around the conference room like a fool.

Damn this outfit, she thought.

She wanted to stretch the leather and yank off the fringe and kick away these high heels forever. But, according to Kieran, she might not have to do any of that. She could just simply set it aside, and walk away.

He'd offered her a job. No, more than that. He'd taken her idea about female customers, mulled it over, shared it with Fletch, and they'd just pulled her into a discussion about it. He wanted her to help implement it.

Good God. First the rose petals, now this.

Her breath caught again, and she started to feel lightheaded. Tenderness filled her until she wondered if she'd burst. Across the table, Kieran stared at her. He'd said something about needing to talk more. Good Lord, she wasn't sure how much more she could take.

"I know this is an odd time," he began, his deep voice filling the empty room, "but there's something else I need to ask you. It has to do with what I started to say on Sunday. About what happened when we first met."

Audrey could feel her eyes widen. She thought she'd been more than clear with him that she didn't want to talk any more about their past, and yet here he was broaching it again. And at the dealership, no less.

Kieran held up a massive hand, clearly reading her expression. "I'll only ask you this one more time. Will you please hear me out? And when I'm done, if you need to leave, you can have the rest of the day off."

"Why would I need that?"

"Because what I have to say doesn't just affect me—it has to do with your family. You need to know the truth."

"My family?" she asked. "My parents are dead. All I have is Casey."

Kieran's pressed his lips together so that they almost disappeared. He simply nodded—once.

Audrey's warm excitement was instantly replaced by cold fear. It settled on her like an autumn fog rolling in from the river. Her whole body was rejecting the idea that

Kieran should say anything at all. Or that what he had to say could somehow involve her sister.

Oh God, she thought, what if Kieran and Casey had fallen for each other at some point, and that was why Casey wanted her as far away from Kieran as she could get?

The idea was baffling. And horrifying. It couldn't be true...could it?

Don't talk anymore, she wanted to tell him. *Let things be simple. Whatever happened doesn't matter. Let's just be friends and let it end there.*

But that was an impossible idea. Willa was right. Audrey was going to have to listen to this man. And then she was going to have to pray that her heart didn't end up dried and crumpled—in danger of being blown to oblivion from even the slightest breeze—when it was all over.

But even if it did, she had to take this chance. She had to seize this moment and face whatever it was that Kieran was trying to tell her.

Her voice shook as she tried to speak. "All right," she said, staring at the chiseled lines of his face. "Whatever it is, let's hear it."

"It's hard to know where to begin," he said, "but I think it starts with me having a gambling problem. And needing money. That's where your sister, Casey, comes in."

The name of her sister on his lips was so strange. Worse was the sadness lining Kieran's face. She wished his eyes would storm with anger, wished his muscles would clench with fury. Something about him being angry was far less scary than the sadness that was radiating off him.

Kieran took a breath. "I'd better start again."

Audrey listened as he poured out his story, her heart

plummeting farther into her body with every word until it was lodged in her heels and she was certain it would never beat inside her chest again.

"My sister?" she whispered. "She paid you to leave?"

Kieran nodded. "She thought I was a no-good. Not worthy of you. And in a way she was right, Audrey. I had a gambling problem. And I'm not sure I could have faced it if Casey hadn't sent me packing."

Audrey shook her head. She wanted to dislodge the information.

Kieran was a gambler. He had lost the money meant for his *sick mom.*

"I don't..." She started to form a thought, then stopped. As awful as it was to think of Kieran gambling away money meant for his mom, she was somehow less addled by that than the thought that her own sister had sent Kieran packing. The notion of it had her stomach roiling with nausea. Did her sister honestly think so little of her? Could that really be true?

"So why not just tell me?" Audrey asked, swallowing back tears. "Why not just tell me the truth?"

"Because then I wouldn't get the money," Kieran said. "Five years ago, I had to pick the money or you and I chose..." Here, his voice trembled dangerously. He took a breath. "I chose the money."

"But Casey knows you're back," Audrey said, grasping at logic. "So you violated the terms of the agreement. Only she hasn't said anything to me." *Ergo you are lying,* she thought. *This is all a bunch of hooey.*

"It paints us both in a bad light, so I can see why she'd wait. Only I couldn't wait. I thought I could come back here and just stay away from you and things would be fine, but that couldn't be further from the truth. I tried talking to her, to straighten things out, but it didn't go very well."

"You and Casey spoke recently?" The idea was dumbfounding.

"Yes. I told her I was going to try to repair our relationship. Needless to say, she wasn't exactly thrilled by the idea."

Audrey was still having trouble grasping that Casey and Kieran had spoken not just five years ago, but in the recent past.

Kieran exhaled. "I knew this wouldn't be easy for you to hear. I know she's your only family. But I will say this. She loves you, and she was only trying to help you. In her way."

"By manipulating my life behind the scenes?"

"Both of us are guilty of that. Not just Casey. If I could do it over again—if I could change my decisions—I would. I'm sure Casey would, too. I want you to know that I care for you so much. I've never stopped."

Kieran's voice was gravelly with emotion. Audrey's nerves knotted at the sound of it.

Audrey looked down at her hands. For so long, she'd wondered if she'd imagined what had transpired with Kieran all those years ago. She wondered if she'd made a mountain of emotion out of a situation that had barely been a grain of affection. If she'd imagined love, when he was imagining lust.

Turned out, she hadn't misread him. He'd cared for her. Their affection had been mutual.

It was almost enough to wash away the fact that he'd chosen money over her.

Almost.

Part of her wanted to rush headlong into his arms, to plunge her hands into his thick hair and pull his face toward hers. She would kiss away the worry etched into his brows. She would smooth away his concerns, absolve him of their mangled past.

She closed her eyes. The other part of her wanted to push him away and continue her course of independence. She hadn't needed Kieran Callaghan for five years, and she could let this conversation be the reason she didn't need him again—ever.

She could do either of these things, she knew. The options were right there, tearing her heart apart in an unwinnable battle. She could wrestle with those options as much as she liked, but the one thing she could *not* do was think that her sister—her closest living relative—had started this avalanche of misery in Audrey's life.

"I need time to digest all this," she said slowly.

"Of course."

"Honestly, I don't know if I believe you."

"Any part in particular?"

"About Casey. I don't—I can't see her doing any of this."

Couldn't she? No. Never.

"Then ask her," Kieran said.

"I will. But you should be there when I do."

"What purpose will that serve?"

Because you're an addict and maybe a liar, too.

"Because then we'll get everything out on the table. All of us. If she's lying, I'll know. Whatever happens from here, it happens with the truth front and center."

Then I'll have proof that I was naïve about many things—my job, my love life—but I wasn't misguided by the one constant in my life. By my sister.

Oh, God, she was almost yearning for Kieran to be making all this up.

"I'm not lying," Kieran insisted, his eyes flicking across Audrey's face.

"Then let's make sure of it tomorrow. I'm meeting Casey at the Paul Bunyan Diner at noon. Can you make it?"

"If that's what you want, then yes."

"It is."

Time passed, but whether it was seconds or minutes, Audrey wasn't sure. All she knew was that, at some point, she couldn't bear to have Kieran's concerned gaze on her another moment.

"I need to go," she said finally. She stood, tottering in her heels. Kieran reached out across the conference table, as if to steady her, then pulled his hand back.

"Tomorrow at noon," Audrey said, trying to sound strong.

"I'll be there."

Not daring to look at Kieran again, Audrey left the conference room. She could feel her shattered heart pressing against her skin—but whether it was broken over the truth about Kieran or the idea that her own sister had orchestrated the most destructive concert of Audrey's life, she wasn't at all sure.

CHAPTER TWENTY

*I*t was early, not even noon, but Audrey wanted a drink.

After the morning she'd had, she figured she might just have *six* drinks.

In fact, she was fairly determined that she wanted to drink asparagus beer until she couldn't remember who Kieran Callaghan was. Steering her car out of the Harley dealership parking lot and into the bright May sun, she drove to the Wheelhouse Bar.

* * *

The smell of spilled beer and old wood greeted Audrey as she opened the door to the Wheelhouse. The space was dim, the jukebox was quiet, and no one else was there. She looked at her watch. No wonder it was deserted—it was only ten fifty. Not even eleven o'clock yet.

This *was* desperate.

Ignoring every voice inside her head telling her to leave now and go for a long run, Audrey shimmied herself onto a worn leather stool at the bar. She was still wearing her outfit from the dealership, and she desperately wanted to peel off the constrictive layers, but she didn't have anything else to put on. She'd reeled out of White Pine Harley, barely aware of anything, much less her clothes.

Now, she was at a bar looking like an alcoholic S&M Barbie.

Fabulous.

Nevertheless, she folded her hands and waited for someone to notice she was there.

After a moment, Dave Englund emerged from the kitchen door to Audrey's right carrying a dish rack full of clean glasses. He stopped abruptly when he spotted her. Audrey couldn't be sure, but it looked like he tightened his grip on the large plastic rack, perhaps to keep from dropping it.

"Audrey?" he asked, his head tilting slightly. If his black hair had been longer, it would have flopped.

"Hey, Dave," Audrey said, smiling too big. She worried that she looked freakish, trying to pretend it was totally normal for her to be sitting on a barstool, dressed in a corset at ten fifty in the morning. "How've you been?"

Dave walked over and set the clean glasses next to the bar's stainless steel sink. "Ah, fine, I suppose." She wondered if he'd mention the other night, maybe chastise her for the way she'd flirted and then run off with Kieran, but instead he was staring at her with something like concern lining his face. "And you?"

His emphasis on the word *you* was unmistakable. The subtext all but screamed: What are you doing here?

"I'm great," she lied. "Never better. I was just hoping I could get a little more of that asparagus beer. I promise to keep it to myself, just like last time. Pinkie swear." She held out her pinkie and instantly regretted it. What was she, sixteen?

Dave stared at her. "Beer came out yesterday. Festival starts tonight, you know."

"Right," Audrey said, pulling back her errant digit. Of course she didn't have to keep the beer a secret—the festival would be in full swing soon, no doubt right about the time she was parading around hoping to be crowned Asparagus Queen.

"Can I just have some, then?"

Dave grabbed a clean glass off the rack he'd just brought in. He pulled the tap's handle, and Audrey watched the golden liquid flow, her spirits already lifting.

Dave placed it on the bar.

"Thanks," she said, and immediately tipped it back. The ice-cold beer went down her throat like bubbly, asparagus-y heaven. After she swallowed, a small hiccup escaped her. And no wonder. She'd consumed half a pint in one gulp.

Audrey looked from the glass to Dave, who was just standing there. "It's good," she offered.

"Best batch I've made so far." He said it lightly enough, but she could see worry creasing the skin just above his dark brows. A moment passed. She took another sip, just to avoid having to look at him.

"You going to hit the festival, then?" Dave asked.

Audrey nodded. "I filed the paperwork to be in the running for Asparagus Queen."

"You don't say."

"Is that surprising?"

"No, not at all. Not that I want that hunky boyfriend of yours glaring at me for saying so."

Audrey shook her head. "He's not my boyfriend."

"Huh. The way the two of you were going at it on the dance floor the other night, I just assumed—"

"He's *not* my boyfriend."

Another moment passed. "Is that possibly the reason you're in here drinking before noon on a Friday?"

"No."

Dave lifted a brow.

"Oh, I don't know," Audrey said, exasperated. She swallowed down more beer. "I feel like I don't even know what's even going *on* anymore."

But of course that wasn't exactly true. She certainly knew that what she wanted—desperately—was to take a chance on Kieran again. But he'd put her in an impossible situation. If he was lying about Casey, then he was just a no-good fibber and gambler, same as he'd always been. But if he was telling the truth, then it meant he and Casey had plotted behind her back and conspired against her five years ago. And to turn the other cheek for them both would require a level of forgiveness she wasn't sure she could reach.

Dave set down his towel and joined her. His strong, lean frame sat on the barstool in one easy motion.

"I don't normally do this," Dave said. "Fraternizing with the customers, I mean."

"But you'll make an exception for me?" Audrey asked, taking in his tight black T-shirt, his black hair, and his brown eyes. Up this close, she could see they were such a rich, golden color they were almost amber.

"We go back," Dave said, shrugging.

Audrey tried to conjure the spine tingles from the other night, when Dave had flirted with her. *Here is an attractive man,* she thought, *and we're alone.* But the idea went nowhere. Whatever sparks Dave had started to ignite, Kieran had made sure they'd gone out. Kieran was so large in her mind and her heart, there just wasn't room for anyone else. Possibly ever.

Audrey barely held back a groan at the thought. The only silver lining in the situation was that there seemed to be a platonic easiness between her and Dave. Possibly he'd also come to the conclusion they'd make better friends.

"I remember in middle school," Dave was saying, "when our English teacher had us write about the person we want to be most like when we grow up. And all the other kids said basketball players or rock stars or actresses, and you said—who was it again? Some kind of veterinarian?"

"James Herriot," Audrey replied, blushing at the memory. "A British author and vet." She stared at Dave's boyish face. "You remember that?"

"I do. It was just so different. At the time, I probably thought *nerd*—"

"Thanks a lot."

"No, but now, when I think back on it, it's really amazing. You had the most individual idea of any of us. You were doing your own thing before it was cool. I admire that. Especially since, well, here I am, tending a bar and the most individual thing I get to do is make asparagus beer once a year."

"But it's so good," Audrey said, draining the rest of her glass.

"I just wish I could do it more often. Make craft beer, I mean. I'd make all kinds of seasonal ales. A White Pine winter ale with nutmeg and cloves, for example. Or a summer shandy with lemons and maybe a hint of lavender from Cleve Ferber's farm. That is, if the lavender worked. I'm not sure it would."

Audrey smiled at Dave's excitement. Even in the dimly lit space, she could see warm color on his cheeks and happiness crinkling the corners of his eyes.

"All I'm saying," Dave continued, "is that I went with the crowds, partied my ass off, barely graduated high school, and now look at me. Bartender at the Wheelhouse. But you figured out how to go your own way early on. Or, at least, you stayed true to you."

Audrey caught a glimpse of herself in the bar's mirror. "I don't know if that's exactly right. I think maybe I'm evolving. Like maybe I was one thing for a while, and now I'm ready to try something different."

Dave got up and went back around the bar to pour Audrey another glass. He set it in front of her.

"You have the guts to try and figure it out, Audrey. And that's what's so amazing. How many people in this town would have the courage to even attempt something like a gig at a Harley dealership after their career imploded? That's what I noticed when you came in the other night. It wasn't just that you looked good—I mean, you did, you *do*—but the more impressive thing was that you'd been brave enough to try something new, to do your own thing yet again. It's admirable."

Audrey stared at the bubbles in her beer. "Thank you," she said, feeling completely overwhelmed by Dave's words.

"I'm saying all this hoping we can be friends," Dave said, wiping the bar distractedly. "I know you like that guy you were with the other night. Obviously you do, or you wouldn't be in here. I just didn't want you thinking any of what I was saying was connected to an ulterior motive. It's not."

"I appreciate that," Audrey replied. "I could use more friends." She said it thinking about Casey, and what she'd do if her sister had been lying to her for the past five years. Would she still want Casey in her life? And if not, how would she fill the gap? Her head ached at the thought.

"For what it's worth," she pressed on, lifting her beer and staring at the glass, "I think this town could use a craft brewery. This stuff is good, Dave. Really good. Betty Sondheim could help you if you wanted to talk about a possible business plan. She's really amazing with that kind of thing."

"Isn't that Betty Lindholm, from high school?" When Audrey nodded, Dave shuddered. "No way. She scares me."

Audrey laughed. "She scares all of us a little. But she's solid. A real friend."

Just then, the door to the bar opened, letting in a sliver of light and a blast of fresh air. A cluster of well-dressed men entered, seating themselves in a booth by the jukebox.

"Ah, the lunch rush," Dave said, grabbing a handful of menus. "And by rush I mean trickle. More of a drip, really."

Audrey giggled. Dave placed one of the menus in front of her. "You eat something, too," he said. "And when you're ready, I'll call you a cab."

"But—"

"It's nonnegotiable. Sorry. I can't have my asparagus beer get you in any trouble."

Audrey thought about Kieran, about Casey, about tomorrow's Asparagus Queen pageant. "I feel like I'm already in trouble."

"*More* trouble, then," Dave said, winking. He walked

over to wait on the lunch table while Audrey studied the menu. She decided on cheese curds and another beer.

She fully expected her pants to pop wide open before the end of it, and she barely even cared.

* * *

She was dying.

No, Audrey realized, she was dead. She was deceased and this was hell, and for all of eternity she'd be punished with this sour taste in her mouth and this sound of six fire trucks blaring through her head.

Where were all these engines coming from, anyway? She struggled to think, struggled to remember where she was. Her brain was sludge-filled and her whole body was rejecting every single movement.

She unstuck one eye. Daylight scorched her vision and she groaned. Slowly, she tried again, opening her eyes a millimeter at a time, until she could see without so much pain. Eventually, she began to glimpse her own curtains. Which meant the engine noises reverberating everywhere were probably her alarm clock.

She reached out, fumbling for the damn thing, trying to find the snooze button. When silence fell, she sighed, relieved.

Until her eyes were fully open and she grasped what time it was.

She sat bolt upright. *Cripes, how many times had she hit snooze?*

It was after eleven o'clock, and she was due at the Paul Bunyan Diner by noon. And she still had to get ready for the pageant.

"Shit," Audrey muttered, stumbling out of bed to the bathroom. Aspirin first. Water second.

I will never drink asparagus beer again, she thought as she uncapped her bottle of aspirin and tapped out three. Dimly she could remember hanging out at the Wheelhouse for hours—drinking, eating cheese curds, talking with Dave, and chatting with random folks, some strangers, some acquaintances, who peppered the bar throughout the day.

Sometime in the evening, Dave had called her a taxi (or *the* taxi, more accurately, since White Pine only had one) and she'd been shuttled home. She figured she went to bed at that point, and had sunk into a drunken oblivion.

Audrey padded from her bathroom to her kitchen, then stopped short. There was an empty wine bottle on the counter and one glass. She closed her eyes.

She hadn't gone to bed. She'd kept drinking.

She cringed when she noticed there were cookbooks scattered everywhere, open to random pages. She could dimly recall wanting to help Dave find new beer recipes. She flushed with embarrassment as she realized she'd scribbled down new ale ideas. They were scrawled on a notepad next to the empty wine bottle:

APpLe CHesTNuT

CUcuMbeR TUrMeriC oAtMeAL

FrIEd OrEo cHeDDaR

Audrey swallowed back both nausea and mortification. *Fried Oreo cheddar?* For a beer? Good God, she *had* been hammered.

Suddenly, her body flushed with adrenaline and her mind sharpened to an uncomfortable point. Had she texted Dave any of this? Her head still pounding, she groped for her phone, eventually finding it in the bottom of her purse. It had been shut off, thankfully.

Dave, she thought. He'd saved her from herself.

He really was a friend.

She turned the phone back on, swallowed the aspirin, and began the painful process of getting ready for the pageant with a massive hangover. At eleven fifty-five, she had squeezed her bloated, aching self into Willa's dress, donned her shabby (albeit recently repaired) heels, and teetered down her sidewalk wearing sunglasses that barely helped dim the glare in her eyes and head. She pulled out the keys to her car, only to stop short.

She *had* no car. It was still at the Wheelhouse.

"Shit!" she cried. Then she clasped her hand over her mouth. The neighbor's kids were out in their front yard. They'd stopped playing to gape at her, their eyes round with surprise.

She didn't even bother saying sorry. Reaching into her purse, she grabbed her phone yet again and dialed the other person she knew was headed exactly where she was going.

Kieran answered on the third ring.

"Can you pick me up?" Audrey asked. "I need a ride to the diner."

Ten minutes later, with chaps on under her dress (it was the only thing Audrey could think of to satisfy Kieran's demand that she wear long pants) and Kieran's helmet crushing what little volume she'd been able to tease into her hair, the two roared over the Birch River and down Main Street, on their way to meet Casey.

* * *

"Wait, Audrey—please," Kieran begged as they walked from the parking lot to the front entrance of the Paul Bunyan Diner. Kieran reached out and grabbed Audrey's arm, even though the last thing she looked like she wanted was for anyone, especially him, to touch her. "Just...*take* a second."

To his relief, Audrey stopped. Kieran wanted to straighten the crumpled, sparkling dress clinging to her body at odd angles. He wanted to wipe away the errant mascara underneath her eyes, and smooth the ends of her wind-blown hair. She'd taken off her sunglasses and now her brown eyes were roving with a manic exhaustion.

She was hungover, there was no doubt. But there was something else, too. Kieran's jaw clenched with the realization that Audrey Tanner was afraid. The strongest woman he knew was barely holding it together as she prepared to face her sister—and him. Together.

He wanted to pull her to him and kiss away her fears. He wanted to reassure her that it would be all right, that he would always be there for her. It was of no comfort to him that the woman he cared for most in the world was about to find out the truth about what he and her sister had done. It would hardly acquit him, and it might crush Audrey.

Frankly, she looked half crushed already.

He saw Audrey take a deep breath. She smoothed down her dress, which helped a bit, but not much. "All right," she said, and more light came into her eyes. Kieran was relieved to see it, even if it was a small victory. "We're already late. Let's go."

She walked ahead of him and he followed, clenching his fists. He felt like he was going into the ring and this was going to be the fight of his life.

CHAPTER TWENTY-ONE

Her stomach roiling, Audrey reached out and grasped Kieran's arm for support. She didn't want to enter the diner like this—unsteady in her glittering dress and clutching Kieran Callaghan—but in this case she had no choice. It was either that or topple over.

As the pair entered the diner, Audrey hoped it was her imagination that the clank of silverware and the murmur of conversation dropped off. What wasn't her imagination, however, was the picture of Casey's mortified face from a nearby booth—her open "O" of a mouth, and her eyes glazed with shock.

Lifting her chin, Audrey forced a smile and headed over. Kieran followed next to her, propping her up.

Audrey's smile vanished when she realized Casey wasn't alone. There was a man in the booth with her, wearing a smart charcoal suit and an asparagus-green tie. He looked up and his eyes visibly widened. Nevertheless, he stood to greet her.

Audrey glanced quizzically at her sister. Casey's face had gone bleach white and her hands were trembling. "Audrey," she managed to croak, "this is Kyle Williams, the principal at Eagan High School. Kyle, this is my sister, Audrey Tanner."

"Hello, Audrey," Kyle said politely. Nausea crested in the back of her throat. Audrey reached out to take Kyle's hand.

"P—pleased to meet you," she managed.

Casey looked like she was either going to faint or erupt. "I told Audrey you were coming *when we chatted on the phone last Thursday*," Casey said through clenched teeth. "Perhaps she forgot."

Audrey's stomach sank. Last Thursday. The conversation at the county offices. The one where she'd barely been listening.

"I'm Kieran Callaghan," came the deep voice from beside her. Audrey turned, grateful for the distraction. The two men shook hands.

"He's a friend," Audrey said quickly. "He's…ah, helping me today. I'm entering the Asparagus Queen pageant. Thus, the dress."

"Oh, I see," Kyle said. Audrey noted he was in his fifties, with salt-and-pepper hair and kind, pale blue eyes. Guilt washed over her.

"I didn't realize you…that this…" Audrey trailed off. Her foggy, asparagus-beer-coated brain didn't know what other words to form.

"There's clearly been a mix-up," Kieran offered, somewhat unhelpfully. Casey narrowed her eyes at him.

"It's no problem," Kyle said graciously. "Perhaps we should just chat a different day then."

Chat about what? Audrey wanted to ask. But of course she knew already. Casey had no doubt set up a pre-interview with Kyle to try to lure Audrey away to Eagan, to be their track coach. Never mind that Audrey didn't know if she wanted the job. Never mind that she'd said as much. It was what *Casey* wanted, so she was pulling strings again.

Just like she did with Kieran.

Audrey fought the idea. She would *not* jump to conclusions.

"Kyle, I'm so sorry," she said. "My sister had the best of intentions, but I clearly wasn't tracking on them. I guess I got pretty wrapped up in the Asparagus Queen pageant."

And I don't want this job, she thought, but held her tongue.

"Certainly. Best of luck today," Kyle said. "Take care." With a final nod at Casey, he exited the diner.

Which left the three of them, bewildered and angry, all staring at one another.

"Sit down," Casey hissed at her after a moment. "Right now. And get this loser out of here. I can't believe you'd bring Kieran along! As if he hasn't done enough to this family already."

Audrey closed her eyes and willed herself to stay calm. Part of her wanted to agree with Casey and shove Kieran out the door, right behind Kyle Williams. But instead she sat, pulling Kieran into the booth next to her. "He stays," she said evenly.

"You're going to argue with me?" Casey cried. "After what you just did? Audrey Tanner, what has gotten into you? How could you show up looking like this? It's bad enough on any day, but on the day when the *principal* of Eagan High was here to meet you for a job that y—"

"Shut *up*, Casey."

Audrey squared her shoulders and placed both hands on the smooth, worn wood of their table.

The lines on Casey's face deepened with anger. "Excuse me?"

"Please, just pipe down," Audrey said. Next to her, Kieran relaxed slightly. For some reason, the motion gave her courage. It was as if Kieran knew she was finding her strength—or trying to—and he was more at ease because of it.

Casey pressed her thin lips together. Clearly her sister had words, but she held them back. Audrey took the opportunity to flag down Pauline for a cup of coffee. "And bacon. And hash browns." Anything greasy sounded like heaven. Kieran got coffee as well. Casey stuck with water.

Audrey took a moment to collect her thoughts. She wrapped her hands around the ceramic mug Pauline brought her and watched the steam rise from the hot coffee.

"I need to ask you some questions," Audrey said finally. She met her sister's gaze firmly.

"What questions?"

"Questions about what happened five years ago. When Kieran and I first met."

Casey's already pale face whitened even more. "What about it?"

"Did you give Kieran money? And did you give it to him on the condition that he leave and never see me again?"

Casey laughed, but it was a hollow, terrible sound. "*No. Of course not. No.* Did he tell you that?"

Audrey nodded, watching her sister closely. She could remember when they were kids and Casey had taken ten dollars from their aunt Lodi's purse. It was so the two of them could go see a movie together, which their aunt never would have allowed normally. After they returned from the matinee, Lodi had noticed the missing cash and confronted them both. Audrey had clammed up in terror, but Casey had lied convincingly, smoothly. Only Audrey had noticed what gave the lies away: how her sister repeated certain words.

"So you and Kieran have never talked privately?" Audrey asked. "You've never discussed the topic of, say, *me* when I haven't been in the room?"

Casey gave an exasperated sigh. "Audrey, this is ridiculous. I don't want to have to defend myself against this. It's ridiculous."

Curious. "Which means," Audrey pressed on, "that your bank records wouldn't show payments from Kieran over the past five years, reimbursing you for the thousands you'd given him?"

"Audrey, you've gone mad. I can't believe this. No. You're mad to ask such a thing. Mad."

She wasn't imagining it. Audrey could feel tears stinging her eyes. Or maybe it was just exhaustion. Or the fact that the awful truth she suspected was erupting to the surface of her life.

She looked at Kieran. She didn't know what she'd see in his pale green eyes—victory or maybe even vindication—but she was startled by the compassion there. By the layers of emotions. The love. The loss. He knew Casey was lying, too. And his heart was breaking right along with Audrey's.

Audrey took a deep, shuddery breath. Her whole body

was sore—a feeling like she'd been dragged through rocks and mud. Her sister had manipulated the course of the last five years of Audrey's life.

"Casey," Audrey said, searching to find the right words, fighting to make them mean something, "I don't believe you. I believe Kieran."

Casey huffed. "Then you're making a terrible mistake if you trust that lying, gambling man before your own sister."

Kieran stiffened, but remained silent. Anger knotted Audrey's stomach at the insult. A hot wave of intense fury, and then her mind went blank with sudden realization. "How did you know he was a gambler?"

"What do you mean *know*? Of course I know. Everyone knows."

"I didn't," Audrey said softly. "Not until recently."

Casey opened her mouth, then closed it.

"But you knew," Audrey said, hating the terrible, true words, "because of the deal you made."

"To help you!" her sister cried. "To protect you from him."

Audrey swallowed back tears. She wanted her sister to take it all back, to undo the terrible rip she was creating between them. Instead, Audrey pressed ahead, willing Casey to hear her, to understand and to apologize. "But I didn't need you to. Not like that, anyway. Not without talking to me."

Casey's body went rigid. "Anyone could see that this man was no good. He was a risk. And you were foolish. Honestly, you should be thanking me. I saved you."

"Saved me from what, exactly?"

"From the world, Audrey. A huge, hurtful world that would have crushed you if I hadn't been there. You being on the track team, you getting into college—all because of me. There were days growing up that you wouldn't have eaten because of me. So don't you dare sit there and say that suddenly you don't need me."

Audrey's heart sank. Casey had always been her protector. She'd sacrificed so much just so Audrey would have a decent chance in life. Audrey could still remember the feel of her sister's arms around her at night, comforting her while Audrey sobbed, wondering what would become of them without their parents.

Casey was the one who had ensured everything turned out all right.

"I do need you," Audrey whispered. "I always have. Just not like this. Not with you lying to me and trying to make my life into what you think it should be. It's not your choice, Casey. It's not your path."

"It was always my path," Casey said tightly, "because it was *our* path. You and me together."

Two girls against the world. The memories of what they'd been through together crushed Audrey and had resentment burning through her at the same time. No matter the past, it wasn't fair for Casey to take her options away before she could even consider them.

"But at a time when you needed to let me find my own way, you didn't. That was a mistake."

Casey's eyes filled with hurt. But in an instant, she blinked it away. "The mistake here is yours, Audrey. Not mine."

The offhand way Casey was able to dismiss her tore at the fiber of Audrey's being. She could practically hear the tiny rips. She barely held back the sobs that wanted to break from her throat.

"Then I guess this conversation is over for now," Audrey said, pushing past the pain. She stood. Kieran got to his feet, too.

Casey stared into her water glass, pretending not to notice that they were leaving. Audrey blinked back tears, wishing her sister would at least say good-bye—never mind sorry.

Just at that moment, Pauline brought their food "Breakfast is on *her*," Audrey said, lifting her chin in her sister's direction. And then she turned on her shabby heel and left.

* * *

Outside the diner, Audrey let her tears fall, ruining what was left of her mascara. Her shoulders rounded as she buried her face in her hands, sobbing next to Kieran's motorcycle.

Hungover and bawling in a parking lot, she thought to herself. *Perfect.*

Dimly, she was aware of Kieran pulling her into his arms. She didn't fight it. Her brain was such a jumble of thoughts she hardly knew where to begin. Especially with him. He'd taken money from her sister and left all those years ago.

But he came back and told her the truth.

And he said he still cared.

She wanted to close her eyes and just go to sleep to the sound of his heart. She'd sleep for days if she could against his strong form. Yet, when she opened her eyes, could she really be sure he'd still be there? He'd confessed his past, it was true, but how sure could she be that he'd changed and wouldn't run out on her all over again?

There was another nagging thought at the edge of her mind as well. She pulled away and stared at Kieran. She was missing something. There was something she was supposed to be—

"Oh my God, the *pageant*!" she cried. "What time is it?"

Kieran pulled out his phone. "Five after one."

"I'm late!"

Audrey slung her purse over her shoulder and immediately started walking toward the festival at the center of town, just a few short blocks away. Kieran fell into step beside her.

"Audrey, I don't mean to rain on your parade here, but are you sure this is a good idea?"

Audrey quickened her pace. "Of course it's a good idea. I entered. They're expecting me."

"Sweetheart," he said softly, and she nearly faltered at the gentleness of the word on his lips. "You are hungover, and you just discovered your sister has been lying to you for five years. You are lovely, but right now, I have to say, you're not at your best. Are you sure you want to do this?"

Audrey was trotting now, jogging as best she could in her tattered heels. "I am one hundred percent sure," she said.

Kieran jogged next to her. To his credit, he didn't argue further. But outside the pageant tent, amid crowds wearing asparagus crowns and drinking asparagus beer, he grasped her hand. "I'll be watching. If you need anything, I'll be there."

She nodded, not sure what to say. Two children barreled past wearing green bath towels as capes. When no other words would come, she ducked inside the pageant tent, leaving Kieran staring after her.

CHAPTER TWENTY-TWO

*T*his was the definition of the phrase *train wreck*.

Kieran threaded his way past all the festival-goers as tent flaps snapped and fluttered in the breeze, looking for any sign of Audrey's friend. What was her name?

Willa.

He needed to find her—or, hell, find anyone who could help him pull Audrey off of the festival's plywood stage. Women were already lining up, heels clacking on the wood, all as candidates for Asparagus Queen. A man in a dark blazer and dark pants was directing them where to stand.

Hungover, rumpled, tear-stained, and emotionally fragile, Audrey was going to be a pageant mess. Not to mention that dress of hers was going to pose a problem.

Kieran loved it in theory. It was glittering and beautiful, elegant and polished when it was clean and crisp. But today, the dress was out of joint. It was rumpled from the motorcycle ride and stained with mascara-heavy tears. Audrey's old, leather heels didn't work with it at all. Next to the other women onstage, Audrey was going to look unkempt and undone.

Kieran stopped and stretched to his tiptoes, straining to see over the crowd. It was futile. He'd be lucky to recognize Willa one-on-one. In this throng, there was no way he'd find her.

Which meant it would be up to him to help Audrey.

But what could he do?

And who was to say she even wanted his help?

"Good afternoon, ladies and gentlemen, and welcome!" The man on the stage had a microphone in his hand and was grinning at the crowd assembled in front of him. "Welcome to the thirteenth annual Asparagus Queen pageant! I'm Leif Jenssen, your emcee for the event. And also your friendly neighborhood mechanic, so remember to *bring your car to Jenssen's and we'll give it attentions.*"

The crowd cheered and Kieran swallowed. Blessed beads of the rosary, the whole town must be here. The whole town except Audrey.

He counted six women on the stage. None of them were her.

Where was she? Hope ballooned inside Kieran that perhaps she'd decided to forgo the whole affair entirely.

"As you know," Leif said, pacing the stage in his dark suit, "we ask our contenders a series of five questions each. Our esteemed panel of community members will judge the answers based on city knowledge, civic pride, service ethics, and overall integrity." He pointed to a folding table where four locals were smiling and waving at the crowd.

From behind Leif there was a thud and a shuffling noise.

He turned, along with every set of eyes in the tent, to
see Audrey struggling to find her footing on the makeshift
steps off to the stage's side. She was grasping the railing
and trying to get her foot off the last step and up onto the
plywood, a task made nearly impossible by the glittering
hem of her dress.

"Well, looks like we have a late contender!" Leif said
graciously. He walked over to give Audrey a hand, which
she accepted, sweating and huffing. Kieran held his breath
as Leif pulled Audrey onto the stage. The crowd tittered as
they took her in—hair askew, makeup a mess, sweaty and
waxy looking. Not to mention in a rumpled, stained dress.
Leif directed Audrey to her place on the stage, while Kieran
glared at the people closest to him, daring anyone nearby to
so much as exhale with amusement.

"We'll start with our questions to ascertain city knowledge," Leif said, continuing like a true professional. He
pulled an index card out of his pocket. "And our first contender is Jeannie Swanson! Jeannie, come on forward."

A thirty-something woman in a high-waisted teal satin
dress—leftover bridesmaid's attire, Kieran surmised—
stepped next to Leif. Jeannie smiled at Leif, then the
crowd.

"Now, we want to get to know all our contestants a
bit. Also we want to make sure folks know we don't dis-
criminate when it comes to the title of Asparagus Queen.
Women who wear the crown can be either married or single, and you're the former, is that correct?"

Jeannie nodded. "I'm married to a wonderful man, Wil-
son, and we have two daughters, Brianne and Renee."

"Wonderful. Now tell me, Jeannie, for your first question, how did White Pine get its name?"

"Oh, well that one's easy. White pine was the kind of tree that the lumberjacks used to cut around here, then float on the Birch River down to the sawmills."

Leif grinned. "That is one hundred percent correct! Well done. You can step back in line now."

On and on they went, until finally Leif came to Audrey. She was blinking in the dim light, as if trying to stay focused, and she didn't smile as she found her place next to Leif onstage.

"All right, Audrey Tanner. It says here you're a former gym teacher but you are starting your own business. What business is that?"

Audrey licked her dry, lipstick-free lips. Kieran could see the wheels struggling to turn in her hungover brain. "I—uh—want to—uh—do prrmp trmunp," she mumbled into the microphone. Kieran struggled to make sense of the words. What was she saying?

"Pole dancing!" Leif said, his eyebrows nearly shooting off his forehead in surprise. "Well, now that's a first." The crowd erupted into giggles of amusement and murmurs of disapproval.

Audrey shook her head, her hands flailing for the microphone. She hadn't said pole dancing, Kieran realized.

"You misunderstood!" Kieran shouted, but his voice was lost in the crowd's buzzing. Onstage, Leif was anxious to move on, past the unsavory career choice he'd misheard.

"All right, Audrey," Leif said quickly, "tell us what item of clothing the White Pine Historical Museum has that once belonged to city founder Jebediah Stronghouse."

Audrey swallowed. She was so pale that Kieran worried she would pass out. She gave an unflattering tug on the hem of her dress. "His h—hat," she managed.

"That's correct!" Leif said, returning to Jeannie Swanson without another look at Audrey. Kieran's heart crumpled at her horrified expression. Dear God, she looked like she was going to burst into tears, and she'd only answered *one* question. There were four more to go.

Kieran barely moved as the second question was asked of woman after woman: *Tell us about how you've helped someone recently.*

When it was her turn, Audrey blinked at the crowd. Kieran could see Leif standing farther away this time, as if she was somehow unsavory. Audrey's eyes were focused somewhere over the crowd's heads. Silence settled in the tent. You could hear every shoe scrape and every cough. *She's in shock,* Kieran realized.

Pain tore through him. He had to help her. He could not—would not—let her humiliate herself any further.

So he took a breath and did the only thing he could.

He stormed the stage.

* * *

Audrey struggled to breathe. The dress's fabric was too heavy, laden with far too many crystals, and hot against her skin. She was claustrophobic in it, and thought she might overheat. Her limbs were numb and tingling, and she wasn't sure how much longer her legs would support her weight.

To call the pageant a disaster was an understatement. In the crowd, one woman glared at her, then grabbed the hand of her young daughter and yanked her out of the tent.

They think I'm a pole dancer, she thought, her chest tight with panic. Next to her, Leif was saying something, but she couldn't make out the words. Time was wobbling and warping—slowing down and speeding up so she couldn't tell where one moment ended and the next began.

I am such a screwup, she thought, tears pooling in her eyes. The next idea pierced her like a stab wound: *Maybe my sister was right. Maybe I* can't *do anything right on my own.*

She feared that the sudden rumbling in her ears was the blood rushing to her head in scarlet mortification. But then, to her surprise, the rumbling reached a crescendo in *front* of her, and Kieran Callaghan came roaring out of the crowd.

She struggled to stay upright as he vaulted onstage. Beside her, Leif Jenssen went rigid. He lifted the microphone to his mouth but didn't seem to be able to find any words to say into it.

Kieran's thick motorcycle boots clomped as he walked over to Leif and whispered something in his ear. Leif stared at him for a moment, then nodded.

And then he did the most astonishing thing: *He handed Kieran Callaghan the microphone.*

Kieran took it, then stood next to Audrey, who decided she was hallucinating this whole thing. The pageant wasn't really happening. It couldn't be. No way Kieran Callaghan was standing next to her onstage. She would wake up soon, warm in her own cozy bed, and she'd laugh later when she told the whole Knots and Bolts gang what she'd dreamed.

The feel of Kieran's arm around her waist was all too real, though. His muscled body was a tower next to her exhausted frame, and she leaned into him.

When she chanced to look up at him, his sea-colored

eyes churned with a tempest of emotion. He tore his gaze from hers to address the crowd under the tent.

"My name is Kieran Callaghan and I work at the White Pine Harley dealership that opened up recently." His strong, steady voice reverberated in every part of Audrey's body. His grip tightened around her waist. "I don't know many of you, but *many of you do know Audrey*. And because you know her, it'll be clear to you that your friend and neighbor isn't feeling too well right now."

He took a breath, his broad chest expanding. "This is a town filled with good people, and so I'm sure you all will extend to Audrey the same grace and understanding you'd want if you were up on this stage right now."

There were murmurs in the tent. For a moment, Kieran looked like he was going to hand the microphone back to Leif, but then changed his mind.

"Just one more thing," he said, his voice gravelly with an emotion Audrey couldn't quite place. "I'd like to answer the last question Leif asked—the one about helping someone recently—by saying that Audrey Tanner's kindness and faith in me changed the course of my life. She helped me, that's for sure. And I know she's changed many of you out there as well." He paused, as if collecting his thoughts. Inside the tent, people were looking around as if to say, *Who is this guy?*

"I know Audrey Tanner has taught many of your children at school," Kieran said, "and I know she's helped get some young women track scholarships for college. When your kids were in trouble, I know many of you went to Audrey, because she's the teacher who would help. And she's *still* helping your kids, believe it or not, even though the school decided to let her go."

Audrey blinked. Was she really hearing this? Kieran was defending her, and, improbably, the town was listening. She looked out at the crowd and saw softened faces, even a few smiles.

"Audrey Tanner isn't a pole dancer," Kieran continued. "She's a personal trainer. She's trying to start her own business, and if you're smart, you'll support her because she'll be amazing at it. And even if she was a pole dancer, it wouldn't matter. Audrey can be a dancer or an Asparagus Queen or a janitor for all anyone should care. Because she's perfect, just as she is. She is astounding."

He cleared his throat into the mic, sending reverb blasting through the tent.

When the screech of the amplifiers was finished, Audrey could hear clapping and cheering from a small section of the tent. She searched the crowd to see Willa, Betty, Stephanie, and Anna, all whooping and hollering like mad.

The next thing she knew, she was back in Kieran Callaghan's arms and being whisked offstage.

CHAPTER TWENTY-THREE

*O*utside the tent, the sun was blindingly bright. Audrey blinked, only dimly aware of the polka band oompah-ing a few yards away, the charcoal smell of asparagus brats wafting through the air, and the drum major for the parade—a life-sized asparagus with epaulets—readying this year's participants for the short, three-block march.

She was much *more* aware of Kieran Callaghan carrying her, of his arms cradling her close and his rumbling growl of "Excuse me," as he shoved past festival-goers. After two blocks of felted crafts, flapping asparagus flags, and trees wrapped in green crepe paper, he finally cleared the bounds of the festivities on Main Street and stopped at a bench outside of Loon Call Antiques. Gently, his breath coming in low rasps, he placed her on the wooden surface, then knelt in front of her. If she didn't know better, she'd think he was proposing.

"Are you all right?" he asked. He grasped her hands in

his and squeezed—a movement that was both thrilling and reassuring.

Audrey stared at the man who had just rescued her from social suicide in front of the entire town and wondered how to answer. Was she all right?

Her sister had lied to her.

The whole town had briefly thought she was a pole dancer.

She was desperately hungover.

And yet Kieran had saved her, and her friends had cheered for her. Audrey straightened, trying to think clearly. "I'll—I think I'll be fine," she said. She was also going to be embarrassed and horrified for weeks, maybe years. She tried not to dwell on it.

"I'm proud of you," Kieran said gently, rubbing his thumbs over her knuckles. The movement made Audrey's dry throat even more desert-like. If he meant it to be comforting, it wasn't. The subtle brushes had tiny shocks electrifying her bones, creating fissures so the energy went straight into her marrow.

"Proud of the village idiot?"

"You are not," he argued. "A lesser person wouldn't have gotten up on that stage at all. Not after the kind of morning you had. But you got up there."

"A smarter person wouldn't have gotten up there, you mean," Audrey said with a sigh.

"You can get out the cake and balloons, but I'm not going to throw you a pity party."

"Then throw me an *amnesia fiesta* so I don't have to remember any of what just happened." Except, of course, the part where Kieran had defended her and said all those wonderful things. He'd given a speech full of admiration and honesty, kind enough to make her head spin.

"It wasn't so bad," Kieran offered.

"Well, it would have been worse if you hadn't saved me. If you hadn't jumped on that stage and made Leif Jenssen look like he was going to pass out."

"It was him or you."

"That seems dramatic. I was doing okay."

"Could have fooled me. You looked like shit and I thought you were going to barf on Leif's shoes."

Audrey giggled. The sound surprised her. She didn't think anyone could make her laugh after what had happened today.

"Is there a poem you think captures the mood of this moment?" she asked. "A piece of verse?"

"There once was a gal from Nantucket, who went up on-stage and said fuck it…"

Audrey giggled again. Kieran grinned, and inched closer. Part of Audrey suddenly wished him even closer still, but he stayed put.

"You got up on that stage and did the best you could," he said. "I don't think many people would be able to say that. And for what it's worth, you handled your sister at the diner like a damn pro. You did great."

Audrey's muscles tightened. Her sister.

They might never speak again after this.

The world blurred as tears pooled in her eyes.

"My stupid sister," she said. "What a liar."

Kieran watched her. "You figured that out pretty quickly. That she was lying, I mean. How did you know?"

"She repeats things when she lies," Audrey said. "She did it even when we were growing up."

"Ah, so you knew her tell. I should have picked up on it myself, but I think I was just so rattled. It was pretty intense." His gaze was heating up the space between them. She could feel his stare in every part of her body.

"I can't believe she paid you to leave," Audrey said.

"What's worse is that I can't believe I left. That part's not her fault, you know. She put the offer out there, but I'm the dickhead who took it."

Audrey smiled ruefully. "You were a dickhead."

"The biggest one ever, maybe."

"Would you have come back again if it wasn't for the job?"

Kieran pressed his lips together briefly. "Honestly? I doubt it. When I first saw you at the dealership, my one goal was to stay away from you and just keep the past in the past. I figured I'd gotten over you, after all."

But you hadn't, Audrey thought.

"It took me coming back to realize what a jackass I'd been, and that you were the only thing that had ever been good in my life. I want you to know how sorry I am. For the mistakes I made five years ago, and for those that I've made since I've been back. You deserve such a wonderful life. I don't even know if I am the right guy to give it to you. But I'd live the rest of my life trying to be him."

Audrey studied Kieran's earnest face, and let his steady words settle in her addled brain. *The rest of his life.*

He had feelings for her: both in the past and right here on this bench. And maybe far into the future—if she'd let it go there.

Her conscience twisted. Could she ever love Kieran Callaghan again?

She gazed at his long, strong fingers clutching her hands. Heaven help her, had she ever stopped?

She was an exhausted jumble of nerves and questions and wasn't sure what to do about any of it.

"You need to rest," Kieran said gently. An emotional enigma she clearly wasn't. "You should go home and sleep. But tonight, I want you to meet me. If you would, that is."

"Meet you where?"

"At the Asparagus Festival. In the music tent. I want to dance with you again."

Audrey's pulse raced. Dancing with Kieran Callaghan at the Asparagus Festival. Just like when they met five years ago.

It's only a dance, she told herself. And yet she knew it would be so much more. He would hold her against his broad chest and they'd move together, erasing the past five years with every sway and turn. It would be like the moment when Kieran's bike surged forward, his feet lifting off the ground and the two of them flying down the road. *The moment of takeoff.*

"If you don't come," Kieran said, "I'll understand. I talked with Fletch this afternoon and the dealership is in fine shape. With your help, it'll only get better. Come Monday, the main office has another gig for me in Brainerd, if I want it."

It seemed impossible that Kieran could leave so soon. Her body tensed, rejecting the idea.

"If I do meet you, and I'm not saying I will, what time?"

Kieran's wide mouth broke into a shameless grin. His white teeth gleamed in the May sun; his eyes glinted like the Birch River. He was so handsome that her breath caught. "Eight o'clock."

She willed herself to say yes, but the word wouldn't come. Not yet, anyway. She didn't dare believe that a single, one-syllable word could start a chain reaction that could have Kieran back in her life, caring for her with his whole heart. And that she could give him hers in return.

Could it really be that simple?

She didn't have much time to think about it. Because tearing down the sidewalk, the sun illuminating her blonde hair like a halo, came Betty. She was waving a dish towel and hollering loud enough for all of White Pine to hear: "Emergency Knots and Bolts meeting!"

* * *

"Hair of the dog," Betty pronounced, setting a small glass of Scotch in front of Audrey. "Drink up."

"I think I'll throw up if I have any more booze," Audrey said. The liquid was deceptively beautiful: a rich color that reminded her of worn leather and polished oak barrels. She'd paint the darn glass if she could, but drink its contents? No way.

"You won't hurl," Betty said, pushing the Scotch closer to her with a practiced hand. "It's medicinal at this point. And that's the good stuff. So just shoot it back."

Against her better judgment, Audrey tipped back the Scotch and grimaced as the peaty, fiery liquid lit up her esophagus and stomach. "Yeesh."

Stephanie opened up a cupboard door. "Can I get one of those, too? The twins crayoned the flat-screen television again."

Betty nodded and handed her the bottle. "Take it and pass," she told the five women crowded into Knots and Bolts's kitchenette, all of them leaning against the counters, the walls, or the small table where the hot dishes were set out. Audrey wasn't sure why they weren't at the big red table, but she wasn't about to argue. This felt tighter—safer.

Her throat pinched unexpectedly. With she and her sister fighting, these women were more like family than ever. She felt fresh tears collect at the thought.

"All right, spill it," Betty said, "because that pageant was a shit show to end all shit shows. And I want to know what caused it."

"Betty!" the women chorused. Audrey could only smile. *Betty said things that needed saying.*

So she opened her mouth and told the story of Kieran's confession at the dealership, about Casey's lies, and about the terrible fight at the diner. "I was just so rattled by the time I got to the pageant that I wasn't thinking clearly. I was a mess. If Kieran hadn't stopped it—"

"No offense, Audrey, but he could have had any woman in the crowd today," Stephanie said, pouring another Scotch. "You should have seen how the ladies were looking at him. Like he was a white knight who had just rescued you."

"He *did* rescue me," Audrey confessed, thinking of his heartfelt defense of her onstage. If the day wasn't a complete ruin, it was because of that.

"Well, I saw plenty of people looking at Audrey," Willa said, her green eyes mischievous, "especially now that she's a pole dancer."

Audrey put her forehead in her hands. She would never, ever live this down.

"I wouldn't despair just yet," Betty said, patting Audrey's arm. "Willa's right. People were looking at you. Which means your plan might have just worked, albeit in a backwards way. I heard plenty of folks say they wouldn't mind some personal training lessons from you, not to mention some dancing lessons, pole or otherwise. You may have hit on something."

Audrey looked up. "Seriously? Dancing?"

"Well, it's exercise, isn't it?"

"I—I guess." Audrey chewed on her lip. She couldn't pole dance, it was true, but maybe she could teach a fun, hip-shaking dance class, like Zumba or salsa. She'd done both in college, and she knew there was certification available for both.

If she started reaching out to potential clients, like Caitlin and Sonja's moms, she could offer more than just weights and running. She could offer something cardio that felt...*fun*.

The idea slammed into her. She never would have even considered a dance class before this.

Maybe the pageant hadn't been a waste after all.

But even if she got a thriving personal training business out of the whole ordeal, it still wouldn't make up for the fact that the most important relationship in her life was still a mess. Casey had misled her—had *lied* to her. Casey had been a first-rate jerk.

She groaned. "What do I even do now? I don't know how to fix things with my sister—or if I even should."

"That's part of why I called this meeting," Betty said. "I have an important proposal for the group. I motion that we let Casey Tanner into the Knots and Bolts recipe exchange."

The women all stared at her. "For real?" Audrey asked dumbly. "But why?"

Betty shrugged, her expression casual even as her eyes were sharp. "I think she needs us."

Anna's forehead was creased under her dark hair. "I don't know, Betty. She hurt Audrey pretty badly. Maybe give it some time?"

Audrey was going to agree, except there was a nagging shard of an idea that wouldn't loosen from her brain. Kieran had been a liar. He had been a gambler. Five years ago, those things had all been true, and Casey had *known* it. He was reformed now, but...

Her fingers twitched around the Scotch glass as she envisioned a marriage where Kieran was stealing from their retirement funds to gamble.

In her own messed-up way, Casey had saved her. In a strange way, maybe she'd even saved Kieran, too.

"Listen," Betty said. "Audrey has told me some about how she and Casey grew up, and it wasn't easy. Casey had to be an adult before her time, and that's hard on any kid. I think what she needs are some friends. Some people to show her how to be a sister. She screwed up, no doubt, but I believe she did it in Audrey's best interests. Call me sentimental—"

"No one would call you that," Willa interjected.

"Fair enough. But either way I think Casey needs us." She turned to Audrey. "Listen to me. You don't have to forgive her until you're ready. You don't have to make plans with her. We'll just invite her to Knots and Bolts on Thursdays and see if she comes, and we'll go from there."

Audrey stared at her friend. Betty might be tough and outspoken, but she might just have the biggest heart of all of them. Audrey remembered how, when Willa joined Knots and Bolts, Betty had her own road of forgiveness to walk. Willa had bullied Betty for years in middle school and high school—and maybe Betty knew that there were good things on the other side of giving someone the benefit of the doubt.

"I'm for it," Willa said, as if reading Audrey's thoughts. "I think she should come."

"I think Audrey should have the final word," Stephanie said. Anna nodded in agreement.

"I'll sleep on it," Audrey said. "I think I need some breakfast and a nap, and then maybe my head will be clearer."

"Fair enough," Betty said. "Let's exit stage left, ladies, and let this poor girl get home."

The group put away the Scotch and headed for the back door. Audrey was rooting for her keys when she stopped short—again.

"Can someone take me home?" she asked, exasperated to the limit. "My stupid car is still at the Wheelhouse."

CHAPTER TWENTY-FOUR

Audrey studied her reflection in the mirror.

Her knee-length sleeveless black dress—the one she'd worn to every school awards ceremony or special occasion for the past three years—hugged her shape in the same familiar way it always had. Her comfortable flats were scuffed but sensible, and she wore her favorite bra—a soft pink satin affair that was delicate but didn't push her boobs into her throat.

Audrey swished her hips a little, and couldn't help but smile. Her hair was down, but not erupting all over her head. Instead, she'd curled it so it tumbled in soft auburn waves that ended just above her shoulders. Her eyeliner and mascara accented her deep brown eyes, but didn't go as far as being Egyptian. More like Egyptian light, she thought.

Her Harley-Davidson clothes and position hadn't been the answer to her new look, her new life, but they'd helped her find it. Now, for the first time since she'd been fired from her track job, Audrey felt like she was seeing—*really seeing*—herself. The woman looking back at her wasn't a mousy gym teacher, and she wasn't a vampy motorcycle model. She was just...Audrey.

She stared at her shape and tried to picture this woman walking through the opening of the music tent at the Asparagus Festival, and letting herself be pulled into Kieran Callaghan's arms. Her skin prickled at the thought of his hands on her, of his wide mouth pressing against hers and her every curve fitting just right against his strong body.

If they came together now, it wouldn't be for some hot sex.

She shook her head, knowing she could tumble into bed with Kieran again and again, but she'd always feel much more than the raw pleasure of it. She couldn't have part of Kieran and not wish for more. This whole notion that she could allow herself a trickle of feeling for him and not have it turn into a wave of affection was ridiculous. The click was always there—ever present, like a playing card in a bicycle's spokes.

The question was, would she let herself go to him now, in order to hit the reset button on their relationship? Would she gather together every ounce of faith she had, and step off the cliff in front of her, trusting that she wouldn't fall—but fly?

"Yes," she said into the space of her empty house. Her heart pounded in her chest; her body was humming with the potential of this night.

Tonight, she would dance with Kieran Callaghan. Tonight, she would let herself fall.

And tonight, she would trust that he would catch her.

* * *

Audrey stepped from her front door into the dusky evening and inhaled the sweet spring air. Crickets and frogs were singing along the banks of the nearby Birch River, and a gentle breeze carried the smell of lilacs and freshly mown grass. Lights from neighborhood homes shone warmly in the deepening night.

She started for town, wanting the walk and the fresh air to help keep her head clear. A walk would force her to know with certainty, with every step, that she wanted to risk her heart to Kieran Callaghan all over again.

It was only when her heel slipped slightly that she looked down and saw her walkway littered with another batch of rose petals. In the thickening darkness they looked black, not red. Her neck hairs stood at attention as she studied the hundreds of teardrop shapes, their edges curling as they dried on the gray cement.

She swallowed back nervousness. It was a romantic gesture—but she was oddly unsettled by it.

She stared at the dark shapes until it dawned on her that Kieran couldn't have left them. She'd been home all afternoon, and she hadn't heard the rumble of his Harley. He also didn't seem like the kind of man to keep repeating the same trick. Petals once? Awesome. Petals twice? Overkill. At least she suspected as much.

It must have been Dave Englund, she thought, but even that idea didn't sit right with her. He'd professed to liking her platonically.

Audrey shrugged. It could be anyone, really. A neighbor she didn't know. Someone from the dealership she'd helped. And until he showed himself, she wasn't about to dwell on it.

Crushing the petals without remorse, she started out, returning her focus to Kieran. Every step of her sensible heel on the pavement was a confirmation of her instincts to trust him. Right—*yes*. Left—*yes*. The hem of her skirt swished at her knees. On and on, over and over, until she crossed the Birch River and even the water's rush echoed the sound of an audience cheering in agreement.

Tonight, she would be with Kieran Callaghan again.

Tonight, she would let herself love him.

She smiled, already hearing strains from the music and beer tents. Main Street's squat brick buildings were just on the other side of the bridge. She'd turn left, toward Knots and Bolts, and then just keep going—dipping her head as she entered the tent, crossing from under the stars to stand under the strands of white lights inside.

For the past five years, she felt as if her life had been leading up to this moment. This was what she had wanted, even if she'd never let herself desire it consciously. She had longed for Kieran's return, had longed for his heart to be big enough to encompass her own. And now, it was.

Now, she was his.

She smiled to herself as she reached the end of the bridge. When a hand shot out of the darkness and grabbed her arm her smile didn't fade—not immediately, anyway. *Kieran,* she thought, and turned, expecting to find his familiar shape next to hers.

Instead, she came face-to-face with the blackness of Hunter Haglund's eyes, and the thin line of his cold smile. "Audrey," he said.

She jerked back with shock and fear, trying to pull away, but he'd anticipated the struggle and had clamped down on her. She screamed, twisting her body, but Hunter was

as unmovable as bare iron. With his other hand, he produced something white. In her confusion and fear, Audrey
thought it was a Kleenex. She was briefly baffled, until he
brought the Kleenex to her face.

It wasn't a tissue at all, she realized. It was cloth.

She screamed again, then knew immediately she'd made
a terrible mistake by intensifying her struggle. As she
pulled air into her lungs, she smelled a sharp chemical
odor. The edges of everything started to fade.

No, she thought.

She resisted, fought to stay conscious, but the pull into
darkness overtook her.

The lights around her extinguished completely.

* * *

In the center of the music tent, a fiddler and a washboard
player soloed their instruments, and a large bassist kept
up the beat. Kieran listened to the twang of the music,
watched couples whirling on the dance floor around him,
and took another sip of his asparagus beer. He glanced at
his watch. Eight fifteen.

She would come.

Any minute, Audrey Tanner would walk toward him,
the inky night silhouetting her from behind and the tent
lights illuminating her from above, and he would capture
that moment in his mind's eye to hold the rest of his life.
He'd play it back to himself when they were eighty years
old, having grown wrinkled and stooped together, and he'd
always see a young, beautiful woman striding toward him
on a warm night.

He'd believed so firmly she would come when he'd

knelt in front of her on the wooden bench earlier today. The softness in her honey brown eyes was unmistakable. *She cared for him.* And he would spend his life endeavoring to be worthy of that care.

Audrey Tanner was the most incredible woman he'd ever known. She was kind and compassionate and strong and forgiving—all wrapped up in a smoldering hot package. She'd believed the best in him five years ago, when she'd had no reason to. She'd trusted him, and he'd let her down.

Come hell or high water, he would never let it happen again. Ever.

And when she arrived tonight, her eyes sparkling and her perfect mouth turning into a smile, he would tell her as much. If she let him, he'd show her as much.

He took another sip of beer, trying to wash away the thoughts of how, exactly, he'd show her. He could imagine his hands trailing along her sweet skin, up her shapely calves to her thighs, then to the soft flesh between them. He would part her there, and slip a finger inside, then two as she heated for him. The heavenly feel of her would engulf him as he pleasured her. He could almost hear her weak moans, could see the way her thick hair tumbled as she arched her neck.

He would pay for his sins in strokes and kisses and thrusts. It would be a glorious repentance.

He shifted, hoping his aching hardness wasn't visible to everyone around him. Instead of fantasizing about Audrey naked, he pictured them in Boston instead. He'd take her to his favorite oyster shack on the harbor, and they'd drink good Boston beer. He'd introduce her to his brother, show her Southie, and even point out the crumbling brick apartment building where he'd grown up. He'd reveal all of his past because there wasn't a single corner of his life he wasn't willing to bare to her, nothing left that he wouldn't show her or confide in her.

Not anymore.

The tent was getting crowded. Someone bumped his shoulder, and irritation flared. He wanted everyone to clear out so he could see Audrey the moment she walked into the tent.

If she walked in.

He clutched his drink, pushing away his worry. There was no *if*. She would come.

Wouldn't she?

He was straining for another look over people's heads, scanning the throngs for Audrey, when two teenage girls approached him.

"Hey, we saw you in the pageant," one of them said, her dark ponytail swinging. "And it was *amazing*. I mean, the way you carried off Ms. Tanner? It was awesome. Are you guys in love?"

Kieran studied the long-limbed girl. She was familiar somehow.

"That was seriously the coolest thing ever," said the other girl. Her blonde hair was pulled into twin braids. "The way you rushed the stage? Incredible."

He studied the pair until it finally dawned on him. The tall one. He'd been at her house. With Audrey.

"I saw you the other day," he said evenly. "Audrey was there to talk to you. About a guy."

"Oh, totally. I'm Alexis, this is my friend Sonja. We run with Ms. Tanner on Sundays. And a couple weeks ago, my dumbass ex-boyfriend Hunter stalked us, and Ms. Tanner was amazing about the whole thing."

Of course she was, Kieran thought. Audrey was amazing about most everything.

"Things are straightened out, then?" he asked, realizing that he hadn't been able to follow up with Audrey after visiting this girl's house.

"Once Ms. Tanner got involved, Hunter totally stopped being a jerk, even when I dumped him," Alexis was saying. "It was amazing. I mean, I didn't think anyone could get him to leave me alone, but she totally did. It was tough because I had to tell my mom and the school principal, but then, *poof*, just like that he stopped. I think it's because Ms. Tanner has super powers."

Kieran smiled at the way the girls adored Audrey. And no wonder. If he'd had a teacher like her, he'd be babbling about it, too.

"He even knocked off the crap with the rose petals," Sonja was saying. "Ms. Tanner got Hunter to quit everything."

Sonja flipped one of her braids off her shoulder. "God, it was so dumb anyway. Hunter would leave rose petals on Alexis's front walkway, and she'd have to clean them up before her mom got home. He thought it was super romantic, but it was more like super annoying."

"Yeah. Never do that to a girl. It's messy. Seriously. Just save the money you'd spend on flowers and take her out to dinner."

Kieran smiled, thinking that he'd do all that and more for Audrey. He'd empty himself out to help her see how much he loved her. By giving everything he had to her, he could be filled up by her, near to bursting, every day.

That is, if he got the chance. His eyes flicked to the entrance again, but all he saw was darkness.

"When you see her, tell her we said hi," Alexis said. Kieran nodded, even as his guts twisted. With every passing minute, he became increasingly worried she wouldn't come. That he'd misread the whole situation somehow. Or that she'd changed her mind.

Alexis elbowed Sonja, and the pair made their way out of the tent. He watched them go, his stomach sinking. He could picture the tilt of Audrey's head, the brightness in her eyes if they danced together tonight.

If she came. If she forgave him.

If.

He glanced at his watch. Nearly eight thirty. His chest ached as the minutes stretched on and on.

CHAPTER TWENTY-FIVE

Audrey awoke to soft light and warm surroundings. She straightened her stiff neck and struggled to get her bearings—and make sense of what had happened.

The bridge. Blackness. *Hunter.*

She twisted her head to look around—which was a mistake. Nausea rolled inside her, and she was forced to stay still until it passed. When she could, she turned slowly, to get her bearings. She was alone, seated on a plush leather couch. There was a fire crackling in a fireplace made of smooth, gray fieldstones. Polished hardwood floors gleamed in the firelight, and enormous windows looked onto the black water of a nearby lake.

She blinked. Where was she?

More importantly, where was Hunter?

She stood unsteadily, forcing her brain to think. To process this logically.

Don't panic. *Find a way to get out of here now.*

She looked down—her shoes were still on her feet. But her purse was gone, and so was her cell. She looked around for a landline, but couldn't see any kind of phone.

The fire popped. She jumped. Clapping her hands over her mouth, she fought to keep from screaming. *No,* she told herself, *you will not lose it. Not now.*

There was a hallway off the high-ceilinged room she was in, but no obvious door to the outside. She took a breath, the traces of the chemical Hunter had used on her still in her nostrils.

She would just have to bolt down the hallway and pray she could make it to a door before Hunter caught her. Wherever he was.

She swallowed, wondering if he was watching her right this instant. She tiptoed closer to the room's only exit.

She couldn't hear anything above the crackle and pop of the fire.

Taking a steadying breath, she was ready to sprint when she heard his voice.

"Ah, you're awake!"

She froze. He appeared at the end of the hallway holding two glasses of wine. "Your shadow gave you away," he said, flicking his sandy-haired head toward the wall, where the outline of Audrey's body flickered in grays and blacks. Her shape was hunched and contorted with fear. Anyone coming down the hallway would see it.

She forced herself to straighten, to stay calm.

This is Hunter—he's a kid, she thought. *Let him know you're the teacher and he's the student.*

He kept his black eyes on her as he set the two glasses of wine down on the sleek coffee table. "Sorry about the bridge," he said casually, as if he'd accidentally bumped her shoulder and not drugged her. "I wanted to make sure we could go somewhere private. To talk."

"What do you want, Hunter?" She kept her eyes on him, kept her voice even. She struggled to remember the training all the teachers had when they'd prepared for an emergency at school. It was an active shooter training, and Hunter didn't have a gun that she could see. Still, Audrey recalled as much of the training as she could, keeping her hands visible, palms out. Only as a last resort were they supposed to engage the person—to confront him or her in any way. They were supposed to flee, or hide quietly. Too bad those weren't options right now.

"We needed to be together, obviously," Hunter said, his sharp cheekbones lifting as he smiled. "I thought you'd like it here. You enjoy the outdoors, right?"

There was an eerie, disquieting calm to Hunter's dialogue. He was so sure about their being here—about being together. It was as if he couldn't imagine that she'd disagree with him about it.

"We're at your cabin, then," she said, trying to redirect the conversation, to get more information about her whereabouts, in case she could find a phone. Or a road, so she could just run. "What lake is it on?"

"I knew you'd like it," Hunter said. He brought one of the wineglasses to his lips and took a sip of the smooth, red liquid. He motioned at the other glass, but Audrey stayed rooted in place.

"This is an Oregon pinot," he said. "Organic grapes. Pressed the old-fashioned way. You wouldn't think it makes a difference, but it does. More flavor."

"Hunter," Audrey said, making sure to use his name. "I need to get home. My sister's coming over, and she's going to be wondering where I am. She's older than me, and when we were kids, she took care of me." She was lying to give Hunter personal details, trying to get him to hear who she really was, not who he thought she was. Another tip from her training.

Too bad this detail singed her heart. She was in danger of never seeing her sister again—and they'd left their relationship in such a horrible state.

Not to mention Kieran was probably waiting for her at the festival, thinking she'd never come. Her heart twisted.

"We have plenty of time," Hunter said. "You should sit down."

"You need to let me go, Hunter. I can't be here."

Hunter's eyes darkened. He studied the wine in his glass, twirling the red liquid around and around. "I hope you liked my rose petals. I've done that before, you know, leaving rose petals for girls, but it never felt right. But for you—it felt perfect. Girls like Alexis look so silly next to a real woman like you. I can't believe I ever wasted my time with them."

He set down the glass and took a step toward her. Audrey squared her shoulders. "No," she said firmly, "do not come any closer, Hunter. I am going to leave and you're not going to follow me or lay a hand on me. Do you understand?"

Hunter's slow smile returned. It was ice cold. Outside on the lake, the trembling, eerie call of a loon echoed across the empty water. Audrey shivered.

"Older women are so much more exciting," Hunter said, taking another step forward. He studied Audrey's legs, his eyes raking over her body, slowly.

She assessed him, too—but quickly, calculatingly. He

was strong and solid for a teenager, but she might be able to overpower him if she landed a few choice blows. If he drugged her again, though . . .

Audrey's chest heaved as if she'd been running. She had to get out of here before Hunter did something even more reckless.

He took a step closer and there was so little room left. Only a couple feet. Audrey had to take control of the situation now, or she was going to be in even more trouble. Her thoughts flailed, and she desperately tried to control them.

Think, dammit.

She looked at the wine. It was Hunter, playing at being a grown-up. Playing at the two of them being together. *Playing . . .*

She stilled. Her thoughts crystallized. Her resolve grew, and became razor sharp. If he wanted to play, she'd give him the role he wanted.

And when she did, she'd make her break.

"All right, Hunter," she said, her heart hammering so loudly she wondered if he could hear it. She lowered her voice. "Why don't you sit down and let me take care of things? I'll stoke the fire, maybe put on some music. We'll talk."

His black eyes glinted. "That's more like it. I knew you'd come around."

"Yes. You knew because you're smart. Anyone can see that."

She forced herself not to scream as he reached out and closed the remaining space between them. His fingers landed on her bare arm and squeezed. His skin was only just warm. Room temperature, she thought, like a lizard's.

"You let me do all the work. You've already done so

much." She led him to the couch, motioning for him to sit. Behind her, the fire flickered. The flames sent her shadow dancing on the wall all over again. The fireplace was just a few feet away, she assessed, glancing at the fieldstone behemoth. But more importantly, the set of fireplace tools—poker, shovel, log hook, and broom—were right next to it. They might aid her self-defense if she made a break for it.

When she made a break for it.

"Does your family use this place often?" she asked, closing the distance to the fireplace as if nothing were wrong.

"Not really," Hunter said. "That's why I like it."

Audrey swallowed a sob. The place was not only remote, there was little chance of someone else showing up. She focused on the tools in front of her, on the weight and heft of them.

She picked up the poker and pulled the screen away from the fireplace. The heat blasted her face; the logs popped with the sound of gunfire. She jumped, then stabbed at the wood halfheartedly, wondering what to do next.

Her palms were sweaty. They wanted to slide off the slick wood handle.

She had one shot. She would *not* drop it.

She took a breath.

God give me strength, she prayed.

Then she whipped around and bolted for the hallway, yelling for him to stay away or she'd hit him with the poker.

She heard more than saw him jump off the couch. His footsteps were heavy behind her. When his hand clawed at her shoulder, she screamed, swinging the poker blindly.

Then she heard more than saw the heavy iron connect with Hunter somewhere above his shoulders. He grunted once before he collided with the wall, then stumbled backward and landed in a crumpled heap.

Horrified, she stifled a cry as she sprinted away. She came to a wide foyer with an antler chandelier hanging from the ceiling and an enormous cream-colored rug on the floor. The front door was right there and, next to it, on a small walnut table, was a phone. She picked it up and dialed 911. When the operator answered, she yelled for help, then hung up. She knew 911 protocol would have them sending officers to the premises when they called back and didn't get an answer.

As long as Hunter stayed where he was and didn't answer the phone, that is.

She wasn't about to wait to find out if that was the case.

Throwing open the door, she stumbled into the night. She was dimly aware of a shrill sound, and realized she was screaming. She ignored it, eating up the miles on her runner's legs and never looking back.

* * *

Officer Reynolds raised an eyebrow at Kieran. "So you saw Audrey this afternoon, but now you're worried about her because she didn't meet you at the festival?"

Kieran wanted to wipe the smirk off the man's face. They were standing outside Audrey's home, which was dark and empty. Kieran knew how it looked. He seemed absurd, calling the cops and overreacting because his date stood him up. Supposedly.

Probably.

He was struggling to find a way to explain to the policeman what he suspected: that Audrey was going to come to the asparagus tent tonight, but even if she'd changed her mind, surely she'd still answer a call from him.

But her phone had clicked to voice mail each time he'd dialed. It wasn't until he'd stopped at her house to see if she was all right that he'd discovered the rose petals.

The kind that Alexis had described.

The kind that her stalker ex-boyfriend had left her.

"Can you just check inside?" Kieran asked. "See if there's anything amiss? There's someone I think may have been following her."

Officer Reynolds shook his head. "At this point, not without a search warrant," he said, tapping his police notepad with a pen. Kieran noticed he had thick fingers— same as his thick neck. And thick head, for that matter.

Dread crawled along his spine as he remembered how Alexis said Hunter had backed off from following her so suddenly. What if Hunter hadn't stopped stalking Alexis so much as he'd found a new target? And what if that new target was Audrey?

Easy there, he told his racing brain. *No one needed to jump to conclusions.* If this were a bet, the odds would be extraordinary that anything was wrong with Audrey or that this Hunter kid was anywhere near her. And yet, his gut told him this was a bet he should take.

His body went cold, thinking that Audrey could be in danger.

The officer was staring at him, forehead wrinkled with irritation. "So?"

Kieran blinked. "I'm sorry. What were you saying?"

"So does this stalker have a name? The guy you think is after your date."

"Hunter something," Kieran said. "I know I've heard his

last name, but I can't recall it off the top of my head."
Reynolds jotted something down, then looked off into the
distance, as if bored. Kieran's anxiety mounted.

"I really need you to help me find—" Kieran was cut off
by the squawk of Reynolds's walkie-talkie.

"Fifty-five and 67, we have a 10-42 at 9945 Moccasin
Lake Drive."

Reynolds pressed the switch on his walkie-talkie. "Fifty-
five copy."

Kieran clenched his fists with frustration as Reynolds
blabbed inane code. Leave it to the White Pine police to
start getting a bunch of calls during the Asparagus Festival.
Probably some drunk guy chasing the asparagus drum major was his guess.

That is until Reynolds turned to him, the sarcasm gone
from his face. "Just got a 10-42 for 9945 Moccasin Lake
Drive. Any of that ring a bell?"

Kieran shook his head. "No. What's a 10-42?"

"A 911 hang-up. That address is for the *Haglunds*. They
have a kid, name of Hunter."

Haglund. "That's it. Hunter Haglund."

"Moccasin Lake is where their lodge is."

Kieran's throat went instantly dry. The officer clipped
his talkie back into his belt. "It's probably just Hunter and
his friends stirring up trouble," he was saying, "but we'll
look into it."

"Can I follow you out to that cabin?"

Officer Reynolds shook his head. "I can't give you any
kind of escort. But if you wanted to keep a respectable distance behind me as I drove, I suppose that's all right."

Kieran had his helmet on and his keys out before the officer got halfway to his car. He took in the slow pace of

the cop, ambling to his vehicle as if nothing in the world were wrong, and swore under his breath. At this rate, they wouldn't be there for ages. He took out his phone and typed in the address. Within seconds, he had the route to the cabin.

Not waiting for Officer Reynolds, he revved his engine and tore out of the drive. If he heard shouting and yells of protest, he ignored them.

Instead, he opened his throttle and raced toward Moccasin Lake, the cool air whipping around him and his headlights cutting through the inky night. The town's streets quickly gave way to farmland and forests. The darkness got thicker, closer. He imagined if he turned off his bike, the silence would be deafening.

Glancing at the GPS on his phone, he took several turns before finding Moccasin Lake Drive. It was a potholed dirt road with cabin names written on crude wood signs. Harry's Haven, the Brown Beach Bums, Olsen's Landing. And there—he spotted the Haglunds' Lodge. This was it. He was just giving his bike more gas when a shape came racing into his headlights. He hit the brakes so hard his rear wheel fishtailed. Gravel spewed in an arc. He nearly lost control.

Hunter, he thought, and leapt off his bike. He would smash Hunter's throat if he'd laid a finger on the woman he loved. Hunter Haglund would rot in a jail cell if he'd harmed one hair of Audrey's head. He was tensed, ready for a fight when, to his shock, he saw it was Audrey barreling forward, waving her hands. "Help me! I need you to call the police!"

A primal surge rolled through him, something so visceral he felt it beyond his bones—he felt it in his every cell. Her hair was disheveled, her dress was torn. She was sweating and panting—terrified. Seeing her frightened, seeing her reeling, gave him an awful knowing, a terrible realization, of how very much he needed her. In a blinding, crippling flash he suddenly understood that he would never, ever be able to live without her. He would die protecting this woman. He would give his life for hers a thousand times over.

"Audrey," he managed to say above the rumble of the Harley's engine. Her face contorted with shock.

"Kieran?"

He lunged forward and grabbed her, pulling her into his arms. He crushed her to him. Dear God, what had she been through? What had happened?

He allowed himself only a moment. He tore himself from her and ran his hands over every part of her body. "Are you hurt?" he asked.

She shook her head. "N-no. I'm fine."

"What happened? Are you being chased?"

"I don't think so. I ran pretty fast, and I knocked Hunter out."

If she'd knocked Hunter out, things had gotten bad indeed.

He lifted her up, placing her roughly on the bike. "We're getting you out of here," he said. Over the motorcycle's rumble, he could hear police sirens. They'd be here soon, and they could deal with Hunter. In the meantime, he was taking the woman he loved away from this mess.

But she clutched his wrists, her hands clawing into his flesh.

"No," she insisted. "If those are sirens, we're going back to the house with the police."

Kieran stared at her. "Why? They can handle that kid."

"Because I want to document what happened. I want to be at the scene. He's sick, Kieran. This kid needs help. Serious help."

"He's not a kid—he's practically an adult," Kieran growled. "And he doesn't need help. He needs to be behind bars."

"The courts can decide that," Audrey said. "In the meantime, we are going back. I'll run once to save my life—but I'll be damned if I run twice. From anything."

The sirens were close now, and he could see the police lights approaching, casting eerie shadows through the trees. He drove the bike to the side of the road a ways, and let the squad cars race by. He and Audrey coughed at the cloud of dark dust they kicked up.

"Go," Audrey insisted. His heart collapsed on itself. The woman he loved had defeated her stalker and was going back to *confront* him. He swore in that moment she was made of iron and stone.

She was a lion roaring through life, and he wondered how he could ever keep her safe. How could he ever keep her from being hurt?

And then he realized he couldn't. She would fight when she needed to fight. She would swing her sword when she had to, and that was part of what he would always love about her. She didn't need him to ride in and save her.

She just needed to know he was there when the battle was over.

And by God, he would be there. Always. Every day.

He kicked the bike into gear, and raced after the police.

When they're not looking, he thought, *I'll punch that little stalker in the face.*

CHAPTER TWENTY-SIX

$\mathcal{H}$unter was still out cold in the hallway. He was sprawled on the floor, his head tilted to one side. Audrey realized she'd sprinted for two miles, cutting through yards and bushes to try to lose him in case he chased her, and here she could have just stayed in the foyer, waiting for the police by the phone. Hunter hadn't moved.

"Do we need to call in a rape kit?" the stocky one, Officer Reynolds, asked. His partner, Officer Collins, tall and with wire-rimmed glasses, kept anxious eyes on her, waiting for a reply. She shook her head. Next to her, Kieran exhaled audibly.

"I'm all right," she said, taking his hand. Kieran was a tower of barely contained fury. She knew he wanted to dunk Hunter in the lake and possibly smash his skull against the fireplace's fieldstones for what she'd been through tonight. But she wasn't about to let the cops show up and have Hunter mislead them about what had happened. "I couldn't let them find this scene and not explain," she said to him, letting her tired eyes find his storming ones, letting the warmth from his strong hand flow into her. She was still shivering, still afraid of what would happen when Hunter actually woke up, but by God she was done running.

"I'm here," Kieran said, his voice so low it rumbled at the base of her spine. It was exactly what she needed to hear to help her stand up straighter and face Hunter.

"He's a minor," Audrey said to the cops, "so you'll need to phone his parents."

"Thanks," Reynolds said. Collins slapped Hunter's face to try and wake him. Audrey didn't hate the sharp sound it made.

Hunter bolted awake with a grunt. "What?" he yelled, standing to his feet. He was confused and panicked—not a good combination. Audrey felt sweat break out on her forehead.

"Hey, easy there," Reynolds said. "Settle down. We need to ask you some questions." Audrey had told them the abbreviated version of events as they'd approached the house. The police hadn't drawn their weapons when they'd entered, but she'd seen their hands tensing over their holsters. She'd explained where she'd left Hunter, but they'd made her and Kieran wait outside until they were given the all-clear. That was when she'd come back in to find him still passed out.

"That bitch hurt me!" Hunter cried, pointing at Audrey. He held a trembling hand to his head. A visible egg-sized lump had already formed just underneath his hair.

Reynolds called for medical assistance on his walkie-talkie. Collins stood near Hunter, his lean figure towering over the teenager, hands on his hips. "What's your name, son?"

Hunter glared at the cop. "Screw you."

Audrey closed her eyes. Hunter wasn't doing himself any favors, and it was a reminder that he was still just a high-school kid. Albeit a sick and dangerous one.

"She brought me out here to seduce me," Hunter said, glaring at Audrey. "Don't believe anything she says."

"This lady has already cooperated with us by telling us her name," Collins said, "and I suggest you do the same."

"Hunter Haglund," he said, never taking his eyes off Audrey. There was so much hate and anger there, Audrey shivered. But she wouldn't back away from him.

"How did Ms. Tanner come to be here, Hunter? Did she drive? Because I don't see a car out there."

"She made me drive her here. She *made* me do it."

The cop nodded, and jotted something down. Audrey hated the lies, hated Hunter's brutal tone, but she stayed silent, and clutched Kieran's hand for strength.

"And she made you pour that wine there, too? Two glasses' worth?"

"She poured it," Hunter said. "She poured it for *me*."

"My fingerprints and DNA aren't on either of those glasses," Audrey said calmly.

"Fuck you," Hunter spat.

"Enough with that language, Hunter," Collins said. "We're going to have a civil conversation here. No more swearing."

"Fuck you," he repeated defiantly.

Collins took a breath. "Okay, Hunter. Let me ask you this: This man here"—he motioned at Kieran—"was looking for Ms. Tanner tonight and says he found her running on the dirt road out here. See how her dress is torn and her shoes are all muddy? How do you think she got that way?"

"She ran away after hitting me with the fireplace poker. End of story."

"She says her purse and phone are missing. Any idea where those are?"

"No."

"She also says she was drugged. Any chance you know about that?"

"She's a psycho. Aren't you *listening*? She hurt *me*. Not the other way around."

"So if we had a look around, we wouldn't find any rags with traces of chloroform on them, or anything belonging to Ms. Tanner here, like her purse, would we?"

Hunter hesitated. "No."

"Good, so how about we poke around and you sit tight."

"You need a warrant for that. Don't think I haven't seen all the cop shows."

"We don't need a warrant to search your car, Hunter. We've got probable cause for days, so Officer Reynolds is going to go out and take a look inside of it, and he'll let you know what he finds."

Hunter paled visibly. "You can't do that."

Collins stood to his full height. He towered over Hunter. "Trust me—we can and will."

Hunter narrowed his eyes. "You don't touch. My. *Shit*."

"It's too late for that, son."

Hunter's face contorted with rage. "Yeah, but it's not too late for this," he said, and slammed his fist into Collins's face. The officer's glasses went flying across the room, landing with a clatter on the hardwood floor.

Kieran pushed Audrey behind him instinctively. Reynolds leapt on top of Hunter to pin him to the floor, wrestling with plastic handcuffs at the same time. Hunter kicked and bucked with manic strength. Reynolds got an elbow to the eye and shouted with pain. Hunter jumped to his feet, sweating and swearing.

For a horrified moment, Audrey wondered if she was going to have to defend herself all over again. Adrenaline surged, readying her for the fight. She clenched her fists. She would punch him in the balls repeatedly if she had to.

But then Kieran waded in, his eyes burning with fury. He kicked out Hunter's feet, and then pinned him to the ground by the neck. Hunter gave a strangled cry as Reynolds entered the fray again, cuffing Hunter's hands behind his back.

Collins turned to Audrey, rubbing his jaw. "Werr ned you to cerm durn to the staton," he said. "Gerve a stat-murnt."

Audrey nodded. "All right."

Collins retrieved his glasses as Hunter was led out of the room, handcuffed. She felt no victory at the sight of the troubled teenager. A tight grief clutched at her chest. She wondered suddenly what had happened to Hunter to make him this way. What had gone wrong?

Her only comfort was Kieran, who wrapped his strong arms around her. His chest pulled in ragged breaths as he held her close. "Almost there," he said. "Just one more stop and then we can get you home."

Audrey nodded. "Let's do this, then," she said, drawing strength from Kieran's spicy, warm smell, and the way he stared at her as if she were a thing he was worried would break.

No one had ever stared at her that way.

I'm stronger than you think, she wanted to tell him.

Instead, she placed her hand in his, and walked back into the darkness, ready for whatever was next.

CHAPTER TWENTY-SEVEN

Audrey sat on the edge of the exam table, hands folded in her lap. Underneath her, clean white paper crinkled. This could be a normal check-up, she thought. The only thing that would hint that it wasn't was the way her dress was ripped in several places from running through the woods. And maybe the way her flats were coated with a thin layer of gravelly mud. And perhaps how pale she was—at least when she'd looked at herself in the mirror a few minutes ago.

She studied the poster of the human body on the exam room wall, at all the interconnected muscles and bones and organs, and wished Kieran could have come in with her. She wanted his strong shoulder pressed against hers as she chatted with her doctor. She had insisted on coming to the clinic after she'd given her statement at the police station. A quick Google search had revealed that chloroform leaves the body quickly, and she wanted to make sure she documented traces of the chemical in her system before it was all gone.

Thankfully, the town's urgent care clinic had been able to take urine and blood samples immediately.

Audrey hoped she would never need to use them, but she'd made up her mind at least to *get* them after a pot-bellied lawyer in a well-made navy suit had showed up at the police station. Hunter's lawyer, in fact. He was there even before Hunter's parents. He'd waved a hand when Hunter started to defend himself, and silenced the teenager with one word: "Enough."

After that, Hunter didn't talk at all.

Audrey knew they would need these lab results if she pressed charges against Hunter. She was barely employed and didn't know what kind of legal counsel she could even afford. Not that she wanted to sue anyone. She just wanted Hunter to get help. Even after what had happened, she prayed he'd get the right medication and counseling.

Even if he did, she knew that this night would still stay with her for a long time. If she was lucky, it would heal over with time, scarring thickly enough so it didn't smart every time she glanced at it.

But she also knew that other parts of this night would remain, too—and those she wanted to keep close. The picture of Kieran racing down the road, hell-bent over his bike to save her; his massive torso stepping between her and Hunter when things got chaotic at the cabin; the leather of his motorcycle jacket creaking every time he reached out to touch her at the police station; the nostrils of his smooth, aquiline nose flaring at the more difficult questions they'd asked.

Did he force himself on you?

No.

Did he penetrate you in any way?

No.

Did he harm you physically?

Yes.

She'd heard the sharp intake of Kieran's breath when she'd showed the officers the bruises on her arm, from where Hunter had grabbed her on the bridge.

She could put away this event, she knew, if she had Kieran's strength mingling with her own, like smoke and fog twisting together on a damp night. She needed his contradictions, maddening as they could be. But only Kieran could be tender enough to care for her, and rough enough to fight for her. Only Kieran could whisper fragments of poetry to her and then shout at the police to go find her. She'd heard how he'd called officers to her home when she hadn't shown up at the Asparagus Festival, and she was beyond grateful. She *was* going to be there, she'd told him.

Before it all went so terribly wrong.

She might be able to picture Hunter in her mind's eye, but just as clearly she could see Kieran on his motorcycle on that dark road. Her breath came in razored gulps, ragged and uneven. He'd been the one person she'd needed to see, and he'd been there.

He would always be there.

She knew it now, of course. She'd fallen and he'd caught her—just not in the way she had expected.

Not that it mattered. He was right in front of her, hers for the taking, if she decided to reach out and accept what he offered: his heart, his love.

She'd be a fool not to.

And life was too short for foolishness like that.

There was a soft knock on the door and Audrey turned. The doctor entered, her steel-gray hair pulled into a neat knot at the base of her neck. Her tiny frame was cloaked in a white coat.

"We'll send your tissue and urine samples to the lab," she said, looking at notes on her clipboard. "It'll be a few days before we have the results, but certainly less than a week. Everything else, health-wise, checks out. Your heart rate is still a little high, but that's to be expected. You've had quite a shock. Best to go home and get some rest."

"Right," Audrey said, feeling like she might never be able to sleep again.

"Do you need something to settle your mind a bit?" the doctor asked gently. "I can give you a prescription for a sedative, if you think it would help."

Audrey shook her head. The last thing she wanted to be was groggy and out of it. Sleep would find her eventually.

"No, thank you," she replied.

"In that case, you're all set. Your family is waiting for you."

Audrey hopped off the table. "Family?" she asked, wondering if they thought Kieran was her husband. Or perhaps the Knots and Bolts crew had somehow gotten word of her predicament.

"Your sister, Casey. She's in the reception area."

Audrey's abdomen constricted. How had Casey known to come? She wracked her brain, trying to remember if Casey was listed as the next of kin on any of her medical paperwork. But even so, there was no cause to call next of kin. She wasn't dead, for crying out loud.

Still, relief flooded her. Casey was here.

No matter what had happened, her big sister was still by her side.

* * *

She thanked the doctor, then headed toward the waiting room. Pushing her way through the lobby's door, she caught sight of Casey in one of the cheaply upholstered waiting-room chairs. She was ready for her sister to lecture her on safety and the importance of carrying Mace and how she could have avoided all this if she hadn't agreed to meet Kieran—but what she saw instead stopped her in her tracks.

Casey was crying.

No, not just crying.

Casey was sobbing—huge, shoulder-heaving howls that echoed in the otherwise empty room. But it wasn't just the tears that anchored Audrey to her spot on the waiting-room carpet. It was the fact that she was bawling on Kieran's shoulder. And he was patting her sympathetically, like you would a friend.

Except these two were *not* friends.

"What is going on?" Audrey asked, stepping forward cautiously. Casey's head shot up and her mascara-streaked face went slack with relief.

"Audrey," she said, standing. She was wobbly on her feet, and Kieran stood, too. "Oh my God, I'm so glad you're okay. I heard what happened and I—"

"How?" Audrey asked.

Casey's mouth pursed in confusion. "How what?"

"How did you hear what happened? How did you know I was here?"

Casey jerked her head in Kieran's direction. "He told me. He called me."

Audrey's confused eyes found Kieran's steady ones. He nodded. "I figured she should know."

Audrey's already overwhelmed brain struggled to make sense of this. "But after what happened," Audrey started, "why would you—"

"We make mistakes," Kieran said, waving a hand. "All of us. But family is still family. She needed to know, Audrey. She's your sister."

Audrey wanted to argue further, but she didn't know what to say. Deep down, her arms ached to hold her sister, for them to cling to one another like they had when they were kids.

"I—I'm fine," Audrey said after a moment. "I was taken...there was a fireplace...I just had some tests...."

She was scrambling her words, struggling to communicate what had happened, and to say that she was all right. Only none of it was coming out correctly. It was as if she'd swallowed all the pills the doctor had offered to prescribe.

Before she could process what was happening, she felt her sister's arms around her—bony, even through the fabric of Casey's light jacket.

Her heart surged with relief. Things weren't perfect between the two of them, but they were going to be all right.

Casey tightened her grip. "I couldn't believe it when Kieran called. He said you'd been kidnapped and the police had gotten involved. For heaven's sake! When he told me you were at the urgent care clinic, I panicked. I got here and he told me the whole story but it didn't help me feel any better. I thought you might not live. I worried you'd *died*, Audrey."

"No," Audrey said as the two of them separated, "obviously it was nothing so dramatic as tha—"

"But you could have died," her sister insisted, "and I would be the horrible person who let you pass away without telling you what a jerk I've been. I've been thinking about you constantly since the diner, but I was too afraid to call you and say anything. And then to find out someone had *taken* you. I could only ask myself what I'd do if I never saw you again."

Audrey was filled with pity at how disheveled, at how broken, her sister looked.

Casey's hand fluttered to her throat. "And when I thought about the answer to that question, I knew I would have lived the rest of my life with deep regret that I hadn't been a better sister. I would have rued the day I didn't tell you I was so, so sorry for interfering in your life. I would have carried remorse with me like a prisoner's shackles, wishing I could go back and let you love whomever you wanted to love."

Audrey struggled to digest what she was hearing. She had never heard her sister say she was wrong about anything—ever. She looked at Kieran, whose keen eyes were already on her.

"People aren't always lucky enough to get second chances," he said gently. "But I knew your sister was looking for a way to make some of this right."

"How could you know that?"

"Her *other* tell," he said simply.

"Which is?"

"She frowns the same way you do when you're not sure about something. She was doing it when we left the diner. It's this little off-to-the-side movement."

"I do not do that," Audrey said, fingers touching her mouth self-consciously.

"Yes, you do."

"While I appreciate the two of you talking about me like I'm not here," Casey interjected, "Kieran's right. About me being unsure, anyway. I just wanted to help you, Audrey, and I was doing it the same way I always had, even though we weren't kids anymore. I guess part of me wanted to know you still needed me. I know I went too far. With Kieran, with that principal, Kyle Williams. I don't know if you can believe me, but deep down I really did want the best for you."

The deep lines of worry and sorrow on her sister's already creased face were heartbreaking. *Harrowed* was the word that came to Audrey's mind.

"I apologized to Kieran, too," Casey said, glancing upward to Kieran's chiseled face.

"But I told her she didn't have to," Kieran added. "The debt we hold is to you, Audrey. We hurt you, not each other."

In the middle of the medicinal-smelling room, Audrey searched for the right words to say next. It didn't feel right that she held any debt at all. She didn't want whatever they felt they owed her. She just wanted to move forward.

But how was that supposed to happen? Should she just trust her sister, the same way she'd decided once again to trust Kieran?

And then she remembered the Knots and Bolts offer from Betty.

"Things need to be different between us," she said to Casey, "but I don't think anything will change if we do the same things over and over. Quick lunches, brisk phone calls. So starting next week, we're doing something totally out of the ordinary."

Doubt flickered in Casey's eyes. "Which is?"

"You're coming to a recipe exchange with me. I know I've told you about it before. It's at the fabric store in town, Knots and Bolts. Go in through the back. There's a room there, and that's where we meet. It will be me and four of my closest friends on Thursday evenings."

Casey's face shadowed with doubt. "You're inviting me to hang out with your friends?"

"Yes."

"Why? Won't that just make me odd man out in your clique?"

"It's not like that," Audrey insisted. "These are good people. And they know how to model good friendships. And right now, Casey, you and I need to figure out how to be friends."

Casey looked like she was going to argue further, but managed to stop herself. "Of course," she said. "I'll be there." Then, after a moment, another question: "If it's a recipe exchange, what should I make?"

Audrey smiled slightly. "I thought it would be obvious."

"You'd better tell me. I'm new to these kinds of things."

Audrey was grinning fully now. "Humble pie, of course."

CHAPTER TWENTY-EIGHT

$\mathcal{A}$udrey's hands shook so hard she couldn't get the key into the lock at her front door. "Here, let me help," Kieran offered, gently steadying her hand. When they were inside, he sensed that both of them were relieved to be away from the rose petals on the front walk, the tear shapes heavy with early-morning dew and disintegrating on the cement.

"Can I get you coffee?" Audrey asked, stepping through the neat front room—with its loveseat and secondhand coffee table—and into the kitchen. Kieran followed her, leaning on the counter as she grabbed a filter and a bag of grounds from the cabinet.

He watched her try so hard to be normal, acting like this was just any other day and he was stopping by for a chat. He could see the strain in her face, but knew better than to push her. He'd probably want to act like everything was fine, too, if he'd been through even half of what she had.

"If I say no, you're just going to make coffee anyway, aren't you?"

Audrey stopped and fixed him with a smile. After everything that had happened, it was a dazzling sight. He wondered at her beauty, even in a torn dress and muddy shoes.

A pressing silence filled his ears. He realized how very alone they were.

"Audrey, I don't want coffee."

Her smile faltered. "I guess it's silly, isn't it? Coffee when we're both so wired. What would you like instead?"

In two steps, he'd crossed the kitchen and pulled Audrey into his arms. The grounds fell from her hand to the floor with a dull thump. "I want *you*," he said, closing his eyes against the anguish that bubbled up in him—the breadth of a thought of what it would be like to live in this life without Audrey. "I never want to feel like I might lose you again. I want you near me, Audrey. Always."

He opened his eyes to find her gazing at him. "Always?"

"Yes, sweetheart. Always. I can't be in this world and not have you by my side. Forever."

"I—I want that, too," Audrey said, the words filling a gaping hole in him. "I want to be with you, Kieran. I want to trust that this is real. That we're real."

"We are *so* real," he said, the wonderful truth of it making his chest hurt. And then, to prove it, he placed his lips on hers gently—a kiss of promise and hope and affection and everything his gambler's heart had risked and won in a last, desperate hand.

She knew the truth about him and wanted him anyway.

The thought had him pressing his mouth against hers more earnestly. He inhaled her sweet vanilla-and-detergent scent and nearly saw stars. On another woman it would be too simple. But on Audrey it was perfect—uncomplicated but desperately alluring in the way it mixed with the scent of her hair, her skin.

He pulled her lower lip between his teeth, and she let out a sigh of pleasure. Her breath was warm on his skin, and his hunger surged. Unable to stop himself, he turned their kiss into an open-mouthed firestorm. He wanted her impossibly close, wanted his tongue to tell her how deeply he cared for her. He pressed himself to her. She trembled against him.

He slid his hands up her arms, savoring the feel of her soft skin underneath his fingertips. He pushed away the dark tendrils of her hair until he had exposed the long length of her neck. Leaving her mouth, his lips found the sweetness of her clavicle, the hollow of her neck, up to her ear until she was twined against him, just to stay upright.

"Kieran," she whispered, her eyes hot with pleasure, "I don't want to do this in the kitchen. I want to go to my bedroom."

Scooping her into his arms, he carried her down the short hallway. He knew the way. Morning light streaked in through the white curtains on her window, illuminating the cream and robin's-egg-blue stripes of her tasteful bedspread. Stacks of books were piled on a side table, and framed pictures lined her simple dresser. Above the bed was a reproduction of Picasso's *Two Women Running on the Beach*. In the image, the women raced in the sand, their heads flung in delight, their clothes tumbling as they held hands, exuberant and free.

He'd seen the print before. The last time he was here. When he'd asked her about it, she'd told him that it combined the two things she loved the most—friendship and running.

Now, she watched him watch the painting. "That's how I feel," she murmured. Her hands plunged into his hair, pulling his head to hers. "When we're together. I feel so undone, but in a good way. Like I could just...fly." She kissed him then, running her tongue along his lower lip and sending flames shooting through his entire body. He worried he wouldn't be able to hold her any longer, so he placed her on the bed gently. Then he settled his weight on top of her.

She moaned as he kneed apart her legs, her black skirt riding to the tops of her thighs. He ran his hands up her shapely calves, her warmth and scent surrounding him like an unbearably sensual blanket. His hands rose higher until he'd pushed the bottom of her skirt all the way to her waist. "I want this off you," he growled, longing for there to be no clothes, no layers between them. She raised her arms above her head, allowing him to pull the dress off her in one seamless tug.

He blinked at her figure, kneeling between her legs as she lay back on the bed. "You are so beautiful," he said, taking in her glowing skin, the perfect shape of her breasts in her pink satin bra, her glossy hair tumbling around her shoulders. He reached out and put a palm on her cheek. She kissed his wrist.

"You act like you're going to break me," she whispered, her breath hot on his skin.

He swallowed the tide of emotion that rose in his throat. "Some days I worry I almost did break you," he said.

She simply smiled at him. "You hurt me, yes. But break me? Never." Then she reached out and untucked his shirt from his pants. Sliding her hands underneath the fabric, she flat-palmed his skin. Her touch had him hissing in breath.

"There was a time when I wondered if I'd ever feel your skin again, though," she murmured, running her hands from his abdomen to his belt. "I didn't bet on it."

Betting. His vice—and in the twisted turn of events, also his salvation.

"I have bet on a thousand things," he said, watching her begin to unfasten his belt buckle, "but for so long I didn't have the courage to bet on us. In the end, I had to risk everything on the idea that you could know me and still care for me."

When his belt fell away with a clink, she unbuttoned his jeans and slid the zipper downward until his erection sprang forward through the hole in his boxer shorts.

She placed her soft hand on his stem. The feel of her flesh burned with immeasurable pleasure. She stroked him once, twice, then sat up and gently—oh, so gently—placed a kiss on the tip of his aching penis.

"I care for you very much, Kieran Callaghan," she said, her shining eyes meeting his. "Frankly, I don't know if I ever stopped."

Something like joy surged through him. Unable to keep his skin from touching hers for one more instant, he pulled off his shirt and tossed to the floor. He eased her backward, returning her to the pillows, so she lay before him, gorgeous and alluring—so free and unbound, just like the women in the painting above them.

That is, nearly unbound.

He slipped a hand behind her back and worked the clasp of her bra. He tossed the pink satin to the side, and stared at her beautiful, naked breasts. "You are incredible," he said. He meant the beautiful bareness of her chest, he meant the golden glimmer in her honey-brown eyes, he meant the softness of her skin and her fresh, uncomplicated smell—but most of all he meant the largesse of her heart, and her unfailing capacity to care for those around her. To care for *him*.

He nuzzled the shallow place between her breasts, then worked his way over to one perfect tip, sucking until it pebbled at his touch. Audrey gasped with pleasure, twining her fingers through his hair. With one hand on her skin, he used the other to work her panties off, until she was naked.

"No fair," she murmured as he let his tongue slide along the tip of the other breast, savoring its sweetness. "I'm naked and you're not."

In a half second, Kieran had changed that, kicking off his pants and boxers, and resettling between Audrey's thighs. She cried out softly as the tip of his penis pressed against her soft flesh. He could feel the wetness of her most private place, could feel the heat from her core, and as much as he wanted to plunge into her, to ravish her until they both cried out, he had other plans. This would not be fucking on the riverbed; this would be making love.

"My lovely woman," he murmured, trailing one hand down her beautiful abdomen, playing with the soft patch of curls between her thighs. He slid one finger inside her and nearly emptied himself on the bedspread. "You are so tight," he groaned, "so beautiful."

She mewled with pleasure as he inserted another finger. Her neck arched and he sucked in breath at her beauty. She was so vulnerable in his hands, and he vowed he would never take it for granted. She would never regret baring herself to him.

"I will always take care of you," he murmured against her skin, trailing kisses down her torso, to her belly and hips, all while plunging and stroking inside her.

"I know," she gasped as his lips found her center. He licked her and felt her emotions building with his own. This woman was everything to him. He would spend his life loving her and keeping her safe.

She was so hot and wet and lovely. He closed his eyes and gave in to the reckless passion of tasting her innermost flesh. He couldn't get enough, couldn't get close enough.

"Oh, Kieran!" she cried as he lost himself in feasting on her center. She lifted her hips, her hands working madly through his hair, her breath ragged. He could feel her pleasure, could feel it building in his own body the same way it was building in hers. He inserted a third finger and she cried out again, eyes shut tight, murmuring his name. And then she shattered in his arms, her ecstasy coming in waves that crashed over them, sending them tumbling into currents of desire.

She pulled his face to hers, placed her lips on his, no doubt tasting herself there. She wrapped her strong legs around his waist. His body was taut against hers. His rock-hard penis rested against her center, but he didn't push.

"I missed you," she said, her brown eyes finding his. His throat thickened at the gentleness and affection there. "For five years I missed you and never had anyone else. There has never been anyone else."

"And you have always been the one for me," he said, gently sweeping back a piece of her molasses-colored hair. "You changed me, even after just two weeks. I was a better person for just having met you. If this moment never happened, I would still be better."

Audrey smiled at him, and the sight of it was so transfixing that he couldn't hold back. He entered her in one fluid motion, groaning at the warmth that welcomed him. "I need you," he growled, pressing himself as far in as he could, getting as close to her as he could.

She cried out, meeting his demand with her own. She wiggled underneath him, and he saw stars. He imagined their muscles and bones and ligaments fusing together—becoming one person instead of two. "I love you, darling," he said, his body twined with hers. "I love you forever."

The words were the most honest thing he'd ever spoken. He wondered why he'd been a gambler for so long, dodging certainty, when the truth felt this good.

Audrey's body was working rhythmically with his, her muscles rippling beautifully under her skin. "I love you, too," she cried as he grasped her bottom and pulled her to him, wanting more—wanting *everything*.

He thrust into her deeply. The bed frame cracked against the wall. Her fingers gripped his shoulders, clutching him as she met his need with her own. Her brown eyes were dark with hunger, her mouth open as she panted his name. He fixated on her face, on her loveliness, then caught her mouth in his.

Kieran felt her pleasure as she seized around his penis. She moaned, her lips against his, her skin damp and glowing. She was like pink-tinged clouds from behind which the sun bursts on a summer day. He closed his eyes as a torrent of ecstasy rained down on him, pelting his senses, tightening his muscles, making him shout her name until his throat was hoarse. He stormed against her until the tide of his orgasm ended. Finally, when his mind was as quiet as the room, he opened his eyes and found her smiling at him, her face sated and relaxed. Her breasts rose and fell underneath him.

"Audrey," he said, saying her name, loving the sound of it on his lips with her body twined around him. He wanted to stay with her, like this, forever. He rolled off her so as not to crush her, then pulled her to him. Her smooth, supple body had him swallowing down more desire, and she kissed him hard enough to make him want to take her again.

But then she quieted in his arms, like a boat coming to rest at the end of its moorings after a storm. Kieran sank into the feel of her—of them together—and drifted off in a sea of pure happiness.

* * *

Audrey awoke to long shadows in her room. She rubbed her eyes sleepily and realized it was late in the afternoon— after three o'clock. Which meant they'd been asleep for hours.

Both of them.

She sat up on one elbow and stared at the form of Kieran Callaghan next to her. Her heart thundered at the sight of his dark red hair, his wide mouth slack with sleep, his limbs touching hers.

They'd made love. In her bed.

And he hadn't left.

What was more, he'd told her he loved her.

Audrey put a hand to her mouth. She felt drunk with happiness. Dear God, she'd told him she loved him, too.

And she'd meant it.

She placed her fingertips on his forearm, loving the feel of his warm skin and the dark, downy hairs there. This was the man she cared for most. This imperfect, hulking mass of contradictions was hers. And she never wanted to be without him.

Suddenly, Kieran opened his sea-green eyes and pulled her toward him. "Are you watching me?" he growled playfully as she landed on his solid chest. She shimmied so their bodies were pressed together—her legs on his legs, her stomach on his stomach. His jaw clenched and she could feel his sudden, raging hardness. It sent a jolt through her.

"I am watching you, making sure you never leave again," she said playfully, wriggling again just enough to make him groan.

"God, with you feeling like that, I'm not going anywhere."

"Not to Brainerd, then?" she asked, trying to keep from sounding worried. Kieran's job kept him on the road, and she understood that. But the thought of him roaring away on his motorcycle again—even if it was for a legitimate reason—made her stomach roil. If there was a way he could just stay in White Pine...

Kieran placed a calloused hand on her face. She loved his rough hands—a working man's hands. "A few weeks ago, my boss in Milwaukee told me that he'd talk to corporate about making me the sales manager if I wanted that. There's even an opportunity to invest and for me to become part owner. At the time I told him to stick it."

"But you've changed your mind?"

"Possibly."

"Because you like me," Audrey teased.

"Because I *love* you," Kieran corrected, kissing her gently. "And I'm not going anywhere."

Audrey's heart surged. "You mean it?"

"More than I've meant anything in my life."

"And you're not sad? To be anchored in one place?"

He searched her face, watching her watch him. "I couldn't be happier. I want to be where you are. I want to be with you forever, Audrey. No more leaving. Not unless you're coming with me, that is. I want to—" He paused, his throat working. She watched the movement of his Adam's apple, and the stricken look on his face, as if he were overcome with emotion.

"What?"

He clasped her hand in his. His grip was crushing. "Sweetheart, I want you to know that I'm all in. That's what they say at the gambling table when it's your last play and you're going for broke. There's nothing left if I don't have you."

Audrey's eyelashes fluttered and she felt tears on her cheeks. All in. It was Kieran or nothing for her, too. She could hardly breathe.

"Are you all right?" he asked. She was quiet for so long he probably wondered if she was horrified.

Quite the opposite.

"I'm wonderful," she said, her voice thick. "I make the bet, too. I'm all in."

He kissed her then, deep and long. Her skin ignited with pleasure, her center heating. Sitting up, she adjusted herself on top of him. Legs anchored on either side of his waist, she opened herself, her body awash in spine-tingling bliss as she took him inside of her.

"I want you to work there, too," he whispered as she

rocked on top of him. "I want you to stay at the Harley dealership. You and Fletch will make a good team."

His hands slid across her flesh, cupping her breasts. The afternoon light wobbled as he sat up, placing hot kisses on her, pulling one nipple into his mouth and sucking gently, then the other.

"I want to start my own business," she gasped, losing the thread of the conversation to pleasure. As if understanding she was sliding into a place where he couldn't reach her, Kieran stilled her hips. He kissed her throat gently.

"You can do both," he said, staring into her face with a mix of adoration and admiration that made her flush. "You can work at the dealership part time if you need to. Start your business and help me sell motorcycles. But don't leave me there alone. I need you."

"Business partners *and* lovers?" she asked teasingly. He answered by tilting his hips in a way that made them both moan. He pulled her against his chest and ground against her wet, aching core. She felt it in every part of her body, down to the tips of her fingers.

"Lovers first," he whispered, increasing his pace. She closed her eyes, letting him lead the way to her breaking point. "Lovers always. Forever, Audrey. I'm not going anywhere. I can't, because you have my heart in your hands, and if I walk away from you, I'll die."

"I won't let that happen," she murmured, leaning back slightly. He held on to her, letting her find just the right angle. And then he was crashing inside her at exactly the right place, and she came apart all over again, her heart shattering and becoming whole as he held on to her and never let go. Everything crumbled and turned to ash that glittered in her deepest parts.

And when the flame of passion had burned off her inse-
curities, her doubts, and her fears, she opened her eyes to
find warm afternoon light streaming into the room.

There was Kieran, his grass-green eyes shining into
hers. His strong arms were wrapped around her. "I love
you," he whispered.

"I love you, too," she answered.

And deep inside, she heard the click—the sound of two
puzzle pieces snapping together.

Forever.

EPILOGUE

August had settled onto White Pine with a thick, heavy heat that wilted leaves and dried up streams and corn stalks in the field. It also had Audrey running at ungodly hours of the morning, just to beat the temperatures.

The farmers said it was one of the warmest stretches they could remember. Audrey hated the sun's glare on everything, bright enough to make her head hurt.

So what in the world White Pine Harley was doing hosting an outdoor event in this weather was beyond her comprehension. But Kieran had insisted upon it, saying that renting a tent and inviting women to a clothing expo would be good for business. She'd disagreed, saying no woman wanted to try on leather jackets and gloves in this weather. But as a new co-owner of the dealership, he'd insisted it was important—finally pleading with her to trust him—and she'd relented.

"I'll take care of everything," he'd promised, placing both hands on either side of her face. "There's an events manager up at headquarters who's said she'll help me. We'll take care of the details. I just need you to show up on the day of and schmooze." His gentle touch was enough to turn her to liquid. She couldn't say no.

So now, wearing a simple white sundress and with her hair up off her sweaty neck in a ponytail, she parked her car and made for the tent, her cheeks already pink from the afternoon heat.

Not that she was complaining, exactly. Not really. Things at the dealership had been incredibly exciting and fulfilling, and every day she saw more and more women in the store. Up until today, the most challenging part of her job had been keeping her hands off Kieran when she passed him in the hallway, or when his fingers grazed hers underneath the conference room table. Some days they'd tumble out of bed together, throwing on whatever clothes they could before racing to work, trying to space their arrival but still making it in so neither was late. The eye rolls from colleagues, especially Fletch, told her they didn't always do a convincing job of it. Not that it mattered, because being with Kieran was a heart-pounding joy that nothing could diminish. And working with him—solving problems with him and making the dealership thrive—was deeply fulfilling.

If he wanted to throw an ill-timed expo under a tent in the center of town, so be it. They'd find a way to make it work.

They always did.

She was smiling slightly when she heard the first strains of music. Kieran hadn't told her there would be a live band. She bit her lip, wondering at the expense. Couldn't they have just played songs from an iPod plugged into speakers? Her brow furrowed at the type of music as well.

Her clientele enjoyed classic rock, or sometimes country-western. Her massive amounts of research meant she was well versed in her market segment, and she knew their likes and dislikes as much as her own. The fiddle, banjo, and washboard she heard were too bluegrass-y. She held back a groan, thinking that now they were putting women inside a hot tent and asking them to try on hot clothes and not even playing the music they liked while they did so.

Sweet Joseph of Arimathea, she thought, borrowing one of Kieran's famous Irish expressions, they were in for it now. Squaring her shoulders, she pushed back the heavy flap of the tent, expecting to confront angry customers right away. Instead, a blast of cool air hit her face, and she blinked at the sparkling white lights and her friends underneath them. Not Harley clientele.

"What the..." She shook her head at the scene, her words fading. All around her were wooden asparagus cutouts, painted green and propped up, smiling. The band on stage was the Shiny Happy Trio, the same band that had played at this year's Asparagus Festival. And in the corner of the tent was a keg that was labeled, improbably, as asparagus beer.

Suddenly Betty was next to her, threading her arm through Audrey's. "Buckle up, kiddo. You're in for a hell of a night."

"What is all this?" she asked, searching her friend's face.

"I think you'd better let *him* tell you that," she said, motioning toward Kieran. He was striding toward them, two pints of beer in his hands.

"I'll take it from here, Betty," he said, winking at her friend.

"Kieran," she started, "what in the world? I thought this was supposed to be an expo."

His wide mouth split into a grin. "That's what we said to get you here. But in actuality, it's a do-over."

"For what?"

"For the dance we missed at this year's Asparagus Festival. You were going to come. And I was waiting for you. Only we didn't get the chance. So I'd like to change that."

Audrey stared at him. "All this? For a dance?"

Kieran handed her a pint. "A beer and a boogie. What do you say?"

She took the golden-hued drink from him and sipped. *Asparagus beer.* Her taste buds sang with delight.

"How in the world did you do this?"

"Dave Englund. I gave him a discount on a Forty-Eight. A great ride. Got him good financing, too."

"But I mean *all* of this. How did you—"

Her question was cut short by Alexis and Caitlin, who flounced into their conversation, along with their respective moms.

"Oh my God this is so *romantic*." Alexis practically swooned. "Mom, isn't this so amazing?" She glanced at her mom, who had the same long limbs as her daughter. Mrs. Belten—Veronica, as Audrey had come to know her—smiled.

"I should take that beer away from Audrey for the workout she gave me last week," Veronica said. She patted her thighs. "So many squats I can hardly sit down on the toilet."

Audrey was barely able to swallow her beer before laughing. She'd expected personal training to be many things, but dramatic wasn't among them. At least not initially. Now she knew that good-natured complaints and eye rolling were part of training many of her clients. She fit them in on Friday, which was her day away from the Harley-Davidson dealership.

"Oh, leave her be," Caitlin's mom, Samantha Granlund, said. She was also among Audrey's clients and, in the three months Audrey had been working with her, she'd lost more than thirty pounds. She'd even started running with their group on Sundays. "We should stop moaning and groaning for five minutes and let Audrey have her night. She deserves it." They raised their asparagus beers in a toast, and then the band struck up a slow song that sent chills along Audrey's skin.

It was "Stand by Me" by Ben E. King, an old song Audrey had confessed to loving and that Kieran had played for her one night using an old record player and a forty-five he'd salvaged from a garage sale. She'd loved the ragged, worn sound of it, while Kieran held her tight as they swayed together in her living room.

Now, he gave her a knowing glance, and she set down her beer to dance with him at the grassy center of the tent. In her periphery, friends blurred together—Casey and the Knots and Bolts crew (especially Willa, whose hand rested on her now-round belly), plus Fletch from the dealership, Paul Frace and other school faculty members, and personal-training clients—all watching as Kieran pulled her close.

"This is a lot of effort for just one dance," she said, smiling up at him. He pushed the errant end of her ponytail off her shoulder. The feel of his fingers on her flesh gave her chills.

"I wanted that dance," he said, his voice low. "I needed it."

A funny word, *need*, Audrey thought. Six months ago, if anyone had suggested that she needed Kieran Callaghan, she would have snorted. Now, clasped in his muscled arms, the idea of being without him bent her brain the way certain science articles did, when they talked about universes on top of universes in an infinite tableau of multiverses. It was incomprehensible.

"I need *you*," Audrey said, watching shadows shift across the rugged stubble of his chin.

Kieran swallowed visibly. "We didn't get our dance this year at the Asparagus Festival, but I wanted you to know that I will always give you what is in my power to give. And today, some lights and a tent—I can do that. But, more importantly, Audrey, I will give you everything that I have. Forever. I'll show you my darkest parts and trust that you can always see the good in me. Because if anyone can—it's you."

His eyes sparkled. Audrey's breath caught at the magnificence of his features, of the feel of him against her, and the smell of grass and cool air all around.

Suddenly, in the blink of an eye, he was down on one knee. She was vaguely aware that the band had stopped playing. Bodies shifted around them, silent shadows.

What was happening? Was he going to—

From his back pocket, Kieran produced a velvet box. He opened it to reveal a sparkling ring. She gasped, her fingers flying to cover her mouth. This wasn't real, she thought. It couldn't be. This was a dream and no way had he just re-created the Asparagus Festival to propose to her. It was too much.

"Audrey Tanner, I love you and I want to be with you forever. Will you do me the honor of becoming my wife?"

The tent had gone stone still. She stared at Kieran, still unwilling to believe that this man loved her, that they had somehow fought the odds to come together after five long years apart.

And yet, they had. The cards were never in their favor, but they'd played their hands and trusted that the other was all in. And she would play the same hand again, if she had to. She'd go to the betting table holding nothing, and she'd trust that she and Kieran could still walk away clutching not riches, but each other.

"Yes," she whispered. "Yes, I will."

The entire tent erupted into a cheer, and Kieran swept her into his arms and kissed her so deeply she wondered if their mouths would ever separate, if perhaps they had fused together with love and passion.

Of course, the kiss eventually ended. And then there was music and dancing, even a toast from her sister. "To Audrey's happiness," Casey had said, her eyes shining as she held a pint of asparagus ale. "May nothing ever stand in your way." She'd hugged Audrey and kissed her cheek, both of them struggling not to cry.

"Let me know if you want to go dress shopping," Casey said. "If I can come, I promise not to offer too many opinions."

"Unless I make her dress," Betty interjected from nearby.

"Save it for the recipe exchange, you two," Willa cautioned. Audrey was so delighted she hugged her sister again, then her Knots and Bolts friends, then her current and former colleagues, and everyone else she could pull into her arms. All the while Kieran stole more kisses that were so sweet she thought she would die from the pleasure of them.

And occasionally, she would lift her asparagus beer and think that the cardboard asparagus cutouts along the wall were winking at her. It might have been the twinkling lights or the joyous, delirious knowledge that she was Kieran's forever, and he was hers. Either way, she winked back, and silently promised to carry a bouquet of asparagus down the aisle when she wed.

Asparagus Hot Dish

From the kitchen of Audrey Tanner

Ingredients

- 1 pound asparagus
- 1 cup wild rice (uncooked)
- 1 pound boneless, skinless chicken breast
- 2 cups chicken stock
- 1 tablespoon butter
- 1 tablespoon olive oil
- 1 teaspoon dried onion
- ½ teaspoon garlic salt
- ¼ teaspoon salt
- 2 (10.75 oz) cans cream of mushroom soup
- 8 slices swiss cheese
- 1 cup french-fried onions

Directions

1. Pre-heat the oven to 350 degrees.
2. In a medium pot, mix wild rice with two cups chicken stock and 1 cup of water, cover and simmer about

    30-35 minutes, until rice is tender and all liquid is absorbed. Uncover and fluff with a fork.

3. While the rice cooks, mix butter and olive oil in a skillet on medium heat. Place asparagus spears into skillet and sprinkle with the garlic salt and dried onions. Sauté until cooked but slightly firm. Time will vary depending on thickness of asparagus spears, but will likely be between 10-15 minutes. Once cooked, set aside.

4. In a large skillet, cook chicken and then cube the meat. Then add the cream of mushroom soup, cooked wild rice, pepper, and salt.

5. Spread the chicken mixture on the bottom of a 9-by-13-inch baking pan. Layer the cooked asparagus over the top, then layer the cheese on top of the asparagus. Finally, add the french-fried onions.

6. Bake at 350 degrees for 25 minutes or until onions are crispy and the cheese is bubbling. Serve and enjoy with an asparagus beer!

Eternal good girl Casey Tanner moved to White Pine for a fresh start. Her mission: to *finally* have fun with a bad boy. And after one long, lingering look at sexy firefighter Abe Cameron, Casey has found her man . . .

A preview of *Every Little Kiss* follows.

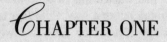CHAPTER ONE

$\mathcal{C}$asey Tanner had never before had colleagues who played practical jokes. She was used to a silent corporate water cooler over which smiles were rarely traded. She was once so startled when a receptionist cackled loudly while watching an online video about grandmas smoking pot that she'd spilled a nonfat latte across her keyboard.

So it was only slowly, over many long, uncomfortable moments that Casey wondered if she'd been had. If she'd been punk'd, for lack of a better word.

Because surely the intern with the wide eyes and trembling chin was joking about having just called 9-1-1.

"Tell me once more why you thought this was necessary?" Casey asked the young girl—Ellie, if she was remembering the name correctly—whose cropped ginger hair was in disarray around her head. The poor thing could be barely more than a first-year in college.

"The CO_2 detector in the basement was *screaming*. We

should open windows or get everyone out of here *right now.*"

The girl's words might be dramatic, but her face was serious. If Casey had wanted this to be a hilarious prank, it sure wasn't turning out that way. Cold fear crawled along her spine, but she focused on Ellie and worked to stay calm. Ellie already looked like she might pass out.

"All right," Casey said, "easy does it. I want you to take a deep breath and—"

"I don't want to breathe deeply if the air is poisoned!"

Casey pressed her lips together. She had only just started at Robot Lit, a youth literacy nonprofit, two weeks before. She was still trying to figure out where the extra copier paper was stored, never mind what do to in a CO_2 emergency. Ingrid, their director, was out taking her ten-year-old daughter to the doctor, which meant Casey was probably the most senior person in charge. Never mind that she was the newest.

At that moment, though, none of it mattered. If the building was filling with CO_2, she had to get her colleagues out safely. Without causing a panic. Her mind raced.

"Okay, Ellie," she said after a moment. "Most everyone should be on the third floor here. So I want you to calmly—very calmly—let people know that we are being extra careful about our CO_2 levels, and folks should stand outside for a bit while the fire department gets here. While you're doing that, I'm going to make absolutely sure the rest of the building is clear. Does that make sense?"

Ellie nodded, her eyes enormous in her small face.

"Don't forget to check the restrooms, okay?"

"Yes."

"And no freaking out, right?"

"Right."

"Say it with me," Casey said, grabbing the young girl's hand. "We're being what?"

"Extra careful."

"And what should folks do?"

"Stand outside."

"Should they panic?"

"No."

"Good. Go tell them."

Casey breathed a small sigh as Ellie walked away, grateful that Robot Lit only had six employees. And there weren't any kids there at the moment. For once, their small staff would be an asset.

Casey grabbed her coat, her eye catching the white of a snow-covered day outside her window. At least if she had to spend time in the cold, she'd get to look down Main Street and see all the holiday lights twinkling.

She heard sirens in the distance as she wound her way down to the conference rooms and kitchen on the second floor, looking for anyone as she went. The rooms were empty, so she headed into the lobby on the first floor. All clear. Through the door's wavy glass, she spotted Ellie along with the other Robot Lit employees outside, clustered in a small circle. She knew she should join them. Instead, pushing aside a prickle of unease, she descended into the belly of the old warehouse on Main Street, all the way to the basement.

She wasn't going to just let a fireman rumble into Robot Lit without knowing what was the matter. It was her job, after all, if Ingrid wasn't there. She would simply find out if the CO_2 detector was really going off, or if it was something else entirely.

Careful, a small inner voice cautioned. It was this need to know everything—and, okay, maybe control everything—that had come close to unraveling her life a few short months ago. Casey had screwed up so badly that she'd left a good paying job in a Minneapolis suburb for a chance at a new start in White Pine and to be closer to her sister, Audrey. Now, she was working at Robot Lit for a fraction of her former salary and living in a creaky Cape Cod instead of her sleek city apartment.

It was all worth it, of course. Casey would do just about anything to atone for her past. She grimaced as she remembered how selfishly she'd acted just a few short months ago, nearly ruining Audrey's chance at true love.

She wasn't about to make that mistake again. She figured she could, however, spare five minutes to figure out what was happening with the CO_2 detector.

Its shrill beeping pierced her ears as she flipped on a small overhead bulb in the basement. She inhaled the dank air of dim space. CO_2 was odorless—she wouldn't be able to smell anything—but she took an inventory of her breathing, of her vision, of any pains in her head that could signal toxic levels. At her body's first sign of symptoms, no matter how tiny, she'd be out of there.

Unless she collapsed in a clueless heap first.

Hoping for the best, she followed the beeping to a small box on the wall. The sirens were louder now. The fire house was just up the street, and the firefighters would be here in no time.

A light was flashing, strobe-bright in the dim space. *Head fine, vision clear,* she thought, accounting for her every breath and movement. Using the flashlight app on her phone, she trained a blaze of light on the panel. There were three lights—green, yellow, and red. But only one of them was flashing.

Yellow.

Service.

The damn thing was low on batteries.

Casey groaned as the thunder of heavy boots came down the stairs. Three firefighters swept into the room, their tanks and gear making them seem like giants. They weren't wearing their oxygen masks, meaning she could see their faces. Two men and a woman.

"What are you doing down here?" the tallest of the two men asked. His hazel eyes were sharp. The bridge of his nose was slightly crooked, like it had been broken in a fight.

"I just wanted to check and make sure things were all right," she said. "I was looking—"

"You should be outside with the others. This is a potentially dangerous situation."

"I know," Casey said, feeling small and silly, "I was trying—"

The fireman shined his flashlight into her eyes. She blinked. "Do you have a headache? Nausea?"

"No, this is all a misunderstanding. The detector is—"

"Did you make the call?"

Frustration needled her. The man hadn't let her finish a sentence yet. "*No*, that's what I'm trying to tell you. An intern called when she thought something was wrong. But the thing is out of batteries. That's all."

She stepped aside so the massive firefighter could take a closer look at the white box on the wall. Underneath the smoky, chalky smell of his gear, Casey detected a scent like wood chips and cinnamon.

The other firefighters stayed a few feet behind, sharing a look that signaled to Casey this wasn't the first time they'd had a false alarm on a CO_2 detector.

"Write it up, Lu?" the woman asked. Her dark eyes were striking in her pale face.

The man's name was Lou, Casey realized. It seemed an odd name for him—like calling bulldog Fluffy.

"When was the last time this device was calibrated?"

"I'm sorry, I have no idea. Lou. Or is it Louis? Louie?" Casey figured she'd better get on this man's good side, and fast.

"Lu is short for lieutenant," he replied, eyes sparking with irritation. Underneath the visor of his helmet, the lines of his face were granite hard.

"Oh." She could feel her cheeks redden. "I'm sorry. Look, I just started here a couple weeks ago."

The lieutenant trained his jaw at the ceiling. His flashlight beam slid down an old copper pipe. "You got a sprinkler system installed?" he asked.

Was he not listening to *anything* she said? She was a brand new employee, but he was still grilling her. It may have been her imagination, but Casey could swear the other two firefighters had just groaned quietly.

"I don't—I couldn't tell you," she stumbled. She checked the time on her phone. The employees had been standing outside for a while in the Minnesota cold, and she figured she ought to herd them down the street to the Rolling Pin and buy them all hot chocolate for their trouble.

"Are we settled here? Can I go back upstairs to the others?"

The lieutenant tore his eyes from the copper pipe and looked around the basement—past the boxes of stationery and the old phone books and an oddly placed plastic hula hoop.

"I want to take a closer look at things," he said. "Quinn and Reese, you two head upstairs, check and see that the smoke detectors all have working batteries and the fire exits aren't encumbered. I'll be up in a few."

Casey watched the female firefighter open her mouth, think better of what she was going to say, and close it. Together, the two firefighters tromped back up the steps in their heavy gear.

"So…can I go?" Casey asked, unsure of what she was supposed to be doing. The lieutenant frowned, a motion that bunched the chiseled lines of his face. He'd be handsome, Audrey thought, if he wasn't so completely abrupt about everything.

"If you would, I need you to answer a few questions."

Casey shifted, feeling suddenly like she was under investigation. She quickly texted Raif, their program coordinator.

All clear inside. Take everyone to Rolling Pin. Buy hot choc. I'll be there in a few.

She hit send as the lieutenant made a low rumbling in his throat. The noise involuntarily sent goose bumps up and down her arms.

"You have a smoke detector down here?" he asked, making his way deeper into the basement. He flipped on buzzing overhead lights as he went.

"I don't know," she replied, trailing in his wake.

The lieutenant made the low rumbling in his throat again, and it struck Casey that the sound was of disapproval. Her jaw clenched with irritation. Why were they still down here if this was just a case of low batteries?

Casey tapped her toe on the scuffed cement floor. She watched the lieutenant scan the pipes and boards all around. She caught a flash of blond under his helmet. The lock of hair looked thick and wavy in a way that had her fingertips itching to touch it. At least until he made the low rumble in his throat a third time.

"Can't find a single smoke detector down here. You'll want to change that."

Yes, your highness, she thought.

"I'll talk to the director," she said instead.

"And a fire extinguisher. You'll want one of those, too."

"I'll add it to the list."

"What's your name?" He was staring at the pipes on the ceiling again. As if he couldn't be bothered from his all-important inspection to focus on her.

"Casey Tanner."

"What brought you to Robot Lit?"

It's complicated.

"Job change," she said. "I moved down here from Eagan."

She pictured the bare walls of her new house, the naked wood floors, and the stacks of boxes she needed to empty, and held back an overwhelmed sigh. The mountain of work ahead of her was daunting, made more so by the fact that she was desperate to find her Christmas decorations. It was December first already, and not a single ornament was in place, no matter that she had taped a label on every box, listing all the contents of each one in Sharpie. But the boxes she'd identified as "Holiday"—inventoried with bullet points like "fake snow, tinsel, Rudolph figures" and more—simply couldn't be found.

"Are you a tutor at Robot Lit?" This time the lieutenant looked up from his writing, and for a brief moment the strict lines around his mouth and eyes relaxed. Casey's breath caught unexpectedly.

"I'm an accountant," she managed. "They brought me on to help get their finances in order. And keep them that way."

She left out the part about taking a huge pay cut to come here and trying to rebuild her relationship with her sister. In other words, the part where she was blind and selfish and in need of a shake-up.

She squared her shoulders, trying to seem more confident than she felt. The lieutenant might have rugged good looks, but she didn't want him knowing anything about her. The way he was finding every flaw in this building probably translated to finding flaws in people. And Lord knew she had plenty for him to uncover.

She glanced at her phone as a text message from Raif came in.

Everyone at Rolling Pin. Text when you can.

"Almost finished?" she asked, reading the text message again so she didn't linger too long on the almond shape of the lieutenant's eyes.

"For now," he said. "On our way back up, let's take the elevator. I want to see how the emergency call button is functioning."

Casey blinked. She didn't even know Robot Lit had an elevator. Which was just as well. Small spaces always caused her heart to pound and her head to hurt. Elevators especially.

She tamped down the lump of worry. It's not as if they were shooting up to the top of the Empire State Building for crying out loud.

Nevertheless, her throat was dry as she followed the lieutenant into the elevator. Above the collar of his fireman's coat, she caught a glimpse of his neck. The skin was golden enough to have her picturing droplets of honey on a sunny day.

When the doors slid shut behind them, the lieutenant hit floor three, then punched the brass button with the fireman's cap on it. The elevator jerked into motion. He kept his finger on the panel, waiting for some kind of response. To take her mind off the cramped space, Casey studied the fine blond hairs on the back of the lieutenant's enormous hand. They looked so delicate in contrast to the rest of him. His spicy smell was back, so much so that her head was all but filled with it. She told herself the pounding in her chest was from the enclosed space.

The lieutenant pressed the fire call button again and again. No response.

"Has anyone used—" the lieutenant began. But the words died on his lips when the elevator squawked to a halt, and they were plunged into darkness.

* * *

Casey couldn't breathe. The blackness was thick and all-consuming. Blinking, she swiped at the heavy nothingness, as if to push it away.

"Help!" she cried, pawing at emptiness. "Help us!"

Strong fingers wrapped around her forearm. She looked down, but couldn't see even an outline of a hand. "Easy there," came the lieutenant's deep voice. "It's okay."

His unrelenting grip should have offended her. *What right did he have to touch her?* But instead, it grounded her reeling mind. Fragments of logic pierced through. *I'm in an elevator. This man is a firefighter.*

Still, her breath was ragged. She couldn't get enough air. The space pressed against her. She was aware she might be panting.

"Casey, listen to me." The lieutenant had stepped closer. She could feel him acutely. "I want you to close your eyes and count to ten."

"We need to get out of here. I have to leave. Why won't the door open? It's time to go." The words were a tangle. The darkness was in her lungs, fighting with all the air. She was beginning to get light-headed.

His grip vanished. She was unmoored, reeling and lost in the smallest space possible. *Come back*, she thought wildly.

Then a flashlight beam sliced through the inky blackness. The lieutenant held it, even as both of his hands came to rest on her shoulders. Heavy and strong. "I'm going to take that breath with you," he said. "Both of us. We're going to do it together." His face was lined with shadow. It reminded her of face paint at a carnival.

The hand that wasn't holding the flashlight slid palm-down from her shoulder, along her biceps, all the way to her fingers. He pulled her hand through emptiness until it came to rest on his chest. "Now you know if we're breathing together. You'll feel it. In and out, okay? Just like me."

He held her hand tight against his sternum. His heartbeat was there, too, steady underneath his fireman's gear. "In and out," he said. "Easy does it." The rise and fall of his chest was like the waves on Lake Superior—great swells that rolled along, one into the next. She squeezed her eyes closed. She pictured the lake, concentrated on matching her breathing to his.

"Good," he said. The rumble of his voice was so near she could feel it. If his chest was a rolling wave, then his voice was rich sunlight full of heat. "You just keep breathing like that, and I'll keep holding your hand. I'm going to use my other hand here to set down this flashlight, then I'll call for help on my radio. The rest of the fire crew can get us out in no time. I need you to speak and tell me you understand what I'm telling you."

"I understand," she managed. He squeezed her hand. In the cramped space, it should have made her more claustrophobic to be this near to a stranger, touching like this. Yet she found that she suddenly wanted to wring the last ounce of distance from between them.

The radio was on the lieutenant's shoulder. He turned his head as he spoke into it.

"Dispatch from unit sixteen, we have an elevator entrapment. It's a single elevator, and we're between floors one and two."

"Dispatch copy. Do you have any injuries on scene?"

"No injuries. There are two other firefighters here also from unit sixteen, responding initially to a CO_2 concern. We don't need a cruiser—just an elevator tech."

"Unit sixteen, message received. We'll get a technician en route."

"Copy. Thanks." A pause, then: "Lieutenant to firefighters and unit sixteen, go to channel two."

A crackle of static. "Yeah, Lu. What's up?" It sounded like the female firefighter.

"I'm in an elevator entrapment situation. I called dispatch, they have an elevator tech en route."

"You doing okay?"

"Yeah. Just try to get the stupid elevator going from

your end if you can. And somebody wait outside for the elevator tech, help them get to the scene."

"Copy that, Lu. We'll get you out in no time."

"Copy. Thanks."

The conversation was over, apparently. The flashlight beam was a tiny lamp in an ocean of black.

"They need to call the elevator company to get those doors open," the lieutenant said. "They'll get a tech out here, and we'll be out in no time."

How long? Casey trembled, wondering if she'd suffer for minutes or hours.

"My name is Abe Cameron," the lieutenant said after a moment.

Casey's brain fumbled, trying to process how to respond. Where were her manners? She couldn't remember what to say. All she knew was that she couldn't think past the four walls pressing so close around her.

"I used to spend a lot of time at Robot Lit," he continued when Casey didn't say anything. "I was tutored here. When I started, I was in fifth grade and could barely read."

The idea had emotion swelling in her chest, though she had no idea what to do with it. "My teacher, Mrs. Wills, brought me to Robot Lit after school one day. They had time to spend with me that she didn't. She really helped. This *place* really helped."

The clouds in her mind broke enough for her to wonder if that's why Abe had been such a stickler in the basement. Because he cared about the place.

For some reason, the idea of Abe being gruff because of affection for Robot Lit calmed her. Moment by moment, Casey became aware of the present, of what was right in front of her, which included Abe's skin against hers.

She could picture the blond hairs on his forearms, the tiny pores, the blood warm underneath. His breath was so close. Every exhale was a whisper of reassurance.

Abe's fingers were steady and firm. A working man's hands, Casey thought. Not like the hands of all the other accountants at her last job.

"You're doing great," Abe murmured, leaning forward and speaking the words into her hair. Casey's breath nearly vanished again, but not from fear. It was the fact that his lips felt mere inches away.

She wasn't used to being this near anyone, let alone a firefighter. She tried to recall the last time she'd been kissed—been held—but the fog of time was too thick. She couldn't glimpse through it.

Casey was suddenly grateful for the darkness so Abe wouldn't see her grimace of shame. There was a word for women like her, she knew. *Spinster*. It might not be the 1800s, but the label fit. *Spinster* even had the right sound to it. The spitting, biting consonants were the perfect reminder that she'd been living a prudish, uptight existence for far too long, batting back the part of her that secretly wanted to break free and live with abandon. With adventure, even.

"Easy now," Abe said. "Just keep relaxing. The tech is coming."

Casey stilled, figuring she must have tensed up just then, and Abe had felt it.

"I'm—I'm doing okay," she replied. Her voice sounded small and tinny.

Abe shifted, his leg grazing hers. An unexpected jolt shot through her nerves. There was so much of him, Casey realized. He must be at least six-foot-four, whereas she was barely five-foot-five. Unlike her sister, Audrey, she didn't have an athlete's body underneath her clothes. All she had was her plain brown hair and her plain figure from being a plain office worker for the past decade.

Here in the darkness, though, maybe it didn't matter. She shifted just slightly, inching closer to Abe. She couldn't be sure, but she thought she heard a soft grunt from him.

Time either slowed way down or sped up. Casey couldn't tell. She had no idea how long she'd been pressed against Abe when there was a scuffling sound from above them. Casey jerked, wondering if the elevator ties were finally going to give way, and they were going to go plunging downward.

"That's just Quinn and Reese working with the tech to open the doors on the floor above us. While they do that, I want you to tell me about a place that you love," Abe said. Was it her imagination, or was he clutching her more tightly? "We're going to picture it together. You're going to tell me all about it."

Tears prickled her eyes. Surely it was the claustrophobia jerking her emotions from one extreme to another. That's why she was getting so worked up over a silly question.

And yet, her chest ached as she tried to think about a place she loved—as she tried to think about *anything* she loved, frankly.

There was her sister, of course.

Audrey was generous and kind and beautiful, and Casey had loved her so ferociously it had almost ruined their relationship. Casey's stomach twisted at the memory of how she'd driven a wedge between Audrey and the man Audrey loved, Kieran Callaghan. She'd done it out of fear, out of a need for control, and it had been terrible. Ruinous, even. Fortunately, Audrey and Kieran were married now, and Audrey had forgiven Casey. But Casey wasn't sure if she had yet forgiven herself. She wasn't sure she'd earned it.

Then of course there was Christmas. Since she was a little girl, Casey had adored Christmas with its sparkling tinsel and glittering streets and freshly cut trees and warm cookies and spiced cider.

So yes, there were things she loved—but a *place* she loved?

The answer seemed impossible. She'd never traveled much outside of Minnesota. Her life up until now had been composed of *getting* places, of ensuring a specific course on a road to success. She'd never stopped much along the way.

"You're awfully quiet," Abe said. She could hear the smile on his lips, trying to lighten the moment. As if he somehow understood what a battle this question was.

"I don't…" The words faded into less than a whisper. She had no answer.

"It's okay," Abe said. His hand was on her shoulder again, the other still clasping her fingers against his chest. This man was stronger and steadier and calmer than anyone she'd ever met.

There was a shout above them, and a scraping noise. Casey cringed.

"The place *I* love," Abe said, "is a little German town called Freiburg. The British messed it up in World War II, gutted it with bombs. But the town was rebuilt with these efficient, logical roads and bike paths that you can take anywhere. There's also a train, and it always runs on time. *Always*. And there's all this green technology through what are called passive houses. They don't require any kind of furnace or device to heat them. They essentially heat themselves. It's efficient. It's incredible."

Casey thrilled at how thoughtful and ordered it sounded. Until a small inner voice reminded her that being logical and ordered is what had almost ruined her life. A straight-laced existence had nearly been her undoing, and she wasn't about to repeat the pattern. She'd moved to White Pine to do the opposite, in fact.

"When were you there?" she managed to ask.

"Never. I've only read about it. I'm saving up to go, but—well, it's a long story."

And based on the shouts and noise above them, there wasn't any time to tell it.

Abe's radio squawked. "Crew to lieutenant. Elevator tech is here. He's going to come in from the top. We'll get you out with the ladder."

"Message received."

"They're coming in though the fire access panel above us," Abe said. "The elevator door to the first floor is just a foot or so away, so they're going to pull us out of the top of this thing, then pull us onto the first floor. Does that make sense?"

"Yes."

Abe's stubbled cheek pressed against hers. The rough feel of it had her muscles weakening. "You're almost there," he said. "Just a few more minutes."

Before she could gather her next thought, Abe dropped her hand and stepped away, just as the panel in the ceiling above them opened. A flashlight beam pierced through, brighter than a hundred camera flashes. Or so Casey thought as she squinted against it.

"There are better places for a party," said the firefighter

above them. "This one is kind of hard to get to, and I'm not sure the DJ would fit."

"Get a ladder down here *now*, Reese." Abe's voice was back to being razor sharp. Audrey wrapped her arms around herself, thinking she'd liked it much better when he'd murmured.

The flashlight beam bounced as a ladder was lowered into the elevator car. "Reese will hold it from above," Abe said. "I'll grab it down here. Go ahead."

Casey took in the firm set of Abe's lips, the rugged edge of his jaw, the hardness in his eyes. His kindness, his gentleness was seeping away—that is, if it had ever been there in the first place.

Not that she was about to stay in the elevator one second longer to wonder. She grasped the sides of the ladder and hauled herself up the rungs until Reese helped her stand on top of the stalled car. Golden light poured onto them from the open doors just a few above. Inside the wide doors was the female firefighter, Quinn.

Audrey gulped air, relieved to be away from the confines of the elevator's four walls.

"You hardly have to move now," Reese said, smiling a lopsided grin. "You just raise your arms and Quinn is going to pull you up."

If she had any doubts that Quinn was strong enough, they were gone within seconds. Before she knew it, strong hands had lifted her into the safety of the building. It was all she could do to smile and thank her rescuers. She wanted to collapse onto the floor and kiss the solid ground beneath her feet.

"Casey!" Her director, Ingrid, was racing down the wood-planked hallway to get to her. "Oh my God, Raif called me just as I was dropping Heidi back off at school. I got here as soon as I could. I was so worried!" Whole sections of her white-blond hair had come loose from her ponytail. A number two pencil was tucked behind her ear, its yellow wood indented with teeth marks.

"I'm fine," Casey managed. "I just don't like small spaces much."

"What an ordeal. Take the rest of the day off. Please."

"I'm sure I'll be all right."

"Just do it, okay? It'll make me feel better, anyway."

She hugged Casey just as Abe's voice sliced through the commotion. He was directly behind her. "Get the ladder hauled up. Talk to the mechanic. I want it logged in."

"Yes, Lu." The firefighters scurried to get their tasks finished.

"Abe!" Ingrid said, waving at him. "You saved our girl here. Thank you."

Casey was momentarily confused as to how these two were acquainted. Abe had been tutored at Robot Lit years ago. Had he stayed in touch with the staff?

"You guys know each other?" she asked dumbly.

"Abe's a good friend to this place," Ingrid said.

Recognition dawned. Casey hadn't been around non-profits very much, but she was beginning to understand that *friend* meant donor.

Abe smiled at Ingrid—big enough to show two rows of gloriously straight white teeth. Casey's heart jerked. "Happy to help," he said. "You two take care."

He started off, radioing more commands. He wasn't leaving, was he? The thought had her stomach clenching unexpectedly. Casey gave Ingrid a hang-on-a-minute gesture.

She trotted after Abe. "Thank you," she said, sliding in front of him to stop his forward march. "You kept me calm down there and I'm grateful. You were great. Are great, I mean. At your job, that is." Her brain still felt tangled, her words twisted into each other.

Oh, God, what was she doing? She should have just let him go. She was making an ass of herself.

If Abe minded her babbling, he didn't show it. In fact, his eyes flashed with emotion and, if Casey didn't know better, she'd say it was warmth. Maybe even something hotter than that—a light closer to flame.

"Happy to help." Then he tipped his helmet at her and walked away, barking orders at the other firefighters. The sound of his fireman's boots on the warehouse's wood floors grew more and more distant.

The connection she'd felt between them stretched thin as he retreated, like taffy pulled too far apart. She felt a pang of hollowness, an unexpected disappointment. Did he really have to walk away like that? He'd been so comforting, so calming in the elevator telling her about Robot Lit and the German city he loved. Underneath all those layers of fireman's gear, she thought she'd glimpsed his tender side, and it left her wanting more.

She thought maybe he'd seen something in her that he wanted more of, too. The way he'd pulled her close, the way he'd murmured into her hair.

But apparently not.

Apparently he was just doing his job.

She pulled in a breath. It was just as well. Abe Cameron was a stranger to her. In her frazzled state in the elevator, she'd simply contrived a connection to a man she barely knew. Even worse, she'd turned him into something he clearly wasn't—gentle, caring, even sexy, a *hero*—and when the hard light of day hit her again, she'd been left staring at something that had never been.

It's all for the best. She wasn't looking for someone whose lifelong dream was to visit an orderly German town. Practicality was not on her list of sexy attributes. She had enough of that in her own life, thank you very much.

Casey knew that to permanently shed her spinster status, she was going to have to find a man who was her complete opposite. Fun-loving, carefree, adventurous—everything she wanted to be.

She stepped out into the darkening afternoon, the snow swirling and the holiday lights twinkling, and reminded herself she was back in White Pine to change. To be better.

A man like Abe Cameron would be nothing but trouble.

CHAPTER TWO

$\mathcal{T}$he morning sun crested over a snow-covered hill, igniting the icy limbs of the cedar trees in a fiery orange glow. Abe Cameron gulped down the cold air, lungs burning as his hiking boots trundled through the fresh powder on the trail. His hands clutched at the straps on his backpack. Sweat dripped down his neck in rivulets that froze almost as soon as they formed.

Three miles in. Five to go. Eight miles every other day along this trail, rain or shine, carrying a backpack filled with weights and a rock or two from along the path, when he felt like throwing them in.

It was the hardest workout Abe could think of. It was also the only one that made sense to him. Because if something was challenging, you did it. It if was tough, you tackled it.

Abe shifted the backpack slightly, ignoring the ache in his shoulders and neck. He'd long ago stopped asking himself how he felt about things. If he focused on the pain, the hurt, the desire to stop, he'd never do anything.

He'd never run into a flame-engulfed building.

He'd never hold the hand of a car-crash victim and tell them to hang on.

He'd never breathe air into the lungs of a drowning victim, willing himself to bring them back.

In White Pine, fire and rescue were wrapped into one, meaning he could get called on everything from a house fire to a sprained ankle. Doing both meant he'd seen his share of broken bodies and tragic situations.

He pushed himself down the trail harder, as if trying to outrun the memories of the middle-of-the-night calls when someone stopped breathing, and the pain in the family members' faces as they helplessly watched him work.

An icy wind blasted his face. He turned into it, welcoming the raw cold. His job should have made him grateful for every day he was alive and healthy. Oddly, it had done the opposite. It had numbed him, in a way, to his life. It could all get taken away so easily, so why get invested?

It's part of why he kept himself cordoned off from any relationships that got too deep or too heavy.

That's just the way it is, he thought bitterly. Then immediately wondered how he'd gotten so jaded. He didn't much like the hardened cynic who stared back at him every morning from the bathroom mirror.

He stumbled, nearly losing his footing. He threw out his arms, fighting for balance. When he righted himself, he took a deep gulp of the crystal air. His thoughts were too heavy, too coarse. He knew this. All this existential clamor about feelings was useless. He should stop right now.

But at the same time, he felt a heavy weariness he

couldn't shake. God, but it was exhausting work, sealing yourself away from the reality that life was tenuous, even delicate. It could all end—poof!—in a single moment. A fire. A misstep. A piano falling from the sky.

This truth had kept him on the edge of his own existence. It had given him his nickname at the station: Ninety-eyed. "Eyed" was a homophone for "IED." Every relationship he'd ever had blew up after ninety days. Ninety-*IED*. He blew up the connection to the women he'd pursued. He pulled the trigger. He knew it. The guys at the station knew it. And the parade of women through his life certainly knew it—if not at first, then certainly by the time they'd dusted off the rubble and got over the shock.

For years, he'd enjoyed the nickname because he'd been happy. Hot sex for a while, then an explosion before things got complicated. But now, he was beginning to wonder if he wasn't happy as much as he was...indifferent. It was hard to be too bummed about anything when nothing really mattered.

He grunted, straining under his pack. For the first time in memory, he was experiencing feelings he didn't want to bat down. A tiny spring bubbled inside him every time he thought about Casey, the woman from Robot Lit, and he was doing a half-assed job of damming it up.

The memory of her soft hand inside his while they were trapped in the elevator had his heart pounding more than it normally would along this section of the trail. He followed a fork to the left into a cluster of birch trees, ducking amid low branches.

If he'd been put off by her reckless decision to go down to the basement when they first showed up, he'd warmed to her when she said she was an accountant. He respected the logic of numbers. And then to find out she was working at Robot Lit was an added bonus. The place had been able to teach him to read, had emphasized the wonder of books when most of his teachers had simply shrugged off his struggle for literacy, saying the words would be there when he was ready. Robot Lit mattered to him, and he liked meeting people who felt the same way.

It also didn't hurt when those people had thick auburn hair and wore form-fitting sweaters that emphasized just the right curves.

A pheasant took flight from nearby brushes, startling him into a full stop. His lungs heaved as he watched the bird warble into the air, snow falling like stars from its wings. An ache pressed behind his sternum, and he instinctively brought his gloved hand to his chest.

What the—?

Chest pain. Only, surely it was just a little bit of heartburn. He brushed it off. After all, the call yesterday had scared him more than he wanted to admit, and he was probably just a little worked up as a result. He'd been extra gruff when his crew arrived because the thought of anyone on the Robot Lit team being in harm's way made his stomach twist. Secretly, he felt badly for turning a low-battery warning on a CO_2 detector into a full-blown inspection, especially when that wasn't even his job. Ty Brady was White Pine's fire inspector, and Abe knew he had no business stepping on Ty's toes. That's why Quinn and Reese were irritated about the whole call, though they'd dutifully checked out the building even when they didn't want to. He didn't blame them for being miffed. But he wasn't going to pass up a chance to make Robot Lit as safe as he could.

He started back down the trail, his breath puffing white in the cold. He'd been high strung about the call to begin with, which was probably why Casey Tanner was affecting him more than she should. They'd shared several minutes in a dark, confused space, and Abe knew better than anyone that trauma could forge bonds with people that normal situations didn't. That's why he'd pulled her closer than he should have, why he let his guard down for a few minutes, speaking into her hair and letting his cheek graze hers briefly.

The problem was, he was still having trouble erasing the picture of her in his mind. Especially when she'd thanked him after it was all over. She'd still been pale and shaken, but her golden brown eyes had been clear and focused. She hadn't felt sorry for herself or milked it for drama. She'd been gracious and grateful and he'd stomped away. Like an asshole.

He didn't want her to know how much he'd enjoyed being trapped in that space with her.

Abe pushed himself up a small incline that deposited him into a wide clearing. Above him, the wind-swept sky was patterned in pale blues and pinks. Ahead, a snow-covered field stretched for miles until it ended in another cluster of woods. He flexed his numb fingers and toes, trying to work more blood into his extremities. He grimaced as a flash of pain ignited underneath his rib cage.

He wondered briefly if he should get it checked out. Chest pain was no joke. Then again, this was probably nothing. Just an overreaction to yesterday's elevator situation.

In the meantime, he blew breath onto his gloved hands and stamped his feet. He'd welcome some warmth to his limbs all right, but his emotions needed to stay frozen. Abe knew firsthand how dangerous feelings could be. They could cloud your judgment, they could keep you from running into the burning building because you were afraid or unsure. Feelings could let you think that you had any control at all over this life.

He thumped his chest once. Hard. A warning shot to his heart. *Do your job,* he wanted to say, *and nothing more.* Abe was a confirmed bachelor, he didn't get worked up about women *ever,* and he certainly wasn't going to start with Casey Tanner.

If there was a prickle of disagreement from deep within, Abe ignored it. He focused on the last few miles to his Jeep, the snow and ice as cold as he willed his insides to be.

Fall in Love with Forever Romance

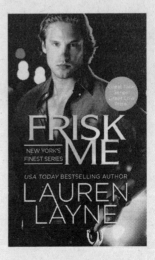

Fall in Love with Forever Romance

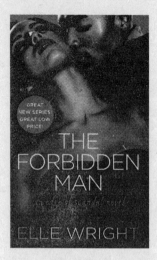

THE FORBIDDEN MAN
by Elle Wright

Sydney Williams has forgiven her fiancé, Den, more times than she can count. But his latest betrayal just days before their wedding is too big to ignore. Shocking her friends and family, she walks out on her fiancé... and into the arms of his brother, Morgan. But is their love only a fling or built to last?

THE BLIND
by Shelley Coriell

When art imitates death... As part of the FBI's elite Apostles team, bomb and weapons specialist Evie Jimenez knows playing it safe is *not* an option. Especially when tracking a serial killer. Billionaire philanthropist and art expert Jack Elliott never imagined the instant heat for the fiery Evie would explode his cool and cautious world. But as Evie and Jack get closer to the killer's endgame, they will learn that safety and control are all illusions. For their quarry has set his sight on *Evie* for his final masterpiece...

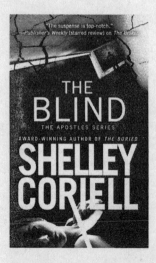

Fall in Love with Forever Romance

THE LEGACY OF COPPER CREEK
by R. C. Ryan

In the *New York Times* best-selling tradition of Linda Lael Miller and Diana Palmer comes the final book in R. C. Ryan's Copper Creek series. When a snowstorm forces together the sexy Whit Mackenzie and the heartbroken Cara Walton, sparks fly. But can Whit show Cara how to love again?

AND THEN HE KISSED ME
by Kim Amos

Bad-boy biker Kieran Callaghan already broke Audrey Tanner's heart once. So what's she supposed to do when she finds out he's her boss—and that he's sexier than ever? Fans of Kristan Higgans, Jill Shalvis, and Lori Wilde will love this second book in the White Pine, Minnesota series.

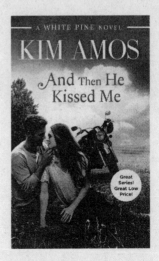